UNREST

A NOVEL

SANDRA ANN HEATH

Library of Congress Control #: 2016900712

Publisher's Cataloging-In-Publication Data
(Prepared by The Donohue Group, Inc.)

Names: Heath, Sandra Ann. | Rivard, Seth, illustrator.
Title: Unrest : a novel / by Sandra Ann Heath ;
illustrations by Seth Rivard.
Description: First edition. | Duxbury, Massachusetts :
Sandra Ann Heath Publishers, [2016]
Identifiers: ISBN 978-0-9965517-1-7 (paperback) | ISBN 978-0-9965517-2-4
(hardcover) | ISBN 978-0-9965517-0-0 (ebook)
Subjects: LCSH: Children of military personnel--Iran--Fiction.
| Iran—History—Revolution, 1979--Fiction.
| Teenage girls--Iran--Fiction.
| Coming of age—Fiction.
| Historical fiction.
Classification: LCC PS3608.E38 U57 2016
| LCC PS3608.E38 (ebook)
| DDC 813/.6--dc23

Visit me @ sandraannheath.com

DEDICATION

For my husband, Greg,
and my sons, Ian and Connor

To read is an adventure

A Coming-of-Age Story Beneath the Alborz Mountains

CHAPTER 1

JUNE 1978, TEHRAN, IRAN

God is most great
I bear witness
There is no god but God
I bear witness
Muhammad is the prophet of God
Come to prayer
Come to well-being
Prayer is better than sleep
God is most great
There is no God but God

"The Azan Call to Prayer"

It's been said that birds can sense an approaching storm. And cattle often run for higher ground before a flash flood. Yet I hadn't been gifted with a similar sixth sense, had no preconceived notions about how it would look, other than my father's carefully worded descriptions, a few photographs, and introductory materials mailed to us before our trip. I sniff the freshly stamped swirls and dots of blue ink on my blue-vinyl passport, the way a child might do in school. I hope for the aroma of mimeograph ink, but there's nothing.

Once into the cavernous main terminal, I look around, wipe moist hands on linen slacks. And my throat hurts, as if a too-large peppermint candy has lodged there. Several men wrapped in long, murky robes slither past me wearing turbans—coils of cotton-stuffed cloth—reminding me of the fabric bowls I'd once made in elementary school. A couple of women are similarly shrouded, faces exposed just enough for clenched teeth to clutch back draping robes. My breath hitches a notch.

On the plane, I'd noticed a few Iranians—how the color of their skin matched my mother's coffee with extra cream. And most of the men had dark hair, prominent noses, lean jaws, and heavy eyebrows. Some wore thick beards or mustaches planted above full upper lips, like hedges. But the people on the plane happened to be wearing clothes I could relate to—a business suit on the father, a stylish dress on the mother, who was also wearing an air of mystery in her large doe-eyes; two nut-brown-haired children in denim overalls sitting on either side of her, snacking on hummus and pita chips. But now in the terminal, it seemed like an approaching storm—swirls of cloth everywhere like storm clouds in the sky—musty heat so suffocating it smelled like rain off hot pavement—*black*—like I was only used to at church.

I notice now that my sister Debbie's elbow is buried in my side, and it's tickling me. She's nodding over at a man who is loitering beneath the Mehrabad Airport sign. He is staring at us, ogling us. My smile evaporates as his gaze slides down the length of me. I wheel around in the direction of my younger brother, Frankie. He's there, thank God, lagging behind us just a couple of steps. He is towheaded to the point of appearing albino, and today his tanned skin and vivid blue eyes, framed by eyelashes so thick and dark, seem to give his hair color. He's wearing a god-awful pair of plaid seersucker shorts, a pair of Speed Racer sandals. His sunglasses have slipped down the bridge of his nose, and he's hardly uttered a word since arriving in the terminal. His eyes are as wide as saucers. I wonder if I should stop to offer him moral support, but I look to Mother.

Like many of the women in the room, her expression is veiled. She's always been skilled at hiding her feelings, pretending for Dad, or for us, that everything was okay. And today is no different. So many times I'd wanted to tell her that she didn't have to pretend ... for us.

Today, Mother is stylish in a smart navy pantsuit. She's brunette with a slight tease to her hair, a kind of tamed-down beehive, and the long aquiline nose so often seen on the well heeled or the well educated. *A Jackie O.* I notice the fabric of Mother's blazer is sticking to the small of her back, and the metal handle of her rolling carry-on case has slipped from her hand. I think I hear her swear, which surprises me. Mother wipes her palm on her hip. "Please, kids, wait!" she calls out. Her voice rises an octave, and she points across the terminal. "We should head over there. Yes, over there." She nods confidently once she's spotted the sign with the luggage symbol.

Up ahead Debbie is fiddling with her camera, tucking her sweat-dampened blond hair around her ear. She resembles a dressed-down professional photographer, ignoring Mother's instructions to dress for travel—to avoid taking photographs in government installations, like airports.

Boys at school had always told me how cool my sister was. "Uh-huh," I'd said agreeably, sitting still on the army green dugout bench, wiping my thick Coke-bottle lenses with the hem of my ragged T-shirt.

Today, Debbie is wearing a ripped Cincinnati Reds T-shirt herself, and peace sign-patched Levi's—and yes, she does look cool, but *holy cow, do we ever stick out like sore thumbs.*

"You guys—there's Dad!" I point to my father near the baggage carousel. Several handsome young Iranian men in jeans and T-shirts hanging around a bank of pay telephones turn to stare. I blush, but their expressions are friendly and inquisitive. They have infectious laughs, and their bell-bottoms accentuate their lack of height. Compared to them, I am a giant.

Dad waves at me, beams like the sunlight off the silver planes outside. Usually he keeps his emotions in check—unlike most of the Iranians in this airport, with their dark tented

3

eyebrows, clipped strides, and excitable shrieks of *Salaam! Haleh chetore!* And all the kisses and emotional embraces.

"Look, there he is!" I yell over my shoulder, break into a gallop, stop short, suddenly shy but drinking him in. A sight for sore eyes.

Today, instead of his Air Force dress blues, Dad is wearing a large flower-splashed tropical shirt. With his head bare where a navy-blue triangular Air Force cap might have covered it, my father looks heavy and lumpy, like a worn-out mattress. My heart aches. I decide I should forgive him for all the black robes now swirling around us. For forcing us outside the bounds of our prior predictable comfort.

Dad had been itching for a new assignment after being stationed at Wright-Patterson Air Force Base for five long years, when a typical tour of duty might last only two. My parents had broken the news of our move while we'd been perched on the edges of our matching lime-green couches set on our gold shag living room carpet. I remember how I was forced to stare up at our round burnished-orange lamp hard enough to keep tears from escaping my eyes—how I saw blurred orange light instead. *Iran? Isn't it in the Middle East?*

"Technically, Asia," Mother had said, and her voice had wavered like the lamp on its wrought-iron hook.

"You've got to be kidding me. I graduate in sixth months!" Debbie had wailed.

Move? It couldn't be true. Hadn't I just begun to feel nonmilitary? To refer to my friends as long term for the first time in my life? And I'd been liking it.

"What about Boy Scouts?" Frankie had complained. "Will they have it there?"

His face had turned a faint shade of pink.

We were supposed to be good at this moving thing. But we never were. "Treat it as an adventure," Dad had encouraged—a coach reinvigorating his team forty-eight points down. "A chance to see another part of the world." But Mother's eyes had been fixed in a deer-in-the-headlights stare, and she'd remained oddly quiet at my father's side.

Colonel Patterson, an experience like this comes along only once in a lifetime, Dad's superiors had said, though they'd assigned him to a workstation absent from his preference list. *Your chance for a promotion to full Colonel.* Dad's shoulders had squared when he told us this; his eyes had carried a look of ambitious resolve.

Meanwhile, it was decided that our fond farewell to our school friends would be postponed for six months so Debbie could graduate. It was as simple as that; we'd join Dad later. Over the moon about this then, we'd never thought about how much we'd miss Dad while he was away. And our Christmas tree had dropped needles as fast as he had to report for duty.

But why the rush? Still, the reprieve for the rest of us had been a heaven-sent gift; it had allowed us to wrap our heads around the move.

"Annie, get over here, silly!" Dad demands now, laughing, arms open wide. Ashamed, I hurry in for a bear hug and a lungful of Old Spice. "You're so grown up!" he exclaims.

"But Dad, it's only been six months!" And at the relaxed familiarity of his face, thoughts of all the lecherous sneers encountered so far in this terminal zip away like the suitcases through this crowd. I giggle and step back, and Debbie and Frankie swoop in to greet him like two friendly monkeys, all kisses and hugs, tangled pale arms.

Almost bouncing in her navy-blue pumps, Mom patiently awaits her turn, but then she can no longer stand it. "Jack!" she squeals.

"Donna!" Dad pulls Mom off the ground and twirls her around like in the movies—another surprising show of emotion. And she's beautiful as she giggles, even though tears are brimming like the rheumy eyes of a child, and scarlet splotches have formed on her cheeks. It's difficult to believe my parents have lived apart these last six months as inseparable as they usually were. In their marriage, there was mostly we, not I—and we kids were along for the ride, or because of it. But this minute, it felt right to be together again as a family.

A group of women rush by us in a fog of perfume. They are wearing brown leather boots and above-the-knee colorful skirts; they have long chestnut hair, streaked in blond or hennaed highlights, or cropped short into stylish shags and shiny bobs. They remind me of the women back home at the mall. I stare after them wistfully, thinking they looked so normal.

"How've *you* been?" Mom asks, caressing Dad's face. Then she pats his stomach. "Too many Hungry Man TV dinners in there?" She smiles affectionately and gazes down at his cheerful Hawaiian shirt.

He lowers his voice to a whisper. "My work uniform is underneath this shirt."

"They don't want you to show your uniform?"

Dad sidesteps Mom's question, says instead, "I've missed you." He kisses her a quick 'we're in public' peck on the nose, the same nose that had captured Dad's attention at an Upstate New York drive-in theater back in 1957. Dad had spied my mother perched on the back seat of a powder blue convertible with her friends, freckled nose upturned. He'd mumbled something about getting popcorn, left his date alone watching Jayne Mansfield on the immense movie screen, made a beeline for my mother as her friends giggled. Mother's smile had captivated him, her cherry-red lipstick so vivid in the dusk. And because he looked like Elvis Presley—same dark hair, defined eyebrows, shape of nose, and curled lip—my mother and her friends had imagined he could sing. And to my mother, he could.

But now the lipstick of choice is dusty rose, and Mom sighs as Frankie and Debbie run ahead to the baggage carousel. Dad asks, "Debbie didn't mind so much about graduation, did she?" I can hear the ache in his voice.

"That you couldn't be there? I don't think so." Mother clears her throat, fiddles with her hair.

Too new on the job to travel back for Debbie's graduation, Dad had supplied Debbie with gifts of guilt—a shortwave radio, a Nikon camera. He'd agreed to let her take a year off before college. A good deal, I'd thought.

"You coming, Annie?" Dad asks.

Like a fly in ointment, I stand stock still. A man in a short-sleeved cream-colored shirt brushes past me with yet another leering stare, has me wondering if my blouse has fallen open. His round belly creeps out of a stretched waistband, his hair so greasy you could fry bacon on it. I look away, uncomfortable.

Another robed woman scurries past me. There is no need for her to anchor this robe closed with hands or teeth—it drapes her from head to toe, concealing her body and her face like a fencer's mask. Two patches of black netting cover the woman's eyes and mouth. I wonder if she'd suffer heat stroke once she stepped outdoors, remembering the blast of heat that hit me outside the plane like a blowtorch to my face.

"What's she wearing, Dad?"

"A *burqa*. The other women have on *chadors*, which are more popular with Iranian women."

The *burqa*-clad woman glides over to a tea kiosk.

But how in the world would she ever drink?

Outside the airport, the afternoon light is dimming to dusk. Yellow lights shimmer along the mountains like strings of tired white lights on a Christmas tree on New Year's Eve. We've crowded like sardines into our metallic-blue Honda Civic shipped over from New York, and the car feels like home. *Except this is home now.* And it is blistering hot.

"What's it, three hundred degrees in here?" Debbie complains, and she rolls down her window so fast it's as if she's afraid she'd suffocate.

"It'll cool off once we get going," Dad assures her.

"I'm telling you, we should have bought that used Pinto with air conditioning," Debbie says.

"But Dad said that Pintos are firetraps in rear-end collisions," I tell her.

"And Frankie is sitting on his suitcase right now without a seat belt," says Debbie.

"That's okay. I love this Honda." Frankie caresses the cloth-covered seat. "Reminds me of a bug." My brother often hunted creepy-crawly things and trapped them into ice-picked metal-covered jars—ants, grasshoppers, orange salamanders, and an occasional lightening bug. More often than not, he'd cause them an early death, though he meant only to study and appreciate them.

"I miss our paneled station wagon," Mother adds, though she had received a fair price for it, despite its dented bumper. "The roominess of it."

I wipe away sweat from my brow, in agreement with Debbie about the heat, and with Mother about the station wagon.

Dad shifts into reverse, checks the rear view mirror, then frowns. I turn around. A police car has pulled up to one side of our Honda, and the officer inside is jerking his head upward. Dad gives him a polite nod, lets his foot off the brake, and continues backward. Inexplicably, the police car advances, and Dad hits it squarely. We all lurch forward in our seats, and our hitched breaths signal the same thought, *what on earth was that*?!

Dad jolts the Honda back into the parking space, and Frankie slides headlong into the front seat on top of the gear shift. "Ouch."

Dad jumps out of the car, arms spread wide, palms raised. "Sir? Didn't you just let me go?"

The policeman shouts back in a heavy accent. I shift in my seat, worried for my father. Wiry black hair covers the tops of the police officer's thick veined hands, sneaks out the neck of his muscle-strained shirt. The officer points to the driver's side door, pulls a fat wallet from his back pocket while his holstered pistol jiggles on his thick muscled hip. He points to his wallet, then to my father. I can't seem to look, so I busy myself strapping a seat belt around Frankie who is back on top of his suitcase.

"Excuse me?" Dad asks. "Not much damage here, not to our Honda, anyway." The pitch of Dad's voice rises several octaves. "You see? Just a small ding on your door."

The policeman points again to my father, then to himself. He raises a cupped palm, rubs a fat brown thumb around the tips of his sweat-dampened fingers.

"You want money?" Dad asks the police officer.

The officer nods. He wants money.

Dad grabs out his wallet from his back pocket, fumbles through it. Hands the policeman several colored papered bills. Sighs.

"*Bishtar*," the officer says.

"More?" Dad asks and pushes a few more bills into his hand.

"Sir, *merci*. No more are you *gonah-kaar* (guilty)." The police officer laughs, tips his hat, climbs into the hardly damaged vehicle and speeds away.

Back in the Honda, Dad pulls a linen handkerchief from his pocket, wipes sweat off his forehead. "Can't think of an easier way out of a motor vehicle accident, can you?" He laughs, but his bright blue eyes remain serious in the rear view mirror.

The route to our apartment is pencil-straight, a wide and empty highway through barren desert. Not a single building, just miles and miles of dust. Dad drives at breakneck speed, as if by the sole act of speeding, we'd overlook everything that was so different outside our windows. The breeze that flows through the lowered car windows cools us. My thoughts shift to something other than heat.

"Everything looks … so … medieval." I smile, tentatively picking at the seat's tweed fabric.

Mother says, "But I've heard Tehran can be quite cosmopolitan. Isn't that right, Jack?"

Dad shrugs, probably thinking more of the drink than Mother's thoughts of sophistication.

"I'm hoping for an adventure," Debbie says.

"Atta girl, Debbie! Hope is alive and well in spring," Dad says.

And yes, it is spring—the second week of June. Temperatures of hundred degrees Fahrenheit, parched-dry mountains looking chocolate brown in the gathering shadows, fragrant lilacs and fat, round raindrops left behind in Ohio. Dad had warned us about culture shock. But the word 'foreign' didn't feel big enough.

Just outside the window are two robed women bent over a murky drainage ditch. They are rinsing clothes and dishes in it. Alongside them another woman holds up a soiled cloth diaper. I cringe.

Dad rolls up his window to cut the road noise. "You know how we've got gutters back home?"

Debbie nods.

"Here they have *jubes,* wider than our gutters," he says, trying to explain. "Like a sidewalk before the concrete is

10

poured. The *jube* system carries water from the mountains through the city. It's flushed twice a day. Irrigates those sycamore trees you see lining the sidewalks. A word of warning though." Dad shifts in his seat. "Sometimes the *jubes* carry unfortunate things besides murky storm water." We didn't ask what, knowing the answer would be bad.

The sky behind the shadowed mountains has turned a deep shade of coral pink, but the pure white snowcap of the tallest peak preserves the evening light. I notice a man alongside the road standing with his back to us. His elbows are raised, and his hands have disappeared in front of him at groin level.

"What the heck?" my sister hisses.

"He's peeing!" I hiss back. Disgust fills my gut at this, and all the offending smells—burned meat, heated blacktop, exhaust, *urine*—my own sweat. I craved fresh air.

Debbie sniffs, nostrils flaring. "*Gee-sus*, Annie, you stink." And she's right. I do. I clamp my arms tight against my sides as if this might help. My face burns.

"Who says it isn't you?" I ask.

Debbie plugs her nose. "Girls, please." Mother wheels around in her seat. "Debbie, watch your language."

We approach a massive traffic circle surrounding a lighted fountained concourse. "The Shahyad Monument," my father announces, "The Gateway into Tehran". I crane my neck out the window. Backlit magnificently by the coral sky, the enormous tower of marble and stone straddles the boulevard like it had legs. Beneath the tower, a mosque-like arch is decorated in a pattern of thousands of turquoise-colored diamonds. Hardly like our Washington Monument with its simple lines and no ornamentation—this monument was nothing less than regal and intimidating.

Closer to downtown the traffic thickens like smog. Orange taxis, yellow and red Fiats and Peugeots, two-tone white and powdered blue Volkswagen buses and bugs dart past us and turn in tandem across lines of streaming head-on traffic. I watch as the outermost vehicle acts as linebacker, running shotgun for the rows of cars that also turn across the wide boulevard to an intersecting, narrow alley.

"You can't be serious," my mother says.

"It takes some getting used to," says my father.

The staccato bleating of horns out our opened windows is deafening.

"See that car over there?" Dad yells out over the road noise, pointing. "That lemon yellow one? The car that just sped through the red light? A Paykan. Iran's national car—means arrow in Persian. Paykans all share the same five keys—which means one thing … they are often stolen."

To me, the car looks too funny to steal. I wouldn't want it. And all the cars were running the red lights, ignoring them as if they didn't matter.

Now the pedestrians in front of us are darting in and out of the slow-moving vehicles like a good game of dodge ball. And I think, *Oh my God, aren't there crosswalks here?* Even if I hadn't harbored my own irrational fear of crossing any street since I was a small child, this chaos deserved reasonable fright. I couldn't wait to reach our new home. *Safely.*

Dad had already explained to us that our new apartment was situated on the "economy", not secluded on an American base, like most places we'd lived, other than Ohio. At Iraklion Air Force Base in Greece, we'd lived in a mobile home on base—steel and round as a bullet—brightened by the hot pink blossoms on the oleander branches that overhung it.

On Long Island, we'd lived in a 1920s' brick duplex surrounded on each side by a lattice-fenced balcony you couldn't walk on or you'd fall through. It was "base" housing for area Air Force personnel at Mitchel Field. Decommissioned in the 1960s, the former base was chock full of abandoned brick buildings with broken-out windows. On weekends, we'd poke around them—avoiding shards of glass and pests, and playing hide-n-seek. After school, we'd race our bikes down an oil-stained parking garage ramp, fly remote control airplanes on the cracked unused runway, turn cartwheels on our green patches of lawn. On windy days, we'd blow gossamer-like thistles from milkweeds growing near rusted metal hangars. In winter, we'd ice skate on wobbly ankles on the hosed-down vacant gas station lot after it had frozen over.

And just as quickly had come the assignment to McClellan Air Force Base—the visceral pain of saying good-bye to a very best friend. After our parents had exclaimed, "California or Bust", we'd begun the cross-country drive, pulling our tent trailer behind us to avoid the expense of motels. I remember I'd blubbered like a baby alongside Frankie, who cried for his bottle. But Dad had promised a sightseeing trip like no other, culminating in visits to Disneyland, Hollywood, and the San Diego zoo.

In Sacramento, I'd made a new best friend named Leslie, got used to a carport, played on scrub-covered hills under large-limbed trees for yet another two years—until we were forced to move again. If we could make the best of the abandoned barracks and rundown buildings, meet new special friends, couldn't we do the same here? Mother always said that once you got used to a place, you'd come to love it.

Now thinking about the arid desert near the airport that had seemed to fly by us in earthy brown streaks, I couldn't be so sure.

Dad is saying, "The Greek Parthenon was once an Islamic mosque, kids, then a Christian church. Likewise, Iran has the ruins of Persepolis." I had a vague recollection of Debbie and me dressed in flowered sundresses posing in front of the ancient stone remnants of the Acropolis.

Mother is saying brightly, "Girls, Iran is Greece without the Mediterranean. There are oleander and orange trees here, too!"

But instead of Greece, the desert landscape reminded me of Route 66 out West, the Mother Road according to John Steinbeck, miles and miles of rim-rod straight highway through barren desert. *But maybe it reminds me of the end of the world.*

I shrug off the thought. To be positive, I grasp onto the idea of Greece where in photographs we appeared happy. If we weren't stationed in front of some ancient statues or ruins, we were posing for the camera at some birthday party. Certainly not being hit over the head like a two-by-four from culture shock, like now, but I'd been too young to understand it. Mother had told me that all my so-called memories before the time I was ten had come from photographs, now wrinkled and faded in a shoe box, with ripped scalloped edges. To think Frankie may have no real memory of Ohio, except in pictures. But he'll be able to remember *this.* I sigh.

"You'll hear the Call to Prayer from our neighborhood mosque tonight at dark," Dad says now, driving past an opulent mansion enclosed behind tall wrought-iron gates. The grounds are lush with green grass, spruces and pines.

"Niavaran Palace," Dad says.

I gasp.

"Where the Shah lives?!" Frankie asks.

Dad nods.

I can't believe we are traveling past the palace of an autocratic monarch. And this is our new home.

Dad signals left at a sign tacked on the side of a tall brick wall labeled *Baharestan,* pulls into a narrow alley. Even the bricks look different here, blond—some almost appearing pink in the late evening light. We slow in front of a high concrete wall, and Dad presses a button on a gadget hanging off the rear view mirror. The gate opens, and to my delight, the drive borders a lighted inground pool Dad has told us about, then disappears into an underground garage. Debbie asks, "Why the security wall, Dad?" but Dad just shrugs.

"Hollywood is filled with security walls," Frankie says seriously.

And this suddenly makes sense to all of us, with the walls and the pool, we were now being offered the chance to be elite. A positive thought.

Once we'd all piled out of the car, Dad shows us our new half bath.

"What's this? A hole in the ground?" Frankie asks. We stare down at a porcelain-encased pit flanked by a coiled red rubber hose.

"An Iranian half bath," Dad says.

"Where's the toilet?" I ask.

"There isn't any."

"What about the toilet paper?"

"There's the hose," Dad says, clearing his throat.

"Something to get used to," Mother explains breezily. *Among other things.*

"It's not possible to go in that," Debbie complains.

"Yeah, it is," Frankie says.

"But you're a boy!"

"Think of it as a French bidet," Mother encourages.

And there it was again, a chance to be elite. And our new home looks fancy, like the White House—same wedding cake color, columned facade—all the exterior balconies. And I'd begun to learn a little about rank—the higher the rank, the better the house.

Inside, I find a conventional toilet fixture in the single full bathroom and breathe a sigh of relief. I follow my mother into the kitchen. On each white square of ceramic wall tile is a large orange circle. Mother whispers, "Mmm. Interesting. At least there's a white refrigerator here." And I am forced to stare squarely at the fridge to stop the abundant dizzying circles of orange, like wall fruit, from turning my vision cross-eyed. Mother gasps, but unlike me, it is in approval of the six-burner gas-fired countertop range in the new kitchen, the stainless-steel double wall oven—compared to the avocado green electric range and matching refrigerator back home, and the olive felt-flocked wallpaper Mother never mustered the energy to strip.

The cabinets in our new kitchen are metal; one of them is seriously dented. "Why metal?" I ask.

"Not much wood in Iran. You noticed the concrete telephone poles?" *Yes, I saw the concrete everywhere.*

I peek at my bedroom, large with a balcony door and painted a deep chocolate brown, so different from the dingy white walls in the military housing I was used to—pockmarked from countless, careless movers. I set to making the bed, pulling out stale smelling sheets, thin blankets, and pillowcases from the boxes stacked in the corner. Carefully, I smooth out the wrinkles across the yellow tulips and the white daisies. I wait for the familiarity of my linens to transport me back home. But the new bedroom lacks bookshelves, and it is claustrophobically dark, unlike in Ohio, where a street lamp had cast warm yellow light across the foot of my bed. I feel displaced here, a different person even. Like I'd never be the same.

I flick the pink gingham bedspread I'd had since I was five over my flowered sheet, the one I'd always jerry-rig into a tent with a long-handled American flag I'd been handed at a Memorial Day parade. It served perfectly as a tent pole. The flashlight had glowed my bed tent hot pink as I'd read deep into the night, until Debbie had complained about the light, how I should get some sleep for church.

Back then my mother, sister, and I had always worn bonnets to mass, sometimes delicate gauzy veils like doilies you'd find under a chocolate brownie, even a simple square of veil, similar to a napkin, clipped to the tops of our heads. Was this why some Iranian women covered their hair, not just at prayer time, but always—hidden away from the sun's bright rays or the cool drops of rain? The appreciative gazes of men? But then their stares could be more than appreciative. Like at the airport.

I cross barefoot over my chilly marble floor and fling open the balcony door. Then comes this mesmerizing, hypnotic chant, song-like and tremulous, but deep and slow, beckoning me to heed the musical prayer. My parents enter the room, and we listen together at the balcony door:

Allahu Akbar, ahhh, ahhh allahu Akbar
Allahu Akbar, ahhh, ahhh allahu Akbar

Ashadu anna la ilaha illa Allah
Ashadu anna la ilaha illa Allah

Ashadu anna Muhammadan rasul –
Aahhh

Ashadu anna Muhammadan rasul –
Aahhh

Aha, aha, aya

Haiya 'ala al-salat, ah, aya, ah
Haiya 'ala al-salat

Haiya 'ala al-falah, ah, ah, ah, ah
Haiya 'ala al-falah, ah, ah, ah, ah

Al-salat khayrun min al-nawm

Allahu Akbar
La ilaha illa Allah–ah, ah, ahhhhhh

Mom breaks the hushed silence. "Beautiful," she says when the Call to Prayer had finished.

"Wow," Debbie says, already in her T-shirt pajamas, her face shining with excitement. Debbie and Frankie had wandered in to listen, and I hadn't even noticed, so intent I'd been on hearing the musical prayer.

"The Call to Prayer?" Frankie asks timidly.

Dad nods.

"Weird," Frankie says, dressed in his "Western" p.j.'s, decorated with cowboys lassoing cattle and Indians aiming bows and arrows. He is standing before the opened French door where the tall slender spires of the minaret pierce the sky like beacons. "Hold that pose, Frankie!" Debbie squeals as she sprints out of the room.

"But it's beautiful, Frankie," Mother encourages. "Think of the passion it takes to wail like that."

Debbie returns and clicks off dozens of photographs as if Frankie were a child model. He smiles but looks tired.

"Off to bed young man and get some sleep. Everything always looks brighter in the morning. You too, Debbie. We'll be in to say good night in a minute."

Debbie shoots a couple more photographs, then she and Frankie shuffle out of the room. Mom turns to me. "Would you like me to flip on the air conditioner?" I nod.

After my parents had kissed me good night, I focus on the rumbling wall unit's hum and icy chill. I pull my blanket beneath my chin and shiver. But then I want to say a prayer myself—one I can recite in sturdy, monotone whispers like I'm used to—instead of the throaty, emotional wails I'd just heard.

Our father who art in heaven,
Hallowed be thy name....

But exhaustion wins as the words of my prayer ride away on the numbing coattails of sleep.

CHAPTER 2

AMIR AND REZA

There is an alley
where the boys who were in love with me
still loiter with the same unkempt hair
thin necks and bony legs
and think of the innocent smiles of a little girl
who was blown away by the wind one night...

Section "Another Birth", by Forugh Farrokhzad

I awake to a dull ache in my shoulder, keeping my eyes closed from the harsh light I sense at the top of my eyelids. I am still tired and uncertain whether the pain is a result of all the suitcase lugging I've done the past two days—first for the flight to Frankfurt, then during the connection to Iran. When I think about it, my shoulder hasn't felt right since those yellow fever and typhoid booster shots ten days ago. Or was it after the shot for malaria?

I open my eyes. The sun's white glare hits me full in the face though it's not yet seven in the morning. Without shades or curtains on the French doors, I give up on sleep, shuffle over to my balcony door.

Tehran, the City of Walls, box-like and linear. I step outside. The morning sky is crisper, smells fresher than last evening. The snowcapped Alborz Mountains surround three sides of the city, and this morning they offer a majestic forgiveness to the buildings they tower above, which appear grimier in the bright morning sunlight. Our kidney-shaped pool strikes me as the likeness of the puddle of cerulean blue paint my mother had spilled on our concrete garage floor back home.

I set off to the kitchen for juice, and Mother is already up organizing. The rubber soles of her Keds squeak on the kitchen floor as she turns from box to box. She has unpacked a single china teacup and saucer from a box tumbling gray packing paper and is drinking fresh-perked coffee.

"Morning, Annette, early riser, how'd you sleep?" Mother has always savored the contemplative early morning "me-time" with a hot cup of coffee as everyone else slept on in the quiet of their bedrooms. But this morning, Mother seems pale and out of place as the Middle Eastern landscape looms outside the kitchen window. She looks as if she could use some company.

"I slept okay," I fib. Actually, sleep had eluded me in the new surroundings. I'd been caught up in memories of my friends back in Ohio—Cindy, Diana, Shane, and Marc, who had gathered on the slope of our front lawn to say good-bye just days ago. I remembered how Diana had hung onto our spindly crabapple tree in awkward silence while I cried. Would I meet similar good friends here? I didn't know.

The focus on my friendship with Diana had always been literary. At thirteen, we'd wiled away a camping trip reading thick paperback copies of *Gone with the Wind.* This had produced no guilt for us, because an Ohio campground meant a graveled, treeless, viewless *Kampground of America*—the sole recreational amenity a motel-sized pool. If we could dream of far-off lands, even if only the rich red soil of Georgia, wouldn't that be a cure for the slight haze of boredom that had just begun to creep in?

Debbie had confessed only a couple of weeks ago that she couldn't wait to leave Ohio for that very reason—no natural recreation, no lakes anyone could get to easily—no mountains, no ocean. I remembered the brown vacant fields after corn harvesting, dead stalks bending like crooked elbows as far as the eye could see. It was true there was the Ohio River and water-skiing. But the Ohio River was rumored to be dirty, and the motorboat lake near school was covered in turquoise foam. But still the farmland was fertile and green in spring and early summer. And it was predictable to us.

"Where's Iran?" my friends had asked, mispronouncing Iran as *Eye-Ran*. I remembered how I'd opened up a World Atlas and outlined Iran with a shaking finger, frightened about how it was surrounded by dangerous places. Russia for one. A big one.

Once Dad had already been living there, my World History teacher had written "Iran" on the blackboard one morning in large, bold strokes of dusty white chalk. He'd scribbled arrows to a diagram of "Nazi Germany", "Great Britain", and "Russia".

Handsome, melodramatic, Mr. Sweeney.

I remembered how he'd cleared his throat and begun to discuss the United States increased involvement in Iran during and after World War II. How during the war, the Allied powers, Great Britain, and the Soviet Union had invaded Iran because of Iran's neutral stance against Germany in the war (but was it neutral?), and because of Iran's refusal to allow supplies and arms to be shipped across it to Russia. Called the Anglo-Soviet invasion, it had occurred in August 1941, after Germany had invaded the Soviet Union in June. Britain, Russia, and Allied troops encouraged—some say forced—Reza Shah to abdicate in favor of his son, Mohammad Reza. The new son Shah came to power in September 1941, allowing the use of the Iranian Railway to transport supplies to the Soviet Union, oil to Britain, taking part in a treaty that allowed a temporary "occupation" in Iran for the war effort, agreeing to help with aid, but holding firm to Iran's neutral stance in the war. As promised, six months after the war ended in 1946, British troops began their withdrawal from Iran, but Russia refused to initially. After diplomatic pressure from the United States and the United Nations, Russia withdrew months later.

"And what had this signaled?" Mr. Sweeney had asked the class rhetorically, slapping his chalk down on the ledge of the dusty chalkboard. "The early stages of the Cold War."

And wasn't this the reason my father was in Iran? And oil.

After the history lesson had ended, Cindy's hand had shot up high into the air. But before Mr. Sweeney could notice and call on her, she'd announced to the class, "Annie's going to live over there, you know. Her dad works in Iran."

I had blushed red when all eyes in the classroom had turned on me.

"Oh, Annie, how interesting," Mr. Sweeney had said. "What does your dad do there?"

"Procurement."

"What's that?" Mark Swiller had asked, a boy I hardly knew, who'd always sat in the front, looking bored, his long jean-covered legs stretched out in front of him. But that day he was interested.

"Oh, purchasing parts and equipment for the Air Force. Contract administration," I'd answered with some pretense at authority. "That kind of thing." I remembered clearing my throat. "He helps to train the Iranian Imperial Air Force officers in Air Logistics Management."

And blank stares had come back at me.

That last day, Marc and Shane had also come to say good-bye. Each had been pursuing me, beginning about the time I'd put away my books for nights out in old town Dayton, developed curves, traded in my thick-lensed glasses for contacts—too much oxygen in my incubator at birth had made me severely myopic. I wondered if I deserved their attention. But then I never had to choose between them. We moved.

"Annette?" My mother asks, interrupting thoughts of my nonmilitary Ohio friends—lucky enough to have the chance to live in one place their entire lives, unlike me. I sigh, open the fridge and lean on the door.

"Where's the milk?" I glimpse no half gallons. I see that Dad had stocked up on juice, eggs, and cold cuts at the commissary—our military grocery store.

Mom holds up a crystal vase to the light. "Oh no, a chip." She sighs. "There's no milk, Annette. Only the powdered or evaporated kind, in a can."

Even the little things would be different in our new lives. I grab a Twinkie out of the familiar Hostess box in the cupboard that slams with a clank.

"For breakfast?" Mom asks. She narrows her eyes and purses her lips.

I smile, shrug, unwrap a yellow cake, and take a bite. "Need some help in here?" I knew I had frosting on my lip.

"I got this. Why don't you concentrate on the boxes in your bedroom?" Mom points to my lip with her coffee cup as if in a celebratory cheer. But then the cup slips from her hand, smashes on the hard marble floor. "Damn!" Her hand flies to her mouth, and she scrambles to pick up the large pieces of broken apple-splashed porcelain. I bend to help. Her face is flushed, and she has cut her finger. Bright red blood drips on the marble floor. She looks surprised, incapable of action. I grab out a Band-Aid from the metal cabinet, wrap it around her finger, sponge up the blood smear off the floor with the efficacy of a nurse. Mother sinks down in a kitchen chair. She sits perfectly still, and I sense the turbulence in her thoughts as she stares at her bandaged finger. Apparently for my mom, things didn't look all that bright this morning. I rummage around in a box for another cup and saucer, pour her more coffee. Mother seems to appreciate that I am tending to her.

"Thank you, sweetie." Mother rubs the bandaged hand through her hair absently. "Suppose our neighbors have heard me? I forget these walls aren't our own," she says as she leaves the kitchen, her contemplative "me-time" over.

The Burnetts are our first floor neighbors. Our apartments share a glass atrium that reaches from the ground floor to the roof, and glass encircles each apartment level overlooking an interior courtyard. The ground floor holds a garden of rocks and plants—like my dentist's office back at home—with its two-story lobby and a water fountain that bursts water all the way to the second-floor windows.

But was it elite to share a house?

Out our large kitchen window, I see a commotion. Chickens are tottering around the yard on quick, spindly feet, squawking. A thin, dark man brandishes a shiny metal ax with a long red handle. I tuck my head beneath my arm and shout, "Oh, God, Dad! They're sacrificing chickens outside!" I lift my face in time to witness their unfortunate wild and headless dance.

"They tussle with chickens like this almost every morning," Dad says, coming up behind me, which makes me jump. "Iranians eat their main meal at lunchtime. Then they nap. You're lucky today. Sometimes it's lamb." I wonder if my face had turned a deep shade of apple green.

Once I finish unpacking, I poke my nose into Debbie's room. She's stringing long strands of glass beads from her doorframe, hanging posters of Aerosmith and Pink Floyd on her salmon-colored walls. Her psychedelic Lava lamp already rests on her bed stand in the corner, the globs of paraffin wax looking glutinous like I felt. "Want to explore?" I ask.

"Sure. Guess I could use a break." Debbie stands up, dusts off her knees. Still she's a good five inches shorter than me, with an ampler figure and a Marilyn Monroe beauty mark stationed above her thin upper lip. I am envious of her more conventional looks. My lips at the very least could be described as full, instead of the thin lips that all the popular girls perpetually rolled raspberry lip gloss over. Like mine, Debbie's eyes are blue—sea-like, but the darker blue that comes after a storm, and squinty, as if she were looking at the world with criticism. At Prom, Shane had described my eyes as the light blue of a Husky dog. But my mother had always claimed they were the same pale blue of her antique milk glass if caught just right in the afternoon sunlight, a description I preferred.

"Are you okay, Debbie? Just wondering—you sad about Josh?" I ask gently.

"Nope, it was about time. I didn't have the heart to tell him I'd lost interest. But now he has plenty of time to forget about me." Smiling, she flicks off a piece of gray lint from her shirt, the way she'd just rid herself of a boyfriend.

Debbie had demonstrated a pattern of being embroiled in serious relationships with boys, hand holding in the school hallways, kissing near the stairs. While Mother was at work as an executive administrative assistant in Downtown Dayton, I'd spend afternoons on my homework at the kitchen table listening to Debbie and her boyfriend in the next room giggle and tickle each other, silly in their infatuation, feeding each other bites of peanut butter and jelly sandwich. *My boy-crazy sister*, I'd think, intent on adding fractions with common denominators. But at the same time, I was jealous of Debbie's success with boys and my lack of it. I wanted to feed a boyfriend, too. But so far I'd only gone to Prom, experienced a perfunctory kiss after, had a few dinner dates with Marc, ending in hot and heavy kissing in the back of his brother's VW van, and that was it, no commitment, no preparation of tuna fish sandwiches while a boyfriend lounged on the couch. And similarly, Debbie was jealous of my good grades, secured without the distraction of a serious relationship, and my parents' delight in them compared to their disappointment in hers. And everything had been amplified by the fact that Debbie had been held back in the seventh grade. There was a side of me that had always wanted to make everything easier for my parents. To compensate for Debbie's bad grades and non-conforming behavior. To be the good daughter.

And Josh and Debbie had seemed so serious, I'd wondered if they had ever … done it. Gone all the way. Made love. Now I giggle at the grown-up phrase, but also wonder what it might feel like. Once I'd asked Mother while we were cleaning up dinner dishes alone in the kitchen. Mother had ignored my question at first, focused on drying a plate carefully with a striped dishtowel, ordering me to rewash one of the pots because I'd missed a spot of dried-on spaghetti sauce. She finally said, "It's nice when you are married and in love." Her gaze was soft, dreamy even. And a few nights later, I received a full-blown *birds and the bees* discussion at my bedside—like I hadn't already learned the mechanics of it from Health-Ed.

At first I hadn't liked Debbie's boyfriend Josh at all, the way tattoos had littered his arms, how his too-tight tank T-shirt had showed off his ripped muscles. The surge of something almost fluttery I felt deep down when I stared at them. But now, Debbie was going to let their relationship fade, and I felt sorry for him. At least he'd made a commitment to her. I liked that Josh preferred Debbie to other girls because she'd ride on the back of his motorcycle. That he'd loved how she'd spend long Saturday afternoons skeet shooting with him. How she never minded when she'd break a nail on the rifle's trigger.

Now Debbie and I wander into the kitchen in search of Mother. I see that the men out back have climbed into several hammocks strung up in the pleasant shade of the verandah. Some of them are lying flat on pads of cornmeal-colored sisal, and I notice their stomachs rise and fall, imagine the bee-like buzzing of their snores. Unable to find Mom in the kitchen, we locate her in the dining room leaning deep into the atrium. "We're going out," I say.

Mother turns and hisses, "Cats!" holding a finger up to her lips. She's wearing the same disgusted look I'd had for the *jubes.* "Cat pee!" she exclaims, pinching her nose. I lean in and see our neighbor's two indoor Siamese cats roaming around among the plants down below.

Outside, our father is struggling with a long-handled net and chemicals. "Have fun—be careful. Don't stray too far," he warns.

We head out the security gate towards the east end of our alley, wander past similar walled-in compounds and down to a large construction site. Beyond the steel skeleton of an incomplete building lay a large tract of open land bordered by a cluster of low-slung coffee-colored structures. The wind kicks up dust in our eyes.

"What's going on over there?" Debbie asks.

Two teams of dark-haired men are playing an energetic game of soccer, and so we cross the brown dusty field to watch. Shirtless players are running and passing, sending the dirt-covered ball upward in graceful arcs, or blasting it outward in straight sharp kicks. The artful receivers handle the ball with either the side of a foot, a stab of a knee, or a push of the head. The game is raucous—players tripping over extended legs, tumbling and laughing, calling out *"boro be jahanam"* ("go to hell"), or *"madar sag"* ("your mother is a dog"), as goals are scored or missed entirely. Iran had just lost in the first round of the World Cup in Argentina. Despite the loss, the excitement surrounding the Iranian team's presence in the World Cup for the first time was generating a wave of soccer playing throughout Iran, like this game, on this dry, dusty Tehran field.

After the match breaks up, two players pull on shirts and amble over to us. *"Salaam,"* they say in unison. One wears a navy-blue T-shirt labeled NYC; the other has on a black T-shirt printed with a picture of Van Halen. Debbie smiles radiantly at the two of them.

Their broken English manages to communicate the question, "Are you from America?"

"New York," I answer.

The man in the NYC T-shirt says, "Ah yes, New York City!" pronouncing City as "Ceety", nodding frantically and smiling widely.

Being Air Force brats, Debbie and I had begun to describe our hometown as my father's, which was Watertown, New York—too difficult to explain we had no real hometown. But worse, we couldn't disappoint these two excited men by admitting we'd come from upstate New York dairy country, rather than Manhattan.

The thinner man in the Van Halen T-shirt pulls a cigarette out of his Adidas duffle bag, places it in the corner of his mouth and squints as he lights it. I sigh, thinking that smoking seemed so grown up. The man has a strong aquiline nose and dark, almond shaped eyes. Between his eyetooth and his right incisor is a narrow space, and a tiny spot of blood marks the edge of his pupil. None of this detracts from his looks. His grin is wide, and he ducks his head impishly. His build is wiry like his jet-black hair, now wet with sweat and parted in the middle. He asks, "You like?" gesturing towards the field with his cigarette-free hand, "The football?"

"We call it soccer. But yes, I do. Very exciting," I say slowly, in case he's unable to understand me, smothering a laugh, in case he's read my mind. "The game," I gush, "is very exciting." I sound as if I'm speaking to a child rather than the eye-catching soccer player standing before me. I giggle, then grimace mentally.

"I am named Amir. That's Reza." He points, then draws on his cigarette. The crow's feet around his eyes deepen as he blows out smoke from one side of his mouth. I wonder about his age. Amir and Reza are roughly my height, maybe a little shorter, but Reza has a stubble of beard, and his shape and features are round. They didn't look like brothers.

Debbie introduces herself also, says, "We just arrived here. It's all so new. I'm taking a year off before college." She points to me. "Annie's seventeen. She'll be a senior this year." She points again with a finger-bitten nail across the dusty field. "We're out exploring?" She stations her hand above her eyes in a kind of Christopher Columbus salute. "You know … looking?"

A half-smile plays on Amir's face. "Yes, I know … *looking*," he says, now smiling widely. "My friend, Reza, and me—we shall help you *look*." He points to a black, convertible Mercedes at the edge of the field. "Would you care to be our guests for a Persian wedding in July? We would be most grateful." He looks sincere. "A wonderful opportunity for us to show you—things along the way." He laughs, having some difficulty with the "th" combination and "w"— saying, "vonderful", and "tings along the vay". I clear my throat, saying nothing, always such a good girl to obey my mother's warnings to be careful of strangers.

But as if he's read my mind, Amir explains, "Reza and me—we have finished school also, like Debbie. We are *hej-e-deh*—eighteen. We work, play football."

And I imagine he'd say next, "And we are such good boys." But his expression has softened at the fear in our eyes. And Reza has also recognized our tentative tap dancing around an answer. He declares, "*Che me farmoid*, I am thirsty. Want drink?" He nods over his sweat-dampened shoulder toward the low-slung buildings.

"*Baleh*", Debbie says, which she'd learned meant yes from our embassy introduction package, along with a list of handy expressions in the official Iranian language, Farsi, and tidbits about the Persian culture. But so far the words on the page hadn't translated literally enough to our new life, hadn't described how unsettling everything would be.

Amir and Reza throw their soccer balls and bags into the Mercedes. We cross the street to a narrow alley. On either side are storefronts in squat concrete block buildings; some are closed for business and are protected by rusted metal gates. Laundered clothes hang across windows or from clotheslines like flags; patterned-sheets billow in the wind. *Chadors*, dresses and bright men's shirts hang damp and limp. The aroma of grilled kebab and spiced rice floats in the air. Young boys in cropped, military-style haircuts, dressed in odd pairings of loud-patterned buttoned-down dress shirts and soccer shorts dart past us, laughing. Suddenly, one of the boys stops short in front of me. I wonder what he wants. I look over at Debbie, but her attention is entirely focused on Amir. I smile at the boy kindly, and he surprises me by reaching up and touching a strand of my hair. His angular jaw drops open. *"Salaam. Khoshgel."*

Reza laughs with a sparkle in his eye. He explains that the boy thinks my hair is pretty, and it seems Reza does also.

"Merci! Thank you!" I call after the fleeing boy, flushing. *"What's your name?!"*

Reza shouts after him, translating.

"Nouri!" the boy calls over his shoulder. And dust flies as he chases his friends.

We duck into a narrow storefront, and inside is a cooler full of Pepsi's. Amir pulls out several sodas, hands them to Reza, who brings them to the counter. Amir pays a stooped old man in a black suit and a knitted wool cap, seated on a round stool behind an outdated cash register. *"Merci,"* he says. *Pepsi* is printed on the glass in English, beneath which are the swirling words of Farsi. The old man at the cash register smiles widely; his grin stretches the wrinkles on his face, which give him the sweet, unfortunate countenance of a walrus. "You from Amrika?!" he asks.

I nod. The old man shakes his head vigorously like my Cincinnati Reds bobble head doll, and he's silenced by the language barrier but is still grinning ear to ear, as if I were a Hollywood celebrity. "California? Hollywood?" His teeth are stained dark.

"New York."

"Ah, New York, too, is very good. *Salaam!*" he says.

"*Salaam!*" I reply.

"Boy, this is good," Debbie murmurs, interrupting all our head bobbling. Bubbles of condensation cover our glass Pepsi bottles like the sweat forming on our foreheads. And then we continue through the store past overflowing bins of produce, outside into the gathering heat.

"You are lucky to have vegetables in your *kuche*," Amir says.

"Vegetables in my *kouchee*?" Debbie asks, offended.

But Amir's laugh is pure and contagious. "*Kuche* market, rather." He explains that kuche in Farsi is an alley. And it's the first time I notice that Amir's expression is perpetually amused, as if he's carrying around a wonderful personal joke.

Outside the shop, a weathered old man in a white peasant shirt and burgundy velvet pants sits crossed-legged on a fringed striped blanket. A few battered pieces of copper and brass rest before him. The man is dirty from head to toe, and he gazes up at me with a wide, toothless grin. His right eye is foggy—all white where normally there'd be the color of a pupil. His upper eyelid sags as if he has no energy to keep it raised. He whispers something I can't hear. I bend closer, wonder if he wants to engage in a barter or ask for spare change. Unexpectedly, he reaches up, grasps my left breast. I flinch, and then I feel the blood drain from my face. Amir shouts, "*Shoma ra cheh mishavad,*" and he steers me away. Over my shoulder, I see the man spit on the sidewalk, cackle to himself while his good eye registers venom. The heat of shame burns off my neck like steam.

Eyes downcast, Reza says, "Most people in Iran… Are very good. That man … is very bad."

Amir is also apologetic…. "*Be-bakh'shid.*"

"That's okay," says Debbie, smiling, and she is stunningly pretty. But I throw her a look, suggesting the question, *who just got grabbed here?*

As we make our way back to the field, the children who are frolicking in the dust-choked alley congregate around us like moths to wool. They ask Debbie and me the same question, "Are you from Amrika?" wearing wide endearing grins.

"Yes!" I say, honored at their idolatry.

Back at the field, Amir urges us again to join them for the wedding party. I am taken in by his grin—his warm brown eyes—as if there was no question he could be trusted. Even so, I glance over at Debbie. But, a split second later she shakes her head yes. We agree to meet the two men at the edge of the field, the morning of Thursday, July sixth, at ten o'clock.

"*Inshallah* (God willing)," Amir says, backing away. But it seems his gaze is focused on Debbie and not on me. "May peace be upon you," he says. I blush, remembering his touch, the long draw on his cigarette with beautiful full lips.

"*Khoda ha Fez,*" I say, as we turn towards home. And I am lost in thoughts of Amir's almond eyes, how the muscles in his abdomen had tightened like ropes as he ran.

"I really like that Amir," Debbie confesses. And my heart sinks because I liked him, too. *Maybe I should have said it first?*

CHAPTER 3

SUMMER IN OUR VILLA

Life is perhaps
a long street through which a woman holding
a basket passes every day

Selected Section, "Another Birth",
by Forugh Farrokhzad

We remain mostly within our compound walls doing everything we'd be doing in Ohio—swimming in a pool, reading, listening to records, sauntering around in our bathing suits and shorts on the heated tile of a concrete pool terrace till our callused feet no longer burned in the blistering heat. Long and lazy summer days bathed in chlorine. If we weren't lounging at our "villa", we were hanging out at the Gulf District, a walled-in, "base-like" compound east of the Shah's palace, its entrance safeguarded by a manned security booth. It was home to a movie theater, a teen center, a motor pool, several playing fields, tennis courts, and the officers clubs.

But instead of the Americanized Gulf District, Dad works at the Iranian Air Force Base called *Doshan Tappeh*. Dad tells us it's huge, an expanse of military land on the outskirts of the city, enclosed in chain link fencing topped by rolled razor wire, supporting several nondescript military buildings and two long runways. For security reasons, the United States and Iranian Imperial Air Force military branches each maintained separate locations on base, though each worked daily in teams.

Just the name of the base brings me unease compared to the wholesome thoughts of Dad's former workstation—man's first flight and our surname. But the Gulf District soon becomes a slice of Americana to us in a place that feels so foreign.

"Why don't you sign up for the women's summer softball league, Debbie?" our mother asks.

Secretly, I am envious that Mom directs this question to Debbie and not to me. It's understandable, though, because my sister can pitch a softball faster than my father, and I can't pitch at all.

"A great idea, Mother." Debbie turns to me. "Want to?"

And I nod, excited that Debbie's included me.

I'd been thinking about asking her to walk back to the soccer field with me, wondering if the boys we'd met there played soccer at the field every weekend. I was thinking, though, that I ought to go by myself. Maybe pull back my hair into a high ponytail, wear my imitation diamond stud earrings that gleamed in the sun, the strawberry flavored lip gloss that shimmered like wet kisses on my full lips. But then I remembered that Amir's wide, impish grin had been fixed on Debbie and not on me.

Under cloudless blue skies faded by the haze of thick pollution, Debbie and I join the Gulf District's summer softball league. Frankie comes to watch. Our team is made up of Air Force women who treat us like daughters. And it's nice. After practice, we cool off at the O Club, sit outside a bank of atrium windows on colorful rubber lounge chairs, and sip tall glasses of ice tea decorated with paper umbrellas, watch children splash around in the pool, including Frankie. He swims by himself, plugs his sweet puckish nose with a clamp of two fingers, and sinks underwater, crossing his submerged legs Indian-style, holding up a make-believe teacup in a solitary underwater tea party. He seems lonely—but we all have that air of loss about us. At least we could all feel normal at the Gulf District.

Our family attends an American Embassy orientation on living in Iran. *Careful about taking photographs, no shorts or short skirts and above-the-thigh dresses outside the Gulf District or compound walls. Without question, no discussion of the Shah or mention of his name with any ill will, or suggestion of it.* The cultural differences are explained: *in Iran, to dip the head signifies "yes" and to jerk the chin up means "no."* Was it that Amir wasn't perpetually bashful at all, just agreeable? Hadn't the policeman at the airport lifted his chin at us?

Despite the warnings, Debbie accepts a full-time job teaching English at the Iran-America Society downtown. And each night, she brings home colorful tales about Downtown Tehran—the salads with the creamy yogurt dressing she devours for lunch, the young Iranian boy who delivers paper-thin baked *Lavash* bread to school at lunchtime and has a crush on her.

"There's as much saliva drooling from his mouth as the butter dripping off the warm *Lavash* bread he sells," she brags. "And my students are learning from me. You see, I can be just as good at English as Annie, even if I don't read." Debbie throws me that bug-eyed look she's perfected. Mom objects to Debbie's comment.

"Now, now, Debbie, reading is beneficial. Those library books I checked out for you? They sit unopened on your dresser."

"I read enough at work, Mother," Debbie complains, shrugging. "When I'm home, I prefer to develop my photographs." And she does, hiding away in the garage storage room she uses as a darkroom.

Usually I'm envious of Debbie's work stories. But one day a motorcycle hits her as she crosses the street to her bus after work. This mishap requires twenty stitches to her leg and sends shivers up my spine. But wouldn't you know work for my sister would represent adventure?

One night at dinner, Debbie tells us, "Towards the end of December last year, the Iran-America Society center was bombed."

Mother stops chewing her meat, but then she continues until she is able to speak. "Was anyone hurt?" She is looking a little hysterical, the way she had when I'd run in front of a Trans-Am when I was seven.

"One person," Debbie answers, twirling her fork in her mashed potatoes.

"Seriously?" Mother asks.

Debbie nods, but remains quiet.

"What did they say about it?"

"You're not going to make me quit, are you?" Debbie's eyes narrow.

"Debbie ... go on," Mother orders, exasperated.

"A guerrilla group claimed responsibility for the attack. They were protesting President Carter's upcoming visit to Iran."

"Oh, that's all?" Mother's sarcastic tone belies the stark fear in her eyes. "Guerrillas?"

Although the news worries us, my parents still allow her to work there, adopting the motto of Dad's work unit, *Business as Usual*. And for me, maintaining a problem-free life in our well-protected compound, instead of working, was preferable, avoiding any further lecherous grasps of my breasts with arthritic fingers, or other accidents that could befall me. But I was worried for Debbie. Although she was a pain—nasty to me most of the time—I would die if anything ever happened to her.

The next morning I awake to suffocating heat, grab my suit for a quick dip in the pool, thinking that swimming might now be becoming routine. But how could this be? Outside, the sun bakes my head. After a few laps, I climb out, circle back to the kitchen where my mother is flipping idly through an ancient, dog-eared magazine. She sighs, looks out the window. "Want to go for a drive in the country?"

I hesitate to ask her if she can handle the traffic. I don't want her to think I don't trust her to drive. Outside the kitchen window, the thermometer reads one hundred and seven degrees. I think about the air conditioned-less Honda, but my Mom's face signals she is eager to get out. Like she's mustering up courage. And what's the alternative? Swimming, reading, swimming, reading. Eating Twinkies.

"Sure," I say.

"A trip to a countryside village is just what the doctor ordered," Mother says now, energized, lips stretched into a wide, excited grin.

I imagine lush green grass, farms and cultivated fields, leggy sunflowers on the edge of a vegetable garden, bright red barns. My definition of country.

"Okay," I say, nervously. But Debbie and Frankie like the idea of getting out, so we clamber downstairs to the Honda only after Mother has smoothed on flamboyant cherry-red lipstick for courage.

Once outside the city, when development thins and the landscape turns arid, only then does my mother relax. The sky is low and a pale shade of blue. It seems to touch the flat desert land on the horizon—less like sand than crumbles of chocolate cake batter once creamed with butter.

Along the way, young boys scamper alongside the road carrying sticks and laughing, darting into the street to retrieve wayward soccer balls, one of which has bounced off the Honda's hood. But this makes Mother giggle rather than annoys her. Women in bright turbans trudge alongside us, toting their straw baskets or pottery high on a shoulder, bent forward like sapling trees in a gusty wind. Pack donkeys carry dark weathered men and bulky saddlebags, the stubborn animals allowing them no real progress. They halt and they bray, exposing large and yellowed teeth, their frustrated riders taking to smacking them with willow canes. Of course, this bothers us. But then we leave the wide, paved roadway for a narrow and rutted one. And as we are bumping along, my mother calls out in amazement, "Kids, look at that! A Dromedary camel!" And sure enough, up ahead stands a single-humped beast, comical with its bushy eyebrows, long eyelashes and crooked mouth; and as it chews his cud, its gray lips protrude outward, as if in a kiss. The animal studies us as we skirt by in our small blue Honda, like *we* were the novelty, not it.

The village contains a few scattered buildings, and we stroll about with the customary dirt and dust. A vendor offers us small paper cups of rosewater ice cream with wooden spoons. I peek into his rusted tin cup, see it holds just a smidgeon of coins. The vendor smiles broadly and asks, "You want?" I accept a paper cup from him. My mother attempts to pay.

"No. No money. For you. From Iran to Amrika," he says, his weathered face transparent with eager friendliness.

"*Merci, merci.*" We thank the kind man and wander away. But after a few yards, my mother asks us to leave our ice cream uneaten. "We aren't used to non-pasteurized milk," she says. "We could contract dysentery." I knew she was imagining bouts of vomiting and uncontrollable diarrhea, like the embassy materials had warned about. Or Typhoid? Hadn't I received that booster?

"What? No ice cream?" Tears threaten to spill from Frankie's eyes, like raindrops. I hand Frankie my cup of ice cream, dig around into my pockets, and dash back to the vendor cart, drop several coins into the man's cup, then flee back to my family.

I see Mother studying Frankie's crumpled face as he stares at the two cups of ice cream he's holding. "Oh, Frankie. Go ahead. You only live once. Now you've got yourself two servings of ice cream." And then Mother looks around. We'd seen all there was to see in this tiny village. She stiffens, braces herself for the city traffic again. And out comes the cherry-red lipstick from her purse.

"You did good Mom, taking us out," I tell her.

"I did, didn't I?" she says proudly. And I realize Mother can do anything she sets her mind to without Dad.

Today Dad tells me he's arranged a summer job for me in the Officers Club payroll department. My heart fills with fear, though it would be a real job compared to my usual summer babysitting.

But first there is a vacation to the Caspian Sea with another Air Force family. And of course, there's the wedding. Poolside in my lounge chair, I plan my wardrobe precisely, as if I'm choreographing a fashion show, flipping through *Teen Vogue* and *Seventeen* I'd brought from the States, even dog-earing pages. I wanted to look pretty that day. Although I'm frightened, I'm determined to go.

I stare down at my thighs, made larger by the metal rim of the patio chair I'm sitting in. *Oh, God, I'm fat. Should I swim a few laps?* Frankie is tooling around in the pool in a rubber mask, spitting chlorinated water into a snorkel. Debbie is sun worshipping on a blue inflatable raft. She has inserted a bottle of St. Tropez sun tan oil in the hole meant for drinks. I slip into the water, begin a fast crawl.

"Stop splashing me," Debbie grumbles.

"Come on, I'll race you?" I say. Debbie closes her eyes against the sun, continues to float. Exercise was less important to her than it was to me, I guessed.

Seriously, I needed some friends.

I'd hoped to get to know our first-floor neighbor, Christie, before school began, maybe hang out with her, but she preferred to stay alone in her apartment, outside the fringes, like an apparition. Occasionally, I'd see her peek out the window at us in the pool.

Just now the security door creaks open, and I laugh, because it's Christie. She sees us and quickens her pace, head lowered, avoiding our receptive gazes. Frankie holds up a hand to wave to her, then lets it drop. I hope she doesn't think that I'd laughed at her.

"*Witch,*" Debbie whispers.

"Shhh," I hiss.

Christie is wearing the same pair of gray corduroys and a long-sleeved dark shirt she always wore—her strawberry-blond hair unkempt as usual, as if she couldn't be bothered to comb it. Unlike their daughter, Mr. and Mrs. Burnett are gregarious.

"Call me Mr. Ned," Christie's father had encouraged us when we'd first met him—an employee of the Department of Defense, doing something he wasn't supposed to talk about. Short and round and graying, his stockiness resulted from his partiality to poolside liquor and happy hour food, rather than bench-pressing. His favorite drink was a *Boomerang*, a concoction of beer, limeade, and rum, which he would shake in a used water jug vigorously over his shoulder and yell, "Ba boom, boom, *Boomerang*," as he slopped the green froth into chilled glasses. His wife, Julie, had gray-peppered hair, warm brown eyes, and an easy manner.

Julie's regular job in the States was a food critic, but in Iran she cooked and tested recipes, just now in charge of the military wives' cookbook. Last night Julie had invited us down to dinner to sample a new dish. She'd been seated at her pine dining table in intense anticipation, chin resting on elbows planted firmly before her, studying our faces, then smiling with warm, crinkled eyes when we signaled we liked it with nods and full mouths.

"Now, what did you like about it, exactly?" she'd asked, brows furrowed, eyes eager. "Did the warmth of the goat cheese meld with the sweetness of the cinnamon and nutmeg?"

When we'd all rolled our eyes in ecstasy, Julie slapped the table, satisfied. "Yes, marvelous—that's it! Exactly what I was going for."

The funny thing was that Christie refused to join us for this impromptu dinner, but we could hear her stereo through the closed bedroom door.

Now in the pool, I wonder about all the calories in goat cheese. I quicken my pace.

"Annie, *puhlease*. Don't splash. I'm trying to keep my hair dry."

"But if you get it wet, it'll get those natural highlights," I say, gazing up at the bright sun.

"Okay, splash me then." Unlike mine, Debbie's hair hangs dry and thick.

"You know, I think I have a better idea," I say, climbing out of the pool.

Usually, I'd swim laps each weekday morning while Debbie and Dad prepared for work, before a smoking Iranian driver would come to pick up my Hawaiian shirt-clad father outside our compound. The time Dad left for work varied from one day to the next. Sometimes he'd leave the house at seven in the morning—other days later. Each night before work, Dad would receive a brief phone call discussing times and directions. "You said seven-thirty in the morning? O-seven hundred thirty hours? Roger that."

"Dad, can't you tell them you have to leave earlier?" I'd complain on days he was scheduled to return home late. "We always wait ages for you to eat!" In Ohio, Mother would serve steaming plates of meat—roast beef or pot roast—every night at exactly five thirty p.m., except for Sundays.

41

"Annette, my work hours are different here. Some days are longer than others. It's just the way it has to be."

"Can't you go early every day, Dad? Come home sooner?"

"Sweetie, try to understand, I can't predict my hours anymore. You know how Mom likes us to have dinner together as a family, right? You've got to be patient."

"Fine," I'd conceded. "It's just that I'm always hungry because I'm on a diet."

"A diet? It's unnecessary, Annie," he'd called over his shoulder, clutching the handle of his hard, charcoal gray briefcase, instead of the slim, elegant soft leather satchel he had in Ohio. "You're beautiful exactly as you are," he'd said, stepping into a boxy white minibus occupied by his Iranian driver and a stocky Iranian man in the passenger seat.

"Excuse me, *Khanoum* Annie. May I use bathroom?" the burly passenger had asked once as I'd swum laps in the pool, his turtleneck stretched tight across his thick neck, his black sports coat straining against the bulk of his chest.

"Yes, sir. *Agha* ..." I'd pointed towards the garage before dipping under cover. I spied him unstrapping a holster weighed down by a heavy pistol as he lumbered towards the bathroom. Was he my father's bodyguard? And why did Dad need one?

Returning now to the pool with two cut lemon halves, I hand one to my sister. "Here, dip your hair back into the pool, then squeeze lemon juice on it." What we women do for men, I think as I squeeze hard. And a pale yellow seed narrowly misses my eye.

CHAPTER 4

THE CASPIAN SEA

Listen
do you hear the darkness blowing?
Something is passing in the night
the moon is restless and red
and over this rooftop
where crumbling is a constant fear
clouds, like a procession of mourners
seem to be waiting for the moment of rain.

Selected Section, "The Wind Will Take Us",
by Forugh Farrokhzad

Mother explains that the Caspian Sea is not a sea at all but a large, landlocked saltwater lake three times less salty than ocean water. Debbie has flipped on an atmospheric Persian music station on the car radio, and she's listening to a happy tremulous song instead of Mother. Her blond hair flies out the open passenger side window, and the smell of dust and burnt meat float in the air; the sun shines brightly on her face. She looks happy and beautiful. We stop at a bakery along the main boulevard near our apartment for a loaf of *Barbari* bread. Inside, men are dressed in white and wear thin paper hats and long aprons. We watch them knead dough into long rectangular shapes, slather it with a layer of sauce, then score it with long horizontal lines with rhythmic pats of their fingertips. Twenty minutes later the bread emerges fresh from the oven built deep into the white-tiled wall, baked to a perfect golden brown over red-hot molten coals—smelling like heaven. And there was no other word for it. *Heaven.* But the bread would go to my hips and to my sister's chest, and you couldn't help but devour it, couldn't leave it alone.

We meet the James family outside their apartment house on the opposite side of the city. I am introduced to a boy named John. He's tall with a mop of blond hair, a lanky frame, and clown-sized shoes. He seems caught in that awkward transition between boy and man.

"Frankie, would you care to ride with us? There's more room in here," John's mother offers. Frankie agrees politely, but I sense he wishes he didn't have to. We are driving caravan-style the three hours it will take to reach our booked beach cottage in Chalus. The Honda Civic is overcrowded with blankets and pillows, sleeping bags, barbecuing equipment, and bags of clothes.

Mother is sitting with me in the back of the Honda and flipping through a travel brochure, reading out loud about the formation of the Caspian Sea. She tells us how it's a remnant of the ancient Tetis Ocean, that over time it had lost its connection with the Atlantic and Pacific oceans, became an isolated waterbody, which explains its salinity. I look out the rear window at Frankie who is missing the geography lesson, hoping he's doing okay. I know the feeling of carrying on an awkward conversation with people you don't know. I wave, and I can just see the top of his small white head. He is sandwiched between John and John's sister, Kelly, who is wearing a Texas A&M hoodie, and is chomping on gum. She looks decidedly less feminine than her brother.

Their parents sit in front, silent, eyes on the road. Mrs. James is large-boned with good teeth and straight blond hair cut just above her shoulders. She has a regal bearing, and she's attractive as far as mothers go. Mr. James's bottom lip is puffy as if he's perpetually on the verge of drooling. He's thin and neat, his mousy brown hair cut in a close-cropped Air Force style.

We drive north along narrow roads and hairpin curves. Impatient drivers are passing us—cigarettes hanging from their lips. My stomach lurches at the steep drop to nothing, just inches from the car's side, and I abandon my summer reading book. A few passing Iranians gesture with upright thumbs, *Bilah*, the Iranian equivalent of *flipping the bird*, honking at our desultory pace. But Dad pays no attention, almost slows to a stop to take in the snowcapped magnificence of Iran's highest peak, an 18,550-foot extinct volcano, Mount Damavand. "Kids, look! How glorious!" He sucks in air. It is true that the mountain peak is stunning, the sun bright on its enormous white cap of snow. My ears pop, and Dad shouts over the grinding gears, "It's the mountain peak you see at the beginning of a Paramount Pictures' movie." I recognize its familiar shape from countless films, most recently at the Gulf District theater. This little piece of trivia resonates with me.

"Groovy," says Debbie.

I turn to the expansive valley unfolding below us as we descend from the Alborz Mountain range into a fairy-tale land of verdant fields of sugar cane and rice. *It's green here!* The leafy stalks of cane bend forward in the wind to greet us, as if in a subtle wave, and the cultivated fields are planted as far as the eye can see. Groups of men and women wearing wide-brimmed hats are bent over the crop in the day's suffocating heat.

Mid afternoon we pull into a crowded cottage community. Our unit is contained within a mildewed gray structure that has seen better days. Inside, a checkerboard pattern of large black and white ceramic tile squares covers the floors.

"Wow, we could play life-sized chess in here!" Mom says. "Not exactly the French Riviera, but I'll take it." She points to a bedroom. "Girls, go unpack." I can see the ends of two lumpy twin beds covered in threadbare beige bedspreads through the opened paneled door.

"I heard that the Shah is opening that big new luxury hotel in Chalus. It's all purple and white and modern, has a pool with a bar in it you can swim up to for Pina Coladas," Debbie says as she flops down on a hard lemon yellow vinyl armchair. Mother ignores her and grabs out a broom from a narrow closet and begins to sweep.

Over the noise of her slow, determined strokes, I ask, "May we go to the beach first, Mom?" We hadn't been to a bona-fide beach ever since California. Mom nods, continues sweeping, waving at a few gnats that are attracted to her hairspray, now sticky in the heat. "Sure, pay close attention to Frankie, though, will you?"

Debbie and I pull on shorts and T-shirts over our bathing suits and wander over to the James's cabin with Frankie. Mrs. James invites us in, and the screen door slaps closed behind us, catching the back of my heel. I stumble in. John is slouched in a chair, leg crossed at one knee, reading *The Count of Monte Cristo*.

"Summer reading?" I ask.

John looks up shyly, seemingly amused by my clumsiness, and nods. His sister, Kelly sits on the Spartan, sixty-ish yellow vinyl couch.

"Want to go to the beach?" I ask. The heat seems trapped in the small cottage, and I move my shoulders, unkinking stiff muscles from the long car ride.

Kelly rises up and slaps Frankie on the shoulder. "Want to make sandcastles, kid? I've got buckets." Frankie smiles eagerly.

John and Kelly disappear into their rooms to change, and we stand around and watch Mr. James hammer thick slabs of beef between two sheets of waxed paper with a heavy wooden mallet. Mrs. James sits at the peninsula fingering the stem of her glass of white wine.

"Isn't this grand?!" Mr. James asks us in a flour cloud.

Mrs. James wrinkles her nose. "Yes, if you like *rustic*."

Mr. James ignores his wife's comment, bends to retrieve a pan from the lower cabinets, whistling. "I'm making my specialty from Texas, 'Chicken Fried Steak'," he tells us.

A door slams and John returns. "All set." He is wearing long red swimming trunks and his chest is devoid of hair. A St. Christopher's medal hangs around his neck. Like his mom, he has perfect, large white teeth. And like his father, his bottom lip is puffy, as if he'd been punched. I am waiting for him to develop a crush on Debbie, but his attention is focused solely on me.

Kelly wanders into the kitchen wearing a bright orange two-piece bathing suit, and her hair is pulled back into two tangled ponytails. She holds a few colorful pails and shovels. I wonder how she can manage to look so boyish in a bikini.

"Do you have a cover up for that, Kelly?" Debbie asks.

Kelly shakes her head and gazes down at herself in just the bathing suit and blue Dr. Scholl's, wobbling on that patented ribbed sole supposed to be so good for your feet.

"Kelly, put something over your suit, will you?" Mrs. James orders in her quiet, no-nonsense voice. "You're not going anywhere like that, young lady." Kelly scowls but disappears and reappears appropriately covered.

Outside we locate the trail to the beach, which winds through scrubby oak, fragrant honeysuckle bushes, and wild climbing roses, spills out to an open expanse of beige sand and gray sea. To our right, several women in long black *chadors* bob in the surf. To our left, men are swimming in another roped-off area, in regular bathing suits.

"Should we split up?" I ask John.

"Good Lord, I don't know."

We stand staring, too timid to swim. Dare I strip off my T-shirt and shorts to reveal my hot pink and yellow, plaid bikini? The suit could only be described as sparse compared to the women's black draping garb in the surf. It was a mistake to think my suit would look collegiate with all the plaid. At least, *here*. Was this the women's beach? Wouldn't their water-clogged clothes sink them like dead weight?

A few Persian women lay before us languorously on beach towels wearing bikinis. They are darker, smokier than us, older and more glamorous. At least they looked normal.

I turn toward the monotone-gray water. To think Russia was just over the horizon. Today, it's an empty canvas of gray, but the sun manages to break through the layer of dense darker clouds above us in periodic bursts, teasing us. *Come on sun.* It's warm though, and I breathe in the salt air's briny fragrance.

"Think we can swim here, outside of the tethered beach areas?"

"Don't see why not."

"It's *really hot*," I say, still nervous to break the rules, running a hand through my sweat-dampened hair.

"Come on, scaredy-cat!" Debbie says.

We decide we have no choice but to peel off our shirts and shorts, wade into the sea. Debbie wears her striking lime-green string bikini.

And then a catcall comes.

Two men playing soccer on the beach behind us are staring at us. One has a receding hairline. They are seeing the best of my sister and me. Debbie is straining her bikini top, and I more than fill out my bathing suit bottoms in a Ruben-esque way—blessed or cursed with curvy thighs, depending how you looked at it. Although smaller than Debbie's, my breasts are perky and firm, responsive to both hormones and cold—like now, erect in the sea's slight chill. I feel my cheeks flush.

I remember how after my good-bye dinner with Marc, I'd let him go further than usual, his warm tongue in my mouth like velvet, his body pressed hard against mine. How he'd moved his hands under my shirt before I'd pushed him away.

But only last week, Diana had sent a letter in her formal, flowery handwriting informing me that Marc was now dating Cindy. When I'd read it, it felt like a punch to my stomach. Replaced so quickly? I remembered Marc's hands on me as vividly as if it were yesterday.

Now aware of the men's stares, I dip down into the cover of water. Debbie gives them a look that could kill, and this signals to them that they'd better stop gawking.

Cindy? One of my best friends? But then Cindy was pole-thin, unlike me, and had a thick swath of bright blond hair, not dirty blond like mine. I pictured Cindy standing in our yard in her shorts, thin legs bowed at the calves, knobby knees shifting back and forth, anxious to move on to something more comfortable than saying good-bye. *Marc*? She'd always had a mischievous streak, switching names on a substitute teacher in French, daring me to skip off campus for burgers at Wendy's, dressed in our cheerleading outfits. Sometimes I'd wondered if Cindy was trying to make me more interesting than I was. But then she was more exciting than me, and Marc liked her better.

"Relax, Annie! Have a little fun!" she'd always say. And maybe I should have.

But I didn't, and I couldn't think of it. Of her. Soon enough, the physical act of swimming distracts me. Who needed boys?

"Annie, dive into the waves!" Debbie calls out, and then she and her green terry cloth bottoms disappear into the water. And John wades in to join us. "Feels so good to cool off," he says, then splashes me, teasing me like Debbie, grinning. Surprised and annoyed—my contacts threatening to spill out—I wipe the water from my eyes, splash back and take cover under water, eyes clamped shut. We swim and dive and chase each other in circles, laughing until our sides hurt from it, until we are both out of breath. When we return to shore to drip dry on our beach towels, we notice that Frankie and Kelly are gone. I see Debbie over at the beach blanket of a couple of the few modern looking men around here, one of them with six-pack abs. We are doing a horrible job of watching Frankie, I think.

The cloud cover has pulled away, and the sun feels deliciously hot against my face.

"Are you nervous about school at all?" I ask John.

He shrugs. "Not really. I'm looking forward to trying out for the football and basketball teams. The high school games are all intramural, you know; that's what we've got to do over here."

We sit awhile longer, looking around. I watch the black-cloaked women to my right.

"Sometimes, I can't get over how different it is here," I say.

"Yeah, not exactly Fort Lauderdale on spring break."

"Right." I point to the beaches that are separated by a strung up rope and a dingy canvas tarp secured in place with clothespins and anchored by two tall metal poles. I shake my head and turn to John. "When did you get here?"

"Just before June." John stares ahead at the water, pulling sand the color of wet cement between his fingers near the side of his beach blanket.

"Just before us. But you know so much!"

"Only because our landlord, Moshdeh, toured us around when we first got here. Showed us the schools, the fields."

"You're lucky. We haven't done much touring—beyond this and the Gulf District, anyway. But Dad says he'll take us to see the Crown Jewels. Maybe even a weekend trip to a caravanserai in the Great Salt Desert. I want to see Persepolis and Isfahan."

"What's a caravanserai?"

"An ancient roadside inn. The Shah Abbas Hotel in Isfahan used to be one, now it's a fancy hotel. The Shah stays there sometimes." But Dad had already told us that it would be too expensive for us to stay there if we ever traveled to Isfahan. During our cross-country trip to California, when I was dying for a comfortable bed and a real bathroom with plumbing, rather than the hard tent bed-end of the pop-up trailer and a campground pit-toilet, Dad had let us stay in a motel, though carpet had climbed the walls, and the air conditioning unit had thrummed noisily all night. And I had tried so hard not to act disappointed, thinking it would be nicer than it was, but Dad had been so excited about the deal he got when he'd checked out the next morning.

I look over at John. Recalling our trip to the village, I add, "My mom mustered up the courage to take us on a trip to a little village outside Tehran. We saw a camel."

John pinches his freckled nose. "Ugh," he says, laughing, and his bright blue eyes crinkle at the corners. His hair is so blond compared to the dark of most of the men and women at this beach that he looks almost angelic.

"They smell? We only just drove by it in our car," I say, but I knew from horseback riding that if you ride it, you wear it.

"Yeah. An extremely *nasty* smell from the manure they haul around in the sun."

"I've wondered what those bulky saddlebags held."

"Yep, camel dung. Don't get roped into a camel ride while you're here," John warns, teasing. "They spit. Bite, too." He reaches over and sticks a finger into my waist. I jump. Giggle.

"I won't, then. Definitely not."

And then I lie back on my beach blanket, and John does too. And after a while, John says, almost sadly, "You are lucky your Mom has the courage to drive you to a little village."

I close my eyes awhile, resting them, listening to the waves' soft pull, like a lullaby. And when I reopen them, I see that the sun is beginning to set, a fiery tangerine ball in the sky.

I nudge John, and we sit up on our elbows, watch it drop below the horizon.

"A saffron-colored sunset," I say.

"Saffron?"

"Yeah, Iran's most esteemed spice—it's reddish-gold, like a jewel."

"Exactly like this sunset then."

We hurry to gather up our things, surprised at how late it's become, and scurry back to John's cottage along shadowy trails. To our relief, we hadn't missed supper. Inside, oil is sputtering in a cast iron skillet on the tiny propane stove, and Mr. James is adding flattened flour-coated steak. Mrs. James sits mashing potatoes next to him, talking to my mother about joining the Women's Club in September. A sliced loaf of *Barbari* bread and a small dish of caviar lay on the countertop between them.

"Smells like heaven," I say.

"Why is it called 'Chicken Fried Steak'? Where does the chicken come in?" Frankie asks. Thank God he made it back home. He and Kelly are splayed out on the floor on their stomachs playing "Go Fish."

"It's just a way of saying that the steak is prepared like you'd make fried chicken," Mr. James explains. "An inventive name for the dish, created by someone with a sense of humor." And I like that explanation, and Frankie loves the thought of fried chicken steak I could tell.

I pull the saucer of caviar towards me. "Aren't we fancy?" I tease.

"It's harvested from the wild beluga sturgeon right here in the Caspian Sea," Mom says.

"Therefore, inexpensive here." My father holds up his wine glass.

"Jack, come on. You know how I love luxury," Mom complains. "Don't act so proud of being cheap."

"You are worth more than your weight in gold," Dad says, kissing my mother, now publicly affectionate after a little wine.

I knew that it was almost impossible to afford caviar anywhere else. A delicacy of the rich and the famous. I spread a thin layer of the tiny black pearls of fish egg on top of a Melba toast round, feeling privileged, and pop it into my mouth.

"Very nice." I steal a sip of my mother's wine.

"Annette, you are not of age!"

I laugh, swinging around on my stool top, not particularly enjoying the taste of either the wine or the caviar.

"Shoo, girls, too many cooks spoil the broth—go set the table for dinner." Mom flicks a dishtowel at the two of us, and then Debbie and I carry out mismatched plates, glasses and silverware to the side-screened porch. I place a jelly jar full of fresh flowers on the red checkered table cloth for a centerpiece, long stems of blue irises with yellow centers, and a tumble of sweetbriar and honeysuckle that Debbie had plucked from tangled thickets growing alongside the beach path. Dad begins building a fire in the stone pit just outside the porch, and soon the aroma of creamed gravy mixed with delectable bits of browned steak, wood smoke and sweet honeysuckle perfumes the porch. Even if we didn't eat "Chicken Fried Steak" all that much, it still smelled like home.

After dinner, all of us kids gather outside around the burning fire, leaving the adults to adjourn inside to the living room for rum-laced coffee. Dozens of stars litter the ink-stained sky, and it looks much the same as the sky we'd see on our camping trips in California.

John pulls up a lawn chair next to me, and we sit and talk, listen to the fire's crackle and pop, the insects' deafening drone. While Debbie and Kelly leave to join Frankie in the hunt for sticks to roast marshmallows, John confesses to me that his mother and father are barely coexisting in Iran.

"Mom is so bored—she's too scared to go out into the traffic during the day. Sometimes well before dinner, I catch her with a coffee cup full of wine." John looks up to gauge my reaction, but there is no judgment in my eyes.

"I'm sorry. Maybe she and my mom will join the Women's Club? I heard them talking about it tonight."

"I hope so; she needs some friends." He stares into the fire, then looks up at me. "I think we all need some friends, don't you?"

But I think he's acting as if he wants more than friendship from me. My cheeks burn. "I'll cross my fingers for her," I say, nervously.

A trail of laughter floats out from a neighboring cottage, the cry of a baby and the sounds of dishes banging. Debbie disappears into the porch, brings out three small paper cups of wine from the abandoned bottle left on the table by our parents. Frankie's eyes grow big. He nods over to the cottage, at the tops of our parents' heads, and the sound of Mrs. James's animated laughter trails out the open window.

"Don't worry." Debbie winks, says to Frankie, "It's only a taste." I grab a stick and roast my marshmallow to an even golden brown, sandwich it between squares of chocolate and graham crackers. John and I sip our wine slowly, and it tastes better with the sweet of the chocolate.

Fatigued and lightheaded, more from the sun than the wine, I lean over to check John's watch, pull up the sleeve of his tattered sweatshirt. And as I look up, he bends to me and brushes his puffy lips against mine. I taste the salt of the sea and the tang of sweet wine. But then he bounds up from his creaky lawn chair, smiles, and says good night, and it's as if he's never kissed me.

Early morning, as Debbie and I sleep alongside each other in our hard iron twin beds, I hear the movement of my father in my parents' bedroom. Although it is outside hunting season, an exception could be made for special tourism, and this morning Mr. James and Dad are embarking on an expedition with a Persian hunting guide and five other men. I am upset that Dad likes to hunt, remembering the graceful doe-eyed deer he'd killed in New York, watching them cure on my grandparents' barn door—their stomachs split open from sternum to crotch, dark red blood splotched on the ground below them where they'd hung. I smell the percolating coffee, flop over in my bed. Hunting wild boar seemed more acceptable to me than deer. I imagine the boar's tusked mouth, large nose, and stiff spiky hide. I'd heard somewhere that boar was the world's most dangerous game.

I pad into the kitchen. "You really want to do this, Dad?" I demand at his back. Dad turns to me holding a hot cup of coffee, a ridiculous netted cap on his head.

"I'm a pro now, Annette—hunted at night this winter in darkness before you got here—it'll be a piece of cake in daylight. Don't you worry."

I remember him describing the hunt, how he'd worn special night-vision goggles that made him feel more like a spy than a hunter. The perpetual optimist, I think. I stand up high on the tips of my toes and kiss his cheek. "Careful!" I huff. But he would go no matter what I say.

I creep back to the warmth of my bed. Lying there between mussed up sheets, I remember John's kiss, the imposition of it, but the sensation of soft lips against mine has managed to stir something in me.

Later that morning I catch Kelly smoking a cigarette behind the bathhouse. She scowls, drops the cigarette in the sand so fast it's as if she'd never held it.

"What's up?" I ask her, lips pursed.

"Nothing," she shoots back, glaring. "And who was drinking white wine last night? Don't be so hypocritical."

"But you are only thirteen." When she doesn't reply, I shrug my shoulders, leave her behind. I spread my beach towel out on the sand in the same spot I think we'd had yesterday. I pull *The Grapes of Wrath* from my beach bag and begin to read about Northern California during the Great Depression and the Oklahoma farmers' escape to the west—something I knew would continue as long as there were people, and as long as there was California. I remember our own trip there from New York—tent camping in the Redwood Forest, those towering trees you could drive a car through, trips to the scrub-covered hills of San Francisco, the majestic Golden Gate Bridge, charming Sausalito, the Wax Museum my father wouldn't pay the fee to get into, and how I'd cried. I recall the sourdough bread we'd bought at Fisherman's Wharf, how we'd torn off large chunks of the tangy-sour bread to eat with cheddar cheese—bread I hadn't liked half as much as the *Barbari* bread here.

In the fifth grade, I wanted to be a farmer after my teacher had discussed irrigation techniques and California agriculture, and after I'd witnessed the amazement of the bright red fields of irrigated poppies planted as far as the eye could see.

I rise up on my towel thinking about how much I missed my grandparents' farm. How my grandmother's rectangular patches of vegetable gardens were bordered by rows of fuchsia-colored zinnias that were so bright they could ward off pesky birds better than scarecrows. Down the beach I see that Kelly is playing soccer with two grown men. And to my horror, she's playing in her bikini. A group of people have gathered around her. The women in *chadors* are clucking their tongues and shaking their heads as Kelly's bathing suit rides up one cheek.

I throw on my long, aqua-colored beach dress and take off towards Kelly, sweeping up her cover up as I pass by her beach towel.

"Time-out for a second," I interrupt, breathless, trying to smile, hands raised in a "T"-formation. "Here, Kelly, put this on," I order calmly.

And when the soccer men seem dismayed, I think, *she's only thirteen,* for the second time that day, bile rising up in my throat.

"Kelly, please come with me. Set your towel up next to mine?"

She scowls.

Once back at my beach blanket, I attempt to return my attention to my book. Kelly gives me an attitude, sits up on two elbows and fishes out a baggie of Doritos from her beach bag.

"What did I do wrong, Annie?"

"Kelly, decorum, okay?"

"I don't know what that means."

"You have to be more careful here. We're not playing by the same rules."

"What do you mean rules? It was just soccer."

"Soccer in a bathing suit," I say gently, pointing to the *chador*-cloaked women bobbing in the surf. "At the Caspian Sea, they are mostly used to that," I remind her.

"But there are women in bathing suits. See, over there?" Kelly points to the same glamorous women I'd noticed yesterday.

"Right. But those women would put on their cover up to play soccer. You see? And you are light-haired and blue-eyed—a novelty. Listen, I've got to finish my summer reading." Kelly smiles, likes that I called her a novelty.

I turn my attention back to my book. *"There ain't no sin and there ain't no virtue, there's just stuff people do."* Recalling Kelly's words, "It was just soccer", I realize she's right—it was just soccer. Why must women cover up in long dark robes to swim and risk drowning? Can't a thirteen-year-old girl play soccer on the beach in her bathing suit without a gang of onlookers—wolfish gazes from grown men, disapproval from *chador*-cloaked women? I wonder all this now, reading the same paragraph over and over again. Despite everything, I soften. I sit up.

"Kelly, you did nothing wrong, except the smoking, but remember the cover up next time. And please, stop the cigarettes."

"Okay," she says, watching the game continue without her.

I resume my reading. *"Need is the stimulus to concept, concept to action. A half-million people moving over the country; a million more restive, ready to move, ten million more feeling the first nervousness."*

And a faint uncomfortable sensation stirs in my stomach.

Kelly stands up, says, "I'm bored; all you do is read. I'm heading back to the cottage."

I nod up at her. She's right, and so I place my book face down on the towel. I doze, waking up periodically to smear sun tan lotion on my legs. I feel a growing sense of peace. I could be at Folsom Lake. I flip on my stomach. At the edge of the beach Mother is walking purposefully toward me.

"Annette, where's Frankie?" She's breathing hard.

"Frankie?" I'm confused. "He's not with me."

"He's not?" She wheels around. "I let him wander down the beach path about thirty minutes ago? You haven't seen him?" Mother asks, forehead puckered.

"Should we walk down the beach and look for him?"

"You go that way. I'll go the other." Mother starts to run, something she rarely ever did. Sand is flying. And this gets me worried.

I follow the beach's edge. I scour the water for a white head bobbing, or swimming parallel to shore. Wasn't that what you were supposed to do? Swim along with the current? I start to trot, break into a full gallop.

After a few minutes and no Frankie, legs burning from sprinting in sand, I meet my mother back at the towel. Her hands are on her hips, and she's looking out to sea. "*Where is he?*" Her voice is small.

When we return to the cottage, Debbie's eyes grow as large as our mismatched cottage dinner plates after we tell her we have no idea where Frankie is. "Remember how the Embassy had talked about kidnappings, Mom? That kid that went missing last year?"

"Oh, yeah. That's right. That ransom note?" I say.

"Girls, don't... Don't say these things," she pleads. "I've never heard such a thing." Mother escapes back outside, and the screen door slams shut behind her as if it were angry, instead of her.

"I think I remember that Mother was in the bathroom when they mentioned those kidnappings," I tell Debbie. "We should go after her."

"Mom, wait!" We follow her down a rose-vine clogged path we'd never noticed before. Once we've veered off onto an intersecting trail, I hear what sounds like a creaky swing and deep animated voices. Mother begins to scramble, and we follow, pushing through prickly climbing roses that tear at my pullover. The path leads to a clearing and a square of sand that serves as a playground with a sandbox. It's equipped with a rusty swing set, an iron sturgeon a toddler could bounce on, and a crooked steel slide. Kelly is twirling on a swing, and the two soccer men from yesterday are gawking at her as she twists. Frankie is making sandcastles, loading brown wet sand into a yellow pail with a matching shovel.

Mother shouts, "Frankie, where have you been?!" He looks confused.

"There's sand at the beach, whatever are you doing?" she shrieks. Several weeds poke out from Mom's otherwise stylish beehive. She looks hysterical.

"Hi, Mom, I'm playing," Frankie says, smiling falsely, forehead creased.

The two men slink away, and I see them eyeball Kelly in her tangerine bikini. They wave, speak no English.

Debbie whispers, "How old are those men anyway?!"

Early evening, Dad and Mr. James return hauling the ugliest, deadest wild boar I'd ever seen in the flatbed of their rented rusted truck. Dad describes how one of the men had failed to shoot the pig in its shoulder, had only grazed it. And the angry wild boar, just slightly injured, had charged the group until the tour guide was able to shoot the boar dead just in front of my father.

In the morning Dad and Mr. James surprise us with a trip to Chalus for brunch. We are visiting the new Hyatt Hotel, which had just opened. We stroll into a contemporary lobby of purple and powder white where there are plush leather chairs. Outside the tall glass windows is the swim-up pool bar Debbie had described.

"See, Jim, we could have stayed *here* all along," teases Mrs. James as she grabs my mother's arm and pulls her outside. "Let's go find us some mimosas at the pool bar."

I hear my mother snicker, ask, "Will we have to swim for them?" But no one is wearing bathing suits. After everyone had wandered away, I slink into a wide deep chair, pull out my summer reading book, wonder why John hadn't stopped to sit with me, secretly glad for the peace and quiet. For once, it felt good to be alone.

"*The Grapes of Wrath?*"

I gaze up at an Iranian man dressed in tennis whites standing above me at the back of my leather chair. He is wearing thick black square glasses, and several men in dark suit-coats stand several feet away from him. He must be important. The man speaks English to me in a soft Persian accent.

"Do you like? A most wonderful book, I do say. I've read the Persian translation of it."

I nod back shyly at this friendly stranger who is now stooping to bow in front of me, formally. "Enjoy your stay at this fine hotel." He has strong eyebrows beneath dark eyes, a strong Persian nose, and graying hair that fans up around his temples to reveal a strong high forehead. He rises up stiffly and backs away, sending me a thin shy smile before he joins a contingent of people loitering near the entrance to a large dining room marked *Private.* He crosses over to a lithe attractive brunette wearing a wide tangerine-colored headband and a summer green silk suit. "Farah," I hear him say, launching into a parade of unknown but gentle words in Farsi. And as they stroll away, the woman encircles his waist with a tanned bare arm that seems to stanchion him up.

The Shah?

At brunch I describe my meeting to Debbie.

"No way. Liar."

When I tell my father, he frowns, says, "But sweetie, there are no crowds here today. You certain it was him?"

Now, I couldn't be so sure.

JULY 1978

A moment,
then, nothing.

Beyond this window, the night quivers,
and the earth once again halts its spin.
From beyond this window, the eyes
of the unknown are on you and me.

Section of "The Wind Will Blow Us Away",
Forugh Farrokhzad

Late Sunday night we return from the Caspian Sea, and
Monday I am set to begin work at the Officers Club on the
Iranian payroll, recording names into thick bound ledgers. All
day, I enter the same names, Amir, Mohammad, Ali, Parviz,
and Reza. I wonder if these names are similar to our John, our
David, our James?

I meet a pleasant girl named Janice, and she asks me to
lunch at the Officers Club. We eat Chef Salads in large wooden
bowls filled high with iceberg lettuce, covered by long fat
strips of oily pink ham and orange American cheese, floating in
Thousand Island dressing like they'd swim out of the bowl.
Strips of grilled *Barbari* bread replace regular croutons, which
seems a fitting touch. Probably a thousand calories, I think. I
ask Janice why she thought my new boss, Major Callahan,
asked me to start on a Monday, when the work week begins on
a Saturday.

"So you could feel normal?" says Janice, shrugging.

My new friend would be a senior like me at TAS this year.
She wears her thick strawberry-blond hair short and has a pale

complexion. The blond base of her eyelashes peeks out from the black mascara she's applied to the tips.

"You like Willie Nelson? I love him," Janice declares.

Hadn't I heard about Willie Nelson's reputation for womanizing and smoking too much dope? But anytime I heard him on the radio, I hadn't minded his music.

"I love him, too," I lie, well maybe stretch the truth a little.

"That means you are cool, Annie, dear, despite your father being career military," she says, laying her hand on my shoulder.

I feel a stab of allegiance for my Dad. Was she criticizing him? But maybe I was being too sensitive.

"My dad's a big executive at Bell Helicopter," Janice continues. "Still, I think we're going to be good friends." She wears a satisfied smile and has on a cute green plaid skirt, a yellow blouse, and long white knee socks. "My work clothes. Otherwise, I'm most comfortable in a pair of blue jeans and a T-shirt. You know what I mean?" And then she winks at me conspiratorially.

"Sure." I think about the occasional dress I'd wear to school.

"TAS people are totally cool, dressed-down types," Janice says, "not to worry." TAS is the abbreviation for Tehran American School, a private, nonprofit school in south Tehran, my new school, its curriculum modeled after standard U.S. schools. Farsi was offered, but I chose French instead for my one foreign language elective.

Janice sips her Pepsi. "Want to know why Pepsi tastes so good over here?"

"Why?"

Janice leans in. "*Cane* sugar instead of high fructose corn syrup. Except that the bottling facility here is dirty."

"Dirty?" I imagine germs or bugs.

She whispers, "I heard that once a tiny mouse was bottled up in the Pepsi."

I push away my drink.

"And sometimes, the *jubes* carry sheep heads and innards."

I suddenly didn't feel like eating any salad, despite the *Barbari* bread croutons.

By the end of the day, though, I longed for that Pepsi, for some caffeine. My first day of work had completely exhausted me.

The next morning, still in a fog of exhaustion sleep hadn't cured, I awake to Christie shouting one level below me.

"No way I'm going to that stupid pool party. You can't make me."

"Christie, you've been nothing but rude to the Pattersons since they've moved here. You are going to go, be sociable, and stop listening to Pink Floyd in your room all day." I hear the slap of two shades being flipped up.

"Go to hell, you're not my mother."

A door slams and the music blares melodic angst. *How I wish.... How I wish you were here.*

Julie is Christie's stepmother? Oh, my God. I stuff my pillow over my head, manage to fall back asleep, even as the bass vibrates below me like a late-summer night in Dayton, when a tricked-up car could spew out music as loud as its failing, sputtering muffler.

Now at the Fourth of July picnic, I look around at the successful turnout. Who needed Christie? My father had invited some officers from work and their wives, his secretary Carol, his Iranian driver, Mohammad, and an Iranian Air Force officer, Ali, a pilot with strong erect posture and a head full of wavy black hair. Ali tells Dad how he had to jump through hoops to receive approval from his counter intelligence chief to attend this party tonight.

"I imagine it was especially difficult because it is our Independence Day," Dad says.

Ali nods. "Well worth it, Colonel Patterson, considering these wonderful grilled hot dogs and hamburgers I don't usually have the opportunity to eat!"

Dad is standing before our black Weber grill, in his element, telling jokes to the guys as he flips the burgers like a short-order cook—but he's telling bad jokes.

I wander over to the overloaded buffet table, eyeing the desserts, my gaze landing on Mom's hot fudge sauce that would soon be ladled over the homemade vanilla bean ice cream that had almost thrown out Dad's shoulder as he'd cranked it. Also laid out on the table are bowls of finely chopped pistachios, ripe Persian melons, dried figs and dates.

I sit low in a flimsy aluminum lawn chair weaved in stretched-out green and white fabric. I am attempting to balance an over-loaded paper plate and appear as if I'm not eavesdropping.

Dad is now engaged in deep conversation with Mohammad, who is shaking his head and knitting his black eyebrows together until they are blended into one. Mother is also listening thoughtfully. I hear her ask, "Why is it that the Iranian people seem to revere and fear the Shah at the same time? Why is his picture plastered all over the city, but no one can speak of him?" I had also wondered the same thing myself, whether the Shah was getting a charge out of seeing his own face splashed over every city block, but Mother was breaking the rules, questioning the Shah in public. And I feel guilty I'd thought this after he had stopped to ask me about my book, encouraged me to enjoy my stay at the Hyatt Hotel. Even though no one believed me.

Mohammad explains that the people are not feeling reverence at all. "We are all afraid to speak our minds because of possible repercussions." And I realize Mohammad is referring to SAVAK, Iran's secret police.

"No freedom of speech exists here in Tehran." Mohammad speaks softly as if he's considering who might be listening.

We'd heard for years that SAVAK interrogations were often combined with torture, some of which Mohammad went on to describe, shocking my mother—solitary confinement, sleep deprivation, glaring light, electric shock, and *bastinado*— where the torturer would beat the dissenter's feet with whips or canes. And I had heard of other torture methods used by SAVAK, like cigarette and acid burns, broken glass shoved into body cavities along with boiling water, and worst of all— mock executions. In fact, one of SAVAK's first tasks on the job was to execute fifty pro-Soviet communist Tudeh party leaders, who had attempted an assassination on Reza Shah, and whose political party had been banned.

"Above all, everything now in Iran is so expensive," Mohammad complains, fingering his worry beads. My father had already explained that inflation was a significant problem in Iran because of the extensive and rapid military build up.

"Now imagine this." Mohammad's mouth twists. "The Shah throws himself a birthday party several years after his own coronation, twenty-six years into his reign. Because Iran is no longer poor, it can afford an extravagant party to celebrate two thousand-five hundred years of monarchy. And so the Shah dubs himself the King of Kings, crowns himself at his own coronation, expresses a kinship with the founder of Persia, Cyrus the Great. World leaders and dignitaries attend this celebration beneath a tent at Persepolis, and it costs extravagant sums. And then the Shah commissions the Shahyad Monument in his own honor. Such arrogance." Mohammad's glance drifts to Ali, the pilot, who stands several yards away, but does not appear to be listening.

Mohammad continues, lowering his voice a notch, "The Shah's so-called White Revolution, his emancipation of Iranian women—these efforts did nothing for Iran's working class; some women prefer wearing their *chadors*. Land Reform? Only unfertile land was left for the peasants. Price controls in the bazaars? Bah. Unfortunate bartering still occurs. In fact, I paid much too much for this shirt," he says, fingering the smooth silk.

Father nods and turns to Mother to explain the protests the previous summer he'd never mentioned before. "Mohammad's right. About a year ago, workers had begun to demonstrate for more wages to pay for the ballooning costs of living. Workplace strikes and arsons also began. Tehran's General Motors assembly plant was burned. Strikes spread to the academia. Professors at universities began to write protest letters, and then disturbances occurred at unlikely events like poetry readings—"

Mohammad interrupts, "Many educators, poets, and writers are now being held in Iran's most notorious Evin prison—for speeches or writings the monarchy considered unfavorable." Mohammad's clear, pure hatred for the Shah makes me wonder why he worked as a driver for the United States Air Force. I wasn't about to tell Mohammad or anyone at the party of my chance meeting with the Shah of Iran.

Behind us, a small commotion interrupts the conversation, a burst of cries and hellos as the James family arrives late with their Iranian landlord, Moshdeh, her name meaning *good news* in Persian. John waves to me, but Frankie grabs his arm and drags him over to our underground garage for a game of wall soccer. Dad, who had obviously been feeling a growing sense of unease during the conversation with Mohammad, leaves to supervise the wall soccer after he says hello to the James and Moshdeh.

"*Salaam*." Moshdeh proceeds to kiss each of our cheeks, rushing in a force of positive energy, so needed a minute ago, like a burst of wind on a spring day. She wears a sheer red scarf on her head, a long flowered crimson dress. Elegant sandals peek out from her lengthy, flowing hem—the scent of jasmine floats about her. John had mentioned to me at the Caspian Sea that besides being beautiful, she was an astute businesswoman, owned a fleet of Tehran rental properties she leased to American military and employees of Bell Helicopter, Amoco, and other American and foreign companies in Iran.

She stops next to my mother, beams.

"And how are we managing so far?"

"Fine, magnificently," Mother replies. "We are fascinated by your intriguing country."

"Wonderful." Moshdeh smiles.

"Let me introduce our daughters. Annette's the studious one. Debbie's our creative and adventurous daughter." I hated when my mother did this, forever pegging me as smart, compared to the cooler characteristics of my sister.

"And Frankie is our eleven-year-old son," Mom continues, nodding over her shoulder at the house. "He's playing in the garage."

"What lovely children, Donna," Moshdeh says, warmth in her bright blue eyes. She leans in to me, and her perfume smells like heaven. "Welcome to Iran. How are you enjoying our country?"

Fine," I say shyly. "We just returned from the Caspian Sea … and Darband." Darband's a town at the base of a ski mountain, east of us in Tajrish, supporting a cluster of restaurants and a rambling river that rushes through it, flanked by a sidewalk where tourists saunter holding paper cups of rosewater ice cream, or sit in patio cafes with large goblets of wine. "There's a chairlift you can ride on in summer," I tell Moshdeh. But Debbie had been too frightened to ride on it when we'd been there, similar to how I imagined she'd been on our plane flight here, surprising about her fear of heights, always so risky in other areas of her life.

In Darband, I'd discovered the writings of the Iranian poet, Forugh Farrokhzad. I knew I'd never forget that first reading of her translated poems, the beauty of her writing, mostly about illicit love and sexuality. I'd found a poem entitled, "Later On", about her thoughts of the possibility of her own death one day; I remembered how I'd stopped reading because something hadn't felt right. Then I'd flipped to her bio, discovered that Forugh had died in a tragic car accident at the young age of thirty-two. My heart broke. I bought her thin book of translated poems that day, pulling out some rials from my purse, always nervous to be handling foreign money, especially since the Shah's face intimidated me on the colored paper bill, his gaze fixed some place over my left shoulder. Forugh was buried in Darband's Zahir Ol Dowleh cemetery—a stone's throw from the bookstore I'd been browsing in.

My mother's exclamation now brings me back to the picnic. "Oh, and *Chelo Kebab* at Darband, Moshdeh! Grilled lamb kebab, saffron-spiced white rice with that crusty layer on top that tastes like—"

"Popcorn? Yes, that is called *Tahdig*—the cooked rice that forms on the pot's bottom that is flipped over onto the plate, like a pineapple upside down cake, revealing that orange crust, a delicacy!" Moshdeh says.

"No doubt no one can cook rice like Iranians," Mother says. "This weekend, we plan to tour the gardens at Tehran University—on Friday—the girls are attending a wedding on Thursday with two Iranian boys ... men rather. Ones they've just met." She eyes us with reproach, unconvinced that a wedding with two strangers—men no less—is wise. And she glances back at Moshdeh.

"Ah, the students, they want a voice." And what Moshdeh says next is not in keeping with her given name, the bearer of good news. "Before you arrived in May, the American School was closed for a time. There was rioting—demonstrations downtown. In January, a large rally of seminary students and religious leaders occurred in Qom. Some were killed. It happened as the holy month of *Moharram* was ending—a week after your president's visit to Tehran."

"What is *Moharram*?" Mother asks.

"*Moharram* marks the mourning for the Prophet Muhammad's grandson, Hossein, the third Imam of Shi'ite Islam, killed in the battle at Karbala. His date of death is known as *Ashura*." I'd wondered about the importance of *Ashura*, why military personnel and families were being warned to be especially careful during these kinds of religious holidays.

"Ayatollah Shariatmadari, a revered cleric here in Iran, took up opposition to the Shah after he read a government-inspired article questioning Khomeini's faith, among other things. Afterward the Shah's police raided his home and one of his students was killed. Other ayatollahs joined forces against the Shah."

In front of us, Frankie performs a perfect cannon ball. The splash of water refreshes me in the languid afternoon heat. I wonder if I should go for a swim, but Moshdeh's story is riveting.

Mother asks, "Moshdeh, who is this Khomeini?"

Moshdeh nods. "Khomeini, a Grand Ayatollah, is a supreme religious leader of the Shiite community. After he had denounced the Shah and what he called the Shah's secular policies—he was placed under house arrest, exiled from Iran.

He has been in Iraq for, oh, fourteen years? Khomeini preaches the necessity for a pure Islam state for Iran."

"We're going to learn about Islam and the Koran in our Iranian Cultural Studies class this year," I offer, inserting myself into the conversation.

"Annie, this is marvelous that your school introduces you to the Iranian culture!"

Moshdeh turns back to Mother. "The Shah has recently made some concessions in the face of this growing opposition, releases from Evin Prison, even replacing the head of SAVAK. This has eased some tension, which I am most happy about. But it may have come a little too late." The conversation falls quiet.

Mother sits still, absorbing Moshdeh's news. During the New Year, at a state dinner toast in Tehran, President Carter had referred to Iran as "an island of stability in a turbulent corner of the world." I wonder if Mom is thinking of this. She begins to speak, seemingly more to herself than to Moshdeh, distracted, "But we were told to bring the entire family to Iran and all of our furniture and belongings. We didn't know any of this!" Her eyes sweep the pool terrace for my father. I take this in. She hadn't been told. Dad is heading towards us from the garage.

Moshdeh looks stunned. "Did your government not tell you of the two American army Lieutenant Colonels who were killed by a bomb on their way to work? Did you not hear of the attempt on a general's life almost a year and a half ago?"

"No," my mother answers, uncomfortable. I wonder now if my father had been a replacement for a murdered air force Lieutenant Colonel.

Dad pulls a chair over to us.

"Phew, the Honda dodged a few bullets," he says, breathless.

"Moshdeh has just been telling us about all the deaths, Jack."

"Deaths?" Dad stares down at his feet.

"Yes, deaths." Mother wills Dad to look up, but his shoes, which are stained with a spot of hamburger grease, hold greater interest for him.

Moshdeh regards my mother with sympathy. "I find it interesting, that in Shi'a Islam, a religious ceremony is usually held forty days after a death. And all these demonstrations— they seem to be occurring roughly on that same schedule—in February in Tabriz, others toward the end of March and May. Many demonstrators killed each time. I am reluctant to contemplate what may be coming next."

Dad shifts awkwardly in his metal lawn chair, likely knowing more than he has let on. Mother looks aware of this, too, face red, posture rigid—eyeballing Dad. Yet she remains quiet. Maybe we were both wrong. Could it be that Dad was just the internal optimist, convinced that a Hawaiian shirt that covered his uniform would keep him safe, even though his work pants were fully visible? That a security wall would protect his family? Or was he just confident that it would all work out, that this was the nature of his assignment in Iran? That he must do what is asked of him in his service to the United States? I recall the American Embassy spokesperson discussing past demonstrations against the Shah by university students. "You know those students, always protesting," the man with heavy wiry sideburns had said. "Remember, Vietnam?!"

Thinking about wars now, I ask, "Didn't World War II have something to do with bringing the current Shah to the throne, Moshdeh?" Something I already knew, having learned about it in History, but I bring it up only to impress her, if I could.

"Ah yes, Annie, you are correct," Moshdeh answers. "A woman who knows her studies. In 1951 a man by the name of Mohammad Mossadegh became Iran's first democratically elected prime minister. Mossadegh preferred that Iran control its own petroleum production though it had been under the control of Britain for about fifty years. Soon though, Great Britain forced a global boycott on Iranian oil, froze assets, and banned exports to Iran. Mossadegh's allegiances with the communist party had frightened the United States and Britain. Mossadegh was overthrown in a two-staged coup called Operation Ajax, ordered by President Eisenhower with CIA involvement. Mohammad Reza Shah returned a stronger leader, no longer a constitutional monarch, but an autocratic one. Mossadegh was placed under house arrest, and it was reported that the Shah subsequently imprisoned, tortured or executed Mossadegh's supporters. The new Prime Minister, General Zahedi, formed an oil consortium, which improved the economy, gave the United States and Great Britain the largest share of Iran's oil. The United States began to fund the Shah's government, military, helped to form SAVAK."

The conversation falls quiet. I change the subject to something more pleasant. "What can we expect from a Persian wedding, Moshdeh?" Moshdeh takes a seat beside me, pulling up her dress and dipping her long, olive legs into the water after removing her jeweled sandals from her dainty feet.

She starts to explain, "A Persian wedding begins with the Sofreh-ye Aghd."

"The *Sofreh-ye Aghd*?" I ask. Moshdeh's toenails are painted cherry red to match her dress.

"It is the legal part of the wedding ceremony, usually attended only by family and close friends. A special fabric is spread out onto the ground and covered with treasures: eggs and nuts to symbolize fertility, honey and sugar to signify the sweetness of the marriage union, and gold coins to represent

73

wealth and success. The couple sit beside a mirror and a candelabra, face east towards Mecca and the sunlight. Burn incense to ward off evil. We Iranians are superstitious that way." She laughs.

Moshdeh touches the scarf on her head absently and continues, "During the ceremony, the married women of the family hold a scarf over the bride's and groom's heads. The groom is asked once if he will marry the bride and his answer is *usually* yes." She laughs, continues, "While the bride is asked three times. Imagine that? Finally, the bride will reply yes. It is a cat and mouse game. Meant to symbolize the husband's pursuit of the wife. Interesting, no?" Moshdeh laughs again, a string of melodic musical notes.

Out the corner of my eye I see Debbie walk over to the security gate and open it. To my surprise, Amir and Reza stand there dressed in pressed jeans and dress shirts. Amir's hair appears damp as if he'd just wet-combed it in place. Debbie brings them over to meet our parents, and Amir apologizes for showing up unannounced at our family's doorstep. Both of them seem bashful.

Amir explains, "We were walking by just now, you know? We see all the cars, Reza and I. And we ask ourselves. Now is not ... a bad time? So we knock on your door." Amir laughs.

He has said "valking", which charms my mother, along with his shy smile. The men each hold out a hand to my father and exchange hearty handshakes. They bow to Mother, who smiles brightly, then motions to the food. After some prompting, their refusal to accept her invitation to eat, my confused mother escorts them over to the buffet table, almost forcefully. Moshdeh leans over to whisper to me, "Iranians usually refuse several times before accepting invitations for food or drink. Known as *Taarof,* it is a pretense at being humble, appearing polite, a custom that is deeply instilled in the Persian culture." Amir and Reza seem smitten with the "all beef" hot dogs my father had grilled, checking first to see that they were not pork, "*Man khook nemikhoram?*"—they exclaim, American hot dogs are amazing. "*Khodaye man!*" Debbie translates for my mother.

My father says, "Amir and Reza, do I have a joke for you."

I stand up to greet them, to circumvent Dad's corny joke, but Mrs. Burnett has approached me to offer a "test-bite" of her Middle Eastern Pasta Salad she'd created for her new cookbook, and apologies for her stepdaughter. "Christie's going through a phase," Mrs. Burnett says as she hands me a paper bowl full of macaroni, faintly yellow as if spiced with saffron. "Don't think it's you, okay?" Mrs. Burnett says brightly. "To be honest, Annie, Christie is having a difficult time adjusting to this country. She misses home. Her mother died recently."

"I'm sorry to hear that. I didn't know."

"That's okay. Christie's seeing someone to get her through this."

"And her mother—" I stop as Mrs. Burnett's eyes cloud over, and I don't press. We notice Mother struggling with a tray of canapés. Mrs. Burnett hurries away, offering to help.

Later, during a novice fireworks display over the pool, we listen to the Cincinnati Symphony Orchestra play John Philip Souza's *Stars and Stripes Forever* on my parents' cassette player. Mr. Ned has consumed a number of *Boomerangs*. He is fiddling with the volume. Dad walks over and lowers the sound.

I wonder about Marc back in Ohio. Was he watching a sky full of exploding color, lying on a blanket, legs entwined with Cindy's? I couldn't think of it. I turn my attention to the guests, some of whom are already leaving. Reza is engaged in deep conversation with Ali. They speak in Farsi, but I can hear animated talk of F-14 fighter aircraft, Phoenix missiles. Amir's eyes are glazed over, decidedly more animated by food than discussions of fighter airplanes—the hot dogs and homemade fudge—eyes that had shone at the mini fireworks display— "Like our *Noruz*!" he had exclaimed at the small burst of color above our pool—and I remember how he'd laughed at the splash of Frankie's cannonball, how he'd been ready to jump into the pool fully clothed before Debbie had stopped him.

Near the security gate, Mrs. James stumbles in her high-heeled sandals. She's consumed a variety of drinks during the night, including the lethal *Boomerang*. And now she's arguing with her husband.

"I'm not quite ready yet. I haven't finished my drink!" Mrs. James complains.

Mr. James removes the *Boomerang* from her hand. "Lisa, you've had enough. Let's call it a night."

"*I'm fine,*" she says, flinging him off like a distasteful insect.

John steers his mother toward the doorway. His cheeks are flushed deep red. "Thank you, y'all." He looks over at me. Kelly shuffles past in her blue Dr. Scholl's.

Ashamed of the lack of real attention I'd paid John tonight, I say, "Let's get together before school starts, you want to? We could play tennis."

John nods, gushing, "That'd be great. I got new tennis shoes at the Co-Op. See?" He lifts up his squeaky clean, pure white sneaker.

"You've got to get those things dirty," I tease.

And then Moshdeh takes my hand. "Peace be upon you and Debbie on your travels. You girls are most lovely." I laugh out loud—a high-pitched and girlish giggle for a woman I admired so much.

I catch Amir looking my way. Still sitting poolside with Debbie, he stares at me, chuckling a little. We lock eyes, then turn away, Amir to listen to Debbie complain about work, me to examine my cuticles. I see Amir sneak a second glance. I blush, then feel a light squeeze on my shoulder. I look up. It's John. "See you soon." He stares at Amir dismissively and leaves the compound.

After most guests had gone, I realize I'm tired, even lonely despite the party. What's the saying—"*all alone in a crowd*"?

"*Shab be kheyr*," I say.

"Night," Amir and Reza call back simultaneously.

"Jinx," I say, then enjoy their quizzical expressions. Amir smiles his boyish grin, blows me a kiss. I blow one back. "See you Thursday."

"See you," Amir says, and his gaze seems serious. I turn, face on fire. I smile to myself and skip upstairs.

Frankie is already tucked in bed, bedroom door closed. My parents are sitting in the living room. Two glasses of white wine rest on the shiny brass coffee table they'd purchased in Greece. They're listening to Vivaldi.

"Did you have a nice time tonight?" Mom asks.

"I did. It was fun." I sigh, wandering to a French door, which overlooks the pool.

"Oh, my, Annette. Are you missing home?" she asks, sympathetically.

"Kind of." I'd been missing my friends and the larger-scale fireworks we'd have viewed from Marc's father's motorboat on the Ohio River. Maybe I was still missing Marc, maybe not, angry with him for dating Cindy so quickly.

"It'll seem more like home once we can shop at the new commissary," my mother says. "We'll go together like we used to at Wright-Patt."

The new commissary was expected to be a state of the art facility in North Tehran compared to the older one on the embassy grounds in South Tehran that resembled a 1950's institutional building, like a school on acres of tended lawns and mature trees, where the American Ambassador, William Sullivan lived. The embassy had even been nicknamed

Henderson High by employees, after the American Ambassador to Iran at the time, Loy Henderson. To me it looked like a hospital campus, the kind where elderly people would sit on benches clutching their canes or feeding pigeons, an oasis in an area of South Tehran already over-crowded with those same, box-like buildings. The embassy held a small cramped store, called the Co-Op, and the commissary.

All military personnel and their families were permitted to use Tehran's commissary facility. Usually, the branches of the military were segregated on their own bases; base stores were either called the PX (Post Exchange) on Army bases, or BX (Base Exchange) on Air Force bases—each was a type of department store/pharmacy. Here, the mission was tri-service: Army, Navy, Air Force, all who'd train and provide assistance—therefore it was dubbed the U.S. Army Mission and Military Assistance Advisory Group, or ARMISH-MAAG.

"You know we really don't have it all that bad," my mother continues. "Sure, this house isn't convenient to a base, and it's apartment style, but it has a pool. We can shop here, buy American food, always find clothes at the Co-Op—you'll be going to an American school."

"Janice at work told me about her friend's family, who isn't military," I say. "Her friend was saying that everything is so expensive here. She shops at those narrow markets like on *Dowlat*. There are sour plums, cherries, and pomegranates. But, because the fruit vendors sometimes wash their fruit in the *jubes*, you've got to be careful to use a special fruit cleanser."

My mother looks to be recalling the women we saw rinsing out diapers in the *jubes*, alongside their dishes. "Sounds unsanitary," she says, "washing fruit in *jubes*."

"Yeah, but they think that because the water flows a certain distance, it's clean."

"That explains it, then." Mom smiles wryly, swirls her Chardonnay around in her glass. "How pleased we are that you've met a nice new friend in Janice, Annette. Invite her over sometime." I nod, wondering if Janice would agree to come.

"Tonight was fun." I think about past holidays back at home. All the colorful explosions lighting up the night sky. The staccato *pop, pop, pop* followed by that screeching *whine*. The quiet in between, when the only thing you'd hear is the soothing rattle of leaves in the breeze, the murmur of just a few people talking, laughter rippling in soft waves. Sometimes a band might play Tchaikovsky's "1812 Overture" during the fireworks' finale—everyone gasping at the brilliant display of red, white, and blue bursts of color, as if a box of crayons had just exploded... But there was something to be said about the magnificence of a saffron sunset. I yawn. "Night. I'm tired. I'm going to bed. Love you."

"Night, sweetheart, sleep well. Love you, too." Mom blows me a chaste mother's kiss.

That night I leave my balcony door open to sleep. A soothing cool wind drifts off the mountains. It feels much better than the chill of a closed off, machine-conditioned room. But The Call to Prayer begins and convinces me to stay awake—less about the noise, more about the intrigue—like a novel too good to put down. And then I remember that our priest would sometimes sing parts of the mass. *Maybe this kind of praying is not so different after all?*

Sometime in the night, a staccato burst of noise sounds outside. *Clack-clah-clack.* Fireworks? I climb out of bed, blinking like an owl, wondering about the noise. I grab my glasses. My perch on my balcony offers me a decent view. In the gloom of night, I can just make out the silhouettes of several young Iranian boys scampering down the street towards the empty field east of our apartment, their fists raised triumphantly skyward, choked-backed giggles trailing after them like scarves. The boys congregate at the construction site, like rugby players going into a game. They chant something indistinguishable, certainly nothing musical.

I hear it again.

"*Marg bar Amrika!*" ("Down with America!")

The boys point something into the air. The motion-sensored mercury vapor light at the construction site now flickers bright to reveal the glint of steel and a black pistol's muzzle. Next come the same sharp staccato bursts I'd heard earlier from my bed.

The boys fire off several rounds into the sky, take off towards the low-lying dismal buildings across the field where we'd met Amir and Reza, had felt so welcomed.

I rush to my parents' room, breathing hard.

"What's the matter, Annette?"

I describe the noise, kids running, gun shots. Dad leaps out of bed, struggles into his pants, hops awkwardly as he stuffs his boxers into his waistband and scrambles out of the room.

I sit on the edge of my parents' bed, wondering suddenly, if the boy who touched my hair—Nouri—is one of those boys with the gun.

My mom, disheveled and half asleep in her flowered nightgown, slips out of bed. She holds a finger to her lips. "Shush, let's not wake Frankie or Debbie." Their air conditioners whirr in their bedrooms like purring cats.

We peer out into the black night from my balcony door. The spooky glow of Dad's flashlight illuminates the pool area. The security gate creaks open.

"He's not going out there, is he?"

"Your father is a tall, strong man. He'll intimidate those boys." Mom wraps an arm around my shoulders.

"Intimidate boys with a gun?"

"They're playing, showing off, Annette, testing us, bored with poverty across that field. Access to guns. You know, the inner city life in Dayton? Gangs. Nothing we're used to, coming from Forest Elms."

Playing? Nothing we're used to? Mom!

I clear my throat. "We had some of that at school in Dayton." Some classmates in our high school hadn't liked us at first, those tough girls in the bathroom with cigarettes hanging from their lips, smoke so thick in the air you could cut it with a knife. At first I'd wondered why there were so many high school students from Downtown Dayton. The landscape surrounding our school was so rural. In between acres of farmland, long empty weedy lots were long offered for sale but never sold, the brokers' signs forlorn and hanging sideways. Except for the mobile home parks that lingered alongside Valley Pike and all the gas stations, there was little development around our school. One of the service stations housed a 7-Eleven that we'd hike to for strawberry or Coke-flavored Slurpees, red hot or sour green apple sticks, hiking the several miles just for something to do. I learned later that our school district had instituted mandatory busing to promote racial balance.

You will become well-rounded, able to experience all walks of life and ethnicities here, instead of only white-skinned Caucasians, Dad had said when we moved to Forest Elms. *Plus houses are cheap in this part of town.*

Dad was right about becoming well-rounded. Debbie and I had each adapted to the cliques. We knew what places and people to avoid, made long-lasting friendships from all walks of life. But sometimes in our school there was tension. Fights. Grudges. Teachers losing control of their classes. I couldn't help but feel that my sister and I were increasingly living on the cusp of danger. Frankie, still in elementary school, had been protected so far, thankfully, now asleep in his bed. I stare outside for signs of my father. I see the glow of the flashlight, hear him climbing the stairs. Finally, he returns, tells us about the fresh scrawl of red graffiti on the outside of our security wall.

"What does it say?" I ask.

"Bad, bad, Amrika," Dad answers.

At least they'd written it in English.

CHAPTER 6

THE WEDDING PARTY

I shall wear
a pair of twin cherries as earrings
and I shall put dahlia petals on my fingernails

From "Another Birth", by Forugh Farrokhzad

Handing gold coins to the marauding band
Getting lost in the midst of the bazaar land

From "Love Song", Forugh Farrokhzad

...the scented branches of jasmine!
The flames of your kiss, on my cold lips—

Forugh Farrokhzad: A passage from "The Dawn of Love"

The sixth dawns a beautiful summer day, bright blue skies without a single cloud, heating up, but pleasantly dry. The thermometer on the kitchen window reads ninety degrees, already.

When Reza and Amir arrive in pressed dress shirts and no-name jeans, we show them the ugly scrawl of graffiti on our concrete security wall. Dumbfounded, Amir declares, "I shall clean it for you! No worries!" Apparently, he's been scrubbing off graffiti with growing frequency from the brick wall of his father's business in South Tehran. His dad, whom he calls *Baba Jan*, partners with his brother, Amir's uncle, in an auto body shop business, employing many first and second male cousins. Amir's father had worked in Iran's General Motors Assembly Plant before it had burned down.

Mother had become nervous about our outing after the conversation at the cookout with Moshdeh. But Amir had

treated my mother with the polite reverence befitting a suitor
(*Khastegar*) of her daughter, and that night Mother had made
the decision to trust Amir and Reza. Amir had offered to bring
her *Barbari* dough to use for pizza crust. She'd encouraged the
men to pick up her daughters at the house instead of the field.

"How did you know where we lived?" Mother had asked.

"We saw very many cars."

She cocked an eyebrow and tilted her head. "Anyone could
be having a party."

"The license plates showed the cars were American
military," Amir had said. We didn't know. We had been unable
to read the Arabic numerals.

Amir had explained that they had hoped to see us, to talk
about Thursday, to meet our parents before the wedding party.
They thought we might come to another soccer practice, but we
hadn't. We were at the Caspian Sea.

This morning, the incident with the wall and gunfire still
fresh in her mind, my mother wanted our trip canceled. We had
no way of getting in touch with Amir and Reza, so they arrived
blissfully unaware of our tumult, promptly, at ten a.m., as
promised, holding a plastic bag filled with a white lump of
Barbari bread dough. After depositing it in our refrigerator, the
men spent several minutes convincing my mother to let us go
as planned.

Amir says, "Mrs. Patterson, the American celebration of
July Four is just wonderful. The fireworks! Ah, so lovely. So
colorful. Your homemade fudge sauce was ... how you say?
Fabulous?"

Mother blushes.

"Decadent," I say, catching on.

Reza rubs his stomach, smiles. Amir brings his long, olive
fingers to his lips and kisses them. "*Kheili khoobe*". His
guttural "K" rolls off his tongue like a Frenchman, "Ah, and

Mr. Patterson's hot dogs! Or should I say Colonel Patterson's?"

My mother laughs, relenting. "All right, girls—if you must, go, but please be careful. Home by midnight."

Debbie and I are thrilled. *Midnight?*

I have on a navy-blue polo and a pair of Levi's, straight-legged compared to my sister's bell-bottomed jeans, the customary red tag tucked into the seam of my back pocket. Debbie wears a hooded sweatshirt that pulls tight across her chest. I have carefully folded my bright red evening dress, bought at the Co-Op for a deep discount, into a duffel bag. Its sweetheart neckline points deliciously to the center of my breasts; its tufted skirt has folds of red chiffon that I'd hoped would fan out around me perfectly to expose a little bit of knee and a lot of leg, should I ever dance a Foxtrot with a spin, like in the movies. Debbie had decided on a pantsuit with lace-like netting on the arms and at the neckline.

"You have dress clothes?" Amir asks. I lift up my bag. "Please no," he says, motioning to me, "hang them on the car door, or spread them out flat in the trunk." He waves his ever-present cigarette. "There is room because I have removed the Persian carpet I usually stow in there for picnics." He grins. *A picnic on a colorful Persian carpet?* The romance of it makes me smile—and the fact that he cares about wrinkled dresses.

Once on our way, Amir explains that he and Reza used to work with the groom at a used car dealership in Tehran, refurbishing foreign cars for resale—mostly Audis and Mercedes. Amir raises the soft canvas top to shield us from the sun. "The men in my family possess an automobile background," Amir says proudly.

I smile at his enthusiasm, trying to forget the number of times my mother had warned Frankie that he must study and attend college or he'd end up being nothing but a garage mechanic.

"After the *Aghd* is the *Aroosi*, or party, which is for us," Amir says. "Very much food, cake, music, and dancing. Sounds very good, no?" Debbie and I both nod yes. "We shall get going then." His smile is wide and generous.

And then the Tehran landscape flashes by us—a continuous streak of dismal gray concrete colored by the vegetable and fruit stands that line the sidewalks—the bloodied slabs of meat hanging from butcher shop windows, the dust-muted red store signs indecipherable on dingy brick walls. Amir drives fast; one hand rests on the steering wheel, the other shifts vigorously. He blows cigarette smoke out a cracked window, smiles mischievously at us in the rear view mirror as we jostle together. I fumble for my seat belt, cough back smoke, nervous about his erratic driving, but then he grins over his shoulder, stubs out his cigarette, and slows down at our concerned faces, his eyes softening.

We cruise down *Pahlavi* Boulevard, Tehran's longest avenue running north to south through the city, known to be the longest street in the Middle East. Large, majestic sycamore trees throw off a luxuriant, cool shade—their leafy branches rise up and over the boulevard in a tunneled vegetation canopy. Amir explains that, in Iran, the sycamore tree is thought to be sacred. "The Shah had all these trees planted." He waves at the knotty, light gray trunks where the bark has peeled off in places, resembling my father's camouflage pants. We pass by several expensive boutiques where fashionably dressed mannequins stare back blankly at us from the storefront windows. Several restaurants have chairs stacked high on their patio tabletops.

"You would like shopping here, yes?" Amir grins in the rear view mirror, and the ash of his cigarette has grown and falls off as he waves it toward all the boutiques.

"Eh," Debbie says, grimacing. But I gaze at the colorful, chic clothes hanging on the mannequins with longing.

"Oh, I don't know, the clothes are awfully pretty."

"Annie loves to dress up. In fact, she's been practicing her Foxtrot every night in her new red dress, in hopes someone will ask her to dance tonight."

I gaze down at my hands, embarrassed.

At the Tehran Grand Bazaar, we wander through long corridors filled with stalls holding wares. Above me, fresco-like paintings of art decorate the ceilings. Other ceilings are arched or fitted with skylights, which allow filtered shafts of dusty light to seep into an otherwise darkened ancient space. The corridors teem with people. The pungent odor of frying onions, garlic, and grilling kebabs fills the air.

In the jewelry aisle, I examine pieces of silver, pure and white gold jewelry laid out on black velvet cloths. I spot an unusual ring made up of multiple interconnected loops. The shopkeeper asks me something in Farsi, and his tone is insistent and harsh. He seems ill tempered, pointing to the person in line behind me to step forward when I don't answer.

Amir pushes his way through the line of people behind me. He asks the shopkeeper gently if he would take out a ring to demonstrate the tricky assemblage, more of a puzzle than a ring. The shopkeeper slams a ring on the counter, motions for me to try it myself. Amir bends to help. His soft breath at my neck tickles me until he manages to assemble the rings into a shape I'm able to push onto my finger. "You like?" Amir asks. "I will buy it for you, then. This is no trouble for me." His grin is wide and toothy. He is eager to give, like a child.

"*Bishtar* (more)," the shopkeeper replies and repeats until Amir and he settle on a price. Flushed red from the heated arbitrations, but in good spirits, Amir appears satisfied with his purchase. Gold puzzle ring in hand, Amir hurries me away before the shopkeeper can yell out once again, "*Bishtar*!" Amir reassembles the ring, slips it on my finger, almost in the dignified manner of a betrothed.

"Thank you," I say warmly.

Witnessing this interplay, Debbie rushes up to take his arm, steer him off to the bazaar's Persian carpets. I let them go, follow Reza to the spice section's abundant baskets, in search of saffron, so my mother can make authentic Persian rice. And Reza tells me how his own mother makes his favorite dish of *Khoresht-e-Gheymeh*, flavored with a blend of saffron and turmeric.

Mid afternoon we travel to the medieval industrial town of Rey to view a public wash and dry of Persian carpets at the warm water spring at Cheshmeh Ali. When we arrive, there are a few onlookers. Men with brooms and sticks brush and beat on numerous rugs at the edge of a large pool. Several women kneel down in the water and wash and rinse them. Once they are cleaned, the rugs are spread out to dry on the face of flat rocks that form a high ridge around the spring. To me, a cliff entirely covered with Persian carpets is like the dressing up of the outdoors. "You like?!" Amir asks. We nod. And the wet wool glimmers in the sunshine. "You must take photographs, Debbie!" shouts Amir. "Have you ever seen such color?"

We arrive at the *Aroosi* before dinnertime. The party is in full swing in the backyard of the groom's parents' apartment house, where the newly married couple will live. A large patio of stone pavers holds an expansive white tent, beneath which are several tables covered in white tablecloths and surrounded by painted white chairs. Miniature tea lights hang from tree branches and surround the fence top like jewels. A band plays Persian music, and several couples are dancing. A long buffet table is loaded with Persian dishes unrecognizable to me, one labeled *Jahaver Polo*, colored by a mix of green pistachios, orange peel, brown almonds and red berries. "Jeweled rice," Amir says, rubbing his stomach, grinning. "*Kheili khoobe.*"

A beautiful bride dressed in traditional white, eyes rimmed in kohl, approaches us. *"Tabrikat!"* ("Congratulations!"), Debbie says to the bride, extending her hand. The bride clasps my sister's hand in hers, "Fatima," she says, smiling shyly. The bride appears young. I had heard that women married at young ages in Iran, but it still comes as a shock. Debbie introduces me, then the groom, Parviz, introduces himself, asks if we like Iran.

"Baleh, Iran keshvarezibai ast" ("Yes, Iran is a beautiful country"), Debbie offers, proud of the Farsi she has already picked up teaching English to her students. *"Farsi man bad ast,"* Debbie apologizes.

"Negaran nabash" ("Don't worry"), Fatima says, squeezing Debbie's hand encouragingly.

I signal to Amir and point to my casual clothes. He speaks to the groom in Farsi, who motions to his cousin to help us, a shy girl with almond eyes and long chestnut hair, wearing a festive chartreuse-colored dress. She escorts the four of us into the house to change our clothes.

Debbie enters a small bathroom off the living room, and I wait outside in the hallway. Minutes later, Amir enters the room, begins speaking to a group of people already gathered there. He has changed into a crisp, dark blue suit and a narrow dark tie. He looks so handsome; my heart flutters.

An American voice booms from the group, a man dressed in jeans and cowboy boots, the only ornamentation a bolo tie. The cowboy's cheeks are full of chewing tobacco, and his arms are crossed over his chest. He's loud, and instantly I know Amir's in trouble. The man wears a tight gray T-shirt, and his sleeves strain at his thick-muscled arms. A large, inky tattoo marks his right bicep.

The cowboy nods over to me, says to Amir, "Iranian women ain't good enough for you, Abdul? Can't get into their chained up pants?" He gives a vulgar clutch of his crotch, stumbles over his words as if he'd been drinking, or smoking something. A crowd gathers.

Embarrassed, Amir starts over to me, shirks off the cowboy who grabs his arm and pulls him back.

Enraged, I stride over to the two of them. "*Leave him alone*," I order between clenched teeth, the cowboy now close enough for me to sniff his overbearing knock-off cologne, his stale beer breath. Debbie appears by my side. "Get out of here, you creep," she shouts, icily, standing tall in her high heeled shoes, legs spread wide, fists raised, ready to deck him cold if she had to.

The cowboy turns to Debbie. "You're the sister slut?" At this, Amir removes his sport jacket and slams into the cowboy with his full body weight and a quiet, controlled anger. "Do not talk to my friends in this way." The protruding veins in Amir's neck pulsate as he pulls the cowboy's tie so taut the man chokes.

"*Vaysa!*" ("Stop!") Reza has appeared from the bedroom. He grabs Amir's hands from the cowboy's neck and shouts, "Not on Fatima and Parviz's wedding day."

"Leave!" Fatima cries at the cowboy. She is standing just behind us and has witnessed the entire argument. The man glares back at the gathered crowd, pulls at his bolo tie, raises up his middle finger, then slams out the back door.

"*Moteassefam!*" "Sorry!" Fatima weeps, explains how the cowboy had come to be invited to the party. How last month she and Parviz had noticed the man entering and leaving his apartment building. Soon after, they'd struck up several casual conversations as they were coming and going, organizing the wedding and after party. The cowboy, who works for Bell Helicopter, was prone to complaining about how expensive things are for him—rent, food … so on and so on. After she'd learned that Amir and Reza were also bringing Americans, she thought to invite him. *So much for Yankee camaraderie.*

Amir pats Fatima on the shoulder, murmurs something in Farsi, then deposits two kisses on either side of a cheek. She smiles weakly, then returns outside to the patio to attend to the partygoers.

"*Delbar*, Annie, your pretty red dress. Go ... put it on," Amir encourages, accent throaty.

Once I'm dressed, I study my face in the oval mirror above the sink. My pug nose and make-up free skin make me look like a child. I take a tube of lipstick and apply a bright red swath of cherry-red color to my lips to match my dress, brush on a light coat of black mascara from a tube labeled "noir", a subtle shade of taupe eye shadow to my lids. "There, that's better," I say to my reflection, snap my lips together, feeling lovely and sophisticated in my cherry-red party dress.

Back outside, we pick at snacks from the long cloth-covered buffet table and sit in chairs facing the dance floor. At first we are content to sit and watch, but eventually, Reza invites me to the dance floor and then Amir asks Debbie. We dance in circles together, at first bashful, but growing comfortable and breathless as the exotic Persian music courses through our veins like adrenaline, forces a dancing style that is more exercise than anything.

Fortunately, as the night grows older, and the dancers grow tired, the music slows. Once the ballads begin, Reza waltzes palm-to-palm with me in dramatic, exaggerated steps. I can hardly keep up. Before each song's final bar, he twirls me around a few times and bends me back for dramatic flair, as if I were an ice skating partner, minus my skates. I pantomime back and neck trouble to him, and then he stops the charade, dances seriously and carefully with me, cheek to cheek, while his scruffy beard tickles my face. The fragrance of dahlias and jasmine perfumes the night air, but the moon's milky light reminds me that we should think about leaving. But Amir and Debbie are dancing song after song like a broken record skipping, and I am reminded of a Frank Sinatra song: *You have danced with him since the music began, won't you change partners and dance with me?*

Later, when an unfamiliar man approaches me to cut in, Reza refuses to give me up. Amir laughs from his table near the dance floor, and my sister leans in, lays her head on his shoulder. Two iced glasses of clear liquid, I guessed was Russian vodka, rest in front of them. Suddenly, Debbie raises her face and kisses Amir full on the lips. A lump forms in my throat. But Amir appears as stunned as I do, and, curiously, he takes a moment to see if I'd been watching. We lock eyes before we both turn away.

I whisper to Reza that this should be our last dance—it is getting late, I tell him, but I can barely speak. *Can't you see I am longing to be in her place? Won't you change partners and dance? You may never want to change partners again.*

Debbie rises up from her chair and files through the maze of round, candle-lit tables; she disappears into the house, a blur of royal blue. I close my eyes as Reza and I dance to yet another ballad. But then I feel Reza's body turning away from me, and when I open my eyes Amir is standing there, tapping at his shoulder. My mouth falls open. "May I?" Amir asks. I stare at Reza, who nods and relinquishes me, bowing. I smile back and curtsy. My legs are putty. Unsteadily, I move into Amir, but then he wraps his suit-cloaked arms around the deep curve of my chiffon-covered waist. I drape my own arms around his shoulders, rest the side of my cheek against the smooth of his face. He nods over to the band, which begins to play a Foxtrot number. I bite my lip as he twirls me around the dance floor and my red skirt fans out just as I'd imagined it would. Dizzy by the dancing and the masculine fresh fragrance of Amir's cologne mixed with the aroma of sweet jasmine in the cool night air, I close my eyes for a second and smile. I can feel Amir's grin press the side of my cheek, and I glimpse Reza wink at me from his table on the edge of the dance floor. All too soon the song is over. Amir grabs my hands, steps back, extends my arms, then drops them. His grin is as wide as I'd ever seen it. He bows and I curtsy back, follow Amir to his table where Reza sits, watching us curiously, one eyebrow raised, a sparkle in his eye. Moments later, Debbie returns. "You guys ready?"

CHAPTER 7

THE KHWANSALAR

Human beings are like parts of a body,
created from the same essence,

When one part is hurt and in pain, others
cannot remain in peace and be quiet.

If the missing of others leaves you indifferent
And with no feelings of sorrow, then you
can not be called a human being

Persian poet, Saadi

(as recited by Jimmy Carter at the State Dinner in Tehran,
New Year's 1978)

Debbie and Amir sit cross-legged in the shade of the sycamore sapling beside our pool studying English. A notebook rests on Debbie's lap, and she writes something across the page for Amir. Their heads are bent forward in heavy concentration—Debbie's long dirty blond hair shines warmly in the sun; Amir's wiry black hair glints silver black, and a soft breeze lifts their hair like feathers. My heart tightens at the sweetness of the scene.

It's August first, Debbie's nineteenth birthday. We'd celebrate with dinner at the Khwansalar restaurant tonight, an atmospheric, cave-like dining spot that caters to foreigners, mostly Americans, providing belly dancers for entertainment, and the kind of Persian food foreigners liked best. Amir had spent the morning removing the graffiti from our concrete security wall after the *Agha* handyman that my father had hired had never showed, the one who was specifically assigned to our alley to miscellaneous odd tasks—to cart away trash

94

(*ashghal*), and shovel off snow (*barf*). My father had informed us that the *Agha* handyman was more reliable in those endeavors, yelling, "*Barf, barf, barfie-a!*" in winter and collecting good money from shoveling off snow from all the flat roofs. Such an unfortunate name for snow in Farsi, I think, laughing.

Today, my father is grateful that the eyesore and billboard advertisement for the country's burgeoning sentiment has finally been removed from our wall after three long weeks. He invites Amir to dinner for his diligent work at Debbie's delight, and mine.

"Thank you. *Merci*, Mr. Patterson. But, no, I am… busy," Amir says, winking. Dad winks back and thanks Amir for his hard work, "*Khasté nabāshee.*"

I shout good-bye to Mother, pass Debbie and Amir by the pool. I am carrying a bag full of tennis balls, a fluorescent-orange terry cloth towel, and my racquet—bought for the sleek panther on the vinyl cover. I stop to study the swirls of Farsi, English and pictures in the notebook. *August* is written in Debbie's careful script, beside it—*Mordad*—in Amir's graceful, masculine penmanship.

"Who's teaching whom?" I ask.

Debbie laughs. "We're teaching each other. Where're you going?"

"To the Gulf District. I'm taking the bus to meet John to play tennis."

"Whoa, oh, oh," Debbie teases. "John and Annie, sitting in a tree, K-I-S-S-I-N-G." I blush at her immature singsong.

Amir studies me intently, shades his eyes from the sun with a long tanned arm. "Must you go alone?"

"Oh, it's fine, Amir. Really." His expression suggests he doesn't agree.

"Want lunch, Amir?" Debbie asks. She grabs his arm, smiles at him possessively. Her pupils are cat-like in the strong sunlight.

He turns to her, fidgets. "Yes, please. Many thanks. I must eat more for *Ramazan*. Build up my strength."

My family was acutely aware that *Ramazan*, the Moslem fasting holy month, was approaching on the fifth of August. Dad had brought home a memo from work that instructed us to keep a low profile during the holiday. "Do you really fast for a month?" I ask Amir.

"Don't be silly, Annie," Debbie says. "Dawn to dusk. You really expect someone wouldn't eat for a whole month? They'd die. For a book worm type in honors' classes, you're incredibly stupid."

"I wasn't thinking."

"Yea-aahh," she drawls, voice dripping sarcasm like honey.

"Debbie, Annie is very smart. You must know this." He pulls at the collar of his NYC T-shirt.

"Yes, but she lacks street smarts." Debbie glares back defiantly—that signature bug-eyed stare she's perfected. "And you must stop writing English right to left!" She slaps his hand.

I ignore Debbie's unkind words and the beginnings of a faintly uncomfortable duel over me. "Speaking of streets," I ask Amir, "do you beat yourself with chains and march in them? I've heard about that."

"No, only fasting and prayer. We eat mornings before dawn—mostly bread, eggs, jam, sometimes dates. We drink tea. This is called the '*Sahari*'."

"Tea, of course, what else?" I smile.

He grins back. "But the real reward comes at night." Amir closes his eyes, rubs his stomach. "In the evening, after fourteen hours of fasting, is the '*Iftar*'. A very large dinner. Then the night usually ends in prayer."

"Sounds cleansing," I say.

"It is. One feels proud to give up something. It is a very good feeling."

"Like our Lent," I say.

Debbie rises up from her crossed-legged position on the pool terrace, grabs Amir's hand and pulls him up. "Come on, let me make you lunch."

I study the two of them. He is as dark as she is light, thin as she is curvy, easygoing when she is not.

"Bye," I call out weakly. I wouldn't think of them; I'd think of tennis with John instead.

Nervous about riding the bus alone, I remembered how we'd been planning to take the bus to the park near the university a couple days after the incident on Independence Day, but Moshdeh had stopped us. Instead she'd arranged to join my mother, sister, and me in a picnic, as a sort of peace offering on behalf of all Iranians to her American friends. She demanded to drive us personally to the park. When she'd arrived at our apartment that day, she'd pinched my cheek to near bruising, and cried, "Annie, we Iranians love you, do not fret. Your mother has informed me of the nasty chants and the neighborhood boys' artistry on your security wall. In fact, I have just seen it for myself, and I am disenchanted, my darling girls."

That day Moshdeh had loaded us up in her flashy black Mercedes. And immediately, she lowered the convertible's canvas top, laughed as if she hadn't a care in the world, her white teeth flashing like stars. "You like?" I remember how Debbie had thrown up her hands in the wind, head back, shouting, "Whee!!!" How Moshdeh's dark, long locks had tangled around her head in beautiful curls, how the wind had stretched Mother's smile into a silly but attractive grin, and her hair had remained tidy underneath a summer scarf. What do you know? I'd thought, Mother has made a friend.

Moshdeh drove us south, past corrugated tin huts glinting in the sun as far as the eye could see. "A shanty town," Moshdeh explained over the engine's roar, and the car party quieted as we passed the settlement tucked deep into the valley—rows and rows of ramshackle huts and sheep, goats and donkeys wallowing in the mud. Sewage and litter filled the streets. Blue tarps and laundry acted like curtains; cardboard and tin were substitutes for roofs. Tires, like paperweights, anchored the flat steel and cardboard panels. Everything seemed crooked and unstable like a house of cards, as if a gust of wind might suddenly knock the entire thing down.

I'd heard about Tehran's shanty towns. How last summer, the Shah's government had tried to shut down the ones scattered around Tehran that housed more than one million people. How this had been met with unrest and the police were forced to raid them, arrest occupants, cut off utilities. Several people died. But after failing to move the shanty town dwellers to government housing, the order to disperse had been lifted by summer's end.

When we'd arrived at the park, Moshdeh showed us the entrance gate to the university, its interesting architecture. Next she bought us grilled corn, still in the husk, from cart vendors. She surprised us by confiding that she'd been married and grilled corn known as *Balal,* had been her husband, Hassan's, favorite treat. He'd been working a construction crane at the site of one of the high-rise apartment buildings going up all over Tehran, and it toppled over, leaving him trapped in the cab and partially submerged in a pile of soft dirt. His coworkers had managed to free him, but not in time. Even if he had been freed alive, his head and neck injuries would have been too severe for him to have survived.

Moshdeh had explained that her husband had left her with enough money to be comfortable, but not enough to live the quality of life to which she'd been accustomed—purchases of pretty skirts and pairs of shoes, dangling earrings and trendy necklaces, bottles of jasmine perfume or Chanel No. 5. She'd fallen into such a state of immense grief without the love of her life, and all her luxuries, that she had spent her days in bed, comforted only by her soft and heavy bed covers. She felt she had no one to live for, no prospects for employment—hadn't worked in years—her dreams of having children were dashed. She and Hassan had been trying unsuccessfully for years.

One morning, after Moshdeh had caught sight of her pale, sullen face in the mirror, her eyes heavy with sleep and rimmed by dark circles, her hair unkempt—so tangled that birds could nest there—Moshdeh had decided once and for all to snap herself out of her doldrums. She began walking daily in the park, preparing healthy and simple meals each night, serving them up on her delicate Wedgwood china. She took long, hot perfumed baths, dressed up carefully each day. The hours that extended luxuriously before her were now considered a precious gift. She read in her free time, mostly poetry—Rumi, Sadi and Hafez. Once she had regained her strength, Moshdeh enrolled herself in several real estate courses focused on leasing. She invested her money in a two-unit rental property, sold it several years later for a tidy sum, acquired a second with additional rental units. Moshdeh now owned four Tehran apartment houses she leased to Americans and other foreigners for what were very handsome sums. Now, she was contemplating buying vacation property at the Caspian Sea.

"Have you heard of the 'Lady in Red'"? Moshdeh asked.

"The Lady in Red?" My mother shakes her head no, but her curiosity is piqued.

"Let me tell you about her then." Moshdeh had spread out an expansive flowered blanket on a sunny patch of grass. "Sit," she'd prompted, and we obeyed. She'd reached for her bamboo picnic basket and began to recount the story of the Lady in Red as she handed out thick pita pockets overloaded with white meat chicken salad, tossed with slivered almonds and pale green grapes.

"Beginning in the 1960s, a woman with a gaunt, weathered face, always bright with make-up, would stand in Ferdowsi Square each day, from dawn to dusk, wearing nothing but red. Her shoes, her socks, her handbag, her long dress were all red. Mostly, though, she just stood there, turning her head side to side, searching the street. Sometimes, she would carry a single, long-stemmed red rose. Other times, she would teeter on spiky high heels of red suede or red velvet, or sit on the ground fatigued, casual as she waited, red high-heeled shoes long discarded and resting next to her, legs crossed at her ankles, feet bare—her gaze pensive and sorrowful. As if she were saying, please come already, I'm tired of waiting. Many people who saw her also thought she was expecting someone. A long lost love? Maybe. Everyone was certain she was standing at a long ago agreed upon meeting place. And, for some reason, her lover never showed."

"You speak of her in the past tense, Moshdeh? Did she die?" I'd asked, picking at short, thin blades of green grass alongside the picnic blanket.

"No, it is rumored she stands there to this day. I have not seen her for quite some time now. I am not often in Ferdowsi Square." Moshdeh had rested back on her elbows then, her lovely face raised towards the sun, appreciating the warmth. I'd wanted the story to go on forever. I'd wanted a happy ending.

"I'll go look for her," Debbie announced, determination like fire in her eyes. "I will find out who she's waiting for. Help her find him." And I wished I had said the same, before Debbie. *How romantic would it be to save the Lady in Red? How adventurous.*

And Moshdeh had only smiled. "*Darmet Gham*. You do that, most certainly, Debbie, for I encourage brave, strong and curious young women."

"Annie was the Lady in Red at the wedding we just went to."

"Oh, is this so, Annie?" Moshdeh had teased. "And were you waiting for a lover as well?"

I remember how I'd smiled a secret smile, tried to keep from laughing, as Frank Sinatra's crooning voice crept into my head.

Now on the bus to the Gulf District, I search for splashes of red in the crowd, but the color of choice is black. An older woman sits quietly on the bus opposite me holding a large bag on her lap. She examines me curiously. Two young children sit in front of me and also stare, but happily, grasping for me with outstretched hands. "Your hair," their young mother says, "the color—they like. Streaks like corn silk." She smiles, points to the top of her own head.

I gaze at her children's round, liquid brown eyes, their jet-black hair and chubby faces. "Your children. They're beautiful." Their mother smiles back at me proudly. "*Salaam*," I say to her children and smile. Suddenly, worry knits the woman's brow, and she hugs her children protectively. I had forgotten that Iranians avoid addressing unknown children directly, feeling that their children are in danger if talked to by strangers. "It's okay," I whisper gently.

I find John at the Gulf District courts hitting neon green and orange balls against a green backboard.

"Hi," I call out, slipping out of my jeans and T-shirt to reveal a short, white tennis dress.

"Howdy! You made it. You look great. How was the bus ride?"

"Fine. I was nervous to be alone at first, but got the hang of it. How was your walk here?"

"Not bad, about twenty-five minutes." John's apartment was closer to the Gulf District and to his father's workstation in East Tehran, near the Italian embassy at Ninth *Koohestan*.

"Want to warm up?"

"Sure."

We volley back and forth casually, lobbing the balls easily and politely over the net, until we decide to begin an official game. His serve is difficult to return. I hit it awkwardly off my racquet's rim. The next serve I manage to slap back at him, bouncing it neatly inches from his toes. He's able to lob it up awkwardly, high into the air, then back over the net. I slam the ball back past him with a strong backhand stroke.

"Very nice," he calls out, impressed.

Our game continues in this manner until we are too hot and sweaty to play any longer. We head over to the pool to cool off. I point to the brick office building behind the courts where I work. After a frigid dip into the pool, we grab two lounge chairs and order two Shirley Temples from the poolside waitress. Almost at once she brings over long, tall glasses of cherry-colored liquid, filled high with bobbing maraschino cherries and paper umbrellas. John pays her as I fumble for money.

"My treat, Annie." We sit quietly, taking in the pool's brilliant blue, the carefully trimmed shrubs at the lawn edges that frame the pool area, all very neat and tidy, calming.

"How's your Mom?" I ask.

"She's okay," John says quietly.

"We had a graffiti incident on the Fourth."

"Graffiti?" John furrows his eyebrows.

"Yeah. A group of boys wrote, 'Bad, bad America', in red spray paint on our security wall." This truly bothered me, despite Moshdeh's peace offering. As if my family were hated, instead of the American government, Jimmy Carter ... most all foreigners. I remembered in elementary school when I had learned that Janet Hager from fifth period band class disliked me, and I was upset, my friend Diana had said to me impatiently, her faced reddened beyond the flush of her usual peaches-and-cream complexion, stopping her noisy sipping from her five cent carton of milk through a straw, "Honestly, Annie, you can't be liked by *everyone*." But I wanted to be. I believed in people almost blindly, respecting our leaders, our president, having no true political opinions yet, crying even when Nixon resigned, upset how he'd been surrounded by his beautiful wife and daughters.

"Geez, I'm sorry," John says, concerned.

"Yeah. Amir scrubbed it off for us." My voice rises a notch at the mention of Amir's name.

"That Iranian guy at the party?" John asks warily.

"Yes, Debbie's guy." I shift in my lounge chair, steer the subject away from Amir. "Have you noticed any hostility from any of the Iranians you know?"

"No, not really. Our neighbors are so far still friendly." He pauses for a moment. "Come to think of it, my Iranian friend, Hamid, hasn't asked me to play soccer in several weeks. He doesn't seem the type to harbor ill will though. Our landlord, Moshdeh, well you know, she's great."

We close our eyes, rest on our long, colorful lounge chairs. The Bee Gees are singing "Jive Talkin" on the pool radio. Nothing better than this, I think. Tennis, swimming, music, sweet drinks, and summer … The smell of coconut sun tan oil. It felt so … American.

John takes my hand in his. Too tired to move away, I dream of the pool in Ohio that had a little patch of lawn where I had spread out a towel next to Beth Hurley, after she had taught me to swan dive.

I return home from the Gulf District before dinnertime. Amir has already left, and I am disappointed. I pull on a sheer rust-colored flowing skirt, hang chandelier-style earrings from my ears, slip into open-back sandals. My sister throws on a sweatshirt and jeans, but changes when my mother complains,

"Can't you wear a dress this one time? At least a skirt?" Debbie compromises with a nice pair of cotton pants, and a colorful T-shirt in a turquoise and pink paisley design that adds a touch of formality.

At five o'clock we pile into our small Honda Civic and drive downtown to the Khwansalar restaurant. Once inside, we are escorted to a table set for five in a dark, but lovely space, already crowded with diners.

In front of us is a small stage illuminated by a spotlight shining on a cave-like backdrop. The walls are stone, the floors concrete. A woman wearing a purple gauzy two-piece outfit is dancing, pivoting her hips in wide sensual circles, gyrating methodically to the rhythmic pulse of the Persian music that plays in the background. She raises her hands above her head, moving them together, weaving them in the air like slithering snakes coiling down a tree. I am mesmerized. Her dark hair tumbles over her shoulders. Frankie looks away. "Sheesh."

The waiter hurries over to take our orders. Mother whispers to him that it is my sister's birthday. He seems to tuck away this information for later as a good waiter would do. When our drinks arrive, we hold up our glasses to Debbie. She toasts back, smiling proudly. And out of nowhere, Amir appears behind us. I gasp. Debbie turns her head and a vibrant smile spreads across her face like wildfire. "Happy Birthday, Debbie!" He approaches her carrying brightly wrapped packages.

"Amir, you said you were busy tonight? *Liar*," Debbie accuses tartily, flinging her hair.

"Surprise." Amir leans over and kisses Debbie's cheek. He sits down in the empty seat between Debbie and me, only glancing at the gyrating belly dancer without interest. The waiter brings over another place setting and a glass of water. I understand now why Mother had asked us to leave the chair open next to Debbie.

"Order, Amir. Get something fattening, something that'll stick to your bones," I encourage.

He orders an entree on the menu we'd never heard of. He is wearing the same dark suit he had worn to Fatima and Parviz's wedding with the long thin tie. He leans over to me, winks, and whispers in his heavy accent, "I ordered sheep tongue and sheep brain just now."

"Ugh." I laugh back.

"Amir, when will you take me to meet your family?" Debbie asks.

Amir smiles back slowly, shifts in his seat. He deflects the question by circling his pointer finger around his right ear and says, "Ah, my crazy Iranian family. My Grand *Baba* (*Baba Borzog*), Ali. You will meet him and run back home crying!!"

"How crazy?" asks Debbie.

"Crazy, but, how you say, lovable—not to worry," Amir explains. "Too much Opium back in the day? He drives over our carpets to age them, and he is always losing everything, keys and glasses, his Koran …. Blames the *Jinn*."

"Gin, as in gin and tonic?"

Amir laughs, "No. J-i-n-n. Evil spirits. And my Aunt Laleh! Agh! She has looked for a perfect wife for me ever since I have turned eighteen." The minimum marriageable age in Iran for women was eighteen and for men, it was twenty, thanks to the Shah. "She asks my *Maman's* cousin's daughters, 'How well do you cook? Clean?' Crazy! I shall marry for love," Amir declares, more to himself than to us, folding his arms in front of him. "No third or second cousin, no-*nakheyr!* Two more years of freedom!"

"Was Fatima and Parviz's wedding arranged?" I ask.

"Yes," Amir replies.

"I'm not marrying until my thirties. I want to travel through Europe. Go to college. Write," I say.

"Marrying wouldn't be so bad if my husband were rich. I could travel and take my photographs. I'd hire a maid. You know how I hate to clean and cook," Debbie adds.

"Yes, we realize that," Mom deadpans.

"I'm not getting married, ever," Frankie says.

My parents smile. They had married young for love and because my grandmother on my mom's side was dying.

"Islamic law permits marriages for girls at your age and younger, Frankie, but our government has changed that." The apples of Amir's cheeks redden. "To be fair to Islam, a girl must be old in head and in body," he says as he points to his head and body, puffs up his chest. "Islamic law also permits a man to have many wives, but most men in Iran do not wish for that."

Frankie is uncomfortable with the conversation.

My mother chimes in. "Early marriage is usually only for poor families living in villages, with no hope for their daughters to become educated—who, with a small dowry, can have their daughter taken off their hands, financially, so to speak. Isn't that right, Amir? For those girls who have grown up cooking, cleaning, and doing household chores, without an education, marriage may be the wisest next step for them, however much we don't understand it. Amir is intimating that it may be Islamic law to marry young, but it isn't Islamic culture. Especially in a sophisticated city like Tehran," my mother offers.

Amir nods, but I wonder how much he'd taken in.

"Amir, are you a devout Moslem—deeply or just medium religious?" I ask.

Amir winks and asks Debbie, "You teach me medium?" My sister holds up her hands explaining small, medium, and large by the expanding air space between her palms.

"Medium," Amir replies. "I enjoy prayer, going to mosque. I believe in Muhammad. No pork, *haram*, but a little bit vodka, sometimes." He suppresses a small embarrassed smile. "I like disco. A woman's face in the sun. My wife will be beautiful, if not to others, to me. Her hair will shine outside in the sunshine if she chooses. Her dresses will be long and flowing, or short, as will be her choice. She will paint her eyes or she will not—I will not judge. She will have books in her head. We will read poetry under our mulberry tree in our courtyard garden. Listen to music by the light of the moon. Our courtyard fountain will gurgle water. We shall have four or five children, *Inshallah*. If this is her wish. We shall grow old together in this beautiful country of ours, Iran. Bound in marriage 'til death do us part."

We remain silent. This sentimental discussion was unexpected from Amir.

"Goodness, that sounds wonderful, Amir, you should be so lucky. A toast to romantic Amir," Mother encourages, giggling like a school girl.

We clink our glasses together. Debbie is pouting.

"Books in her head? But you ride motorbikes?" Debbie's expression is akin to someone who has just drunk sour milk. I knew she was focused on two words: *our country*.

"You teach me English do you not?" Amir looks puzzled.

"Do you live near us, Amir?" my father interrupts.

He looks up relieved. "Not too far, Mr. Patterson, several blocks away. My house is different from yours."

"How so?"

"Little furniture (pronouncing little as leetle), many carpets. Pillows. Long pillows to lean on. We eat on the floor sometimes. And we have hard uncomfortable chairs we use only for receiving important guests. All the windows on one side of our house face into *Maman*'s rich garden."

"*Lush* garden," corrects Debbie.

"You eat on the floor?" asks Frankie.

"Yes, but not always."

"Amir, if I had my wish, we'd also possess hard uncomfortable chairs. Fancy antiques, instead of the wood veneer furniture we have now." My mother needles my father with her elbow.

"But your furniture is very wonderful." Amir cocks his head sideways. "Wood veneer is better than no wood at all? Yes?"

Our food arrives, served up on large mosaic plates, the main dish laying on a heap of rice. My lamb is charred to a musky crispiness, and it tastes succulent and wild. Frankie dives into his food in an effort to evade the belly dancing to his left. Dad also digs into his meal, dispensing with all conversation as he was known to do after food is placed in front of him. I am curious about Amir's way of cutting his meat, using the edge of his spoon. I ask him about it, and he shows me, touching my hand to position the spoon just so. I pull back my hand as if I'd touched fire.

After dinner, the waiter brings over *Yazdi* cake, a Persian dessert flavored with cardamom and rosewater. He has inserted a single lit candle into the cake, sets it before Debbie, and sings:

Tavallod, Tavallod
Tavallodet mobarak
Mobarak, Mobarak
Tavallodet mobarak

"A birthday wish in Farsi, just for you," the waiter says in broken English, smiling widely and bowing, one arm tucked behind his back.

"Perfect!" Mother exclaims, clapping her hands and thanking the waiter profusely for his Persian birthday song. He leaves to retrieve cups of steaming hot coffee for my parents and sister, strong brewed tea for Amir and myself.

Debbie begins to unwrap Amir's gifts quickly. First, she uncovers a toy camel with an authentic looking beige hide and a single hump. Another present is a toy doll, a *Chelo kebab* griller. The pint-sized man is dressed in a rolled-white turban, white peasant shirt, and flouncy black velvet trousers. A dark mustache is painted above his upper lip and he is holding miniature steel grilling paraphernalia in one hand, a plastic kebab of skewered meat in the other. "Cute!" I tell Amir while Debbie moves the gift aside. The third package holds a doll-sized mosaic ceramic tea set. Debbie gazes up at Amir, and disappointment is written all over her face.

"Thank you, Amir. But what about the puzzle ring?" She huffs. "We talked about it. You got one for Annie, remember at the bazaar? Don't you know I have an aversion to dolls?" Her face is pinched as she slides the presents over to Frankie on the table. "Here, you still play with dolls." The rest of us sit without speaking, uncomfortable, trying to ignore the awkward exchange. I am amazed at how ungrateful my sister could be at times.

"What?" She asks, eyes bugged, staring at us around the table, not caring that her words are hurtful. "Dolls are creepy."

I pick up the gifts, enjoy how the figurines each mimic real life in miniature.

Amir raises his chin, explains that all the presents are memorabilia of Iran for Debbie—he'd bought the pottery set at the bazaar. Amir's usually full lips are pursed thin and after finishing his tea, he pulls back his chair abruptly, bids us good night. He plants a quick kiss on Debbie's forehead.

"Thank you for your wonderful hospitality," he says and moves around the table to shake my parents' hands, tousle Frankie's hair, and squeeze my shoulder. "May peace be upon you, *Khoda ha Fez.*"

He fumbles in his pocket for money, but my father stops him. "No, Amir, this is my treat for your hard work today on the security wall."

On the drive home, the streets are subdued but still active, the moon looms large, and the air is fragrant with the sweet scent of flowers, not now in competition with the exhaust from the day's heavy traffic.

"You were impolite," my mother says to Debbie flatly. "You're a grown woman, Debbie, and can do what you like, but I'd have hoped I'd instilled better manners in you." My mother always claimed that what we did reflected on *her* character. "Always be grateful for gifts and respectful of the gift giver."

Debbie stares out the car window into the inky darkness, brightened by occasional streams of flashing neon. She folds her arms across her chest.

Once home, I march directly to the dining room hutch my parents had purchased from the furniture store, Levitz, when we'd first moved to Ohio. I grab out a small square of leftover birthday wrapping paper, tape and some scissors, then take them to my room. I place the puzzle ring I'd pulled from the bottom drawer of my jewelry box on the square of gift wrap. After I'd finished, I carry the flat unadorned package to Debbie's room, lay it on her pillow. Washing up for bed, I make a silly face at my girlish reflection in the mirror, promise myself I'd forget about Amir, never feel guilt about that puzzle ring anymore. Debbie's boyfriend had given it to me, and it wasn't right for me to keep it anymore.

"Happy Birthday, Debbie," I call over to her in the living room, where she's listening to music.

"Annie?" she asks.

"Yes?" I ask as I amble over to her, smiling, imagining how excited she'd be at my present.

"Stop flirting with Amir, okay?" she warns flatly. And my smile freezes stiff on my face like ice.

Ramazan begins on the fifth of August. The entire month, we see very little of Amir. I wasn't sure if his absence was because of my sister's attitude on her birthday, the responsibilities of the holiday, or a crazy work schedule. Debbie convinces herself that this was the explanation, the holiday and work. However, exactly two weeks after her birthday dinner, a breathless Amir appears at our doorstep early in the morning before work.

I am heading across the pool terrace in a pleated gray skirt, a crisp white blouse, and black high-heeled pumps. We were having a payroll *efficiency* meeting that morning, and I'd dressed carefully, professionally. I am waiting for the white minibus the Air Force sends around to retrieve their student summer-hires at their homes, when someone outside buzzes our intercom. I open our security door quickly once I hear Amir's voice. Amir rushes in.

"The Khwansalar restaurant was bombed," Amir says.

"What?" My hand flies to my mouth. "No."

"Last night, blown up … to pieces." I perform some mental math, realizing that this happened two weeks to the night we'd celebrated Debbie's birthday there.

"I came to be certain you did not go back." Amir is breathless, fear showing on his face. He stands so near to me I can see the pores in his skin. I close my eyes and touch his shoulder.

The alluring belly dancer dances in my mind—the attentive waiter treading so delicately as he'd brought the Persian cake to my sister, the candle wavering mystically in the breeze but remaining lit. "That nice waiter! The belly dancer! Was anybody killed?" Amir nods. I can hardly tolerate the thought of it.

"I only know that many were killed."

I swallow, nodding. "Well, Amir, we are here. We're fine. It's awful, though." I shiver, feeling that things were beginning to creep in. "Do you want me to go find Debbie?"

"No. I must return to the *Iftar*. I am thankful you are all safe, Annie." He touches my face tenderly, squeezes my hand. "I am taking more professional English classes. I hope to have conversations more worthy of your intelligence." He looks at me again closely, pointing to my clothes. "Why, Annie, you look very wonderful … Your dress for work?"

"Oh, this? Thank you," I say shyly. "Yes. I threw something on today for a meeting we're having." I grin, smoothing my skirt, my face flushed hot. Amir's smile back to me is as disarming as I'd ever seen it. Once again. My heart flutters. *"Khoda ha fez."* The security door clips shut behind him. I stand still, hands curled tight over my lips, breathing in the fragrance of him.

Debbie's voice comes over the intercom. "Amir, is that you? Did you buzz us? Amir?... Amir?" A few moments later, she appears at my balcony door. I signal to her that Amir had gone, with the wave a referee might make as he was signaling, "No good." Or "Out of bounds." A signal meant for me and not for Debbie.

During the rest of August, demonstrations, killings, and bombings occur with alarming frequency. We learn that the day before the Khwansalar restaurant bombing the army had fired upon demonstrators in Isfahan, and martial law had been declared there. I knew that martial law meant an emergency military state. We learn that the SAF organization had claimed responsibility for the Khwansalar restaurant bombing, though I don't know what SAF stands for. The news claimed that seventy people had been killed or injured.

My parents begin to listen to the BBC radio news, morning and night, from their small, old-fashioned, pale yellow radio on the top of our refrigerator. Often I'd enter the kitchen to find my parents at our Formica-topped table listening to that radio, my father pensive with his legs crossed, one ankle resting on top of a knee, my mother sitting across from him with a scowl and her Franciscan Ware teacup, the rim soiled pink by a smudge of lipstick. The only other news available to us was through the Shah's National Iranian Radio and Television Service. I'd watch the beautiful English speaking Iranian NIRT newscaster, Suzie Ziai, announce the news in her measured newscaster's voice, pronounce *Tehr-ha-Rahn* with a breathy "huh" and a roll of her "R", using appropriate phonetics belonging to the more traditional spelling of "Teheran". The news in the paper was never current, censored before publication. We also had access to the Armed Forces newspaper, the *Stars and Stripes*. The Armed Forces Radio and Television Network had ceased operations before we arrived in Iran. My father had also been receiving spotty announcements from work and periodic news through the Embassy and the State Department. The instruction was "business as usual, everything is under control. Go about your regular activities with extra caution. Keep a low profile."

It's my last week in Employee Payroll. I feel I've hardly worked there, knowing my earnings would be just a drop in the bucket for college. Janice asks me to lunch at the Officers Club. The television above the bar shows news footage of a roaring fire. It's in a city in southwest Iran, near the Persian Gulf, named Abadan—a crowded movie theater with people trapped inside, mostly Iranians. The newscaster reports that initial tallies have the death toll at about four hundred people, and there were conflicting opinions about who was responsible, the Shah, SAVAK, or militant Islamists? The theater was found locked at all exits, and the fire department's response had been surprisingly slow. But the theater manager often locked the main entrance door at the beginning of a sold-out show. The Shah was blaming radical Islamists.

"Jesus," says Janice vehemently. "Sometimes these people are such savage beasts."

"Who, Iranians?" I ask.

"Yes, Iranians," Janice says. She requests another glass of water from our Iranian waiter who has friendly, gentle eyes.

"You see how little we pay them?" I say. "You do the books. Maybe they're just unhappy." But our own janitor, Mahmoud, the household head of a family of eight, constantly shoots me his high wattage smile before he bends to empty my trash basket. "Scuze me, *Khanoum* Annie, may I disturb your most important work for just one second," he'd say.

But now I see that a light has clicked off in Janice's eyes. You could never argue with her.

I am supposed to take in a movie at the Gulf District with John in a couple of weeks. I already have a Shakespeare paper due from my summer reading assignment for English Lit; this triggers thoughts of Marc as Romeo in last fall's production of Romeo and Juliet, playing alongside Cindy as Juliet. I can't believe I'd missed the almost imperceptible rise of Marc's body as he'd kissed Cindy, proud of how well he could act. I decide I should skip the movie in case my luck is running out on me here in Iran, but thoughts of Marc and Cindy urge me to go.

CHAPTER 8

AUGUST, SEPTEMBER 1978

Life is perhaps
a child returning home from school.

Life is perhaps lighting up a cigarette
in the narcotic repose
between two love-makings
or the absent gaze of a passerby
who takes off his hat to another passerby
with a meaningless smile and a good morning.

Selected Sections, "Another Birth",
by Forugh Farrokhzad

I am entirely alone at the bus stop on my first day of school, missing Debbie. She had always waited with me at the bus stop since I was in kindergarten. Today, Frankie, so much younger than me, is able to sleep in, go to school later. I'd left him tumbling around in his bed, likely as worried about his first day of school as I was. It feels strange going on with weekday business on a Saturday. But I expected to feel even more off kilter tomorrow in school on a Sunday—as odd as I felt in church on a Friday. Christie Burnett is also absent from the bus stop this morning. I had an inkling why after an early morning argument woke me up from a sleep made fitful by first day school jitters.

"I'm not going to school!" Christie had shouted early this morning in her bedroom just below me.

"You must," Mrs. Burnett had answered back flatly.

"I don't have to do anything I don't want to."

"Yes, you do."

"Shut up, Julie. You of all people? Telling me what to do?"

I'd been morbidly fascinated by their argument; I listened hard in my bed.

"It's all I can do to get that image of you and Dad in Mother's bed out of my mind. Her body not yet cold in her grave—smoking your damn cigarettes. I wish you never happened. I want my old school back. You can't make me go to this stupid foreign one."

"Christie, we've been over and over this. You surprised us that day by coming home early. Skipping class. Don't you see? It was a private moment between your father and me, never meant to have been witnessed. You know how devastated I am about your mom—your father, also, how supportive I've been to you, but dear, I am your father's wife now. I need you to get out of bed. Get dressed. It's an American school, for God's sake. You'll meet friends."

I sigh, sad to have heard such a private exchange. And speaking of privacy, was there any in that house? Did high ceilings and marble floors magnify sound? The day was heating up, and I am thankful for my cool, white cotton sleeveless shirt and the thin beige poplin pants I had put on for the first day of school.

A large commercial bus with a sign labeled "TAS" on its windshield pulls up to the curb. The door slides open. I climb the stairs and turn towards the aisle, to all the kids that fill the bus, those few girls who smile shyly up at me. I return their smiles, think about how odd it is to be riding to school in a commercial bus more suitable for a touring rock band, than for a bunch of school kids. My plush fabric-covered bucket seat is equipped with seat belts never found on a yellow school bus back home. There is a bathroom just behind me.

The Iranian bus driver happily moves back out into the stream of heavy traffic. "Welcome!" he bellows jovially, smiling in the rear view mirror. The serious dark man across the aisle in a black suit coat and jeans reminds me of my dad's bodyguard.

Never had I encountered such heavy traffic on a bus trip to school. The bus driver is vocal, yelling and throwing up his hands when another driver cuts him off. He handles the large vehicle expertly, weaving in and out of traffic, passing cars adroitly, even a truck full of watermelons. He easily avoids a stray, feral dog when the animal darts in front of the bus from between a line of parked cars. "Ah, next time I run over you!" the driver yells, laughing. I had noticed that many Iranians lacked the unconditional love most Americans felt for dogs, considering them unclean. And Mother won't have one, which gives me dog envy, even for street dogs. Iranians' best friend seemed to be the long-haired Persian feline, understandable, considering how cats were always grooming themselves.

Mostly men are out at this hour in dark suits, their starched shirt collars fanning out from their suit coats like the extended wings of a seagull. Their shirts are tucked into thick wool sweater vests, despite the heat, and they are dashing around with either a morning newspaper tucked beneath an arm, or bread. And they nod polite hellos to passers-by, but are intent on their business.

After what seems like forever, but is only an hour and fifteen minutes, the bus pulls into an ugly concrete compound of mostly blacktop and grimy brick buildings. Some entranceways are framed by pinkish, concrete latticework that lends the school a sad 1950's institutional appearance. It's like an urban Catholic school where kids in plaid uniforms might skin their knees on the blacktop at recess. One of the school wings resembles a two-story motel you'd find on a divided highway, on a seedy commercial strip, all colored doors and windows, metal stairs and second-floor walkways. I feel slightly ill.

Immediately, I meet a friend named Alika Aoki in English Lit. She wears rectangular-shaped glasses and a long tunic-style purple flowered shirt. She introduces herself at the pencil sharpener in the back of the room.

"I've never met anyone named Alika before," I say, shyly.

"It's Hawaiian, means defending men."

"Nice, your name. My name's Annette, Annie for short. My parents named us after their favorite actors, Annette Funicello, Debbie Reynolds, and Frankie Avalon."

"My biological mother named me. I'm Hawaiian-American and adopted. To be honest, I have no clue why she chose Alika."

"Maybe she wanted you to be a protector of yourself. Get along in the world without her?"

"Maybe, Annie, a nice thought. I wish I could ask her why."

An uncomfortable feeling lodges in the pit of my stomach all day long. In our dreary cafeteria at lunchtime, I pass a crowded table of girls dressed in flared jeans and rock band T-shirts. I spot Janice among the group, manage to catch her eye, but she looks away. I glance down at my clothes, make a mental note to dress more casually in the future. I turn to see Alika's gleaming black hair. She occupies a corner table by herself and relief passes over her face when she sees me; she waves me over. We eat our home-packed lunches together, compare afternoon class schedules. I am relieved we'd have Writing together.

In French, we learn we'll have to keep a journal—not the typical diary in which to confess juicy thoughts, or complaints about parents or teachers. Our entries were to be one hundred percent French and entirely sensitized.

In writing class, we're instructed to compose a page about ourselves, about our summer vacations, our aspirations in life—what we may like to study in college. We take turns reading them aloud. I describe all our interesting trips around Iran this summer. Alika explains her quest to find her birth mother without hurting her adoptive mother's feelings. How she wants to be a social worker or a psychologist. How she's born to help people.

Just two classrooms in school aren't old and decrepit—the science room with its black tables and stainless-steel sinks, and the geography classroom in a newer brighter building decorated with colorful topographical maps. My writing class lies on the top floor of the school's middle wing, across a narrow metal bridge (clomp, clomp—here come the Writing students). A fire escape covers one of the windows, blocks any scarce natural light that might otherwise find its way into the room to brighten the dreary space where enlightened prose was supposed to happen.

News comes of more demonstrations and the Shah's ill attempts to stem them. On the twenty-seventh of August, Jamshid Amouzegar, the Prime Minister of Iran, is replaced with Jafar Sharif-Emami, the former speaker of the Senate, once a prime minister, and head of the Pahlavi Foundation. His father was a cleric, which signals to many an obvious attempt by the Shah to start appealing to the religious masses. Immediately he releases political prisoners held in Evin prison, reinstitutes the Islamic calendar. He promises democracy.

School barrels on despite the growing discontent. The activity of attending classes and completing homework blurs the sheer enormity of what is happening outside the safety of our own American lives at home and at school.

On the fourth of September, more than one hundred thousand people take part in public prayers to mark the end of

Ramazan. This time the prayers are accompanied by demands for the return of Ayatollah Khomeini. There are mass marches at *Eid al-Fitr* in Tehran, also by Khomeini supporters. On the fifth and sixth of September, erratic demonstrations break out throughout Tehran. The soldiers are ordered not to carry guns.

So far, the demonstrations occurring in southeast Tehran remain distant from our quiet alley apartment in northwest Tehran.

It's Thursday, the first week of September, a weekend day akin to our American Saturday. We are planning to attend a work sponsored chili cook-off with my father's detachment. It's early evening and my dad is hanging by the phone, waiting for the top brass to call it off.

"I can't believe they are going through with this ludicrous plan for a family chili cook-off!" Mother complains. "You said there were security alerts warning of a large demonstration downtown tonight, right?" she asks, arms crossed over her chest.

"I'll attend by myself," Dad says, resolve passing over his face. "The United States Ambassador is coming, General Gasky—close to six hundred people are expected. I must go. I have to. The Iranian police have instructed us to be out of there by nine—not sure why—I'll be fine; I won't be late."

Mother doesn't speak, clatters around pans for dinner. She eats her dinner quietly, rises from the table the moment we'd finished. Later, I see her at the French door in the living room, gazing out.

But just as he'd promised, Dad returns home well before nine, experiencing no trouble.

The next morning, we are relaxing around the house, and I am wondering why Mother hasn't yet showered for church.

Dad is in the dining room on the phone, talking quietly, and I see Mother hanging around him, pacing.

Soon, our parents are gathering us around in the living room.

"Kids … We have news …" Dad clears his throat. "Martial law has been declared in our very own city, Tehran."

"What?" There is a collective gasp.

"The chief of army staff, General Gholam Ali Oveisi, has been appointed the military governor of Tehran. Martial law has been declared in Tehran and eleven other cities." Dad explains that it is only a temporary measure to ensure safety. "It will mean that people are off the streets from nine o'clock in the evening to five o'clock in the morning, every day—to help stop the anti-Shah demonstrations."

Frankie falls quiet. "What happens if my bus breaks down after school. If I can't make it home by nine o'clock?" I wonder the same thing.

"You'll get home in plenty of time," Dad reassures us.

We accept my father's explanation that this was a normal course of action to stabilize unrest. That we shouldn't be worried.

Frankie and I spend part of the morning in the pool. Cheerleading tryouts were being held next week, and I had to create a cheer worthy of the scrutiny of a judges' panel. I struggle with the words as much as I would have done if I were creating poetry in English Lit. What hasn't yet been said in a cheer for football? *Push 'em back, push 'em back, waayyy back.* Taken. *Rebound that basketball, Rebound!* Wrong sport. When I'm finished, I cringe at the cheer's patness and bad grammar, but hope I can tweak it later. I'd try to mask my juvenile cheer with a gymnastic ending; maybe end it in a round-off jump that slides into a perfect split—thighs plastered to the floor with no air space between—something so far elusive for me. I'd be taking a risk. At least I wore contacts, now. I remember how Beth Hurley's father came to one of our games at the University of Dayton. He was photo-shooting for some magazine. I recall how he busied himself importantly, arranging lighting, gathering all us cheerleaders around the basketball court just so, dissatisfied and nervous, until he asked two of us to step aside—me in my thick-lensed glasses and one of the heavier girls on the squad, who couldn't quite keep her bloomers in place, who stood sadly beside me while we watched the prettier girls on our squad smile and say cheese. I knew what it meant—I wasn't stupid. It meant that we weren't pretty enough for the photo shoot.

In the evening we avoid all news to still our nerves. "Isn't it nice to have some normalcy?" asks my mother. "Doesn't this feel normal?"

Normal? Not in the least. Creating a cheer on a day that would end with martial law? How normal was that?

It's after nine o'clock in the evening, and we are all hanging out in the living room, restless. The sudden quiet has crept into our apartment house like a thief. My parents and I are attempting to read; Frankie is fidgeting on the couch, staring into space. Debbie has put on some soft music on the record player at my mom's request to still our nerves.

"Let's go out on the roof," Dad says spontaneously.

Frankie and I frown. Outside? Should we?

Obediently, we climb upstairs, through the sturdy steel door that opens onto the roof. We cross over to the roof's edge and peer out into the street. The night is pitch black. There is no movement, no sound. I hear a caw of a bird (a crow?), the rustle of dry leaves dropping too early from a dying limb. The night is humid. To think we couldn't make a run to the market to buy cheese—but would we have wanted to anyway? Travel to the store for medicine. Even walk a dog if we had one. This makes me claustrophobic, the way I'd felt in our tent trailer during the rain, when the humidity formed tiny bubbles on the tent's underside, inches from my face. There in the enclave of my bed "end", where the suffocating aroma of wet canvas filled my nostrils like chemicals, I'd felt desperate to get out, to go home. Noticing my wide-eyed panic my mother would always say, "Why, Annette, you really aren't a camper, are you?" *But I am, Mom! I am! You've got it all wrong! It's just the canvas. I'm as fun as Debbie.*

My sister asks, "Isn't this exciting?!" She avoids the roof's edge. How could she say this? When we were under martial law? But Debbie is the camper in the family. Adventurous and brave, except for heights. Frankie and I are just plain scared.

That night the telephone rings sharply in the family room. I bolt upright in my bed, wondering, *oh no, what now?* Dad answers it on the second ring. I put my ear up to the wall, but I can't catch what he's saying.

The next day I am preparing for school after the weekend, worried about the Algebra test I'd hardly studied for. My parents are listening to the news on our pale yellow refrigerator-top radio. At breakfast, Mother asks us to sit down. And we obey nervously.

Mother explains, "A large group of demonstrators had gathered to protest in Jaleh Square last night or early morning—not sure if they hadn't realized, or cared, that martial law had been declared. There were soldiers, tanks … helicopter gunships." Mother stares at her hands. "Shots were fired. Many people died."

"Please be mindful that the Shah's army isn't playing around," Dad adds, eyes piercing. "We neglected to tell you so we wouldn't worry you—if anyone is out after curfew, the Shah's army has been instructed to shoot."

But we already knew that. Shoot to kill, we'd heard.

"You're staying home from school today. Last night work called and asked me to stay home."

Rather than processing the atrocity at Jaleh Square, I am selfishly and momentarily thrilled to stay home from school. As the day wears on, though, and as we listen to more news reports about the bloodshed, my initial happiness dims. Early reports by the Iranian government suggest that hundreds had been killed. The BBC was also reporting the same. A French journalist informs us that two to three thousand people had died.

Later, we'd learn the troops that day were not trained to control demonstrations, were not adequate in number. There were claims that the troops had faced "professional agitators"; some were thought to be Palestinian and Libyan guerrilla groups. Although the troops had been ordered to fire into the air, only when they'd been fired upon had they fired into the crowd.

At a meeting of the National Security Council, the day after the Jaleh Square massacre, General Gholam-Ali Oveisi issued a statement:

I swear to God and my soldier's honor that their [referring to clerics or opposition leaders] sharpshooters started the firing into the crowd and towards the soldiers. Since yesterday I have more than thirty soldier families who are in mourning in Tehran alone. They also belong to this country. You have declared martial law, forced me to bring my soldiers into the streets and then His Majesty has tied our hands from behind. We have strict orders not to shoot under any circumstances, even in self-defense. They are allowed only to shoot in the air. Our police is not equipped with tear gas canisters and with modern riot control equipment. The U.S. and other friendly western countries have decided not to sell them to us. You have thrown us into the ring and then tied our hands from behind. The army is being used like a scarecrow. The people are using bad language at my soldiers. They want to provoke them into scuffle and action. How long do you think this situation can last? Which one of you is willing to come to console the families of my soldiers who have lost a dear one these days? What tangible benefits are their families going to receive? Why should they continue to serve in these circumstances? Aren't they human beings?"

Most Iranians did not believe that anti-Shah sharp shooters were planted in the crowd that Friday at Jaleh Square, or that the Shah, or any of his soldiers, was civilized. They remember only that Jimmy Carter refused to sell the Shah's army non-lethal crowd control measures.

School continues on as usual, except for the Iranian army guards who patrol the school compound during the day. At first the guards hold bayonets, then they carry rifles, then the rifles are studded with bayonets and a guard rides on our bus each day with a submachine gun. I am slow to make friends. In the morning the school buses arrive well before the bell that signals the start of classes. All of us are forced to mingle in the school compound. Most people form small consistent groups. The popular girls always seem so amused about everything, their lush hair flinging off their shoulders like drapes lifting in the wind as they laugh and swat each other. Then there are the groups of jocks staring at the pretty popular girls and the hair flinging escalates. There is the no-nonsense group, where people talk with arched eyebrows and focused attention, as if they are solving the world's problems. Then there are people like me, who don't fit any one category, who hardly know anyone. I dread the mingle time before class almost as much as I fear the armed guards who patrol the compound—who gaze at the pretty popular girls and also at me. But at least there was no dread from within the confines of the school, except for cosmetic. No girls lingering in the bathroom to push past while they bumped us with sharp elbows and blew smoke rings in our faces.

Cheerleading tryouts are held after school the second week of September. I'd spent the entire weekend practicing. My impression is that I'd done well, nailing the round-off/split combination with zero air space between my legs and the floor.

When I return home from school, it is late, but well before curfew. As I pass by our pool, the water rolls, a curious phenomenon I don't dwell on. I walk into our apartment and shrieks come from the atrium, like a baby's cries. I open the window, lean in, and see Siam and Meese scampering below. I say hello to my parents in the living room.

"There's a dish of leftover 'Hamburger Stroganoff' in the kitchen on a warming plate for you, Annette."

"Thanks. What's up with the cats?"

Mom shrugs. "Goodness, it's sure deafening."

Frankie strolls in as I finish my last garlic infused egg noodle, slurping the pasta into my mouth like a frog snatching a bug with its tongue.

"How's school going?"

"Okay," he replies without enthusiasm.

"Who do you eat lunch with?"

"No one," he says, slumping in his seat.

"Really?"

"Yeah...."

"What about Kelly? Can you sit with her?"

"No. She's not my type. Too old and smells like smoke." I am depressed that Kelly is still smoking.

"If it makes you feel any better, I sit at lunch with the first person who asked me."

"Not Janice from work?"

"No. Seems she has other close friends at school she knows from last year. Almost sat down at her table the first day, but got the idea they didn't want a new girl in the group."

"Oh, that stinks."

"Yeah."

"You see John much?"

"No. He's in my science class, sits way in the back. He asked me to a movie a few weeks ago, but I canceled. Football starts soon. He's playing. Maybe I'll cheer for him—if I make it. Knock on wood." I rap my knuckles on our napkin holder. *Living here is making me superstitious.* "You should join a team, you know? Then you'd have plenty of people to have lunch with."

"Yeah, I guess."

"Mom!" I yell from the kitchen. "Sign Frankie up for soccer!"

"Shhh. No, Annie, please. I'd rather just get home after school." Frankie's eyes are silver dollars in his face.

"Why?"

"Sometimes I'm scared."

I can relate, but I say instead, "Don't be. Things can't be so bad if we're still getting up and going to school most every day. Dad's still going to work, right? Mom and Dad are still planning their trip to Russia. Even with martial law. And we'll be here *by ourselves.* We're going on a field trip in my Iranian Cultural Studies class, and we're *walking.* It can't be all that dangerous."

"Where?"

"The Reza Abbasi Museum. It has an art gallery, which you know I'll love." I had dabbled in oil painting in Ohio. My parents had surprised me with a wooden easel and a box of paints one Christmas. Had I been so naive as to think that holding a paintbrush would give me talent? I smile. "We're going to eat bag lunches in the gardens outside the museum."

"Sounds boring, except for the lunch part." Frankie laughs, and I smile back at him. I am bored myself without the fervor of Amir around, almost wishing for his reconciliation with Debbie, so I could see him again. True, I'd been busy with school, immersed in homework—having no time to think of anything else. But I was dying to tell Amir about the upcoming trip to the museum—ask him if he'd ever gone there. Tell him how I'd be making *Chelo Kebab* in Cultural Studies. My mind was stuck in a conversation with him, and it shouldn't be. I shuffle into the dining room to start my homework.

Later that night, we learn of an earthquake in the city of Tabas. The damage was devastating, the city flattened, twenty-thousand people dead. I tell my father about the odd shift to the water in our pool that evening. He'd also noticed the china rattling in the Levitz hutch, our framed Van Gogh *Sunflowers* print shifting sideways on its picture hanger.

Don't tell me—yet another worry? Earthquakes? But then I remember the San Andreas Fault, the tornadoes in Ohio, and how we'd have to retreat to the basement, terrified, to lie under a mattress with a portable transistor radio and wait for the all clear signal.

After several days, the tryout results are posted on the cafeteria door. And my name is printed there in black and white, Annette Patterson. It seems I'd made a team! The Phantoms. I scroll up for Janice's name—Janice Hanley—she's made the Vikings. I skim the names on the Raider's cheerleading squad but recognize no one I know. A note on the bottom of the list asks us to make plans to stay after school tomorrow to collect uniforms and practice. Miss Barker, my Writing teacher, is our cheerleading coach.

That night I receive a telephone call from John. "You're my cheerleader. I'm on the Phantoms, too. Isn't that cool?"

Without waiting for a response, he asks, "I was wondering if you'd like to take me up on that movie invitation? *Smokey and the Bandit* is playing in two weeks. I've been wanting to see it." He blows out a jagged breath. Silence. He waits for my answer, but I'm thinking.

"I could do that," I say, relenting. I couldn't steer clear of movie theaters forever. I also didn't want to hurt his feelings. "I guess we could take a bus to the Gulf District."

"Let's have dinner after the movie. I'll get my dad to pick us up after, take us home. Plan for Wednesday the twentieth. Be there or be square."

Did he just say that?

The Reza Abbasi Museum lies several blocks from the American school, and after homeroom, we stroll there along with two other classes, one of which is Alika's. And it is pleasant to march in line beneath the canopy of leafy Sycamore trees, like Madeline from the picture book I'd kept on my Ohio bookshelf next to my favorite, *Make Way for Ducklings*.

Once we arrive, we gather outside the museum. A guide explains that Reza Abbasi, the museum's namesake, was a miniaturist painter from the Safavid period. That the state religion in Iran is *Ithnaashara* or Twelver Shi'ism, established by the Safavid Dynasty in the seventeenth century.

"This branch of Shi'ism recognizes twelve Imams, all of whom were martyred except the twelfth, Muhammad al-Mahdi, who disappeared and is expected to reappear on judgment day with Jesus," says the thin, erect museum guide in a cultured voice.

Inside, various ancient Pre-Islamic and Islamic period artifacts are displayed in tall, glass cases. Muted incandescent lighting illuminates the art and casts a warm glow on the walls. The people-watching was what I was enjoying most; I am admiring the quiet regard of a dark-haired young woman beside me. She is studying a painting, and her head is tilted sideways, her fingers cup her chin. *What was she thinking?* Her tall, thin companion, graced with a handsome chiseled profile, stands next to her at an adjacent piece of artwork. Also studying. A date to a museum seemed so romantic to me.

At noon, we sit outside on benches in the dappled shade of leafy, sycamore trees. I pull a bologna sandwich from my wrinkled brown paper bag. "Pretty interesting as far as museums go," I say, usually more impressed with splashy oil or watercolor paintings by Monet or Renoir than ancient clay pots and animal ceramics. "Iran is so old, so layered with history." I sigh. "Pieces dating back to four thousand B.C.? It's hard to believe."

"I know," Alika says. "The book exhibit. Pages so thick and riddled with age."

I nod, thinking. "Did you hear how Shi'as also believe in Jesus? Is it our Jesus?"

"It is, but as I understand it, Christians believe in the Father, the Son and the Holy Spirit—one God and three persons, distinct, but of the same nature. Shia's believe in a single absolute God in only one person, similar to the Jewish faith. Islam regards all prophets, including Jesus, to be mortal, sharing no divinity. Most Muslims believe Jesus ascended into heaven without being crucified on the cross—a person who appeared exactly like him was crucified instead." Alika attempts to lighten the mood—maybe worried her intelligence is off-putting—and says, "I know one thing, though, you're not catching me marrying my cousin at eighteen, however distant that cousin may be. Has no one heard of the movie *Deliverance?*"

"Shhh, someone may hear you, Alika! Besides, they're usually *very distant* cousins."

"My parents are Japanese Christians."

"Are you Christian?"

Alika shrugs her shoulders and sips from her thermos of powdered chocolate milk. "I haven't decided yet."

I meet the members of my cheerleading squad after school—Cathy, Lindsay, Amy, and Melody. Three of them are lithe and petite, like gazelles; one is tall and large-boned, like me—a perfect mix for building pyramids. I recognize Lindsay as one of Janice's friends at lunch.

Miss Barker gathers us in a circle in the school compound's basketball court. "Afternoon, girls. First of all, congratulations! What an accomplishment on your behalf. The competition was fierce this year. Therefore, we will take this opportunity seriously. Practice hard and abide by my number one rule: have fun. Rule number two: we will not neglect our studies. Especially, and I mean especially, those of you who have me for Writing!" Miss Barker winks at me. "Don't forget the writing assignment next week!" She is wearing a crisp white polo shirt and navy-blue shorts, which reveal a dark tan on her lean, muscular legs. She bends over to sort through the used but cleaned garments, arranged by body type.

"You'll need bright blue bloomers and cheerleading shoes. You can order them through the Co-Op. The shoes *must have* blue trim." Miss Barker hands me one of the larger uniforms just as the Phantoms' football team jogs past us into the gym. I spy John at the back of the line of husky fellows—hefty and strong, himself—in thick shoulder pads.

"Go, Phantoms!" Lindsay shrieks after the players, jumping to her feet. "We are *number one*. We are *number one!*" she yells shrilly, raising her pointer finger skyward. *"Whoo, whoo!"* She ends her private cheer in a hearty round off, but by that time the boys had already disappeared into the gym.

I giggle softly.

"Excellent, Lindsay!" compliments Miss Barker. "I do encourage spunk as a Phantom cheerleader!"

Two weeks later, John and I sit in the cool of the Gulf District movie theater, waiting for the patriotic blast of "The Star-Spangled Banner". We are holding two tubs of hot buttered popcorn on our laps. John's hair is damp, and I recognize the fragrance of Herbal Essence shampoo. I'd also showered and changed, took careful pains to brush my hair out straight. I'd replaced my sneakers with a pair of flat leather sandals. John's sneakers squeak on the sticky concrete floor, and his long legs hit the seatback, like mine. I think about how nice it is to be with someone who is taller than me.

When the movie starts and the theater grows dark, I sneak a peek at John who is already laughing and chomping on his popcorn. The movie is all right, but I'm preoccupied and Jackie Gleason's oddball, loud-mouthed sheriff doesn't make me laugh like it does John.

After the movie, we each order light salads at the Officers Club. We talk about school and grades, and science—how some kids in fifth period chemistry had mixed up a toxic blend of chemicals in a beaker, been overcome by fumes. "We'd know better than that, wouldn't we, Annie?" Often John would wait at my science table to walk me out after the bell, quizzing me on the chemical elements of the periodic table as we went:

"What's Ba, Annie?"

"Barium!"

"What about Be?"

"Beryllium!"

"And what is Beryllium?"

"A metal used in aircraft, missiles, and space craft," I'd say.

"Perfect, Annie."

Our dinners come quickly. John stabs his fork at a thick piece of oily pink ham, jams it into his mouth, which is already loaded with *Barbari* bread strips. He has extricated all the onions to one side of his bread dish, and one has fallen off onto the white tablecloth.

"Not an onion fan?"

John smiles. "Usually, I am. But …."

He waits for me to catch on, and I do.

I stop chewing.

"Remember that night at the Caspian Sea when all I could taste was wine and chocolate on your lips?" He smiles, reaches over the table with his cloth napkin to dab at my chin. "A spot of Thousand Island dressing," he explains.

Is he expecting to be kissing me again? I remember Amir's bare fingers on my cheek that morning I'd seen him last. My heart sinks as John looks at me so eagerly.

"John, I—"

"Annie, don't." He swallows hard, and his smile vanishes. "Let's not ruin the night. All right?" I nod and we finish our dinners in silence. Then the bill comes, and John fumbles for exact change. I set money on the table.

"The tip?"

I nod.

"All right, if you must," he complains. "All set?" We leave the Officers Club and an awkwardness springs up between us like the slight breeze in the air. We wander to the parking lot to wait for John's dad. But five minutes turn into ten, and ten turn into twenty. After an hour, I ask nervously, "Your dad. He knows he has to pick us up, doesn't he?"

"Yeah, I told him."

"Let's sit here near the gate so he'll see us as soon as he pulls in."

We sit on the curb's edge, our arms wrapped around our knees, looking for the Cadillac Seville.

"You know we have thirty minutes until curfew?"

"Yes, I realize this. But let's be calm."

"Okay. But Jesus, where is he?"

John bites his lip. "Please don't worry. How about that Trans-Am in the movie, huh? Wasn't that something?" he says to change the subject.

"A BMW might be nicer?" I tease, embracing humor in time of need. Not really caring all that much about Trans-Ams. Disliking them, even.

"Ooh, la, la, high class lady," John teases back. The humor evaporates, though, when there is no Mr. James. We return to the Officers Club to use the phone. John dials and then holds out the receiver, where the harsh buzz of a busy tone sounds like the horns out on *Dowlat*. I raise my eyebrows.

He stomps his foot. "God, Kelly. She's probably on the phone. This could go on for hours.... Want to walk?"

Two American blondes walking the streets of Tehran? And there was no way we could make it to John's house before curfew on foot. My parents could never get here in time. Things were getting serious. "Let's call a taxi," I say, wondering why we hadn't thought of it before, handing him the card I always carried with me. John slams down the phone, picks it back up, and dials the Orange Taxi Service. We settle down to wait, but the cab arrives quickly.

"Get in, get in! We must get you home," the excited driver cries out the open car window. He smokes a fat cigar. We duck inside. I cough. "Where to?" asks the driver.

John gives his street address. And the cab pulls away like a bucking stallion.

Out on the boulevard, soldiers are appearing for their shifts, dressed in khakis, some jaunty in their army caps, others menacing in hard round helmets, machine guns slung across their shoulders. I swallow hard as the cabbie idles at the corner, and a huge armored tank lumbers past us. Its large caliber gun points skyward in its rotating turret like a gray elephant poised to charge. A soldier is perched on top like I'd only ever seen at a Memorial Day parade. He glares down at us. I check my watch for the umpteenth time, and it's still before curfew. Once the tank has passed, John and I stare at each other, terrified, each of us breathing hard.

The cabbie careens onto a residential side street I recognize is John's alleyway. He screeches to a halt; John throws him a wad of bills. We run inside.

In the kitchen, Kelly is setting a white ceramic bowl into the sink.

"Where's Dad?" John asks curtly. "He never picked us up."

"He's out looking for Mom," she says, pursed-lipped.

"What?" John's eyes are wide.

"Someone at the Hyatt Hotel called Dad. Mom was drunk in the bar. But then she up and leaves before he gets there." She huffs. "Now, he's out looking for her."

"Oh, my God. When did he leave the Hyatt?"

"Maybe an hour ago?" Kelly looks at the wall clock. "It's after curfew." Her eyes brim with tears.

We all stand quietly for a moment. John turns towards me. "Annie, you should give your parents a call. They're probably freaking out." He turns back to Kelly. "Annie's got to spend the night here, obviously."

Kelly nods, her eyes wide with fear.

I dial my house. Mother answers on the first ring. "Annette?! Where are you?!"

"Mom, I'm fine. Listen, Mr. James was late picking us up at the theater is all. We just arrived at John's house—we're safe—made it here just before curfew. I have to spend the night."

"My God, Annette." Silence. "Goodness, I'm just so relieved you called. Will Mr. James be dropping you off in the morning?"

"Yes," I say, but I wasn't sure.

"You have your contact lens case and solution. Right? Glasses?"

"No," I answer, rolling my eyes skyward, slapping my forehead. "I'll look around here for some."

"Always remember to bring them with you, okay? Lesson learned. Don't cut it so close ever again? No more late movies, young lady."

"*Never again.* I'm sorry." Was Mom implying that I should carry along a hostage kit? A toiletry bag with glasses, contacts, contact solution, medicines, Mercurochrome for God's sake? Once I was forced to throw out my eight-hour contacts, how would I ever see? I shiver.

"Amir and Reza brought over *Barbari* dough for pizza," Mother says. "They left a while ago. Amir asked about you. Debbie told him you were on a big date."

My stomach drops like a ton of bricks—was he back with Debbie?

"Did you like the movie?" My mother interrupts my tangled thoughts.

Amir back at our house and I missed him? I twirl the telephone cord around my finger.

"Are you there, Annette? Was the movie good?"

I clear my throat, find my voice. "Yes, it was good. Funny."

"I've always liked Sally Field. No idea what she's doing with that Burt Reynolds, though."

Who knows why anyone chooses a person to love? "Yeah, right," I say laughing, though it sounded fake.

"Okay, sweetheart, night. See you in the morning."

I pause, wordless. Reluctant for her to go.

"You sure you're all right?"

"Yes, Mom," I say, voice wavering.

"Okay, Hon, be safe."

I hang up the phone and wonder if I should have told Mom about Mr. and Mrs. James. That they weren't here. She'd only be worried. And then my thoughts return to John's parents. I hoped they were safe.

We stand there, huddling around the phone. I clutch my backpack and we examine our feet. Kelly is wearing her Dr. Scholl's and her leg is twitching; John's big toe is pushing through his sneaker.

The phone rings shrilly. We jump, startled.

Kelly grabs it. "Hello? Dad?!" She's silent, listening. One hand is over her mouth. John and I eye each other, eyebrows lifted.

Kelly finally speaks. "Okay, Dad. Yeah. Right. We'll call Moshdeh if we need to ...Yes, John's home ... all right. Love you. Tell Mom I love her." Kelly hangs up the phone and turns to us, eyes moist. "Dad found Mom at the bar at the Evin Hotel, just before curfew. He said tanks and armed soldiers were everywhere. They'll spend the night."

"Dad's right. Good they're staying. You didn't mention Annie was here?"

"No. I wonder if Dad forgot about your date. Early to bed for you tonight, he said—your game tomorrow? They'll be home early morning."

John turns to me. "You can stay in my parents' bedroom. Let me show you where it is." He leads me upstairs through a hallway decorated with family photographs. An attractive antique hallstand holds a brass lamp that John flicks on.

"You're so lucky to have an apartment with two floors. Feels like a real house," I say.

"Mom insisted on it though it costs more than our housing allowance. She says it's worth it because it came with Moshdeh."

Dad had explained to us that our apartment modeled the Iranian tradition of building two or more apartments for the entire family within the same structure. The elder parents live on one level, married children on the other and there were two kitchens. Our resourceful landlord had thought to rent his house out to foreigners first, pay off the cost of construction, live in the interim with his wife in his parents' cramped two-bedroom apartment, downtown.

John opens the door to a roomy master bedroom and a large Queen-size bed covered in a plush green-velvet duvet with matching throw pillows.

"This is where you'll stay, but let's go downstairs first, unwind a little." I drop my purse and backpack in the room. We retrace our steps to the kitchen. John pulls open the refrigerator, finds some leftovers. "Want some chicken stir-fry?"

It occurs to me I'm hungry—the popcorn and light salad at the Gulf District already a distant memory. I nod. He places the leftovers in a skillet, heats them up, drizzles some soy sauce over them, serves them up with rice on his mother's white porcelain everyday china, and throws a handful of fresh cashews on top. "Kelly, want stir-fry?" he yells to his sister.

"Nah," she hollers back from her bedroom. "Ate some cereal earlier."

John hands over a plate of steaming stir-fry, flips off the stove, grabs out utensils from a drawer beneath a long countertop of elegant gray-veined marble. I take a bite, close my eyes. "This is fantastic, you cook like your father!"

John smiles, says, "Yeah, I play around. But this is Mom's cooking. I only just heated it up." I look around the house. Real care had gone into the decorating of it—expensive antique furnishings, Louis XIV chairs, oil paintings, Persian carpets, and rich, colorful throw blankets and pillows.

"Speaking of Mom…." John moseys over to the sideboard, brings out a bottle of white wine, two crystal glasses, "Ah, I shouldn't be disrespectful to her. Want a taste? Thinking we could sure use some of this after the stress of the ride home."

"I'll take a small glass," I say. "I understand. About your mom, I mean."

"Come on. Let's take our food and drinks to the roof."

We grab our dinner plates, juggle our glasses of wine, and climb the two flights of stairs to the rooftop. The night is quiet—everyone obeying curfew. Traffic noise on *Saltanatabad* is almost non-existent. We sit around a steel patio table. The porch light illuminates a pot of cheery, red geraniums and some lawn furniture. To his mother's credit, the stir-fry is delicious. We sip our wine in silence.

"I like this wine. It's sweet."

"Yeah, my mom goes for the bubble gum wines, which I don't mind."

"Me neither. I hope your Mom's okay." I don't know what else to say. "If she could do what we do. A small glass, then put it away."

"She's upset. She and my father don't see eye-to-eye on anything anymore. My mom complains she never signed up for this when she left Texas and our ranch."

I stare down at the alley below us, thinking that none of us signed up for this, except our dads. I look up, interested. "You lived on a ranch?"

John nods. "Lived on a ranch—a farmhouse on twenty acres—a stable, barns, riding rings, jumps—the whole nine yards. Mom shows Tennessee Walkers."

"Those horses that prance? My grandmother loves Tennessee Walkers! My grandparents on my father's side live on a dairy farm in Watertown, New York—with cow barns, a pony, a horse that is the spitting image of Black Beauty—tall and graceful, even a white patch shaped like a star above her nose. And so my grandmother named her Beauty." I laugh. "The pony's name is Betty. Her mane is always getting tangled, and she is constantly eating all the sour green apples off the trees in the pasture and getting sick. The thing is that

Betty seems to think she is as beautiful and graceful as Beauty, but her legs are far too short." I snicker again. "Took my grandmother once to a Tennessee Walker show in Ohio while my grandparents were visiting—those quick high steps? Amazing."

"Mom's horses are the flat-shod type, not the ones with those exaggerated tall steps."

"Oh."

"But those are good, too!" John blurts, never wanting to offend me.

"Can't imagine your mother as a rancher—pitching hay and shoveling manure? Well, maybe, but in well-heeled leather boots and a cabled fisherman's knit wool sweater." I smile.

John laughs. "Mom isn't the typical rancher, you are right. No modest farmhouse with peeling paint and ponies for her, just a renovated farmhouse with a gourmet kitchen and Tennessee Walkers. And fine art. That's all."

I remember the colorful oil painting above the sideboard just now.

"But the expense—the horses' care, their feed, the hired hands—the farmhouse renovations—it all made Dad angry. Difficult to support on an Air Force Major's salary." John shrugs.

"But your father likes to cook? Didn't he like the new gourmet kitchen?"

John nods. "But he would've been perfectly happy with our pink electric stove with no cabinetry around it, a single overhead cabinet, a sink you had to pull a curtain around to cover up the pipes."

"Oh." I look over at the shadowed rooftops to *Saltanatabad*, think I see a tank. "We rented out our house back home. Did you ever think about that?"

"No. Something about the line of credit being due." John fiddles with his jeans.

"What about the horses?"

"Boarded back home. Mom can't wait to get back to them." John laughs again. "She's suggested going home early. Especially now. But Dad won't let her."

I remain silent, thinking how nice it was that Mr. James is happier with his spouse around. *Shouldn't that be the norm? It was for my parents.* "I'm convinced that my mom would follow my father to the ends of this earth if she had to," I say, but regret it when I see the hurt in John's eyes. "Anyway, my mom's used to traveling." I pause, watch the tank lumber by. "They met at Syracuse."

The light in the apartment house opposite us flicks off. "My parents met when my mom attended Vanderbilt and my father worked at Arnold Air Force Base. I don't think she ever thought for a minute she'd have to travel halfway around the world when she married him. Your mom like it here?"

"She docs. Makes the best of it. She's a reader—mostly fiction, like me. She always says that if she has a book to read, she's happy—takes one down by the pool and reads during the day while we're at school. Otherwise, to keep busy, she spends an inordinate amount of time carefully ironing my father's cloth handkerchiefs." I giggle.

John smiles. "My dad carries cloth handkerchiefs, too; irons them himself." He pauses, thinks a moment, then says, "I suppose my mom was happy here at first. But once she finished her decorating, she hadn't anything to do." John snorts. "Except drink wine. And once she starts, she doesn't stop—one endless glass until she falls into bed at night." John looks down at his hands.

"Your mom needs a friend, I'm convinced. Sometimes, my mom hangs out downstairs with Julie Burnett, tests her recipes."

"Yeah, I filled up on her Middle Eastern Pasta Salad at the picnic. Never had anything so yellow before."

"Saffron."

"Our saffron sunset." John looks serious for a moment. "Did I tell you how beautiful you looked at the beach, Annie? How when I first saw you stumbling into that awful cottage, I said to myself, I like that girl."

His confession makes me shift in my chair, but I keep on topic. "I suppose Mom has to struggle with electricity outages and our funky dishwasher we hook up to our sink, all the appliance transformers, but she likes being with my dad. She was miserable back home in Ohio without him for six months. Does your mom read?"

"Only those non-fiction books when she's decorating. That kind of reading."

"Oh." I sit awhile thinking about what might help make Mrs. James happy. But I didn't know her well enough. "What do you think will happen here?" I ask, pointing out into the streets.

"Not sure. It'll probably just get worse."

I kick my feet on the low concrete wall that serves as a railing around the building's edge, and ask, "Don't you miss McDonald's? Small town centers—grass?"

John nods, points to his stomach. "Big Macs especially."

I laugh, rolling my eyes up to the inky sky. *What I'd do for a Big Mac right now.*

Simultaneously we both start to sing. "Two all beef patties, special sauce, lettuce, cheese—"

Our singsong echoes into the night, and we quiet down somberly.

"My dad doesn't know how long he'll be here," I say. "He used to think two years. But now, who knows? How long will you be here, you think?"

"It's also supposed to be two years for us."

"It's certainly an experience, though," I say. "What will you study in college?"

"Sciences. Biology or Chemistry, maybe. I want to be a teacher. I like sports. Possibly a coach. I don't know. I'm about to send out applications. You?"

"I love to read and write. Publishing? Is it too glamorous to think I might live in New York City one day, read manuscripts all day long?"

"Sounds pretty glamorous, Annie." He doesn't think I can do it.

"Yeah." I stare out into the darkness. "If we ever get out of here."

The apartment goes dark across from us. I remember football. "First game tomorrow." My voice rises. At least that's something to be excited about.

"Yeah, I know. Guess we should think about turning in."

"Right."

We descend to the second-floor hallway, and John hands me a towel from the linen closet. He takes my dishes. "One problem," John says.

"What?"

"Contacts?"

"Right. God, sorry, but I have to get these things out of my eyes."

"Contact lens solution is saline, right? I'll be right back."

Soon there is a rap on the door. John stands outside holding two small juice glasses filled with cloudy water.

"Saline solution with Morton's Salt—the best I could do," he apologizes.

"That may work. You are my favorite chemist."

John lingers near the bathroom. "I really like you, Annie."

"I like you, too, John." But my smile wavers, and my statement lacks the passion he's looking for. "John—"

"Sweet dreams." He backs from the room.

After I've washed, I find my way back to John's parents' room, squinting. I lay down and cover myself with the soft wool blanket at the foot of the bed. I wonder about my family across town, how the *Barbari* dough tasted as pizza crust. Sleep escapes me, something about an unfamiliar place, a different bed, and unusual sounds.

Early morning, I hear rumblings downstairs—doors opening and closing, ceramic mugs clinking. I check the bedside clock. It's seven a.m. I climb out of bed, shuffle to the bathroom, insert my left contact lens. The sting is unbearable as the lens clenches my eyeball like a vise. Morton's Salt, I guessed, wasn't a suitable substitute for contact lens solution. The pain subsides though as the natural saline of my eye moistens the lens but repeats with the insertion of the other lens. I grit my teeth, and when I can stand it, I gather myself and go downstairs.

"Annie?" Mr. James is banging the kitchen cabinets to locate a clean coffee cup. "Oh, Annie. The movies. I'm sorry. I forgot."

The percolating coffee smells wonderful. On closer examination, Mr. James wears a five o'clock shadow and he has bags under his eyes, still wearing his large, now rumpled shirt and his blue work pants. Yet he's studying me now. "Have you been crying?" he asks.

"No, no, Mr. James. Eye sensitivity. Contacts. It's nothing. It's okay about the movies. We caught a cab home in time."

"Oh, such level-headed kids. I thank you for that." Relief registers on his face, yet he looks sad. "Want coffee?"

"No, thank you. Never touch the stuff, myself," I say. "But it smells great. When you get a chance, though, would you mind dropping me back home?"

"Certainly; it's the least I could do. But, wait. Let me make you an omelet before you go. Goat cheese and herbs. We'll eat on the roof in the morning sun. Does that sound nice?"

"It does, Mr. James. Should we wait for John?"

"Yes, we should," he says, winking, and aprons of gray frame his eyes, hint at his awful night.

"Let me pour you coffee," I say, a lump in my throat.

The sound of running water comes from the half bath opposite the kitchen. Soon after, Mrs. James emerges. She stops dead in her tracks. "Annie."

"Mrs. James." Her hair is undone, makeup running beneath her eyes in raccoon-black half-moon circles; she presses the back of her hand against her forehead. "You know I'm feeling quite ill. I must lie down. My husband and I had difficulty making it home in time for curfew. I see you did too. We apologize for this."

"No problem, Mrs. James. Let me grab my bag out of your room. Don't you want an omelet?" I nod over to Mr. James.

Mrs. James rolls her eyes. "No, thank you. My husband can make a mean herbed goat cheese omelet, he can cook, but he has no sense of direction to save his life! He wanders around Tehran, perpetually lost," she says bitterly, "otherwise we might have made it home last night."

Otherwise? Familiarity certainly breeds contempt, I think sadly. I glance at Mr. James, who is contentedly clanging around pots and pans, to see he hadn't heard.

Back home, I meet my mom in the kitchen. "Hi," I say. She is mixing up canned tuna fish in a yellow-striped ceramic bowl.

"You're back!" She looks relieved. "Did you sleep okay at the James's? We missed you."

"I did. It's a relief to be home though. Scary, almost missing curfew."

"Yes, young lady, I am none too happy about it," Mom says, nose wrinkling. "You know if you're not with me I can't protect you. The way I did the time you almost got hit by a Trans-Am running to the ice cream truck." My mother had recounted this tale of providence dozens of times. She'd been there for me. I'd taken off towards the musical bells of an early ice cream truck, and was about to dash across the street when my mother, who had remained a step behind, was quick enough to tug on my tight pink T-shirt, pull me back to safety. And as she tells it, the rush of air from the speeding car blew corn silk wisps of hair away from my face, had curled up the edges of the *Turbo Popsicle* sticker tacked onto the metal truck's side. But after she'd scooped me up in her arms and had planted fire engine-red lipstick kisses on my little girl's forehead, she crossed the street, looking both ways to the point of exaggeration, and bought me that *Turbo Popsicle*.

But last night I had figured it out on my own. Martial law was making me grow up far too fast.

"Where is everybody?" I ask.

"At the soccer field watching Amir and Reza's game."

"Can I run to the game?" I gush.

Mother rolls her eyes. "But you just got back. Take a shower. Get dressed for cheerleading. Spend time with your mother." She dips a large spoon into a jar of Hellman's mayonnaise, arches her brow.

"I'll only be a few minutes."

"You really want to go? By yourself?"

"It's just down the street."

"All right, then. Tell everyone I'll make lunch. We'll eat by the pool. Do you want something?"

"I'm not hungry. Mr. James made me an omelet."

"Goodness. That man can surely cook! What am I doing wrong?"

Dad was lucky to prepare toast without scorching the crust, never ever did laundry, but he was strong, could fix a car, pay bills, and invest money. I had few complaints, as did my mother. She was only teasing.

"Invite Amir and Reza back for tuna melts! They can eat tuna, surely?" my mother shouts at my retreating back.

"Okay!" I reply, elation building as I jog toward the field. *Would the game be over?* I sprint. Once I'd arrived at the field's edge, I slow, shape my wind-tangled hair in place, let my ragged breathing calm, wish I had on something nicer than gym clothes. Frankie is kicking around a soccer ball by himself. Dad and Debbie are concentrating on the game. I sneak a peek at Amir on the field. His movements are graceful, masculine. My heart flutters. Amir and Reza are wearing red; the other team has on royal blue.

"Who's winning?" I ask.

"Shhh. Reza's and Amir's team," Debbie answers, frowning, concentrating on the game.

Amir kicks a ball out of bounds on the sideline to avoid a corner kick. And Reza is bent over, winded, hands resting on the tops of his thick thighs, head lowered as he attempts to catch his breath. Play resumes and after several minutes a referee blows the whistle.

"That's it?" I ask disappointedly.

"That's it," Debbie says.

Amir and Reza trade handshakes with the other team. They walk over to greet us.

"Hi, stranger, Annie," Amir says. His hair drips sweat; his skin is darkened from the flush of exercise.

"I'm sorry I missed your game. My mom has invited you back for lunch," I say.

Reza answers, "Very well, wonderful." He looks like he could use a tall, cool drink.

"And are you inviting me, too, Annie?" Amir flashes a wide bright smile, but something seems off with him.

"Mom is." I look over at Debbie, smooth down my baggy shirt.

"I heard you had a...how you say? Date? A date last night?" Amir asks, and his gaze is as intense as I'd ever seen it, and I can't look away, until I sense Debbie's presence. Her eyes are narrow.

"Yes, that's the word, date. I did have a date ... with John." I kick the dirt at my feet and fiddle with my shirt collar. I almost want to ask, *What's it to you*? I glance over at Reza as a player in blue from the opposite team strides by and rams a shoulder into Reza's arm.

"*Ah, boro gom sho!*" Reza yells after him as the disgruntled soccer player in blue proceeds to do the same thing to Amir and mutters "Infidel" under his breath. But then my father lurches forward as Amir hauls off and kicks the soccer player in the groin, shouts something in Farsi, then "Maryam?" The player spits on the ground, glares back at us. "Yankees, go home," he shouts over his shoulder. Frankie has stopped kicking the soccer ball around and is staring.

"What was all that about?" Dad asks.

Amir rubs his shoulder. "I am sorry, Mr. Patterson. Afshin. He is, how you say? A sore loser? He runs around the city making trouble. He is a, how you say, disgruntled student. No worries though. He has many feelings for my sister, Maryam. For this reason, we are good. Afshin is a protestor. He looks for demonstrations, likes them. What he dislikes are the Shah's soldiers. So he teases them on their tanks on purpose, even stuffing pretend flowers in their guns. Sometimes, I wonder if he is not crazy." Amir makes that familiar gesture with his finger, encircling his ear.

"You've got a sister?" I ask, surprised. I had no idea. Amir nods, explains that the meaning of Maryam in Farsi is tuberose, a white, amazingly fragrant long-stemmed flower. Apparently, Afshin has been stuffing artificial tuberoses down the guns of the Imperial Army for Amir's sister. "His idea of showing love."

"For Maryam or Khomeini?" Debbie asks.

Amir shrugs while Reza struggles with the equipment Amir has left him to handle. "Ah, this is no fair, Amir, *doostam*, buddy, you are stronger and more fit than I!" Reza complains.

Dad heaves the heavy bag into Amir's convertible, looks at his watch. "We've just enough time for lunch before we've got to get Annie to the Lavizan fields. Amir, did you want to drive over in your car?"

"No, Mr. Patterson, it's closer to walk. I will leave the car here."

We hurry across the field, continue up our alley. Debbie has an arm wrapped possessively around Amir's waist and their hips bounce together as they walk, throwing them off-kilter. Debbie's laughter trails down the street, soft and feathery like velvet. I wonder now whether the public display of affection between an Iranian man and an American woman is a good idea, especially after what had happened back at the field. But soon after, Amir moves away from Debbie, glances back at my father and me, worry knitting his brow. Frankie jogs ahead, his snow-white hair shining in the sun.

"Did you have fun at the James's house, despite your late arrival?" my father asks.

"It was okay," I reply, avoiding his eyes.

Up ahead, the neighbor who lives three houses down from us is in the alley rolling his rubber garbage can through his security door. My dad stops to chat. "Dr. Jamison, hello. How are you feeling?"

Tall and gangly, hair thinning and gray like a spool of almost used thread, Dr. Jamison stands slightly stooped, holding shiny gardening tools in his hand. He wears a beige safari hat and baggy cargo pants, a matching shirt weighed down by large pockets perfect for stowing away compasses, certain to be filled with trinkets or artifacts.

"Feeling fine, Jack, really, thanks for asking."

"How's the treatment going?" my father asks.

"Fine, Jack, it's going well." Dr. Jamison waves around his sparkling spade. "Come in, please, let me show you the hybrid tea roses I'm developing. The old-fashioned variety of fragrant roses that can grow successfully here in Tehran, in excessive temperatures, with a modicum of care, and absolutely no irrigation," explains the erudite Dr. Jamison.

"We saw wild climbing roses at the Caspian Sea," I offer.

"Ah yes, the Caspian, the birthplace of the cultivated rose, more humid with cooler nights than we have here in Tehran." Dr. Jamison points to two bushes, one of which is obviously dying. "Let me introduce you to my no fuss, Middle Eastern rose." The other rose bush was thriving, beautiful stems of bright red rose blooms, rising up to greet my nose as I bend.

"Fragrant. Just amazing," I murmur as I inhale the sweet perfume.

Dr. Jamison snips off a stem with his garden clippers, hands me the beautiful crimson flower with a flourish. "For you, young lady," he says, bowing. He smells of wet wool and peppermint.

"Oh, you shouldn't have, Mr. Jamison. You'll have one less bloom! But thank you."

My father smiles. "This is really quite wonderful. We're privileged to have a stem off this hardy rose bush. Aren't we, Annie?" I nod. "My regards to Mrs. Jamison. Take care of yourself, Daniel," he calls over his shoulder.

"I most certainly will, Jack. These things are sent to try us." Dr. Jamison waves good-bye, then shuts his security door.

"Why are you inquiring after his health?" I ask after we had ambled away.

My father hesitates, then comes right out with it. "He has cancer."

"Oh." I view my new survivalist rose sadly, wishing the same hardy survival for Mr. Jamison.

"Is he a medical doctor?" I ask.

"No, a professor. He teaches Chemistry at the Community School."

"I thought so." A kindly professor or a determined archeologist back from a dig.

My mother has set up lunch poolside and has prepared iced tea. I skip the meal for a shower and a change. Once inside, I plunk my precious rose in my mom's chipped crystal vase I'd filled with tap water. I change quickly and run back downstairs. I am anxious not to miss any free moments with my Iranian friends.

When I reappear in my Phantoms' uniform, Amir grins. He and Reza are holding onto sweating glasses of sun tea. Amir signals for me to perform a cheer, and I do, though I am embarrassed to. I wrap up my cheer with the try-out round-off/split combination I'd perfected at tryouts. Amir and Reza clap and shout, "Bravo!" and I blush.

"Annette, not on the hard pool terrace!" my mother exclaims from her post on our swinging patio chair. Secretly, I am amused by this—marauding bands of protestors and anti-American sentiment out there on the streets. A bomb in a Persian restaurant. Tussles on a soccer field at the end of our street. Soldiers and tanks. Guns. A machine gun-toting escort on my school bus. Remarkably, my mother feels more anxious about a gymnastics routine gone awry than a country unraveling.

Later, I would learn that when Amir and Reza returned to the soccer field that afternoon, a tire on Amir's Mercedes had been slashed. Of course, Amir was handy with a crowbar and could easily change a tire, but his normally cheery disposition was beginning to drain from him like air from a deflating tire.

CHAPTER 9

OCTOBER 1978

Spooky summer [fall] on the horizon I'm gazing at
from my window into the streets
That's where it's going to be where everyone is
walking around, looking around out in the open
suspecting each other's heart to open fire ...
I can't sit still any longer!

A section of "Revolution", Anne Waldman

Despite the turmoil, my parents proceed with their plans for an already-booked trip to Russia with the Burnetts. They read the riot act to us before they leave, for lack of a better phrase. Mom warns us, "No visitors, you hear? You're not to step out of this house after curfew—Debbie, no wandering around Tehran with Amir. You're the big sister in charge. Come straight home after work and school while we're gone."

Mom had been looking forward to their trip—thrilled to be visiting her family's homeland. And Dad had always been the ultimate sightseer, often dragging us around crowded cities or rural towns, a guidebook tucked under his arm. Sadly, our parents had toured the ancient city of Isfahan and the exquisite mosaic tile of the Friday Mosque without us. We'd heard that several American women had worn halter-tops and shorts as they'd toured the mosque, speaking loudly and giggling, creating quite the uproar. But my parents were not afraid that Debbie and I would do the same, Dad's superiors had instructed the men to avoid traveling in groups and together as families for security reasons. Anyway, Dad had been dreading the cost of a family plane fare to Isfahan, so we weren't given the opportunity to go. Even to Persepolis. We'd been cheated out of a visit to our dubbed Iranian "Greek" ruins, something Mom had said would make Iran feel familiar to us. And as things got worse, my parents' rush to squeeze in trips and historic sites was seeming quite irresponsible to me. But they saw it differently. They thought they were behaving quite responsibly, sheltering their children from danger. Had they drawn up a will? Designated our guardians? Just in case anything happened. I don't ask them, reluctant to frighten Frankie.

The first Friday in October, our parents grab a taxi to Mehrabad airport to catch their three-hour flight to Moscow. Mother had arranged for Mr. James to transport me to and from the football games while they were gone. They promised to cut their vacation short if things got worse. I wonder about the exact nature of their trip, knowing that my father was involved in procurement of counter-intelligence equipment at the border of Iran and Russia. Their return flight is scheduled to arrive after curfew.

"After curfew?" I'd asked. "But what will you do?"

Dad explained that taxis could move freely after curfew if they were shuttling passengers from the airport—the drivers carried a special pass. "A soldier might order a vehicle to stop at a checkpoint to look over papers or passports, but almost always, the drivers are waved on." I wonder if this would be the case for my parents. *What if no one waved them on?*

With our parents gone, Frankie and I become caught up in the normal routine of school—and we barely see Debbie. Every night, she'd return home just before curfew, then disappear into her room. She'd sleep late the next morning through our normal preparations for school.

Tonight, Debbie arrives home earlier than usual, shouting at the top of her lungs in the stair hall. "Annie, Frankie!"

Up to my wrists in raw hamburger meat, breadcrumbs, egg, and ketchup, I shout, "Yeah?" She appears in the kitchen, eyes shining with excitement.

"Amir and I saw the Lady in Red!"

"The Lady in Red?! No way. Did you ask her who she's waiting for?!" My breath catches in my chest and I shriek in excitement.

"I did."

"What'd she say?!" I squeal.

"Nothing. She never answered us. Didn't even look at us." Debbie shrugs.

"What?" I am devastated to hear this.

Debbie bristles. "At least we saw her," she says, glaring. "What's for dinner?"

"And what's it to you? You're actually joining us?"

"Yeah, I'm starved."

I smooth the meat into a tin loaf pan, pour a layer of ketchup over the top and insert it into the oven. "Meat loaf. Ready in an hour. Take Frankie for a swim, will you?"

"Annie, I've got to iron some clothes for work tomorrow. Can you?"

"At least pop your head in on him. He's in his room, doing homework."

"God, I'll see him at dinner," Debbie says, flounces away. I purse my lips and grab Frankie for a pre-dinner swim. The evening is quiet except for the sound of the pool water slicing between our fingers. After we'd grown tired of swimming, each of us spread our arms along the pool's edge, backs pressed against the slippery mosaic tile wall, kicking, wondering who could splash the highest.

Once the hooting and hollering had subsided, when everything got quiet and the both of us were lost in our own worlds, Frankie says, "I miss Mom and Dad."

"Me too, Frankie." Sometimes there were no substitutes for parents.

At dinner, I remind Debbie that Frankie and his sixth grade Spanish class are going on a field trip to a Mexican restaurant the next day, and he'd be later than usual.

"He'll be home sometime after six," I tell her.

"I'll remember to be around."

When I return home from cheerleading practice the next day, Frankie had been perched on the toilet bowl for at least an hour. I look around for Debbie. She's nowhere.

"Frankie," I call through the bathroom door. "Are you all right?" He is moaning, and I can hear explosions of diarrhea hitting the toilet bowl, the stink of it finding its way into the hallway.

"No," he says weakly. After multiple flushes, he appears in the corridor, ashen. "Sorry. I feel crappy. My stomach." He whirls around, hurries back to the bathroom, huddles over the toilet bowl and heaves, until he rids most of the Mexican food from his upset stomach.

"Jesus!" And I start to gag, myself.

Steering him into bed, I place a plastic garbage can by his bedside.

"Use this if you're unable to make it to the bathroom, okay?" I rummage around for Pepto Bismol, coming up lucky when I find it lodged behind a pile of washcloths and a box of cotton balls. I open up the crusted bottle top, feed him a spoonful of the pink, gunky goop. "I hope this hasn't expired," I tell him. I tuck the sheets under his chin and set a glass of water on his nightstand.

"I'm going to die," Frankie says. It looked as if he might.

"You are not," I say. "You'll be okay. Either you can't handle Mexican food, or you have food poisoning."

"I have food poisoning," he squeaks.

"Drink the water. You need fluids."

I leave Frankie in bed and go out to settle my own queasy stomach. I'd been famished when I'd walked through the door. But now I wasn't so sure.

I escape into the kitchen for a glass of iced tea, which makes me feel better, enough to think about preparing dinner. I place my mother's tall blue tin pot on the stove for pasta, throw long strings of fresh green beans into a pan, add yellow slices of summer squash, diced red tomatoes, and sauté them until tender. I lay the colorful cooked vegetables over steaming noodles. Once I'd eaten, I save the leftovers for Debbie, hoping she'd show up soon. Before curfew.

I hear Frankie lunge for the bathroom again, heave.

I drum the tabletop with my knuckles. *Where was Debbie? What if I have to rush Frankie to the hospital?* I didn't think I could do it on my own. I grab the Orange Taxi phone card out of my purse, just in case, lay it on the table next to my dish. *Where was she? Maybe she got hit by another motorcycle?* I am thinking she should really stay away from those things.

But I can do nothing but wait. I glance restlessly at the yellow clock, listen to its tick and its tock, a sound that is growing louder with each passing moment, pounding in my ears like drumbeats. I stare back at my reflection in the window, crossed-legged and barefoot on my chair. I look awful. I pull my knees into my chest on my cold metal chair and look up at the ceiling. *Where was she*? I think about bed, but Debbie's keys still lay on the hall table. Groggy, I rub my eyes. *Tick tock. Tick tock.* Time seems to be standing still.

I find myself dozing, but then I wake, coughing back drool. "Debbie?" I ask out loud. Debbie? Nothing. Total silence. I check the clock again—11:30 p.m.? I slam the side of my wrist on the Formica table. *Where is she*? I feel like I'm going to jump out of my skin.

Sometime later, the intercom buzzes. I jump up, stumble to the foyer. "Who's there?" I ask, voice shaking.

"It's Debbie. Annie, let me in! Hurry!" My breath escapes me before I realize I had ever been holding it. I buzz the intercom.

Minutes later, Amir enters the apartment with Debbie. I glare. "Where were you? It's after midnight." My hands are on my head, I am pacing, pulling at my hair, and the last of my restraint falls away. My voice shakes like small arms fire. "Out after curfew?" I yell. "Are you crazy? Don't you ever listen to Mom and Dad? I've been up to my wrists in shit and vomit. Frankie is sick." Amir stands still, sweaty and pale—wordless—averting his eyes from mine.

"Chill, Annie." Debbie is almost yelling at me. "Don't have a cow. I'm an adult, unlike you, worry wart .... We went to Tehran University," Debbie explains.

"You went to Tehran University? For what? Tea and cookies—a lecture?!"

Debbie rolls her eyes. "The newspapers went on strike today. Maryam and Afshin went to watch a sit-in strike of journalists protesting censorship. Amir was worried about his sister so we followed. And like we'd expected, she ran into trouble," Debbie explains, wild-eyed. "We all ran into trouble." Sweat had matted her normally bouncy hair flat to her head.

"What trouble?" I ask woodenly.

"At first everything was good, peaceful, just a bunch of students and professors protesting. But then the troops started firing," my sister cries, eyes already swollen and bloodshot, like a drunkard after a fifth of whiskey. Amir wraps his arm around her, raises his eyes to the ceiling.

I swallow. "Were you in the middle of it?"

"No, we were watching from around the side of a building."

"Is Maryam … okay?" I am concerned for what Debbie might say next.

"Yes. But *I'm* not. Inches away from me, a man got shot in the head. And as I peeked out to see if I could help, I saw him lying in a pool of blood so red, it looked black. And more people were dropping around him like flies. The gunfire was deafening." Debbie covers her ears as if she were hearing it all over again. "And then we didn't stick around to see. We ran. Iranians were marching, holding up signs printed with photographs of Khomeini. Some were chanting, 'Every day is *Ashura*. Every place is *Karbala*. Every month is *Moharram*.' Like I would know what it all means."

I remember Moshdeh explaining that the Prophet Muhammad's grandson, Hossein, was killed at the battle of *Karbala*, on *Ashura*. "Debbie, I'm so sorry." I imagine her watching the throng of people, most of them students, hands and fists raised skyward, shouting unintelligible chants in Farsi, poster-paper placards waving Khomeini's photographs, his stern face, disapproving heavy brow, encouraging the battle against the enemy, the Shah.

Debbie turns to Amir. "It's all your fault. Your stupid idea to protect your sister."

"But that's what brothers do. Protect their sisters," I say. "Older sisters do, too," I sneak in, arms folded across my chest.

"But he didn't do anything, but run." Debbie flops her head over her crossed arms on the table.

"*Everyone* ran," I say. "Sounds like."

"And you are safe. I am, too." Amir lays a hand on Debbie's shoulder, which Debbie flings off. A shadow creeps over his face, and he takes a step back, wringing his hands. "I am not so certain about Maryam."

Debbie looks up at me, tears in her eyes, nodding. "Maryam ran off with her friends in the opposite direction. We don't know what happened to her." Debbie explains that she and Amir zigzagged frantically through darkened streets until they reached *Saltanatabad.*

"How'd you ever get back?" I ask, eyes wide.

"An airport taxi. You know, the kind with a pass to be out after curfew? The taxi driver liked my blond hair. We paid a lot for that ride." She snickers, blowing out snot, wiping it away with the back of her hand. "God. Sorry."

I bring out the leftover pasta. "Have some dinner. I'll heat it up for you." I place a hand on Debbie's shoulder. She shrugs it off.

"I'm not hungry." Turning to Amir, she says, "Call your mom. Tell her you'll be spending the night."

"But she would not approve."

"Think of something, Amir, you can't go home now. It's already so late." Amir leaves the kitchen to use the family room phone. I heat up the pasta anyway in the blue frying pan left on the stove.

I remember my mother's warning to all of us to stay at home; I imagine Debbie flitting around Tehran with her exotic boyfriend while I'm left to take care of Frankie, make breakfast, lunches, and dinner. My voice becomes a fingernail scraping a chalkboard. "You are way out of control, Debbie. I need to tell you that." I spin around and leave the room.

Later, I hear Amir in the kitchen eating my pasta. "Debbie, this is wonderful. You must try it. Your sister is a very good cook." But an argument ensues and then comes the sound of utensils flying. *Gee-sus, what now?*

I awake with a start, shaking. I'd had a nightmare about a violent shoot-out. Not in Tehran, but in downtown Dayton. A young teenage boy wearing a red paisley bandana is brandishing a gun. He waves it high into the air, screaming obscenities, sweating profusely, obviously ready to lose it at any moment, pacing, gun held sideways. Suddenly he pumps out rounds. A young boy in front of him falls listlessly to the ground, like a puppet on a string. His bright red blood splatters on the city building behind him and tinges his hair crimson as he lays dying on the hard gray sidewalk. The sidewalk turns to sand, the sand becomes dirt, the dirt becomes the soccer field at the end of our Tehran alley. The boy is Frankie.

I leap out of bed, hurry into Frankie's room. He is sleeping soundly, mouth open and snoring, his black eyelashes casting shadows beneath his tightly closed eyelids. Dressed in his Cowboys and Indians pajamas and covered by his soft cotton blanket, I recognize how young and defenseless he is. How proud I am that I am attempting to protect him from all that can hurt him.

The stench of his vomit is stifling in the room. I remove the plastic bag from the garbage can and carry it to the kitchen. Debbie is there, peering into the refrigerator. She is wearing nothing but Amir's long-sleeved white dress shirt, and the long tails reach the top of her thighs.

"Debbie?"

She stands up, bangs her head on the freezer door, then whirls around. She blushes pink. "Do not say anything, Annie." She points her finger at me, snatches out two cold hot dogs, grabs two small juice glasses off the counter, and leaves me open-mouthed.

"You left out the Stoli!" I shout after her. I pour myself a glass, take a sip, then spit it out, my throat burning. *Couldn't Debbie have rustled up something more romantic than uncooked hot dogs? Even I could have done better than that.* I discard Frankie's vomit, grab a new plastic bag. Shoulders slouched, I retrace my steps to Frankie's room, reinstall the plastic garbage can at his bedside, open his window wider. Through the paper-thin walls, I hear my muffled sister's voice announce that she had snacks and "shush" because Annie has seen the vodka, and then I hear the stereo's disruptive vibrating bass through her bedroom wall. I escape to the security of my room, listen to Amir caution, "Please, Debbie, Annie will hear," in his deep guttural voice.

"Annie? You're worried about Annie when there's Frankie to worry about?" Debbie almost shouts.

I pass by the still folded sheets on the arm of the family room couch on my way back to my own bedroom. I crawl, exhausted, into bed. Later, I hear Amir murmur good night, and then comes the flap of sheets unfolding in the air outside my door. I take satisfaction in the fact that Amir hasn't chosen to stay with Debbie the entire night.

In the morning, I tiptoe around the sheet-cloaked lump on the couch to the kitchen to make some tea. Minutes later, Amir shuffles in. He wears a five o'clock shadow and looks good, tousled from sleep, or *whatever*, something I didn't care to think about. He is wearing nothing but a sleeveless T-shirt and boxer shorts.

"Hi, Annie."

I refuse to look up from my tea. "Hi, Amir." Still in my short red T-shirt pajamas, *Number One* emblazoned on the chest, I grasp at the hem, pull it lower over my thighs, my long legs helplessly in view. But then I wonder, can't two play this game? *What was my steadfast, studious personality getting me?* I let my hem slip upward.

"May I have tea?" he asks.

"Sure. It's the Lipton tea bag type."

"Very well. *Sobhaneh khordee?* Want I should make food?" Amir asks.

"Breakfast? Sure. What are you proposing?"

Amir eyes me, scratching his five o'clock shadow.

"Proposing. Planning? What will you make?" I snap.

"*Tokhme morgh.* Eggs. Fried eggs on bread. Soft eggs."

"Sounds wonderful." I can barely crack a smile.

Amir goes to work, grabs out eggs from the refrigerator and removes slices of bread from the bread tin, asking me where something was every so often.

I shake my head, bothered by his presence, all of his questions, but I find him a fry pan, a spatula, and some butter. I slap the frying pan on the burner. "Here."

Minutes later, I smell the aroma of frying eggs and toasting bread. When the eggs are still soft in the center, he scoops them out and lays them on slices of warm toasted bread, whistling as he worked.

"You have quince jam?" Amir asks.

"Quince? Jam? Why in the world would we have that? We have Smucker's grape jelly."

"That will do, Annie," Amir says, bewildered.

I retrieve the jelly out of the fridge and hand it to him. He slathers it on top of the runny egg, presses a piece of toasted bread over it.

"Grape jelly on eggs?" I ask.

"Yes, sweet and savory. Try it, Annie. You will like it very much." He smiles.

"I doubt it," I say, shrugging my shoulders. But then I humor him. I take a bite. The mix of sweet and savory isn't bad. "Excellent," I tell him grudgingly. "Juice?"

I reach up high into the top cabinet, bring down two jelly jars my mother uses for orange juice. My red T-shirt rides up on me, exposes pink lacy underwear, but I don't care. Amir stutters when I turn to him, "Eggs—sometimes ... not good." He motions to his face, which is beet red.

"What, not good for skin? You mean eggs cause bad skin?"

"Yes."

"Eggs? No, I doubt eggs do that."

"Yes. Very bad," Amir says again.

"Okay Amir, I believe you. Why then are you cooking eggs?" I bite back a grin, not knowing enough Farsi to explain about oil-clogged pores, non-comedic face lotions, and bacteria. I nod holding up tea. "Cheers! Thank you for breakfast."

Amir gazes at my bare arm stretched out in front of me as I fiddle with my teacup. "Annie, you have very lovely hands," he says, pointing to one of my nails I'd lacquered with *Ravishing Rose* polish—a not so subtle red named after my favorite flower. A shot of heat follows his touch.

I fish out a sugar cube from the container on the table. Before I can drop it into my tea, Amir touches my hand again. "Wait." I watch him pop a sugar cube on his tongue, then take a sip. "Do like this." He grasps the cube between his teeth and swallows the hot tea.

I smile and do the same, let the sugar soften, melt away as I sip my tea, blushing at all the focus on our tongues, mouths and lips. Amir's beard is peeking out beneath the surface of his skin on his angular jaw—still clean-cut, but darker from the perpetual five o'clock shadow. His full lips are perfectly shaped. Funny how perfection makes you stare. But then there was the spot of red on the edge of his eye, that imperfect smile. More importantly, Amir wasn't mine to stare at so longingly. I look away, flushing.

Debbie strolls into the kitchen in sweats and a T-shirt. I am relieved she isn't still wearing Amir's shirt.

Debbie yawns. "What's for breakfast?"

"*Tokhme morgh*," I say. Debbie smiles at my knowledge of the word egg. "Did Maryam make it home okay last night?" I ask her.

"Yes, when Amir called home Maryam had just called from her friend's apartment, not far from the university. She and her friends didn't have to hail a taxi, like us," Debbie says, sitting tall. "Amir's mother was beside herself with worry."

"Yes, and you were crazy to follow Maryam in the first place," I say. "What did Amir tell his mom about where he was staying the night?"

"Reza's." Debbie turns away from me. "Amir, make me some breakfast."

I roll my eyes.

"Absolutely no grape jelly though."

God, I think, she's so demanding.

"I shall make breakfast for you and for Frankie," Amir says grinning.

"Skip Frankie." I slam a plate on the table, but then I remember how dry toast is usually palatable when someone is sick. "On second thought, throw some white bread into the toaster for him. No butter." I stand up to grab another plate.

"Annie, put some clothes on!" Debbie says after she's shoved her hair out of her eyes.

Frankie strolls into the kitchen, hair matted to his head, complexion sallow. My heart softens.

"Frankie! How're you doing?" Debbie asks.

"Better." Amir slides a plate of dry toast over to him.

"Thanks. Why're you here?" Frankie asks Amir.

"Curfew."

"Curfew. Oh, right." And Frankie accepts his answer, grabbing his dry toast and taking a bite. "You got soccer today?"

"Practice. Game tomorrow." Amir's eyes brighten. "Frankie, come. To practice. If you are no longer sick?" he invites.

"Sure." Frankie beams; toast crumbs are lodged between his teeth.

"You too?" Amir asks me.

"I can't, I have a football game today at Lavizan. Mr. James and John are taking me. Actually, I should get ready."

As I leave the kitchen to shower and change into my uniform, I feel Amir's eyes on me.

Later, I catch Debbie alone in her room.

"About last night," I begin.

"Nothing happened, if that's what you're thinking," my sister shoots back.

"Something happened. You wore his shirt."

"That's right. I wore his shirt. That's it." Her gaze is defiant.

"Yeah, right." I don't believe her.

"It's really none of your business, Annie. But, if you must know, he's saving himself for marriage." She crosses her arms.

"Really?" *Ha.*

"Yeah, really. He's trying to abide by the Koran," Debbie says smugly. "But because you're in my business, I will tell you he lacks willpower," she whispers.

"Okay. Stop. I've heard enough." I do not wish to hear any more.

"Why are you so interested, Annie?"

"Stop it! I'm not." And I escape to my room in a huff, secretly relieved he is saving himself for marriage.

Before Amir leaves for home, I give him my dog-eared copy of *The Swiss Family Robinson*, hoping he might like the tale, the cast-a-way theme.

"Why, Annie this is very wonderful," Amir says. "You gave me a book!" And then he flashes the impish grin I love.

The Phantoms beat the Vikings fourteen to three, allowing for only a single field goal. It's the kind of crisp autumn day that gets you thinking about itchy hayrides, orange pumpkins, colorful leaves, and tart apple cider. The aroma of fresh-cut grass brings me back to Ohio. I stand on the sidelines, sandwiched in between Cathy and Melody. I look up into the stands, crowded with schoolmates and parents wearing royal blue and gold. Alika sits in an upper row, her long black hair glinting in the sun, her boxy-style eyeglasses reflecting back light. Everything seems so American here, so normal compared to everything happening around us, outside the Lavizan campus.

Janice is cheering on the opposite side today, and she has barely acknowledged me. Something I've been getting used to. I wave Alika over, and a dark-haired guy seated next to her waves back at me. Had he thought my wave was meant for him? *Oh, God, he did. He is strolling over.*

"I'm Mike," he says when he reaches the fence in front of me. "Mike Morales."

"I'm Annie." I smile, trying to keep cool. "Do you go to TAS?"

"I do." Aside from TAS, there is another school for Americans and other international students called the Community School, originally formed for the children of Presbyterian missionaries, formerly a hospital. The Shah's third wife, Farah Pahlavi Diba, was born there, and Mr. Jamison teaches there. I'd never noticed Mike at TAS, and he was definitely someone to see.

"Saw you at Wednesday's pep rally, looked you up in the program. You're a dead ringer for my girlfriend back home in San Francisco."

"I am?"

"You are."

I stand there awkwardly—a loaded statement to open up a conversation with.

The sun shines bright on his face and he's squinting, but I can see how his brown eyes are flecked with amber. He is gorgeous, out of my league. He has a light beard and wears a brown nubby sweater, faded Levi's and black boots—a biker model for Pete's sake. He explains that his father works for Bell Helicopter. He is a senior this year, like me.

"My father's U.S. Air Force. Do you know Janice Hanley? Her father works for Bell Helicopter."

"Can't say that I do."

"I'll introduce you sometime." I nod over to the field's edge. "Erh. Sorry, Mike. My ride. Sure was nice meeting you."

"Bye, Annie, same here. I'll look for you at school." I watch him saunter away, then look back over his shoulder at me, a slow, gorgeous grin spreading out on his face. He's also a dead ringer for someone. An actor? I can't put my finger on it. But then it dawns on me. He's an American version of Amir, same stature, dark-brown eyes—but not as clean shaven.

"You look exactly like her, you know," Mike calls after me.

I blush. "See you at school." I turn to find John standing there, now out of gear, crossing his arms in front of his chest, a visible flush in his cheeks.

"Sorry." But was I apologizing for keeping him waiting, or talking with Mike?

Alika approaches. "Oh, my God, who was that?" she asks.

"Mike Morales from school."

"He's gorgeous."

I say nothing, and John stands by, silent still.

"Great game by the way," Alika says to both of us. In his quiet moodiness, John doesn't give her the time of day.

"Thanks," I say. "Want to come over to my house sometime after a game?"

"Sure," Alika says. "Next week?"

"It's my birthday on the twenty-sixth." I blush, usually not advertising it.

"Really? Let's have a party," Alika squeals.

"Happy Birthday, Annie!" Mr. James says, his smile genuinely tender.

I smile. "Thanks, Mr. James." Turning to Alika, I say, "Sure. We'll talk at school." I motion to John and Mr. James.

"My ride." I wave bye to Alika, follow Mr. James and John to the parking lot to collect the Cadillac Seville.

"Great game, John," I say as Mr. James hurries ahead to the car.

"That guy? Who's he again?" John asks, hands shoved into deep pockets.

"Just a guy from San Francisco."

When I return home, Frankie sits reading a *Hardy Boys* book on our flowered corduroy couch.

"How was soccer with the Persians?!"

"Awesome," he says, practically beaming. "I met a new friend."

"You did? Who?"

"Nouri."

"Nouri," I repeat the familiar name. Then it dawns on me. "Right, Nouri, the boy across the field—the one who ran by us one day in the alley when we were getting Pepsis. He liked my hair."

"If you think he liked yours, he loved mine," Frankie says matter-of-factly.

"You know it, Blondie. Glad you made a new friend."

"Yeah. He was just hanging out by the field, staring, kicking around a soccer ball, the way I usually do, you know? Amir invited him to play, like he did me."

"That's nice."

"Nouri's my age. We were the only eleven-year-old boys playing. And guess what?"

"What?"

"We scored the only goals." Frankie's eyes shone.

I could just imagine Amir winking and signaling to the other men to let the boys score. I smile to myself. "Where's Debbie?"

"At Amir's."

I shake my head, pausing to find words. "You know, Frankie, how about we don't discuss Debbie's behavior this week with Mom and Dad, okay?"

"I won't say anything," Frankie says earnestly. "I don't want Amir in trouble. I like him."

"I like him, too. Very much."

"Can I have Nouri over sometime?"

"Sure. How're you feeling by the way, Bud?" I ask.

"Fine. Starving!"

"Let me change out of my uniform, see about dinner—all that throwing up has left your stomach empty. See you soon, Bud."

"How come you always call me Bud when I'm sick or hurt?" Frankie asks.

"I must be feeling sorry for you. But now that you are a major soccer star, maybe I shouldn't?"

Hoping that Mike would be at our next game again, he doesn't disappoint me. Just before our half-time cheer, he files into the stands alone again. He waves at me, and I smile back awkwardly. I'd noticed him in the school compound on Tuesday deep in conversation with a thin blonde with long, super neat hair—a Breck girl for Pete's sake—from those shampoo commercials. I'd decided not to say hello to him then, but at least today he was alone, and smiling at me.

"Okay, everyone. Ready?!" asks Melody.

"Ready!"

Come on fans, let's yell it loud!
Bring the noise up in the crowd!
D D Defense!
D D Defense!

The whistle signals it's half time, and we gather in the middle of the field. Today our dance is to *Brown Sugar* by the Rolling Stones. Melody has created a crazy routine—lots of hip wiggling, stomping and clapping, twirling of our royal blue and yellow-gold pompoms to the song's fast tempo. A pair of us at a time will strut to center stage and prance in circles, slap our hands together like in paddy cake, and end our pair dance with a bend towards the audience and a flip of our skirts upward, showing off our royal blue bloomers. This routine embarrassed me but delighted the crowd.

Right before we are set to begin, Debbie, Reza, and Amir file into the stands.

Oh no, why had they come? I am too embarrassed to perform this routine in front of them. *Could I even do it?* But when it is over, Amir and Reza laugh and clap madly, Mike smiles and pumps his fist skyward, but Debbie sits quietly. She has never approved of my cheerleading—any cheerleading, in fact, saying cheerleaders should play the game, not cheer for it. But girls weren't allowed to play football—not yet anyway. Cheerleading, though, was a sport for me.

After the game, I let Mr. James know that I would grab a ride home with Debbie. He looks relieved to be freed of the long ride across town to my home. I glance up into the stands and catch Mike's eye, who waves good-bye and mouths, "Exactly like her!"

On the way home, Amir pulls into a gas station for a bathroom break; luckily, he needs no gas because the line has formed out into the street. I have to go desperately but find the door to the women's room is locked, and someone is stirring inside. I wait awhile, turn to the tall mountains behind me. A crooked orange construction crane rises up into the sky like the skeleton of some prehistoric bird. I see the half-finished apartment building on the hill at the Lavizan field.

I hear the clunk of the lock turning, and a diminutive woman draped in a black *chador* struggles out the heavy bathroom door. I pull the door to help her, but she eyes me coldly, wags a crooked finger inches from my nose, tittering loudly in Farsi—spit spraying on my face like the pool water from Frankie's perfect cannonballs. Her angry make-up-free face is just inches from mine. I'm momentarily confused, but it dawns on me that I am still wearing my cheerleading uniform. I sashay past her into the bathroom, my shoulders erect. I turn and flip up my skirt like I had done during our half time routine, expose my royal blue bloomers, then slam the door shut behind me. Knees shaking, I lose my balance above the putrid pit, my back banging against the grubby tile wall that holds me up. I regain my footing, ignore the red rubber hose on the ground for the tissue I've been keeping in my bra for occasions like this, shoulders smarting. I can't take this anymore.

At lunchtime, early in the week, I encounter the Breck girl in the restroom applying make-up at the mirror, brushing out her long blond hair. She is speaking to a friend. I scurry into a stall.

"He's gorgeous," the Breck girl gasps.

"Where's he from?" I hear her friend ask. I clip the door shut behind me.

"San Francisco."

"No way. Cool," her friend says.

My heart drops. I try to urinate quietly, rip the toilet paper gingerly from the roll.

"I have a secret," the Breck girl confides to her friend.

"Tell me, Mallory!"

"Mike Morales told me I look exactly like his girlfriend back home."

I hover over the toilet seat, saddened, because Mallory and I looked nothing alike. I wait for the girls to leave, then I hurry out to the lunchroom.

I am forced to order hot lunch, fried fish and pale green salad, yellow even, because I had forgotten my bagged one.

Alika sits at her usual corner table, but surprisingly, Janice, who is seated with her usual group of friends, waves me over. I gaze down at my Levi jeans with relief, pull at my sister's cool cotton hooded sweatshirt, *Boston* plastered on the front, and head over to her table.

"Hey, Annie," Janice says. "Saw you chatting with Mike Morales at our last game. What's he doing with a girl like you?!" she asks. Her friends spill into a fit of giggles. I blush, trying to figure out if she is being facetious, where the conversation is going.

"Sit," she beckons. She pats the lunch table seat; her friend Rebecca slides over to make room.

"You're one lucky girl if Mike Morales is paying attention to you. Listen, we're going to the Roller Palace Wednesday night after school for some skating. Think you can charm Mike Morales to meet us there?" She bats her mascara-tipped strawberry-blond eyelashes coquettishly, implying that I should flirt.

"Sure." I twist in my seat. "I can try." My mind reels. I hardly knew him. He is also talking up the Breck girl. Curfew had been relaxed and there'd be plenty of time for evening activities, but I am feeling uncomfortable.

"Great," says Janice. "We're grabbing an orange taxi. We'll pick you up."

I feel ill from the fumes off the fried fish on my lunch tray.

Janice notices. "Hey, don't you usually bring your lunch?"

"I forgot it today."

"Well, welcome to the table with the cool ladies who can afford the blue plate special."

I turn to Alika who sits alone at her secluded lunch table. She raises a hand to wave but then lets it drop, now focused on the sandwich I knew she had pulled from a wrinkled brown bag.

The girls are discussing a party they'd escape to after skating. "Annie, make certain Mike knows about it."

"I will." My trembling leg thumps the cafeteria table. I place my hand on my thigh to still it. I wished I were at Alika's table, discussing her Agatha Christie novel, even though I am partial to love stories.

Wednesday morning I convince Debbie to stay home with Frankie that evening. Promptly at six o'clock, Janice, Rebecca and Mindy, pull up to our security door. Janice's first question to me is whether I'd invited Mike Morales. "I did," I say, struggling with my seat belt. "I also told him about the party afterwards." Janice smiles as she offers me a roll of strawberry-cake lip gloss.

When we enter the rink, lo and behold, Mike Morales, in his brown leather biker jacket, in all of his glory, stands inside watching the skaters. "Annie, you have some *persuasion*," whispers Janice. She eyes me with approval.

"Mike, hey." I scurry over to greet him with three eager girls in tow.

"Hey, beautiful," Mike says. I introduce him around. Almost before we'd finished our pleasantries, Janice grabs Mike's hand and drags him to the rental counter. Once on skates, she monopolizes his company. Occasionally he'd skate by me, tug a lock of my hair, and I was left alone to follow the Persian women skating past me in full *Chadori* dress, their black cloaks trailing behind them like scarves, tempting me to reach out and hang onto their skirts for a ride.

Once my thighs were burning so much I thought I'd die, Janice yells over the *Saturday Night Fever* music, "Annie, party-time!"

Outside the rink, the taxi is waiting for us. Once we'd piled in, the cabbie whisks us away through narrow, dusty streets. I sit in front, and Janice directs the driver from the back,

"*Niavaran, Farmanieh*! *Dasteh Chap*! (Left!), *Dasteh Rast*! (Right!)." Mike dashes behind us on his motorcycle, and his longish brown hair flies out behind him in the wind. The driver says, "Hold on, *voomen*! You *vill* love the ride in *thees* orange taxi!"

The neighborhoods grow tidier with each mile traveled, the houses, too. Eventually, the taxi driver pulls into a wrought-iron, fenced-in residential compound. He continues up a long driveway and into an expansive yard, deposits us outside a columned, white stucco house perched high above the city. Dozens of teenagers are milling about on a granite terrace holding frothy drinks in large, clear plastic cups. Journey blasts from a stereo on the terrace. *Whose amazing house is this?*

"How cool the parents allow beer," Rebecca says. But I wonder. Do they?

Janice and Mike go in search of the keg. I wander to the property's edge, peering down into the valley of twinkling lights. A warm breeze lifts the hair off my shoulders, and someone approaches me from behind. It's Mike, and he kisses my cheek, offers me a beer.

"No, thank you." So far I'd only sneaked sips of bubble-gum wine in private, not beer in a crowd of kids.

Mike feigns surprise and whispers, "The most beautiful girl at this party isn't going to get drunk? Let me make out with her?"

His cotton candy words did nothing for me. Right off his bike, it seemed Mike's eyes had worked the crowd like a bodyguard, falling on every tight T-shirt-clad blonde in the opulent yard. I shake my head side to side. "Nuh, uh. *You've* got a girlfriend back home in San Francisco." I tap his chest, bite my lip to hide a smile. *Would I still be the most beautiful girl at the party if the Breck girl were here tonight? Or his girlfriend?*

"I like it when you bite your lip," Mike teases. He gazes out over the flickering lights in the valley, sighs. "Such an incredible view...."

And Journey was playing "Lights", appropriate that the song was about San Francisco.

"It reminds me of home and my girlfriend," Mike shouts over the electric guitar.

Dozens of bright stars illuminate the night sky. I could almost reach out and pluck one, they seemed so close. *He must miss her desperately, if everyone he sees, or everything he hears, reminds him of her.* I wanted someone to fall in love with me like that. I sigh.

"Did you get a load of the size of that pool over there?" Mike asks pointing to a side terrace. "The Rolls Royce in the garage," he whispers.

"And how about the two stately lions guarding the driveway?" I ask. "Luckily, they're made of concrete." Mike nods, sipping his beer, and we sit awhile, looking out over the valley of twinkling lights, and the city that is laid out before us in all of its glory, miles of terraced, shrub-covered earth, like a Persian carpet that runs down an oak staircase, suggesting something earthy, with all the swirling vines in greens and taupes, amid a background of dusty beige.

"If I squint my eyes, I'm back at home near the Bay Bridge, but without fog," Mike says, then he tells me about his family, his brother, how his Madre makes the best "Shrimp Jambalaya" in the whole world—how he loves the rawness of Iran, the sincerity of most Iranians, their hospitality. He tells me how his housekeeper, Zahra, calls him *Agha* Mike. How she makes him a pot of strong, hot tea every morning. "Madre spends hours each day cooking elaborate Persian meals with Zahra, who's more of a companion than a maid to my mom." He laughs at the idea, a hired friend for his mother.

From out of nowhere, Janice sidles up to Mike. "Dance with me?" Already drunk, she stumbles, drapes her arms around him to steady herself. "*Pleease,*" she whines. "I just *love* this song." The mascara has run off her eyelashes; they are colorless now, which makes her less attractive than usual, her blue eyes almost disappearing into her pale complexion.

I scan the yard, not recognizing a soul, a wallflower without Mike's attention. Suddenly, I didn't want to fit in, to mingle. That feeling of claustrophobia was back. "I'm heading out guys," I say. Had Janice even heard me?

"Already?" Mike asks, disappointed. But now, I understand he has a soft spot for maids and blondes, except for Janice. And he is nice.

Still, I leave him to handle Janice alone. And he's confused, not understanding my overwhelming desire to go, probably used to getting anything he wanted from any girl in her right mind. I wander past the Olympic size pool. *Maybe it was true I looked a bit like his girlfriend?* A thought that made me happy.

I enter the house through the side door and into an expansive kitchen where there is creamy white tile, cherry cabinets, a stainless-steel island, marble countertops, and a butler's pantry so packed with crystal, china and colorful bottles of alcohol no one need ever venture out to a liquor store. *Probably exactly the point.*

"Hello?" I call out. Through the kitchen, a long parquet hallway dressed in paneled wainscoting leads to various parlors and libraries stocked full of books and china figurines. The hall empties into a foyer that rivals the size of my family's entire apartment. On a round walnut antique table is a ceramic vase of ivory and pink gladiolas, red carnations—lavender roses spiking out the center—the fragrance so cloyingly sweet it's oppressive. Unsuccessful in my search to find anyone at home,

I wander back into the kitchen, pick up the wall phone, and dial the Orange Taxi Service from the note card in my bag.

I wait near the wrought-iron fence and study all the other opulent residential compounds on the street. The ones to the south had gated entrances and similar expansive views of Tehran. I recall the shanty town dwellers that lived in filthy squalor amid buzzing flies, those sewage lakes on the way to the commissary in South Tehran created from cesspools built at higher elevations. I hear the roar of an engine, see a taxi careen around the corner and fly by me, screech to a halt before backing up as fast as it'd been driving forward. I fling open the door, jump into the back seat, and call out the name of my modest alley to a bearded Iranian driver.

Do the people who live on this street work for the Shah? Did they get rich from taking what didn't belong to them? I wondered. *Was this a high ranking military officer's home? An American oil executive?* I'd ask Janice at school if she's still speaking with me.

Oddly, this taxi driver drives quickly, eyes fixed on the road, not in the least jovial. The passenger side visor is flipped down and a photograph of the Shah in military uniform is taped there. The driver's shoulders are rigid; he is hunched over the steering wheel, a cigarette dangling from his mouth, and he's all business. He drives quickly and efficiently, his radio sounding every so often. He speaks slowly and deeply into the receiver—almost churlishly. *Perrrk!!* Each time the radio blasts, my heart thumps in my chest.

The ride feels long to me now. I wheel around in my seat at all the storefronts that look the same no matter what street we are driving on. At last I recognize the brick wall of my alley. Relieved, I reach into my pocket for money. "Eight," I call out. But the driver continues past our security door, picks up speed, flies down our alley, past Mr. Jamison's apartment house. *"Vaysa!"* ("Stop!") I shout. At the construction site, the driver finally squeals to a halt in a 360-degree dust bowl. But then he sits there, not turning or speaking, car still idling. *Had he not understood me?* I am too afraid to say anything now—I don't know what to say, how to say it. My left thigh is trembling, and I can't seem to stop it. Still, the driver sits and pulls long and languorously on his cigarette, squinting up at the night sky. I can't tell what smells worse, his Turkish cigarette or the exhaust spilling into the car. He cuts the engine, flips up the visor and the photograph of the Shah, and slaps down the driver's side visor, this time holding a photograph of Khomeini. I stifle back a gasp as he opens his door, gets out, still smoking. When he's smoked the cigarette down to the nub, he throws it at his feet in the dirt. The end glows orange before he grinds it out and starts around to my door. I slide over frantically. My jeans catch on the cracked leather seat. He flings open the door, orders, "Out." I scrape a hand through my hair, but stay in my seat, and clutch the other door handle. "Out!" he shouts. I get out. "Money," he says flatly, extending his palm. I hand him a wad of bills with a shaking hand. He takes my money, slowly smooths the bills out one at a time on a short, thick thigh. When he's pushed the straightened, carefully folded bills into his back pocket, he steps towards me, reaches a hand up underneath my hair and pulls me forward by my neck—his face just inches from mine. I smell the nicotine on his breath, dare not to flinch. He seems uncertain what to do with me. My mind whirrs, thoughts of kidnapping and ransom tumble around in my head like tumbleweed. Had I neglected to bring along my hostage kit, thinking it was just skating? *Would I ever learn? If I screamed loud enough, would anyone hear? Debbie? Frankie?* I stiffen, breath heaving in my chest.

But just as suddenly as he'd grabbed it, the driver lets my hair drop, turns on his heel and returns to his open car door. As he ducks in, he laughs or sneers, I can't begin to tell which, then slams the door behind him. And after, he shouts out the open window, *Begu marg bar* Shah, Carter! I notice now that the mercury vapor light has flicked on, a probable sign from Allah himself, and it illuminates my fear. And as the taxi driver peels away, the car tires spin up dust that settles into my eyes and mouth and chokes me. It is then that I see the taxi isn't orange after all.

I scan my alley, eyes burning. The light glowing from the second-floor windows casts a brightness over the security walls and spills out onto the street. And after the taxi has disappeared from view, I gather the courage to flee to our security door in the dim ochre light, shoulders hunched, head down, sobbing. Oh, how I wanted my mom and my dad.

My parents return from Russia with grand tales—exotic descriptions of Red Square and their excursion on the night train to Leningrad, how on their ride home in the airport taxi the Iranian Imperial Guard had stopped them at a military checkpoint after they'd seen that their passports showed recent entry from Russia. Assured my parents weren't Marxists, the guards moved them on with dismissive waves, as if they had better things to do. The Shah was skittish to have Russia on its border and the now communist regime in Afghanistan to the east.

For gifts, my parents bring back stackable wooden dolls with painted on scarves and crimson lips, and a tea cozy—a hefty looking pink-cheeked Russian woman made from stockings with wild red synthetic hair. With a ruby pout, she holds a plastic tea cup and saucer, sewn into one hand; large pearl earrings hang from fleshy, nylon ear lobes, her wide draping skirt made to cover and cozy a hot tea pot. They call her Vladlena after their Russian tour guide. But even with the gift of the stackable wooden dolls, a slow burn of anger has begun to smolder inside me, like those placards of the Shah being set on fire, burning just around the edges before being fully engulfed in flames. It's one thing to leave your children home alone for a trip to Venice or Paris, but vacationing when a civil war is simmering, and a selfish sister guardian is in charge, that's unthinkable. It doesn't make sense to choose a Honda over a fire-trap Pinto, and then decide to bring your children into this.

Later in the week, I receive a call from Miss Barker that the weekend games would be canceled as a precautionary measure. Some buses carrying Lockheed Aircraft employees had been stoned. I don't mind the cancellation because I am celebrating my eighteenth birthday.

I call Alika. "You think your dad would feel comfortable driving you to my house? It's the Shah's birthday today as well, you know."

"I know. Can you believe you share the same birth date with the Shah of Iran? Your claim to fame. Hold on, I'll check to see if my dad can drive me." I can hear her speaking with someone in the background. But then Alika's voice sounds in the receiver. "I'm absolutely coming—ten o'clock okay?"

"Great. But please don't come just because it's my birthday."

"But then it would be the one reason for me to come, Annie."

Just before ten, I wander downstairs to wait for Alika. I leave the security gate open, and in the alley, I smell a wood fire burning off in the distance.

A few yards down the street, a boy is walking. And as he approaches, I see it's Nouri. He grins.

"Nouri, hi!"

He peers into our compound shyly. "*Salaam*. May I come in?"

"Nouri, what wonderful English! Sure, but please let's wait until my friend Alika arrives, okay?"

And Nouri waits patiently with me until a light gray compact-sized car turns the corner. It's Alika, driven by her father, his hair fully gray, jaw slack. He looks to be of Japanese descent. He smiles at us pleasantly.

"Hey. Welcome." I greet Alika as she exits the car.

"Hey. Happy Birthday." She turns to her father. "Bye, Dad. Get me at—"

"Four o'clock?" I interrupt.

Alika's father nods, leans out the window and waves goodbye. "Happy Birthday, Annie." He pulls away, and dust spins off his tires as he turns the corner. Alika's father worked at TRW, Thompson Ramo Woodridge, shortened to just initials in the 1960s. He's some kind of an aerospace engineer.

"Let's go inside. Alika, this is Nouri. Nouri, Alika." Nouri nods. Alika tries to tousle his short hair, but it doesn't budge. A small white scar shows through the dark stubble on one side of his head.

"Hi, Nouri, please to make your acquaintance." His expression is blank, but then he smiles widely.

We wander past the pool, and Nouri feasts it in with wide eyes. I lead the pair upstairs to our apartment.

"We have the house to ourselves," I say. "Our neighbor, Mr. Jamison, is sick. My parents and our first-floor neighbors bring lunches to him and his wife every weekend." The aroma of baking brownies from the atrium fills the air. Nouri inhales the chocolate fragrance in deeply, eyes closed. It seemed Christie was becoming domestic like her stepmother.

"Frankie," I call from the hall. "Guess who's here?!"

Frankie emerges from his room and stands just outside his door, shifting his knobby-kneed legs back and forth. "Hi," he says to Nouri shyly.

"*Salaam.* Hi," Nouri answers, biting his fingernails, concentrating on his feet.

"Want to build some Legos, Nouri? I have the Galaxy Explorer set."

Nouri nods, smiling, understanding the word *Lego*, and the two boys disappear into Frankie's room.

Alika and I wander into the kitchen and I pull out a can of orange Hi-C from the fridge, grab a couple of juice glasses from an overhead cabinet. We sit awhile, drinking. After we'd finished, I set the glasses in the sink. As I pull open the refrigerator to return the can of Hi-C, Nouri appears behind me. His eyes are wide at the stocked contents; he almost salivates.

"Hungry, Nouri?" I ask, motioning to my stomach, then to my mouth. "Food?"

He nods.

Minutes later, I offer up Amir's special sweet and savory fried egg sandwich, which Nouri grabs for, before I can stop him. I lift up his dirty fingers, turn them to him and say, "Look! Nouri, wash!" He returns to the kitchen with sparkling clean hands, except for the skin beneath his fingernails. He devours the sandwich in several large gulps.

Alika stares, surprised. The hollow of his cheeks and the bowl of his legs signal he is suffering from malnutrition. Alika and I look at each other, eyebrows raised.

I say, "Go ahead, Nouri, you are welcome to anything you like here in our home. What else would you like to eat?"

Nouri nods over at the counter. Alika rises from her chair and grabs a banana off the countertop. She hands it to Nouri. He smiles gratefully, eats it quickly, hands me back the peel. He and Frankie leave to go downstairs to the pool area to play.

"*Merci,*" he says from the kitchen door.

I turn my attention to Alika. "Thanks for coming over. To be honest, it's nice to have a break from games this weekend." I blow out a sigh.

"I know what you mean. I'm a member of the Royal Riding Club—a big commitment. But my parents are making me quit.

Coming home from practice one night, a bunch of Iranian boys in a Paykan tried to run our bus off the road. They laughed the whole time. Should we be more worried?" Alika asks. I consider this for a moment.

"According to my dad's high command at work, the Shah has it all under control," I say. "They've relaxed curfew." I shrug. "I try not to think about it. My dad tells me it's fine."

Suddenly, shrieks sound below us, and I recognize Christie's shouts. We rush downstairs, frightened. Just inside the Burnett's open apartment door, Christie holds Nouri by the scruff of his neck, almost choking the malnourished boy.

"Do you know this kid?" she asks angrily.

Bewildered, I look at Nouri who is wearing a messy mustache of chocolate. "Nouri?"

"*Moteassefam! Motavajjeh nemisham*," he cries, frightened. "This... this is not your house?"

"No, no, Nouri. It is our neighbor's. Did you eat their brownies?" I motion to my lips and point to the plate on the counter.

Nouri nods.

Meanwhile Alika has been studying Christie. "Hey, don't I know you from school?"

But then Christie's expression turns blank as if a wall had closed. Did she want to reject all friends here? To spite Julie!

"Christie, it's me Alika from Algebra. How are you?! I've been loving that pink fuzzy sweater you've been wearing to school lately. It's crazy cool."

"Thanks," Christie says slowly, calming down. "What's the deal with the kid?"

"I'm sorry," I say. "We invited Nouri over. He and Frankie play soccer together down the street. He's been eating ever since he got here. He's starving."

Christie's gaze opens up. She holds out the plate. "Want a brownie?" she asks.

"Sure." Alika takes a dark lumpy square and bites into it, smiling. "Yummy. Very yummy," she says. "Want to come downstairs to the pool area with us?"

Christie pauses, considering the invitation carefully. "To swim? It's a bit chilly, only sixty degrees."

"To hang out, not to swim," I say.

"Okay, I'll be down in a minute."

I am surprised but pleased. It must be that Alika was approachable. Indeed a "helper of man."

"Come on, Nouri," I say, "let's go."

"Nouri?" Christie asks gently, holding out the plate of brownies. "Don't you want another?"

"*Merci*," Nouri says with a toothy smile.

"Okay. See you in a minute." Christie closes the door softly behind her.

Later, as promised, she joins us downstairs in her corduroys, but also in her pink fluffy Angora sweater threaded with tiny bits of metallic silver. She looks bashful but pleased.

"Hi," she says shyly, sipping from a large ceramic mug of coffee, disheveled as usual.

"Hi, Christie. Your coffee smells good," Alika says. "I know Annie isn't a fan, but I love it."

"Want some?"

"Sure."

Christie shoots us a wide grin and returns upstairs to grab Alika a hot mug of coffee and the plate of brownies. Her two cats are running beside her when she returns. "I'm giving these two a taste of freedom." But the cats are more frightened than excited, their short hair elevating off their backs, their ears flattening, as each of them take tentative steps. Frankie kneels down on one knee, splashes them and shouts as they scurry, "See! Cats hate water!"

Christie hands the cup of coffee to Alika. "It's Turkish."

"Aw," Alika says kindly, "Nothing like coffee and animals!" She turns to the boys. "No more splashing," she orders. Siam has crawled up onto her lap. Meese has located a spot in the sun on our poolside strip of grass, and is lazily gnawing on a blade; the grass has grown long in my father's absence.

The security gate buzzes harshly, sending the cats scurrying towards the house, and I hurry over to open it. There stands Debbie, and Amir, who is sucking on a pencil.

"Debbie wishes I should quit smoking," Amir explains. I know that Amir has been smoking forever—but then everyone over the age of twelve in Iran seemed to have a cigarette dangling from their lips—but he wants to please Debbie.

"I am always telling Debbie I don't mind very much that she drinks diet Pepsi," he says, shrugging his shoulders.

"Oh, give Amir a break, Debbie," Christie says. "We should all quit chocolate, then."

Debbie argues, "It's a little bit different. Has no one ever heard of lung cancer?"

Luckily, there is a knock on the security door to diffuse the tension. I open it.

"Hello, everyone, am I missing good food?!" Reza asks.

"Nope," I say, laughing. Debbie grumbles to Amir, "We were supposed to be alone this afternoon." I look over at Reza, who hadn't heard Debbie and was walking towards Nouri, "*Doostam*, my buddy," he says, hand extended, then a quick downward movement at the last moment.

Nouri laughs, his empty hand still stretched out in front of him.

"Reza, *Doostam*!" I can tell his little boy mind is whirring, thinking about a possible joke to play on Reza for revenge.

"Nouri, where do you live?" Alika asks. Amir translates the question to Nouri, who answers back in Farsi. Amir explains that Nouri lives in one of the few shanty towns in North Tehran.

I understood now why Nouri was so ravenous and filthy.

Amir asks Nouri another question in Farsi, and Nouri answers. Amir translates, "Nouri's *baba* drives a taxi, but his company is on strike. His *maman* is a housekeeper at a doctor's house near Niavaran palace. Today, Nouri's *maman* and *baba* sell flowers outside the bazaar. He has many brothers and sisters who help his *maman* and *baba*. Nouri was home alone today. He was bored and walked here."

"How many brothers and sisters, Nouri?" Alika asks. Nouri looks at Amir, who asks him the same question in Farsi. The two of them talk at greater length, privately.

Amir says, "Nouri has three brothers and two sisters. He would be in big trouble if his father knew Nouri was here." Amir explains that Nouri's father is angry at the Shah for attempting to shut down his home—about curfew. "His *baba* makes no taxi trips during the night, and so there is less money for the family. Long gas lines. Now, his company is on strike. He says the Shah is America's puppet."

"Amir, do you think that? Are you mad at us also?" I ask.

Amir shakes his head. "No, I love you and your family. *Kheili.* Very much. You are all my good friends," he says solemnly.

Next to our apartment is a vacant lot that holds an orderly and apparently cared for garden of trees. Frankie has been fascinated with exploring the property, able to peek into a portion of the land from my balcony, or from our rooftop, viewing rows of bent green trees overloaded with large balls of fruit. He has wondered what kinds of trees are over there, but has never mustered the courage to check. But today, Debbie gives him permission to go next door and explore. And he is pleased that he has Nouri to go with him. The two leave our compound, carrying sticks to ward off danger, giggling as they go.

Once Frankie and Nouri are out of earshot, I say, "A rumor that three hundred Americans will be killed as a birthday present for the Shah is spreading. I heard it in school."

Amir says, "Iranians do not want Americans hurt. Three hundred people? No. Terrorist groups have hurt and killed important military people before, how you say, high ranking? Not people ... like you." Amir says this with confidence, then shakes his head. "But yes, it is bad. You are right for fear."

"Amir, my father is high ranking."

Amir looks at me, keeping quiet. None of us have much to say after that.

Thirty minutes later, Nouri and Frankie buzz the compound door, giggling. When I open the door, a dog runs into the compound with them.

"He must smell Siam and Meese!" Christie exclaims.

"Can we keep him?" Frankie asks.

We stare at the pooch, now sitting back on his haunches, almost grinning up at us. One of his ears is standing straight up, the other bends forward. The gray fur on his muzzle resembles a beard. Amir throws him a piece of brownie.

"No chocolate, Amir, not for dogs!" shouts Debbie.

I think of my mother, touch Frankie's shoulder, tell him we could never keep the dog. Amir shrugs his shoulders, and I knew he was thinking—what, other than brownies—do we have to coax this guy out?

Debbie seems to understand this, opens the security door and reluctantly throws another piece of brownie into the alley. When the dog scurries after it, she slams the door shut.

"I feel so guilty," she says.

"I think it has to be a lot of chocolate," I say nervously. "Where'd he come from?"

"He followed us from next door. Azar shooed him away with a broom."

"Azar?" I turn back to the boys, their faces stained purplish red.

"What kinds of trees are over there boys?" I ask, but I figure it out before they can answer.

"Pomegranate!" Frankie shouts. "The lot isn't empty after all. There's a hut behind a wall of trees and bushes." Frankie waves his arms to the west. "And a man, Azar, appeared out of the hut and helped us pick pomegranates. Showed us how to eat them. At first we were scared. But then he ended up being very nice. Azar, the gardener. He's invited us back for pomegranate soup one day. He doesn't live there, only gardens."

I am fascinated to learn that there was someone next door to us to the west after all, if not occupants of a house, a gardener. "Did you know the word grenade comes from the Middle French word for pomegranate?" I ask.

"Annie, only a bookworm like you would know this," Debbie says. I ignore her.

"Now, who wants to go play soccer?" Reza asks Frankie and Nouri.

"I do!" the boys answer back, simultaneously.

"Jinx," Amir says, winking.

And so the boys escape to the soccer field, and the girls are left alone to be girls—gobble up more brownies, engage in prolonged discussions of *boys*. "How about that Mike Morales?" Alika asks.

"The guy ogling Annie at the football games?" Debbie asks.

"Precisely the one," Alika says. I pull out a stack of *Archie* magazines and we flip through them, admiring Betty's and Veronica's voluptuous figures, eyes rimmed in thick swaths of charcoal eyeliner, wearing exaggerated red pouty mouths, and overemphasized curves.

"Excuse me," says Christie, "Can I have a figure like that?"

"Annie, grow a pair of those and you'll have Mike Morales eating out of your hand!" Alika says, and I blush. "That Amir ain't too shabby either," Alika continues.

Debbie throws Alika a sharp glance that stops any further comment, and I stare down at my hands. But then it all turns nice: Christie makes lunch for "the birthday girl and her friends"—leftover *Barbari* bread she had the fortitude to top with Roma tomatoes, prosciutto, and mozzarella. "You are becoming your stepmother," I say.

Alika presents me with a copy of *East of Eden* because I'd loved *The Grapes of Wrath*. "Thanks, Alika, you shouldn't have!" Christie places a candle into one of her brownies, and the girls' sweet, high-pitched voices serenade me, "Happy Birthday, Happy Birthday to you!"

I can still picture a dress-up birthday party in the yard when I was young. Probably in Greece. Two-year-old girls in too-large heels, long skirts and their mothers' pearls. And little boys in humongous suits eating cake, their sleeves rolled thick up their skinny arms while they plucked round fat oranges off a thin-trunked tree. How their ties almost touched the ground. And me in my mother's sparkled ruby red shoes and matching ruby ring for the occasion. Had it been my birthday?

I can hardly believe I am eighteen.

When my parents return home, and after everyone had left, Mom makes my favorite dinner of flank steak and mashed potatoes, a home-baked red velvet cake, sweet swirls of penuche frosting covering it in sugar-hardened peaks decorated with shaved curls of chocolate like an edible hairstyle. I tried not to compare Debbie's birthday and dinner out. I shouldn't care; my Dad didn't want us out in a group at a public place.

Later, reading the assigned novel for Writing in bed, I remember the large brown grocery bag Alika and I had filled to the brim with food for Nouri and his family. I imagine a refrigerator plugged into an extension cord and jerry-rigged to the electricity of an adjacent portico-columned mansion, piggyback splices to redirect power and possible electrical shock; even kids playing around mud covered spliced wire. Is that how it was for the shanty town dwellers?

I recall Christie's brownies. How pretty she is when she smiles. Reza had skillfully disappeared to leave Amir and Debbie alone by offering to walk Nouri home and carry Nouri's over-stuffed bag of food. I'd heard Reza explaining a good joke to Nouri as they'd left the compound, his arm draped over the little boy's shoulders—my father's joke from the picnic. *How sweet.* Immediately, Debbie and Amir had become embroiled in an argument—something about how Amir should be going out with *Reza,* not her. How smoking was disgusting. Amir must have sneaked a smoke and Debbie had caught him. Amir had left the apartment only minutes after Reza, slamming the security door behind him.

The phone rings. It's Alika.

"Thanks for everything. Happy Birthday! Got some bad news to tell you though."

"What?"

"On the way home, someone threw a big boulder at the side of my father's car."

I picture the already battered gray vehicle with a large dent in its side. I sigh. "Was your father angry?"

"Not at all. He was happy I could visit a friend's house. He understands the Iranian people's frustration. He only wanted me to warn you. It happened near your house, at the corner of *Bolvar E Jannat Abad* and *Golestan.*"

"My bus stop," I say.

"Oh no, really? Be careful, Annie."

190

"I know. Right."

"My father flagged down a police officer to show him the damage to our car; he only moved us on, saying we were foolish to be out today."

"I'm sorry, Alika. It was all my fault. It was foolish to ask you over. Selfish of me."

"No Annie, my dad says we must live our lives as we would normally. It's okay. He was fine with it. He says faith will protect us. I'll see you in school. G'night."

"Night, Alika." I wished I had that kind of faith.

Phone in my hand, I remember John and his mother. I quickly dial their number. Mrs. James answers, and I say hello and ask to speak with John.

"Annie, hey!" John says breathlessly when he comes to the phone. "How y'all doing over there?"

"Good! I wanted to tell you about something that might interest your mom. I had Alika over today. She mentioned she belongs to the Royal Riding Club. Does your mom know about it?"

"Not sure. I'll ask her. Great idea," John says. "You're a nice friend."

"Have you ever thought of a housekeeper? Someone at school told me they have one, and their housekeeper is their mother's best friend."

"Who said that?"

I didn't tell him. I change the subject. "It's my birthday today."

"It is?! I wish I'd known."

"That's okay," I say pleasantly. But I distinctly remembered having talked about it with Alika in front of John after the game. Maybe he'd been too preoccupied with Mike Morales.

"Well, maybe I think it's important for me to know the date of your birthday, Annie."

"You could have asked me when it was," I say softly.

"Well then, I hope you had a nice birthday. I'll give you a present when I see you next. I would have today—had I known."

"Thanks, John." I sigh. "I did have a nice birthday. A present isn't necessary. But you're a great friend to want to give me one."

"Did ya'll have a party?"

"An impromptu one."

"Oh yeah, who came?"

"Alika and the usual cast of characters."

"And who are they?" I sense jealousy in his tone.

"Just Debbie, Reza—Christie, by the way, which was nice. And Amir...." His name catches in my throat. I fall silent.

"Amir?" Silence.

"Yes. Amir. *Debbie's guy.*" I manage to get off the phone, confused at my nervousness, my guilt. I don't owe John a thing. He was just a friend.

Speaking of friends, a letter from Diana still lay unopened on my dresser. I take it outside on my balcony together with a cold can of TaB. I rip open the long ivory envelope addressed to the overseas military address of APO, New York, which was anywhere but New York. Her first sentence reads "Annie—are you okay over there?!"

Amir comes by the next day looking for Debbie.

"Hi, Annie," he says when I open our compound door.

"Hi, Amir. Debbie isn't here."

"She isn't?"

"No, she's out with Frankie." She and Frankie had gone to the store across the field for Pepsis.

Amir looks at me. He seems completely focused on me. He bites his lip.

"Come with me to lunch," he says.

"What? Me?"

"Yes. Come out with me."

"Me?"

"Yes, you, birthday girl. I did not know it was your birthday yesterday until Debbie told me after you had gone upstairs to make lunch for Alika. I want to buy you lunch for your birthday. Eighteen is *Hej-e-Deh* in Farsi."

I am thrilled that he wants to buy me lunch. But what about Debbie? I am still waging an internal war with myself—the desire for Amir. The wish to be a good sister. At first the competitive underdog, now a girl with a real crush, and no wish for a broken heart.

"Will Debbie mind?"

"She's angry with me."

"Why is she angry with you?"

Amir shrugs.

"All right. You win. I'll come out with you. Where?"

"*Chelo Kebab?*"

"*Chelo Kebab.* Yes. I'd love that. But where? There was fighting in the streets yesterday."

"I know. It was the Shah's birthday yesterday. Not today. You will go, yes?" He licks his lips nervously, seems poised to flee. To avoid Debbie?

"Let me change," I say, also nervous. My parents had brought the Jamisons some lunch. I wonder if I should ask them if they minded? Instead, I leave a brief note explaining I am with Reza; why throw gas on an open flame?

I change into my favorite orange terry cloth dress, casual enough for lunch, but still pretty, long enough to be appropriate. I check my hair in the hall mirror; my skin appears luminous in my nervous excitement. I return downstairs, careful not to trip. The dress hugs my hips perfectly. I'd left a button undone at my breast, and Amir notices. But fortunately, I am one year older, now—eighteen.

We arrive at the restaurant at exactly noon, and it is perfect timing. Amir holds his hand at my back and guides me to a table. Several diners turn to stare at the tall blonde with the striking Iranian man.

We sit at a small square table decorated with a single red rose in a glass vase. The long white tablecloth tickles the tops of my thighs. Amir's almond eyes are fixated on my top button. I lean forward.

"People are staring at us," I whisper.

"As well they should be," Amir says, pleased we are being noticed, thinking we ought to be.

He winks. "It is because you are as beautiful as an orange Tiger Lily."

I blush, but the compliment animates me.

"Lamb or ground beef *Chelo kebab*, Annie?"

"Lamb."

He continues reading the menu. "Or would you prefer chicken?"

"I'd still like the lamb. Speaking of poultry, Mother is having trouble finding a meat market that sells fresh turkey for Thanksgiving—"

The waiter interrupts us with ice water in bright cobalt blue goblets. Amir orders lamb for the both of us. Once the waiter has left, Amir sits back in his chair, relaxed and happy; his smile is gorgeous.

"Iranians do not favor Turkey for dinner the way Americans do. But I truly enjoy the idea of your Thanksgiving. Celebrating food and family."

"One of my favorite holidays." But I adored every holiday.

"You are a woman who enjoys many things," Amir says, eyes so dark they seemed black.

"I do." I feel my lips purse the rim of my glass. Water, I think.

"You like pretty clothes, lunches in city cafés, shopping on *Pahlavi* in expensive boutiques. Look at your nails. Beautiful. Your hair." Amir smacks his lips as if they were dry and dips his head shyly, the way I was accustomed to. A lock of hair has fallen over my face, and he leans over the table and tucks it behind my ear. "Your hair is kissed by the sun, you must know this."

I take a sip from my water glass, enjoying the compliments, hiding my left hand with its chipped nail polish under the table. I think about the lemon juice I had squeezed in my hair.

"The summer sun encourages these natural highlights," I reply, laughing.

"The sun kisses you here, Annie," Amir says, putting his hand at his heart. "John is. How you say? Not worthy? You know when the sun shines. And there is a bright yellow glow around it?"

"Yes, the sun's aura?"

"And you must place your hand over your eyes because it is so bright it hurts?"

"Yes."

"Annie, this is you. You look at Annie and see sun. You look at John, and there are clouds." Amir continues, "I wear a black tie and hard black boots to see fine art; he wears a baseball hat, jeans, and?"

"Sneakers?"

"Yes, to museums or fine restaurants such as this."

"Right."

"That is John," Amir says.

"John is from Texas, a cowboy type. He is only seventeen. Give him a break," I say gently. "Forgive him." But Amir had just uttered aloud what had been troubling me all along. John likes Trans-Ams for Pete's sake.

I think of Amir's motorcycle. "But you ride a motorcycle," I say in a flirty, accusatory tone.

"Ah yes, but it is a Mercedes motorcycle," Amir says, smiling. He bows his head again. And then there is that impish smile. Those bright almond eyes. "I am a cowboy type, also no? An urban cowboy from Tehran."

"Right. Trade in your motorcycle for a horse, and your street smarts for a Colt .38 and you are the traditional definition of a cowboy."

"And with enough sense to wear dress shoes to a restaurant to impress a lady. Do I impress you, Annie?"

The waiter interrupts our conversation. He sets down two blue-rimmed white porcelain salad bowls, the usual starter of fresh cucumbers and tomatoes swimming in a milky yogurt sauce. "*Mamnoon.*" Thank you. Amir nods.

"*You* are the sun, Amir. You're one of the most handsome men I've ever laid eyes on. How is that for being direct?"

"Direct?"

"Forward."

"Forward?"

"Oh, Amir, just eat." I smile and Amir grins back. "Debbie will have to teach you the meaning of direct and forward." Amir glances up from his meal, an odd look in his eyes. I have no clue why I mentioned Debbie just now. I knew the purpose of our outing. I knew he had interest … in me, and I was electrified, not thinking about the repercussions.

"Yes. Debbie. But, please. Let us eat."

Soon the waiter brings over two plates of steaming lamb on rice. The meat resembles two long brown braids that might cascade down a girl's back. The rice is fluffy and bright yellow, with crusted bits of orange on top, like confetti. "*Tahdig*, my favorite!" I exclaim.

After lunch, Amir suggests a stroll along *Lalehzar* Avenue, a lively neighborhood of shops, movie theaters and restaurants. We browse through kiosks holding newspapers, magazines, books, and tapes for sale, even one of my favorite bands,

Boston. I admire a white pleated blouse in a display window, and Amir offers to buy it for me. We disappear inside a chic boutique. But eventually I think about Debbie and say, "Buy me ice cream instead." Anything bought on this avenue should not give me dysentery. My eye catches a display of earrings and bangles, and I tell Amir I'll meet him outside. I lift a necklace of delicate seed pearls from a rack. The pearls glint in the sun as much as the apples of my cheeks do in the counter mirror. I admire the necklace for a second, then return it to the rack reluctantly. I smile at my reflection in the mirror, giggle, and turn to leave. I feel so happy right now.

Outside the storefront's plate glass window, I see Amir speaking with a young woman. At first he shakes his head no, then he hesitantly accepts a lumpy manila envelope from her outstretched hand. A young man also hands out folded paper pamphlcts. I start. It's Afshin. I wait, hoping he'd move from his post directly in front of the store. But Amir turns to the store window, hands raised in a question. Afshin pushes a pamphlet into Amir's hand and as they speak, body postures become rigid, and I can tell they are shouting at each other. I must go out. I can't stand here forever.

Once I'd emerged from the store, recognition flares in Afshin's eyes like fire, and his complexion reddens. He pushes a pamphlet into my chest, but I let it drop to my feet, afraid but defiant. Afshin steps forward and whispers, *"Allahu Ahkbar,"* his voice soft, but guttural, his hot curried breath tickling my ear, his face swollen by either proximity or disgust. His eyes are the shade of my mother's brown antique glass. The light amber brown unsettles me.

His tongue shoots out of his mouth like a frog, and he licks my ear. I cringe. Amir grabs my arm and hurries me away to the ice cream shop, yelling Farsi over his shoulder.

"What did you say to him?" I ask.

"If he ever comes near you again I will kill him! If he ever touches my car again, I will break his neck."

Inside the ice cream store, I pull open the pamphlet, and the folded paper tears at the staple. Inside is a photograph of Khomeini's face, his dark eyebrows knitted together. I swallow hard. Words in Farsi are printed at the bottom.

"What does it say?"

"'Death to the Shah. Death to Carter'." Amir's face reddens slightly. He steals a glance at me, and I blanch.

Suddenly, I'm no longer hungry for ice cream. It's been growing dark earlier now, becoming cooler in the early evenings.

"Ice cream was a bad idea. I've no appetite for it anymore," I say.

"Let me buy you a roasted beet, instead. You must try. A perfect food for autumn. Much better than ice cream." But I wonder. Amir leans in, peering into my eyes, concerned. "Please, come." His eyes are pools of melted chocolate. He leads me over to a street-side vendor cart and a huge steaming kettle overflowing with bright red beets, some skewered on long wooden sticks. A second mammoth kettle sits next to the beets.

"What are those?" I ask, pointing.

"Fava beans."

I watch the steam rise skyward like coils of smoke curling out of a chimney. The *chador*-cloaked woman smiles as she stirs the pot. "I'll try a beet," I say, picking the lesser of two evils.

The cheerful vendor ladles an oversized beet into a paper bowl, hands me a plastic fork, smiling and hopeful. "You will like," he says, encouraging. "You from Amrika?"

I shake my head no, worried; but suddenly feeling like a liar, I stare down into the warm bowl of beets between my hands amid the smiling Iranians, ashamed. My focus turns to the task of eating a slippery hot roasted beet without burning my mouth. It tastes earthy, but tart.

"You like? Yes?!" Amir asks.

"I love."

"Ah, *kheili khoobe.*" Amir grins ear to ear. He tucks the manila envelope beneath his arm and pays the street vendor.

In the Mercedes, our bellies warmed by the beets, Amir says, "That woman outside the store … she gave me this." He rips open the lumpy manila envelope to reveal a steel-gray cassette tape. He shoves it into the player, tucks a cigarette into the corner of his mouth, and pulls out into thickening traffic. Amir? Still smoking?

"It's Khomeini."

I listen to Khomeini's soft monotone voice, calming, mesmerizing but frightening. I understand nothing.

When the tape ends, I ask, "What did he say?"

"'Do not be afraid to give up your lives and your belongings in the service of God, Islam and the Moslem nation. There will be no compromise with the Shah. Until an Islamic Republic is established, the struggle of our people will continue.'" I sense Amir considering this, listening to the encouraging voice of Khomeini from Paris as the ayatollah sits calm and crossed-legged, clad in his black robe and turban. Was it becoming personal to Amir? A call to arms. It was certainly becoming personal to me, and it was frightening. "*Elahi ghorbunet beram.*" ("I would sacrifice my life for you"), Amir says to me. "Never Khomeini. *Doret Begardam.*"

Around the bend in the road, a small crowd is mingling on the sidewalk around a broken storefront window, the jagged glass a reminder of the turbulence that had also occurred on the Shah's birthday, the turmoil we'd been shielded from in northwest Tehran. So far. Amir reaches around the seat behind him to grab a gauzy headscarf left on the floor of his Mercedes.

"Please put this on, Annie. It's my *maman's.*"

Further down the boulevard, there are more broken windows and people gathering. I smell the burning rubber before I see fires flaming in a row of tires to our right, serving to barricade a street running perpendicular from the one we are driving on.

I wrap the filmy scarf around my hair and duck down into my seat. I am terrified, the trip to my house interminable, though the streets are empty and free of demonstrators. When we approach my alley, Amir pulls over and cuts the ignition. He turns to me. I turn to him. He cups my face in his hands and leans in, kissing me very gently on the lips. I gasp, but my heart swells.

"I am so sorry for all of this, Annie. Thank you for coming out to lunch. Not the best decision, but I adored it." Amir brushes his lip with his hand, and his bottom lip fattens.

I feel a pull of desire, but at the same time I am irritated. Who was he interested in anyway, Debbie, or me? Even so, I lean into him, pull my hands through his hair. And then I stop thinking about Debbie.

He pushes me down onto the car seat, kisses me roughly. I taste salt and cigarettes, the tang of roasted beets. His lips are full and soft, despite the roughness of the kiss. I pull back and ask breathlessly, "But how can you let Debbie wear your shirt one night, then kiss me another?" I had to know.

"How can you have a date with John, flirt with boys at football games, then kiss me another?"

Amir had noticed this? "You mean Mike Morales?"

"Yes, if that is the boy at the game."

I keep quiet. We stare at each other, red-faced and disgruntled, each of us breathing hard, until we are both laughing. "Your red pajamas are stuck in my mind, I think," Amir teases. "Your full lips are now stained even more luscious by the roasted red beets, like the cherry red of lip paint." He pauses. "That night Debbie took my dress shirt off the back of the couch. I had removed it for sleep. She surprised me by wearing my shirt for pajamas."

"I don't know if I believe you," I say without conviction, hoping it had happened that way. The seed of doubt becomes a spore of hope—desperate to rid myself of the thought of the two of them shedding their clothes in hasty passion—the image of Debbie throwing Amir's half-unbuttoned shirt over her messy hair, only to stop midway to inhale his scent, then head to the kitchen for snacks, bare legs hurrying.

"*Delbar*, Annie. It is true. I am regretful you saw her that way. In my shirt. If you have feelings for me." Amir sighs, runs a hand through his thick mat of dark hair.

"John and Mike Morales mean nothing to me." My voice sounds desperate.

"Ah Annie, you are perfect." Amir kisses the tips of his fingers. "You are feminine, smart, athletic. You look wonderful in red." He pauses, thinking. "I picked the wrong sister."

His words fill me with guilt. I say quietly, "Right. But there is Debbie to think about." My voice is small. "We can't kiss like this anymore."

Confused, he stiffens, nods yes to my dismay. "There is Debbie to consider," he agrees, still nodding, posture erect. "But sometimes she is, so? ... so....?"

"Critical?"

"Yes, that's right, Annie. Critical. And I am trying to make her see happiness, but I fear I am failing."

The day after my parents' return, several buses carrying military personnel had been stoned. Dad had received official notification to wear his bulletproof vest from this point forward anytime he ventured out of the house. At the same time, my father's military commander declared it wasn't bad enough to think about evacuation. Despite the word evacuation being volleyed about, our household seems back to normal with my parents home. We keep the escapades we experienced in their absence secret. My lips are still blistering from Amir's kiss, but I keep it buttoned up, close to my heart.

Walking to the bus stop one morning, I find the *jube* dog from the pomegranate orchard just outside our compound. I reach down to give him a pat, but he skitters away, his nut-brown eyes filled with fear.

"It's okay, sweet dog." I open my lunch bag and pull out my bologna sandwich from the waxed paper it is wrapped in. I kneel down and offer the dog a piece. He skitters backwards, and so I place the piece of bologna on the ground and step away. The dog scrambles forward, snatching the dirt-covered morsel in his mouth and again he scampers backwards. Afraid I'll miss my bus, I throw another piece on the ground, this time wrapped in bread, and sidestep the hungry dog. He turns to watch me leave almost gratefully.

Each subsequent school day morning, the hungry salivating dog meets me outside our compound door before I walk to the bus stop. I tell Frankie about it.

"Can I feed him, too?"

"Let's get some real dog food. Give him something healthy instead of bologna."

"Okay." Frankie likes to have a project—a do-gooder like Alika … and me.

Thursday I buy a bag of dog food at the *kuche* market and stow it behind the toy bin in the garage. We set our alarms to rise early like we'd do on a normal school day, instead of sleeping in. I bring down a second-hand china bowl from the kitchen.

"Here, Frankie, you feed him."

Frankie fills the bowl and the cascade of dry chunks rattles in the dish. He brings the bowl to the security door and opens it cautiously. Lo and behold the dog is waiting there, panting a goofy lopsided grin.

"He's here!" Frankie shouts, although I am just inches behind him. I jump, rubbing my ears. My chin quivers—how many times had this poor pup waited outside our security door on a weekend morning and I hadn't come?

"Go on, put the bowl down," I tell Frankie.

"Maybe he won't like real dog food? Maybe he's used to garbage? Bologna?" But, as Frankie says this, the dog is scarfing down the food.

"See, he likes it," I say.

"Can we name him?"

"Sure. What's a good name for an Iranian *jube* dog?"

Frankie thinks for a moment, tilts his head to the side and rubs his chin. "Khoda? For *Khoda ha* Fez?"

"Frankie, that's perfect. Khoda, it is."

Halloween comes and goes without cute little children rapping on our door and exclaiming, "Trick-or-Treat", dressed up as tiny ghosts or precious princesses, or muscled superheroes like Spiderman, Batman, or Superman.

Tehran American School puts on a small Halloween party in the gym in the afternoon. Students are permitted to dress up as they pleased, but I don't. Frankie is permitted to trick-or-treat from classroom to classroom at the elementary school. One of the star football players on the Vikings team named Jeff dresses up as an Indian, goes so far as to shave his head into a Mohawk. He wears fake deerskin bottoms and war paint on his cheeks and is shirtless. Apparently, his house had received the note found all too frequently on an unsuspecting American's door, "Yankee go home", usually scrawled in bad English. "No one's gonna mess with me," Jeff yells in the gym, garnering everyone's attention as he does a little Indian war dance.

I am also feeling nervous, especially after Amir had shoved Khomeini's tape into the cassette tape player, and I heard the angry urgency in the grim-faced ayatollah's tone. Like

Moshdeh, I had hoped everything could be resolved peacefully. This was becoming more and more unlikely.

I overhear my father and mother whispering together in the kitchen—an American couple's car had been vandalized after they had left it unlocked and parked on the street while attending a dinner party. The car's interior was soaked with gasoline, then set on fire.

CHAPTER 10

NOVEMBER 1978

My whole being is a dark chant
that perpetuating you
which will carry you to the dawn
*   of eternal growths and blossomings.*
In this chant I sighed, you sighed
in this chant.

"Another Birth", by Forugh Farrokhzad

It's the first week of November and it's growing chilly outside. The snowcaps on the mountains expand each day, like my backpack, which is full of all the homework I've been neglecting. The city brightens under the snowcaps' cool blue light. The crisp air is a reminder that coziness is just around the corner, and there are things to anticipate—the scent of cinnamon-apple cider, roasting turkey and Grandmother's recipe for sausage herbed stuffing, peanut butter fudge and snicker doodles baking, thick down bed covers, soft wool sweaters pulled from bedside trunks, and pools of melted marshmallows on steaming mugs of hot chocolate.

It's lunchtime, and I am laying in the school compound painting a banner for the next football game. It's peaceful outside and I hear nothing but my paintbrush stroking the paper, Cathy humming, and a bird crying out. I smell a foul chemical odor. The horizon appears darkened as if thunderclouds are approaching.

Just after lunch an announcement comes over the loudspeaker: "Students, please gather your things, proceed directly to your buses for pick up." Alika and I frown. That's it? That's all the information they're giving us?

Miss Barker looks concerned, but says confidently, "Students, we have the privilege of leaving a little early today."

Quietly, we assemble our things. Miss Barker guides us outside into the school compound, where the buses are already waiting.

I stand in line and gaze over the rows of students. There's Mike Morales, who nods over to me; Alika, who waves good-bye. John is also standing near his bus, arching his brow and shrugging his shoulders. He mouths, "Call me!" His fingers wiggle at his jaw. I nod, rush up the bus stairs, escape into my usual seat.

After all the students have been accounted for, our short excitable bus driver strides down the aisle, pulls the bus curtains closed with forceful sweeps of his arm. Before he settles into his large bucket seat, he turns to us and says, "Students... *Listen*... If I tell you to duck down anytime on the ride home this afternoon, you must obey my order, *at once—* please dip well below the window glass. Does everyone understand this?"

Several students answer him wordlessly with confused nods. Up front, Christie has turned back towards me, a quizzical expression on her face. The driver flops down in his seat and hangs over the large flat steering wheel, edging out from the compound gates, looking in either direction as he moves forward, forcing the steering wheel around as if it were the heavy door of a steel vault. The armed guard near the driver stands. He is resting his submachine gun on his shoulder, clutching the steel pole for balance. A second guard stands at the back of the bus, his machine gun also pressing against his muscled shoulder.

The driver accelerates when he sees clear streets ahead, traveling briskly and avoiding the alternate route up Old *Shemiran* Road, where some of the embassies are located. At the next intersection, he jolts to a stop. Through gaps in my bus curtain, I see groups of Iranian men and women hurling stones into business windows: the bank on the corner, the movie theater now ablaze. In an area just alongside the boulevard, crowds are congregating, burning placards of the Shah. The licking hot flames have turned the paper edges brown, and the Shah's face melts away before the poster becomes fully engulfed in flames.

We are stuck in unmoving traffic. Other students are peeking outside through the gaps in the curtains. "Ah, no!" the driver shouts. "Do not show your faces!" An angry mob of Iranians carrying thick clubs starts towards the bus.

Desperately, our driver attempts to inch the bus forward in the gridlocked traffic, wanting to escape. He knocks the bumper of the car in front of us, locks the bus doors. The mob swarms us, raps the bus's side with punching fists, shoves it with their shoulders, rocking it. My heart pounds and saliva begins to drain from my mouth. The dark-haired men with their thick clubs shout obscenities in Farsi, their mouths forming angry rectangles. I can almost see their tonsils. I pull the curtain shut, slink down in my seat.

"Get down!" shouts our driver. The students obey, slumping down as low as possible. I pull up my lumpy backpack filled with poster making supplies from the floor, put it on my seat, kneel on the now empty space, head squeezed against the seatback.

The armed guards on the bus become active. I peer around the seat. Up front, the guard is tapping the gun's muzzle at the windshield. The guard at the back also displays his machine gun. Outside, a short man in a purple sweater notices the guards and yells out. And then the demonstrators begin to file away.

Too frightened to celebrate the men's leave-taking, I am relieved when the traffic begins to move, and the bus pulls forward. Several yards north at the next major intersection, a group of men throw a row of tires in front of the grid-locked traffic, set it on fire. More milling, angry demonstrators congregate in the streets. "*Begu marg bar* Shah" ("Death to the Shah"), they shout.

With some maneuvering our bus driver manages to reach an intersecting alley and turns into it, anxious to escape the melee on the main boulevard, only to find that the Paykan directly in front of the bus has stalled. The distressed driver flicks on its hazard lights, leaves the Paykan, shrugs his shoulders then hurries down the street away from the automobile and the melee on the main boulevard.

"*Ah, boro gom sho!*" our bus driver yells, slamming his hands down on the large steering wheel, raising his arms up in angry resignation, shouting something in Farsi to the armed guards. Next he flings open the bus door, runs down the steps, and disappears down the alley like the Paykan driver had done. I gaze in shock at our bus driver's retreating back, but I notice other vehicles are parked haphazardly in the alley minus occupants, including one that blocks the alley at the next intersection.

Christie turns to me, horrified. The guard at the front of the bus exits through the open door; his dark hair disappears as he descends the stairs, then reappears before he vanishes into a small store on the corner. The other guard remains. "Sit," he commands harshly from his limited bank of English knowledge.

Minutes later, the other guard returns with a short gray-bearded storekeeper, who says to us in a heavy accent, "Everyone, please stay seated. Remain calm. The motor pool at the United States Embassy is bringing another bus. It may be necessary for all of you to hike several blocks to a clear intersection and the new bus. Does everyone understand the situation you are in?" The storekeeper nods to the guards, then leaves the bus. Moments later, he pulls down the steel gate across his store, padlocks it as he leaves, and nods to us as he hurries off down the alley. Our would-be protector/translator has also abandoned us like our frightened bus driver had.

By this time, most students are crying. The smell of smoke hangs thick in the air. I pull out a book from my backpack, begin to read. Hardly focusing, I periodically peer out the back at the billowing smoke, the fire's yellow-orange flames, the thickening crowds of demonstrators. I wait. We wait. Time drags on.

Suddenly, Christie appears at my seatback, breathing hard. Scaring me.

"We've got to do something. We're sitting ducks!"

Just as she hisses this, I hear the woosh of the bus door sliding open. This time both our guards leave the bus and amble to the corner. They pull cigarettes from deep pockets and light them.

"Come on, Annie. We must go. *Now.* Before they lock us up on the bus again." Christie tugs my hand and drags me up the aisle, ripping off a curtain from one of the bus windows.

Out on the sidewalk, Christie tears the blue and white striped bus curtain in half, asks me to put it on, which I do, trying to create the shawl effect of a *hijab*. Once she has her own shawl set firmly in place, she rearranges my head garb.

"What exactly is your plan?" I ask, wringing my hands.

Christie shrugs, face burning. "I don't have one. I was claustrophobic. I had to get off that bus."

Understanding this, but feeling much more desperate outside the bus, my face burns as much as Christie's, hot pink and slick from fear.

"Let's find a phone," Christie says.

"No chance anyone could pick us up in this."

"I could ask Julie to come get us in this mess; it'd serve her right," Christie says with derision.

At the next intersection, I recognize the street name. Amir and Reza's used car dealership is on this street. Amir had pointed it out as we drove to Fatima and Parviz's wedding. I tell Christie.

"You got to be kidding me. This is perfect. Let's try to find it."

The sidewalks are quiet here. Christie and I stumble beneath leafless trees, lifeless and colorless, as if they too were on strike. The day is cool but damp, like humidity hovering over a frozen pond. I look back at the bus, pull my jacket snug around me, not sure we are being wise, no matter how confined Christie felt. Here, the traffic is fairly heavy, the cars detouring from the main boulevard in their attempt to escape the madding crowd.

"It's still early. Someone's got to be there," I say.

And there it was, several blocks down the street. I recognize the grimy brick storefront on the corner, two stories rising above it, flanked by a large open parking lot holding an inventory of used cars. We wander into the building, find Reza and Amir in the shop's garage working, oblivious to everything happening in the streets. *Thank God.*

Amir looks up from the cherry-red Audi he's working on, surprised. "Annie?! Christie?" His face registers concern. "Has anything happened?"

Reza walks over and touches the blue striped bus curtain covering my head. He chuckles. "Why Annie, you are lovely as an Iranian woman."

Christie explains everything happening south of town, the mob that had surrounded our bus, her claustrophobia. "I thought that if we didn't get off, something terrible might happen."

"These are our bus curtains." I motion to my head.

Amir and Reza burst out laughing, and the amusement calms my nerves. They aren't unduly alarmed. The smell of smoke is faint in the building. I look around at the shop area, the oil-stained concrete floor, the dingy concrete block walls. A pot holding hours-old coffee sits on a table by a window. A brass *samovar* sits beside it, and a partially dead plant rests on the window sill—everything seems so normal here.

"Reza and I shall drive you home in the Mercedes." Amir wipes his hands on a towel already black with grease.

I shake my head no, explaining how burning tires are blocking sections of boulevards we would need to cross to reach home, describing the gridlocked traffic, stalled vehicles. "Like the other day—at lunch, but much worse."

"We shall take each of you on the back of our motorcycles then—drive on the sidewalk if necessary." Amir touches my shoulder. "First things first, though. Annie. Christie. Sit. *Tea.*" Amir smiles, concern and warmth in his tone, compared to the armed guard's curt command of "Sit" I'd heard on the bus. I shiver. Amir pours me a cup of tea—Christie a cup of coffee.

"*Ghahveh?*" He slides over powdered milk to Christie. "*Ghaveh ba sheer?*"

"*Chai?*" I accept the hot mug of tea from Amir, thankful that the heated ceramic cup is warming my hands.

"Things are becoming very bad," Amir says. "No one is happy with the Shah anymore. They blame foreigners. Americans. I worry about your families. It shall only get worse. Your fathers must know this already." He pauses, wondering if he'd said too much. "But for now, relax—enjoy your drink."

After we had drained all the liquid from our cups, Reza and Amir scurry to close up, hang keys and make certain the cars are locked on the lot. After they had finished, Amir instructs Reza to take Christie home on his motorcycle. He grabs a pouch of cash and credit card slips, nods over to me and says to Christie, "I shall take Annie on my bike. I must make a deposit." He holds up a flat leather bank bag. "Go with Reza. Return home safely, yes?"

Christie nods, leaves the store with Reza. We follow.

Outside the sky is building towards dusk in gunmetal-gray clouds. Acrid smoke fills the air. Amir hands me a helmet, and I pull it over my makeshift *hijab*. Lithely, he straddles the seat, and I climb on behind him, wrap my arms around his slim waist and rest my head on the backpack he'd slung over his shoulders. Over the engine's roar, he glances back to make certain I am well-positioned before he peels out into the street. I grip his waist as he races down the road and onto another one, no problems apparent up ahead. He pulls onto a wider main boulevard, then slows almost to a stop. In the distance flames roar through several high-rises. Amir pulls over, cuts the engine.

"Oh, Annie, you are right." His face is ashen. "That's my bank." He points to *Bank Sadarat*, which is now in flames. "I used to feel fortunate that my bank was not on strike, but now it is on fire." He starts up the engine, inches forward in fits and starts. The traffic hardly moves and Amir rides up onto the sidewalk, following other motorcycles and scooters. But just ahead, a man dressed in a dark suit jacket, bright white shirt, and jeans, is crouching on the sidewalk and holding a frantic, bleating sheep in one arm, a long silver machete in the other. I cringe at the swipe of his arm, and the bright red blood that spatters onto his dress shirt and streams across the sidewalk—the poor sheep flails as it dies. I grasp Amir's shoulder. Not focused that far ahead, instead concentrating on the crowds of people milling alongside us on the sidewalk, Amir looks up too late, hits the brakes, and turns sharply to avoid the bloodied animal and crazed man. The motorcycle's front-end plunges into the *jube*. I scream in horror as I pitch into the deep murky water, in what feels like slow motion. I am thankful for the gutter water and my school backpack that cushion my fall, but the metallic taste of blood fills my mouth. Amir is behind me in the rust-colored water. "Amir!" I thrash around in knee-deep sludge to reach him, my backpack and *hijab* thankfully still anchored in place. I hug him. *Thank God—he is fine*! In contrast, the motorcycle is a bent heap of partially submerged metal.

We begin staggering westward but find we can't avoid another throng of angry demonstrators. Amir backpedals, moves away from the mob burning things. Everywhere, there are endless chants, signs emblazoned with Khomeini's stern dour face. Police sirens wail in the distance.

"We have no choice but to return to the shop," Amir says. "I have keys to the upstairs tenant's apartment who is traveling. I have promised to water his plants. You may call your parents from his telephone." We stand still, take in all the destruction, watch Amir's company's bank burn. "This is very bad," he says sharply. He grabs my hand and we turn around, away from the flames.

I feel like I'm walking in slow motion, treading water, suffocated by the blinding bright fire and smoke that leave a putrid taste at the back of my throat, like vomit on an empty stomach. There are intimate distasteful odors everywhere—the crowd with raised arms and angry, punching fists is much too close to me, shouting for death—the Shah's, Carter's, and mine.

Water, I think. *I need water.* I remind myself to keep my head down, place one foot after the other—hide my pale skin, blond strands of hair hardly soaked dark from my *jube*-soaked *hijab*. Amir shields my face with a protective crook of arm, but then I can hardly breathe—and I'm already breathing hard. It seems ages before we see the grimy gray of Amir's shop.

Now the detoured traffic is thick, and I cannot muster up the courage to weave through the gridlocked traffic. Amir watches me. "I have you." He sweeps me up and cradles me in his arms. My dangling feet brush the hoods of idling cars. I'm surprised at how easily he carries me, as if I am no heavier than a bag of groceries. Inside the building's darkened foyer, he sets me down, points upstairs, then removes his shoes as he's used to, but I leave mine on, soaked wet to the skin from the *jube* water. We climb to the second-floor apartment and once inside, I let out a gasp of air——trading the sharp inhalation of fear for the breathy exhale of relief.

I blow on my hands and rub them together. Amir busies himself firing up the kerosene heater. I shiver and wrap my arms around me, look around. The tenant's apartment is lovely, marble floors and a fireplace, an ornate mantel. A tidy stack of wood has been left on the marble hearth, as if the tenant had known someone might stumble into his apartment while he was away. A small U-shaped kitchen holds a marble peninsula that supports numerous corked bottles of red wine. A warm red and black Persian carpet covers the kitchen floor. Amir points to the phone. "Tell your parents you must stay the night." I grab it to dial home.

As I explain the situation to my mother, I make it sound better than it is, let her know I am stranded. I assure her I am in the good hands of Debbie's boyfriend. Mother tells me someone from school has already called to cancel tomorrow's classes and explain how bad it is in the streets. That I had abandoned the bus. Mother tells me she's been in a panic, couldn't imagine how she'd rescue me. Unfortunately for her and for me, I am with a man I want more than anything. Maybe I did need rescuing.

"You will hole up there with Amir?"

I wonder if my mother is as thick as a plank of wood, but it's helpful now. "I will. Dad home yet?" I ask.

"No, not yet." Mother sounds anxious. "Nor is Debbie."

I sigh, wishing that both of them were already home, maybe then I could set aside my own worries. "How about Frankie?"

"Yes. He arrived an hour ago."

I breathe a sigh of relief, but remember Christie. "Check on Christie for me? See that she made it home safely? I'll see you tomorrow."

"Okay Annie, stay safe."

She'd called me Annie.

After I'd hung up, Amir calls his family and speaks in Farsi, and so I can't understand him. After he hangs up the phone, he turns to me and says, "Annie, *Delbar'am,* come on, let us go find a change of clothes." He shows me to a sizable, neat bedroom holding a large contemporary-style bed and a long chest of dresser drawers from which he pulls out pajama bottoms and a T-shirt. "Go change," he says, pointing to the bathroom.

In the tiled bath, I throw my clothes in a heap in the shower and turn on the water full force to clean the blood and dirt from them, which reminds me of the dying sheep and the bloodied *jube* water. *Who would slit the throat of an animal? Burn buildings they'd normally conduct business in, destroy places of entertainment, even city landmarks?* The force of the water is a needed salve. I soap up vigorously, desperate to rid all traces of the filthy *jube* water from my skin, the distasteful memories.

After I've finished washing up, scented by the musky-fragrant bar of soap left behind in the shower, I start out of the bathroom. Amir is still unclothed, pulling on a robe. "Sorry!" I say as I retreat and slam the door. My hand shakes at the marble doorknob as I recall the silhouette of his shapely backside, how it had glowed white in the darkened room. After a few moments, heart pumping in my chest, I swallow awkwardly, ask through the door, "Amir, do you need to use the shower, too?" My words elicit a sexual familiarity we didn't have.

"Yes. Are you finished?"

"Just done," I say. I pull open the bathroom door and wince, awkward in the darkened bedroom, fresh out of the shower and in my pajamas. I avoid his gaze, leave him alone to wash up, and return to the living room.

The fire has taken off. It casts a warm glow in the darkened room; firelight leaps up the walls like the burning flames off the torched rubber tires. I sit on the cool leather couch while it slowly takes on the heat of my body and the strengthening fire. Two generous glasses of red wine have already been poured and await us on the glass coffee table in front of the couch.

I toss a balled-up clump of newspaper into the flames to nurse the fire along until Amir finishes. It is blazing hot when Amir joins me on the leather couch smelling fresh and clean. He grabs his goblet of wine, and I pretend I'm not breathing him in like incense. "What does your tenant do for a living?" I ask casually, clearing my throat.

"Jamshid? He works at the Tehran Opera house, doing..." Amir makes motions with his hands like he is hammering wood, painting scenery, and creating sets for operas like *Don Giovanni* or *Tosca*, and so I ask, "Stage design? Building sets?" Amir says, "Jamshid is a director. He directs plays." He laughs. "Only, he is like a woman!" He holds out a limp, bent wrist and smiles gently. "His voice."

Amir is telling me Jamshid is gay. "I have no problem with that," I say.

"I have none either. Look at this place, how lovely it is, the artwork, the plants." Amir sweeps his hand in front of him. I look around, suddenly noticing the splashes of colors within the abstract paintings, the long crooked stems of pussy willows that had been placed carefully into a black ceramic vase. I admire the sleek modern furniture, the antique Persian carpet beneath the glass coffee table at my feet.

"Why did that man kill the sheep on the sidewalk? Was he trying to frighten people? Signal that this could very well happen to us?" I take a long slow sip of my full-bodied wine and curl my feet beneath me.

"None of that. Afshin has told Maryam that sacrificing sheep makes blood in the streets. It looks very bad. A way to blame the Shah, the government, for all the bloodshed."

The embers are glowing hot red beneath the grate. The heat of Amir's thigh, which is resting against mine, excites me, sends shivers up my spine. I watch his lips caress the rim as he sips his wine, and I am staring. Thirsty for him. But before long, Amir grasps my left hand, raises it to his lips, then kisses it.

I gasp.

"Lovely hands, Annie. Lovely."

The wine makes me sensually courageous, and so I lean in and kiss him. I taste the salty softness of his full lips and then bite his bottom lip, suddenly crazy with passion.

"Ow." Amir complains, but he wears a pleasant look of surprise.

"Sorry." I grin back, but kiss him again, ravenously. And then he returns it almost as urgently as I gave it, pulling me into his lap, hands finding the back of my neck, tangling in my hair, tongue slipping into my mouth. We stop, scramble to sit up, face the fire, and attempt to cool down, our breaths escaping our mouths as if we'd both been running a race. I gulp down my wine, embarrassed that moisture is now wetting my borrowed pajama bottoms. I hold out my empty wine glass. "More?"

He smiles, says, "Annie, you are such a sweet, bad girl." He leaves the couch for more wine.

I hear pops outside that sound like gunfire, but then the chanting of the Call to Prayer sounds, and it serves to drown out the noise, which is a relief.

Amir hands me back a full goblet. "Who sings the Call to Prayer?" I ask.

"A muezzin. He sings from the minaret of the mosque several blocks from here."

"I'm beginning to love the Call to Prayer. Will you show me sometime how you pray?"

Amir nods, shameful. "Yes, I should be at mosque more, even now—should bow to Mecca. Pray. Rest my head on the cool tile floor. Especially now." He dips his head, slaps his thighs, then stands up. "Are you hungry? You want food?"

I am, even though the motorcycle crash and gunfire have frightened me.

"Rice with *Tahdig* on top. Would you like that?"

I nod, hug my shoulders, watch Amir poke through Jamshid's cabinets and pull out a long, flat package of rice, whistling, place a large black pot on the stove and pour water into it to soak the rice. He grabs out a blue-striped towel from a cabinet drawer, says, "The key to perfect rice is a towel." He lays it on the counter, grabs out saffron from the cupboard, and his busyness is comforting to me.

I throw another log into the fire, sip from my goblet of wine. Was it right to enjoy myself during all of this turmoil? To feel like a woman with this man who was making me rice, my sister's boyfriend, who has been acting decidedly unattached, or rather very attached to me? But then I'm feeling pulled into the night, protected, ripe for whatever might happen. And with tempers boiling over out on the streets and the feeling that the world is ending—it seemed a good time to embrace being alive.

After the rice had cooked for about ten minutes, Amir grabs out another pot, explains that he is creating the perfect environment for *Tahdig,* drizzling canola oil in it, pouring in water, layering the rice on top, the blue-striped towel placed carefully between the rice and the lid, as if he were making a bed, laying a perfect table. Such capable hands.

"We wait now," he says. "For steam." All the while, he's smiling.

He grabs for the bottle of wine, our wine goblets, joins me at the couch. We ignore the noise outside.

"Don't you want to attend University like Maryam?"

Amir shakes his head. "No. I work on cars to make money for my family. Eventually, I may take over my father's business, but the pay ... it is very good. For Maryam's university. Her dreams are, how you say? Creative. To be a journalist. Maryam is first in our family at University. She has no desire to be a housewife like my mother."

"But she supports Khomeini? An Islamic Republic?" It seems ludicrous to me. "How will she make something of herself, then? Isn't the Shah improving women's rights? You are telling me she will want the fundamental Islamic beliefs and traditions? Where her husband could say 'I divorce thee' three times, walk away from their marriage? Or if her bangs or ponytail creep out of her veil she could be thrown in prison?" I am almost shouting at him.

"Ah, so many questions, Annie. She wants the Shah gone from Iran. If religion can do this, then yes. She argues that Khomeini will make things very good. He will be righteous, but just, and will liberate Iran from the corrupt dictatorship of the Shah. She says that the Shah has been shaping Iranian women into dull, dumb western dolls." Amir falls silent, scrutinizing me, biting his lip. I smile at him gently, not angry at all, except for the idiocy of the comment.

He continues, "Maryam and my *maman* have said that the veil is decency and honor for Iranian women. Khomeini has declared from Paris that any nation who has women as our Iranian women will surely be victorious." A half smile plays on Amir's face. "I have no certainty about Khomeini. The Shah is all I have ever known. But I wonder. An Italian journalist interviewed the Shah, and the Shah told the reporter that in a man's life, women count only for beauty—that women may be equal in law, but not in their ability." Amir pauses. "This made Maryam join the revolution."

I sit quietly for a moment, a sick feeling in the pit of my stomach, trying not to judge. I'd sensed only warmth and intelligence in the Shah's eyes behind his large black glasses. Was I a bad judge of character? I wonder. The Shah did appear extravagant, but extravagance always impressed me, lavish parties, Empress Farah's beautiful outfits and furs, the Shah's fluent French. He didn't seem like a tyrannical dictator to me, but I didn't know and wasn't about to say this now, to anyone. The Shah had stopped to speak with me. "Don't you think the Shah is losing his arrogance in the face of this opposition? He seems distracted, not himself. Ill, even."

Amir nods, says, "We hardly see him anymore." The news had showed a cardboard cutout replacing him recently in the monarchy's motorcade during his birthday procession through the streets. The idea of a cardboard cutout is ridiculous, but understandable in the face of flying bullets. "Maryam would say that the Shah will never lose his arrogance. And Afshin. His uncle was taken by SAVAK one day, in the very early morning hours. Accused of being a political dissenter. Beaten and bloodied in the alley outside their house. Taken to Evin prison until word came that he was executed. A professor. An advocate of Karl Marx's teachings—socialism, anti-capitalism, class struggles, dislike of bourgeoisie, nothing else."

"Oh," I reply, remembering my enjoyment as I'd shopped on the bourgeois *Lalehzar* Avenue, before political activism ruined it.

"I hear the Shah has made donations to the Tabas earthquake fund this year instead of his own lavish birthday party." We both nod in appreciation and watch the fire flicker. Amir changes the subject. "I dread turning older, Annie. According to Iranian law, I must serve in the army for two years. And I am a pacifist. Not like Reza who desires to fight, fly airplanes. Not me. How in the world would I ever kill another person?"

"When? You will be allowed to train for two years first, right? Maybe the war, if it ever comes, will be over by then. When is your birthday?"

"May. I turned eighteen just before you arrived here. I am the same age as Crown Prince Reza. And like our Reza, the Crown Prince likes the idea of flying planes. He is an air cadet in Texas. No matter, Annie. I have a few more years."

"Well, then I'm sorry I missed your birthday." I wonder if I'd be around to see the next one.

We talk awhile, listen to all the noise outside until Amir motions for me to sit at the marble peninsula where we feast on large ceramic bowls of his rice. And it is cooked to perfection, the crust on top a delicacy. After dinner, Amir brings steaming mugs of tea to the leather sofa.

After we've finished, Amir says, "I must go to sleep. I can no longer concentrate tonight. I am so very tired. But you are the most beautiful distraction. Let me sleep here. You may have Jamshid's bed. It is larger."

"Amir, this is silly. I'm taller than you."

Amir feigns hurt pride. "You certainly know how to make a man feel good about himself." We look at each other awkwardly. The desire in the air is so thick you could slice it with a knife. A look of resolve passes across Amir's face. "Then come to bed. Sleep with me, Annie. Nothing else. Will you please?"

I stare into the dying fire—mind racing, but I say nothing. More nervous than reluctant, I nod, accept his offer. Once Amir has thrown the last of his tea on the fire, and it gasps out, he extends his hand to me and I take it, and he leads me back to the darkened bedroom. Thoughts of lost innocence become real, questions filling up my head like balloons. What was he expecting from me? I know I should be thinking of my sister, but I couldn't seem to make myself care about how this would make her feel.

I watch as Amir pulls back the covers of Jamshid's large, neatly made bed. "*Inja,*" he whispers, and then we crawl into an expanse of white, three-hundred-thread count sheets, soft and cool to the touch. After several minutes of lying side-by-side, distractedly aware of each other, eyes affixed to the bedroom ceiling, I give up. I turn to him, study him. In the bedroom's deep dark shadows, his skin is a decadent chocolate brown, compared to my pale arm against his stomach; I can't resist. He says, also, "I cannot help myself, forgive me," as he moves closer, and the hard press of his body surprises me, but I welcome the sensation. He kisses me gently, then forcefully, generous kisses that become treacherous—at first full on the lips, then scaling down my neck and falling lower, fingers tracing the sides of my waist. My soft skin is a road map for his fingertips. I feel bashful as he circles fine tendrils of hair near my ears, now damp with sweat, and says, "Your ears. They're so small ... so perfect." I smile, a flush starting from my chest where his hands had just lingered, to the length of my breastbone his fingers just traced. Delicate, special touches. Then his breath is in my ear and his chest has just the right amount of hair, which pleases me—thick, wiry black hair that funnels down to his waistband.

I look up. Amir pulls back and stares at me; a half smile plays on his lips. His pupils are full and soft, and expressively dark, and he sketches the hollow of my neck. But he stops, moves away, shakes his head no. "Mr. Patterson will kill me." Sitting up in bed now, he runs his fingers through his hair and looks away.

Doesn't he like me? I felt that he did. *What was wrong*? I put my hand on his leg.

"Annie, *nakon*. Don't. Please, let us enjoy sleeping here tonight. Nothing for us to regret."

Foolish at my recklessness—*hadn't Mr. James just called me level-headed?*—I recognize he's right. And my father would indeed have his head. It would be comforting to be together in this large, warm bed—honestly. We had our families' unsuspecting permission to be here together in this apartment. At least we had *that*. No one would ever have to know. And so I relax a little, wrap my arms around his strong, slim shoulders, throw my long leg over his. What's two inches and almost one year? Who cares if I'm taller, American, and we have nothing in common. I stare back at his dark face, so close to mine. *Who cares?*

After Amir had fallen asleep, I sneak out of bed to retrieve my contact lens solution and case from my backpack in the living room; I leave my glasses put. At least I can keep up the illusion of natural beauty, I think, before I knock my hip into the peninsula's edge. The ear-splitting noise outside has elevated to piercing screams—women? I hear sharp rapid fire. *Rat-a-tat tat. Rat-a-tat tat.* The click of reloading. *Rat-a-tat tat.*

I stumble over my sneakers at the side of the leather couch. *Am I drunk?* My eyes fill with tears and I creep back to bed, nestle into Amir's back, and then he turns over, but stays asleep. I steal peeks at him, watch his chest rise and fall, listen to the putt, putt of his breath as he blows out air, watch the rapid movement beneath the thin skin of his eyelids. Too conscious of his presence to sleep, I crawl to the far side of the bed. Only then do I fall into a deep, fitful slumber, filled with dreams of angry men yelling, dying bloodied sheep, buses rocking. I dream I'm kissing a boy who is John at ten or eleven years old, but then he is Shane and we are kissing under the rose trellis at Prom, but then he becomes Mike Morales and the Breck girl is hitting at him, trying to pull him away from me as her long blond hair cascades over her face in loose, sorrowful ringlets. Then someone grasps my hair and pulls my head back sharply....

My eyes fly open; my heart races and my temples pound. I lick my lips and swallow. *Oh God, what a headache. Such a metallic taste in my mouth.* I need water, aspirin, don't recognize where I am. I see the sleek modern bureau against the wall shrouded in shadows. And then I remember.

Without the aid of wine that had taken care of all my inhibitions the night before, I blush. I turn to Amir, lying with his back towards me, sleeping. All this was feeling much too adult. I glance at the bedside clock, can't make out the Arabic numerals. *Was it 3:00 a.m.? 4:00 a.m.?* The room is pitch black. The night has turned quiet. The image of my father's face appears in my head. I sigh. Afraid I'll wake Amir, I slip out of bed, grab a blanket from the linen closet, snatch out my glasses.

In the living room, the fireplace appears messy now, cold with gray soot. Wine and tea glasses litter the coffee table, used napkins. Amir's T-shirt lies on the floor in a heap, and so do my discarded sneakers, so girlish with their pink shoelaces and clashing red ladybugs. I bring the dishes to the kitchen, set them quietly in the sink, fill up my wine goblet with tap water. I gulp the tepid water down, then lie down on the small leather loveseat, curl my long legs into a fetal position, tuck the tips of my toes into the crack between the armrest and the seat cushion. I cover myself with the red fleece blanket and fall asleep with the knowledge that my mother would like this sleeping arrangement much better. And so would my father.

But how I hated the sound of machine gunfire.

I feel soft lips kissing me awake. Slowly, I open my eyes, which are still thick with sleep. Amir stands over me, peering at me.

"Morning," he says shyly, tenderness in his eyes. "You changed beds."

I lower my gaze, look back up. "I know. I'm sorry. The thought of my father bursting in here—suddenly, I felt weird … Thoughts of Debbie, too."

Amir takes my hand. He smiles genuinely, regarding me thoughtfully.

I pat the couch beside me, and the leather cushions groan as he sits. "I don't think I slept a wink," I say, rubbing my temples after he strokes the tops of my slicked smooth painted fingernails.

"You slept. You were dreaming just now. You even snore a little."

"I do?"

"Yes."

"Well, you putt, putt in your sleep," I tease back.

"Putt, putt. Hmm. Am I a Mercedes?"

"You sure sound like one," I say, laughing.

"Take a shower. Breakfast will be ready in ten minutes. Ali has quince jam! You must try," he says, bouncing on the loveseat, kissing me again, laughing, a quick brush of warm lips as he rises from the couch. "Take your time, beautiful Annie—"

"But wait, Amir, don't go. I don't even know your last name." That clichéd sentence often uttered after a one-night-stand.

"Fallahi."

Fallahi. Amir Fallahi. I try his name on like a pair of soft leather gloves. It felt comfortable to me, a nice ring.

"After breakfast, I shall take you home to your parents. I will grab a car off the lot. No more motorcycles for you, young lady." The mention of my parents brings on a bundle of worries. I grab the phone on the bedside nightstand and dial home. Mother answers on the first ring.

"Hi, Mom."

"Annette! Good morning."

"I'm calling with an update. So you aren't worried—"

"I would have thought I'd receive one from you by now—"

"I'm coming home soon. Did everyone make it home okay last night?"

"Yes, we're all fine here, thank God! Christie, too. When can we expect you?"

"Maybe in an hour." I keep quiet about the breakfast Amir is cooking for me—reluctant for her to have an image of domestic bliss. I look down at the mussed up sheets, ears burning.

After I'd hung up the phone, I think of Debbie—imagine her face. I push away nagging, guilty feelings, cross to the bathroom. What was that saying, *all is fair in love and war*? Is it?

Once I'd finished showering, I enter the kitchen. Amir has set up the metal table outside on the balcony. He is staring out over the backyard, absently smoking a cigarette. Once he sees me, he motions me outside. On the patio table he'd set a cup of tea and a quince-covered egg on a piece of crusty French bread. A faint smell of smoke lingers in the air, alongside the bitter odor of Amir's cigarette. It is quiet this morning at the back of the apartment, off the street.

"I worry the bread is stale. Go on. *Eat*. Tell me how you like it."

I take a large bite from the sandwich; it's warm and fresh, not stale in the least.

"It's soft and delicious, lovely with the warm, melted cheese." I pucker my cheeks slightly for emphasis. "Quince jam is sour, but it makes all the difference."

Amir appears pleased, satisfied. "A quince tree grows in our courtyard at home. *Maman* makes jam from it. She adds in much sugar."

I think of the crabapple tree back home in Ohio my mother also used for homemade jelly. Also sour and requiring lots of sugar.

Amir takes an even larger bite from his sandwich, nodding approval as he devours it in a few large gulps. "Jamshid has left us very good with rice, wine, firewood, eggs, quince jam, and even cigarettes. Everything we should want. But, I remember now. I must water his plants."

Ah, the plants. Amir grabs a green plastic watering can and soaks several plants that hang from macramé hangers in multi-color ceramic pots. As I finish my tea, I remember the rumpled bed, and so I rise up to clean the bathroom, hang discarded towels over the shower rack so they wouldn't mildew, make up the bed. And at the same time, Amir is cleaning the breakfast dishes. He leaves a note on the counter for Jamshid, explaining he'd stayed overnight.

"He should not be upset at his landlord," Amir says, smiling.

"You are his landlord? You own this place?"

"I am. I own the shop," Amir says proudly.

The early morning streets are clear of demonstrators, but are littered with trash, firebombed cars, broken shards of glass. There are smashed storefront windows and burned-out buildings everywhere. I am sick to my stomach at the damage.

Amir drops me off at my security door and says good-bye, intent on visiting the *jube* crash site, to discover if he can salvage anything of his motorcycle.

"Do you want to come in?" I ask.

"No," he says quickly, guiltily. And I understand his hesitation.

"Thank you for everything," I say, kissing him discreetly through the car window, on the side of a cheek. He grins, grabbing my hand to his face, kisses it, lets it drop. He pulls away in his Mercedes, waving, now more focused on the rescue of his motorcycle than me. I turn away from spinning tires spewing dust, gather up courage to face my parents.

Before I manage to open the security door, I see Khoda running towards me full throttle. Of course! It's his feeding time. I throw my backpack on the ground and drop to my knees. As Khoda reaches me, he slows, sidles up to me, and I am pleasantly surprised that he would get so close. I sit down with him for a few minutes, wanting to take time with this; my back rests against the wall as I stroke his matted fur. It's as if Khoda had sensed the trouble I'd been in yesterday. I run inside to retrieve his bowl of dog food. He is famished.

Upstairs, I find my mother in the kitchen. She rushes over to hug me. "Annette, you're home. I'm so relieved you're safe," she says, for the second time in two months. "Amir did well to make you stay put."

The heat of embarrassment creeps up my neck, and my temples pulse from too much wine the night before. *Little did she know.*

"Debbie hitched a ride home from a boy named Mahjid in her English class last night. He's still here if you want to meet him."

I do, and so I wander into the living room where Debbie and Mahjid sit cross-legged on the floor in front of the stereo cabinet talking shyly. Debbie's short hair is carefully styled this morning.

"Hi," I say. Debbie looks up, startled. *Was there suspicion in her gaze?* Mahjid smiles obtusely, waves hello. He is dark and handsome, but I'm beginning to think every young Iranian man is. The music is too loud to carry on a conversation. Al Stewart's "Year of the Cat" is playing on the stereo, and Debbie appears perfectly happy. I wave awkwardly and escape to my room to rest; my eyelids are blocks of stone. I crawl into bed, remember the feel of Amir in my arms. The stereo's bass vibrates through the wall, and I hear only what I can describe as appropriate lyrics:

In a country where they turn back time ... in the blue tiled walls near the market stalls ... The drumbeat strains of the night remain, in the rhythm of the new-born day ... You know sometime you're bound to leave her ... But now you're going to stay.

School is canceled for the rest of the week. I am surprised but relieved. The Shah has placed the country under military rule after the disaster that was November fifth. I learn that the chaos that day evolved from another mass shooting the night before; this time ten protestors at Tehran University were killed in the melee. Prime Minister Sharif-Emami has resigned and General Gholam Reza Azhari, commander of the Imperial Guard, has succeeded him as interior prime minister of the military government, until a civilian government could be put in place. General Gholam Ali Oveisi was to continue as the Military Governor of Tehran.

The Shah holds a televised press conference. We watch. "I heard the voice of your revolution," he says. "As Shah of Iran, as well as an Iranian citizen, I cannot but approve your revolution." Was it true that the Shah was becoming humble? Had I been right?

Work is called off for my father. The Americans in our neighborhood take the occasion to organize a party for Mr. Jamison, the kindly professor who had offered me his hardy long-stemmed Middle Eastern rose. Just having been released from the American hospital after throat cancer surgery, his wife thinks a party might cheer him up. John, Kelly, Mr. and Mrs. James, and Moshdeh are invited. The pilot, Ali, who wishes to get to know Moshdeh better after the Fourth of July barbecue, also receives a special invitation.

Mother is busy making an egg soufflé dish when the electricity goes out. I hear her swear softly. I smile. Mother is becoming potty-mouthed here in Tehran, worried about the possible deflation of her masterpiece in the white ramekin in the oven. Within seconds though, the electricity flicks on.

"Thank God," Mother says, gazing up towards the lights. "This must cook so we aren't late. Dinner is early."

"Do I have to go?" Debbie asks.

"Yes, of course, we're going together as a family."

Debbie rolls her eyes. "Mahjid thought he'd come over this afternoon."

"Mahjid? But what about Amir? I can't keep up with you," Mother says, rolling her eyes right back at Debbie.

I look closely at Debbie. She doesn't seem to be blaming me for anything. *Did she know? Could she tell?* I am no better than Scarlett O'Hara kissing Ashley Wilkes at his dying wife's bedside. Debbie shrugs. "I'm too young to settle on any one person. I like playing the field. Variety is the spice of life! Mahjid thinks I'm beautiful. He says I should grow my hair out."

"You just cut it," I say.

"Remember how you led both Marc and Shane on?"

"At least I didn't date and dump half the high school like you did."

"You're so picky, Annie, a real snob."

"Girls. Stop it. No more." Mother flips on the oven light to gauge the inflating soufflé's progress. "Always date someone who loves you more than you love them," Mom cautions.

"That's what I'm trying to do," Debbie says. She flounces out of the room.

Around four o'clock, we head out to the Jamisons. A chill lingers in the late afternoon air. The Jamisons live in an apartment house long and narrow from the street back while ours is wide across our lot. It is decorated with a large antique

Persian carpet in blues and taupe with swirling, tangled vines, splashes of colorful blue flowers. Buddha statues have been placed around the room like chubby, smiling talismans, and ivory-tusked elephants sit on several bookshelves and coffee tables, all of which are overflowing with books. Mrs. Jamison has strung up royal blue crepe paper from the living room ceiling in sweeping, curling arcs. A sign hangs from the fireplace mantel, exclaiming, *Welcome Home, Daniel!* in graceful loops of script.

A grand piano spans the entire living room's width. Mrs. Jamison has covered it in a white linen tablecloth and has spread out hors d'oeuvres and multiple bottles of wine and champagne over the piano's top. Soon a gaunt, weak Dr. Jamison enters the room to claps and cheers, wolf whistles between two fingers from Kelly. I spy John standing shyly across the room behind Mr. and Mrs. James.

A stubby tube protrudes out of Dr. Jamison's neck. Surprised, I eye my mother with concern. She whispers to me that he must have had a tracheotomy. "This allows him to breathe," she says. Dr. Jamison pulls out a small black device from his pocket. He holds it up to his neck. His hello vibrates oddly within the room.

"Thank you all for your well-wishes and joining us in our home during this trying time, not only for me, but for all of you," he says, spreading out one arm to include all the people standing in front of him, his other arm bent at his neck so that his hand could clutch the small device. Mrs. Jamison steps forward to join her husband, hugging him tightly and blinking back tears. She holds up a fluted glass of champagne with rail-thin arms—papery translucent skin hanging off her elbows in generous soft folds—and toasts her husband. Tears fill her faded blue eyes. "He survived! He did it! I am so thankful to have Daniel here at my side. Thank you all for coming, for welcoming Daniel home—please help yourself to the refreshments on the piano." My eyes also fill with tears. Heartfelt displays of affection cut me to the core; the love that Mrs. Jamison feels for her husband is raw, and she wears it on her face like a threadbare shirtsleeve.

I turn to see Moshdeh engrossed in conversation with Ali, who is handsome in a tailored black suit. She wears a long ribbed green sweater that flatters her figure, her filmy long skirt almost touching her ankles that are hidden in fashionable leather boots. She laughs at Ali and her teeth flash white as she smiles; her hand touches his shoulder. He smiles back at her radiantly. They talk intently as if they were the only two people in the room. Her long black hair curls and tangles about her shoulders.

Amir comes to mind. My hair was blond and thin. It did not tumble. It was not exotic. Shouldn't Amir desire someone like Moshdeh?

It is growing dark. Mrs. Jamison has placed candles around the room should the power go out. She has invited everyone up to the roof for more cocktails and sodas for the kids.

I feel a tap on my shoulder. I turn to the vibrating voice box of Dr. Jamison. "Annie, young woman! How are you? I am certain you'd be most happy to know my rose bush thrived until the first frost!"

I step forward to shake his hand, which turns into a hug. The boniness of his back concerns me. "Wonderful, Mr. Jamison, I am pleased you are well," I say, pecking his cheek. "You were successful at hot temperatures, how about creating a rose that can withstand cold temperatures, frost and even snow?" I tease. He smiles and squeezes my shoulder, "To do this, Annie, I'd have to be much smarter. I hear your school is closed for a week. That's wise for now, given the situation, a chance to calm down. The Community School is also closed. I look forward to more recuperation time for myself. Stay well, Annie, so good to see you. Enjoy, please," Mr. Jamison

232

encourages, waving to the tidbits on the piano, wandering off to engage his other guests in conversation as a good host would do.

Christie approaches me holding a plate of Swedish meatballs. She has on a pretty autumn-colored dress in brighter colors than she usually wears, splashes of red, orange, and yellow. Her strawberry-blond hair is anchored back in a French braid. She looks fabulous.

"Hi," she says with a beaming smile. "Guess, what?"

"What?"

"Julie and Ned are sending me back to Ohio to finish out school. I leave this Friday."

"Christie, no." I am so disappointed. I had begun to like her after my birthday party and our frightening bus ordeal the other day.

"It's good. You know how I miss home. It was all Julie's idea," Christie says, nodding over at her stepmother standing several feet away, holding a plate of mini hot dogs swimming in barbecue sauce.

"That's very nice of Julie."

"Julie can be pleasant sometimes. Will you tell Alika good-bye for me, Annie?"

"I will. Where will you stay?"

"With Julie. In our old house, once she packs up here. She's arranging to bring Siam and Meese out with her. She wants them in the cabin; the airline allows only seven pets out per flight."

"Is this okay with you? To live with Julie?"

Christie regards me with shame. "You've heard us fighting, haven't you?" She shrugs. "I have no other choice. At least she's a great cook and I get to go back," she says with a smile. "She's not all bad."

I absorb her news.

After the eating and drinking had wrapped up on the roof, and when the Call to Prayer was about to begin, Dr. Jamison invites everyone back downstairs. The piano had been cleared of all the refreshments, and a violin case rests nearby, next to a music stand. Mrs. Jamison is sitting on the piano stool, and Dr. Jamison has pulled up a chair beside her. He removes a shiny mahogany violin from the case at his feet and winks at me. Mrs. Jamison speaks for her husband. "Ali, Moshdeh, you will appreciate this, but my husband and I enjoy accompanying the Call to Prayer from the mosque. Though, we recognize the beauty of it in its simplest form—without music, we do this...." She smiles. "Ali, if you'll open the balcony doors, please." Ali complies. Mr. Jamison rests his voice box vibrator on the piano's top, begins to reproduce the plaintive cries from the minaret with each strum of his instrument while Mrs. Jamison adds high staccato notes from the piano, and then the music finishes.

I look around at everyone's awed expressions, thinking about how all of us Americans had tried to make the best of Iran—attempted to embrace everything that wasn't ours, so radically different from what we were used to, tried to insert ourselves enthusiastically in this country but remain true to our American selves. Most of us in this room had been taught tolerance, the careful consideration of other people's feelings and views, even if we didn't share them. But we could never belong here. Had never belonged. My father could never have done the good he had envisioned when he had first come. Our stewardship to the Iranian people was tantamount to cancer cells multiplying. Curfew now hangs over our heads like a dark shroud, while more and more hostility creeps in. We are all so frightened.

After dessert, no one is ready to leave, but the guests begin to gather their things slowly, to locate their coats and jackets piled high in a heap in the Jamisons' guest bedroom, to thank the hosts for a lovely evening and exchange good-byes. Outside in their courtyard, Ali takes Moshdeh's hand and squeezes it. My heart swells. Just in front of me, Mrs. James is leaning heavily on Mr. James. Oh no, not again, I think.

Up ahead, John slows to a snail's crawl to say good-bye to me. Mrs. James has also stopped. She turns suddenly and shouts, "John, what on earth do you see in this girl? Can't you understand that she is so *not interested* in you." Her expression is haughty.

Her slurred words sting me like bullets. I feel contemptible for liking him less than John and she think I should. But I am interested in him. I care for him. He is a cherished friend.

"Mom, please…"

"She isn't even all that great," Mrs. James spits out through large gritted teeth.

John looks dumbstruck. Mr. James has overheard and circles back to steer Mrs. James away from us.

"Annie, I'm so sorry," John says. "I don't know what to say."

"It's all right." I lie.

John steers me to a quiet corner of the pool area. "She's been drinking as you can see—got a hold of Mr. Ned's *Boomerangs*." John laughs awkwardly. "Today, my dad forbade her to join the Royal Riding Club with all that's going on. She becomes a different person when she drinks. Please tell me it's okay, Annie."

"It's fine, John. Please. Get home safely." I rush away to hide my hurt feelings and join my family. Down the alley, a dark figure lingers outside our security wall. Was it Amir? I quicken my pace, legs turning to jelly. It felt wrong for me to want Amir after what Mrs. James had just said about me. I turn to see if John is still there. His back is turned to me, he is bent over, hands in his hair. But then his dad puts an arm around him, draws him over to Moshdeh's car.

"Mahjid?!" Debbie asks when we draw closer. She waves us on as the two of them stand a breadth apart, holding hands and smiling, infatuation filling their eyes like the tears that are swimming in mine.

That evening, Dad receives a telephone call from work asking us if we'd house some of the employees who stay at the team house, unsafe as it is for anyone to continue to live there. The team house is located on the corner of *Takht-E-Tavoos* and *Kurosh-E-Kabir*, right downtown, near Tehran University and all the rioting. My dad agrees, and so we are set to accommodate one or two houseguests beginning the next morning.

Sure as gold, my father's secretary, Carol, arrives at our doorstep the next morning—a petite woman with mousy brown hair and large owl-shaped glasses—I don't judge. She lugs a powder blue suitcase through the pool area. As it bangs against her legs, I picture the enormous blue bruises that most certainly will form on the woman's thin limbs. We are still waiting for Tim, a bachelor who also works in my dad's office. Carol and Tim, both captains in the Air Force and each unmarried, stay at the team house rather than living like us in apartments on the economy. But, no longer.

After dinner, my parents ask us to go to our rooms early so the adults can talk. Instead, I sit near the door, anxious to hear their conversation. At first, I can't hear over the noise of my mother clearing dishes, but then their voices carry, enhanced by the echoes off the marble floor.

"What time does the driver show up in the morning?" Carol asks. Work is back on schedule for my father's department, but still school is canceled for us.

"Tomorrow he'll pick us up at seven a.m. The thing is—I wonder about our driver. I'm just not trusting him anymore."

"Mohammad? The one at the picnic?" asks Carol.

"Yeah, Mohammad. I feel him turning, growing colder, icy towards us."

"Jack, I carry a .38 caliber revolver in my brief case," Tim says.

"You do?"

"I do."

I had learned that in Iran it had become United States Embassy policy in 1976, after everybody had attempted to arm themselves when two colonels were assassinated, that carrying firearms on your person was prohibited. Many military men ignored this and carried a gun anyway, usually stowing it away in their bullet-proof briefcase, also useful as a shield. But martial law prohibited anyone to carry firearms anyway. My dad's innate moral code to do the right thing, along with his naïve optimism regarding the state of the Shah's regime, made him carry a metal baton instead.

"Jack, if anything goes wrong, I'll shoot the driver—you hit the bodyguard with the baton, okay? If they revolt."

"The body guard is SAVAK. He shouldn't revolt."

"He may. Who knows any more about anything? I'll shoot the bodyguard if he does."

I hear my father shush them, then their voices lower.

"I buy defense equipment to sell, not to use with my own hands," my father says. "At least not for now." My dad was lucky never to have seen combat, although Tim had, in Vietnam.

Carol is saying, "I asked Colonel Ross if he would reassign me back home, even in Europe—anywhere but here. When he checked with the MAAG the answer was a flat out no. The top brass told him everyone must stay. They say there should be no appearance of not supporting the Shah." Carol sighed. "At least they moved us out of the team house. I could hardly sleep at night with all the demonstrations and noise—the shooting—the women screaming and crying."

"You'll still hear it here," my father says grimly.

"But, the sounds seemed so close, and if you peeked outside, or looked from the rooftop, the streets were empty. Were the screams and gunfire fabricated? To trick everyone to be afraid for their lives?"

"I wondered the same thing," Tim says.

"I was terrified some guerrilla or terrorist organization would pipe bomb us while we slept—so sure how visible we were coming and going. It's not easy to sleep under those circumstances."

I've heard enough. I creep to my room to read and distract myself from the world around me. A few pages into my book, I hear a skittle of stones at my balcony door. I look outside. Another arc of rocks flies over the security wall. I freeze, rooted to my bed. In another life I'd have suspected a friend, even a suitor. I push back my covers, walk quickly to the foyer and press the hall intercom button. "Who's there?" I ask, voice shrill.

"Amir!" he says excitedly. *A suitor.*

I sprint down to the pool area and fling open the door. Amir is standing there, a huge silly grin plastered on his face.

"I was hoping it'd be you!" I almost shriek.

"I wanted to see you. I've been busy at work, but have not forgotten you. I am walking home just now, and I thought to surprise you."

"An easier method of communication is the telephone!" I say, a twinkle in my eye.

Amir takes me seriously. "You know why I am frightened to call."

"I do, Amir, and I have something to tell you."

His face falls. "You regret the other night, do you not?" he asks, kicking at something invisible at his feet, a stone, a piece of discarded litter, his face pale as wax.

"Come on in. Please. Sit." We take a seat on the patio swing. He looks grave. I break the news. "Debbie is hanging out with Mahjid from English class." I gaze down at my sandals.

"Mahjid?" Amir asks. "Really?"

"Yes, Amir. Are your feelings hurt?"

"No, silly," Amir says, laughing a little. Relief shows on his face. "I care about you. Only you. But, seriously ... Mahjid?" he whispers, then leans into me, planting a kiss on my open mouth, his laugh big in the night.

He places his hand at his heart and says, *"I caught the happy virus last night when I was out singing beneath the stars. It is remarkably contagious – So kiss me."*

Laughing, I kiss him. Amir whispers, "Poetry from the famous Persian poet, Hafez." And I like that he is trying to wrap words around me, happy encouraging words that match his positive outlook on life.

We sit quietly for a while, side by side, enjoying the sounds of peace, intimate noises rather than wails and chants, a bug buzzing by our noses, a child squealing happily from a neighboring compound. I almost doze, my head resting on his shoulder.

A screech of brakes interrupts our short-lived peace, doors opening and slamming, male voices shouting. Amir rises up, opens the security door. *"In chist?" More voices are shouting.* "People are climbing over the wall of a house down the street. I am almost certain it is the professor's. Do you have something I can use for a weapon, Annie?"

"My God, Amir, not Mr. Jamison's house," I say, running into the garage to retrieve our Pete Rose-autographed wooden baseball bat. "Here—Amir, hurry, Mr. Jamison's sick. His wife's fragile. Please help them."

Without hesitation, Amir takes the bat and heads down the alley. He wheels around as he runs backward. "Annie, close the door. I'll be back." Fear sounds in his voice.

I peer around the security door, frightened for Amir. The alley is empty, the last intruder just now vaulting over Mr. Jamison's security wall from the roof of an abandoned car. There is no sign of Amir. My heart pounds in my chest. He needs help.

I rush upstairs, where the adults still gather around the kitchen table. "A gang went over the Jamisons' security wall!" My father and Tim take one look at me, then rush for the door.

"Amir grabbed the bat," I holler after them. "There are golf clubs in the bin in the corner!" But then I remembered Tim's briefcase and his gun, Dad's metal baton.

My mother, Carol, and I regard each other with fear. Debbie enters the kitchen. "What's up?"

"The men went to the Jamison's. Apparently a gang went over their security wall," Mother tells Debbie. "Amir is already there helping."

"Amir?" Debbie asks, biting her lip.

"Yes, Amir," I answer, my stare defiant, as if to say, *what's it to you*?

We wait. Mother makes coffee. I try a sip while she paces. I spit it out. Carol lights a cigarette. "Do you mind?" she asks after she has already inhaled a deep first puff. My mother shakes her head distractedly. We wait with nervous dread while the acrid smoke hangs heavy in the air.

After about an hour, the men return. My father explains how they'd found Amir inside, his bat resting on the floor beside him, standing guard on the outskirts of a group of young Iranian men and women who were sitting peacefully in the Jamison's living room. They held cups of tea and large plates of cookies. Mr. and Mrs. Jamison were calmly listening to the group, but at first the intrusion had frightened the older couple.

Mr. Jamison would later say that as the group pushed through his apartment door, and his life flashed before his eyes, he made a mental note to always lock the dag-gone door.

"By God, Dr. and Mrs. Jamison talked them down," my father says, amusement playing in his eyes.

"I did not have to use this," Amir says, grinning, holding up the Pete Rose-autographed bat. "Mrs. Jamison invited the protestors to sit for tea and cookies, to share their concerns about the present regime."

"Which are?"

"Complaints such as Maryam has voiced."

My father says, "The demonstrators asked Dr. Jamison if he knew the price of an apartment near Tehran University. Dr. Jamison said no, but he knew the price of his own apartment, and it wasn't pretty. He told them how he understood their complaints, the overbuilding—apartments only foreigners could afford. He discussed the successes he's been having with his hybrid Middle Eastern rose. Even played some music on the grand piano. The crowd left peacefully, expressing concern for his voice box, thanking Mrs. Jamison for the refreshments. The students explained that he was targeted because he was a professor at a school for Americans and foreigners."

"Hasn't Ambassador Sullivan been pressing the United States to have a dialogue with Khomeini?" Carol asks.

"Yes, but Brzezinski doesn't want that, and he's the National Security Advisor," Tim says. "I'm afraid Ambassador Sullivan envisions Khomeini as a Ghandi, and goddammit that's the last thing he is. And the Russians might be beginning to like him."

Debbie approaches Amir with a flirty smile. "Amir, how brave of you." She lays her hand on his shoulder. Amir sidesteps her touch, avoiding her wounded gaze. "I must return to the Jamison's. I promised I would stay over and keep watch."

"Thank you, Amir," my father says. "So brave of you to act as their protector. Can't tell you how grateful we are. We'll see you again soon, won't we?"

"Amir, would you join us for Thanksgiving dinner?" my mother asks. "Bring Reza with you? We'd love to show you how we celebrate the holiday."

Amir grins, winking at me, "Yes, Mrs. Patterson, that would indeed be wonderful. I shall invite Reza the next time I see him. See you on Thanksgiving."

After Amir leaves, Debbie pouts.

"What's the matter now?" Mother asks.

"I was planning on inviting Mahjid for Thanksgiving. I've moved on from Amir."

"Ask him, too," Mother says. "The more the merrier. I have a feeling Amir's moved on also." She gives me a knowing glance.

Debbie glares at me, then my mother. She folds her arms across her chest. "*Mom*, Amir never just moved on, he's *always* been infatuated with Annie. Her height, her grades. Her weight. *Books in her head*. Like I've none in mine? I was teaching him English for God's sake. Afshin says Amir's a spy. Not to be trusted. That he was paid money to date me. To spy on Dad. For the Shah and for SAVAK."

"Debbie," Mom says.

"Dad is so blind. About Amir. About Annie. Unbelievable that he skipped my graduation! But he'll go to Annie's. 'Cause *she's* the scholar. The pretty one." Debbie flounces away, and I hang my head in shame, flabbergasted at her outburst. I huff, crossing my hands over my chest.

"Debbie, please." Mom calls after her. "You're beautiful! Creative. Don't you see? You must believe in yourself...." Her voice trails off, then rises. "I knew I had you two too close in age! How many articles have I read about sibling rivalry in children not spaced far enough apart!"

"You took long enough to have Frankie!" Debbie shouts.

"Not everyone has perfect ovaries, you know!" Mother screams back at her, losing her cool, which she'd been doing a lot of lately. Mother looks at me then, tilts her head, eyes narrowed and moving over me as if she doesn't like me anymore.

I try to fool her by acting strong. "Let her go, Mom. Amir is no spy." But how well did I even know him? Hadn't he said that the Shah was all he's ever known? Since when does Debbie listen to Afshin?

During the brief school break, Amir and I spend late afternoons at the soccer field. Each day he brings a thermos of tea and spreads out his trunk-sized Persian carpet on the dirt, and we pass the steel canister of warm *chai* between us, conscious of our mouths and lips on the same canister's rim. I had already pushed Debbie's accusations about Amir from my mind.

"*Noon o paneer, mesleh hameesheh* (bread and cheese as always)!" Amir exclaims as he pulls a loaf of *Barbari* and a chunk of goat cheese out of his satchel, my copy of *The Swiss Family Robinson*. Amir asks me to read it, lounging back on his Persian carpet, arms folded behind his head, eyes closed, but listening intently, complimenting me on my voice. But before I can finish, he closes the book, pulls me to him, and kisses me. I see stars. But afterward, our eyes dart around quickly, and I wonder whether anyone has seen us. We decide to play catch. I'd brought along a softball and two baseball mitts from the bin in the garage to teach Amir to play. We laugh at his early clumsiness, but then the natural athlete in him catches on. Afterward, we saunter back hand-in-hand to our compound, swing dreamily on our patio swing set, unable to keep our hands off each other. All worries fade away with each of his kisses. I don't care who may be watching, even Debbie.

But then the construction workers rebuilding a security wall across the street spy us from the scaffolding they are standing on. Moments later, bricks and stones reign down upon us like hail, landing on the swing's canopy overhead with knocks and thuds. Amir runs from our compound in a huff and a verbal scuffle ensues, Farsi expletives flung about like heavy stones. After I let Amir back into the compound, I see that fear is gathering in his eyes like an ominous rain cloud.

Back at school, I discover our football season will be cut short—there'd be a final game, the All-Star match! And I'd made the All-Star cheerleading squad. But John had failed to make the All-Star team. Disappointed that he wouldn't be breaking the banner that Cathy and I had so painstakingly created, my excitement about being selected for the All-Star team is also dampened by the fewer number of classmates in school. Mike Morales has already gone home to San Francisco. I'm not sure about the Breck girl. At last now he could be true to his girlfriend.

At least Alika is still here. I find her in the compound before school, tell her Christie is going back home. "I hope I can get back to Riverside soon, too," Alika says, envious. "Still no word from TRW." She kicks at a crack in the pavement. "I only just started to have this good feeling Christie was turning around, becoming happy. One day before Algebra class we got to talking. She told me how her mother died. In a careless car accident—swerved into the path of an oncoming tractor trailer as she reached for an atlas—got hit head-on. Died instantly."

I'd wondered about Christie's mother, and it is unbearable. I bow my head. "Awful about Christie's mother," I say, looking up with moist eyes.

Alika tucks a black hair strand behind her ear. "Yeah ..." She changes the subject. "We're going in search of a Christmas tree soon. The artificial ones are sold out at the Co-Op."

"A Christmas tree, how great. Keep the faith, Alika. You might have to travel all the way to the Caspian Sea for a Christmas tree, though." I look around at the dreary compound, the Iranian guard smoking a cigarette, gun held at his side. It doesn't seem like it could ever feel like Christmas here. "We have a family ski trip planned to Germany for Christmas break."

"You'll be able to admire the hotel's Christmas tree, then. I'm sure it'll be one of those 22 foot grand ones."

I nod. "Our hotel stands on top of Hitler's bunkers."

"How ironic that Iran means the land of the Aryans. No connection to Nazi Germany's Aryan blond-haired, blue-eyed physical ideal, though. It's just so weird, isn't it?" Alika examines her feet, looks up at me. "What if you can't get back here?"

I think of lunchtimes with Alika and our shared conversations, all the books. Amir's grin also comes to mind, his beautiful skin and mouth, his white teeth and wiry black hair, his zest for life and country, his willingness to please and help our family, not the Shah or SAVAK. "I'll miss you, Alika, if we can't return," I say, grasping her hand. I'd also miss Amir, desperately.

A week before Thanksgiving, I hear the buzz of our intercom. It's Amir and when I go to let him in I hear an unusual commotion. Curious about the clucking noises and sounds of flapping, I open the door. Amir is on the stair landing holding a live turkey, fear and discomfort painted on his face as much as on the distressed bird he can hardly contain. Feathers are flying like at a slumber party pillow fight.

"Mom," I call over my shoulder and duck out of the way. Eek, large flapping birds have always frightened me, and I was not about to stick around for pleasantries.

I hear my mom say, "Amir, this isn't necessary ... Really, I have no idea what to do with this. I wouldn't know how to kill it. Wouldn't want to. Please ... take it away. I have a frozen one." I felt so sorry for him, realizing that he had thought about our conversation at lunch and was, irresistibly, bringing us a fresh turkey.

After Amir leaves the stair hall, and the squawking has finally subsided, I peer outside my balcony door. Amir has let the turkey go, and it is skittering across the pool terrace, skims the tarped pool in a short harried flight. Amir jogs over to the security door, opens it and the gangly bird escapes our compound with its life. He slams the door behind it, wipes feathers from his clothes. Even from my faraway perch, I see relief flood his face. He couldn't kill it, either. My mother wanders to the balcony door. "Poor, thoughtful, Amir."

Mother wakes me early Thursday morning to help her prepare the turkey. "Rise and shine. Many hands make light work!" She is worried about cooking times and altitude, if the turkey would taste as good as it did fresh from the local turkey farm. "You had your chance," I tease. She'd purchased the twenty-two pound Butterball turkey from the commissary, all the while crossing her fingers that the time it took to ship frozen products from New York to Iran—the freeze and thaw of the poultry along the way—would not spoil it, or sicken anybody who would eat it. Debbie is left to sleep in, always complaining too much to be of any help in the kitchen. Frankie would greet the guests and take their coats, I'd help with the cooking, and we'd all tackle the dishes together when the guests had gone.

I shuffle into the kitchen, yawning. Mom quickly puts me to work chopping vegetables; a large pot of water already simmers on the stove. I am a sous-chef under orange kitchen wall fruit, a Japanese Sushi cook julienning vegetables with quick, determined strokes, sautéing them on the gourmet gas stovetop I am growing fond of. A flick of my wrist and the vegetables turn over nicely in the frying pan. Mother dumps a bag of dried breadcrumbs into the now boiling pot of water; she tells me the best way to mix it is with the fingers. Hands burning, I stir until the cohesive lump of seasoned bread becomes moist. I stuff it into our large pasty turkey, tent it with aluminum foil, then slide the bird into the oven to roast. We pray for the electricity to remain on throughout the day.

Hours later, the fragrance of roasting turkey fills the apartment and brings me back to my former home, makes me salivate.

The intercom buzzes.

"I'll get the door," Frankie yells, eyes bright as sunlight as he rushes downstairs to greet the guests. Besides Amir and Reza, Nouri, Moshdeh and Ali are also expected. I study the clock, suddenly confused; it's way too early, just past noon. Our guests are scheduled to arrive at three. A sick feeling overcomes me. *Oh no, not again!*

I bolt downstairs, shouting for my father. My shoe catches on the stair's edge, and I pitch forward. I grab the banister to prevent a fall, shout, "Frankie!" After I recover, I dash through the garage, breath ragged in my chest. "Wait!" I shout, but the security door is already open, the damage done. Frankie stands to one side, weeping, as a crowd of Iranians wearing black armbands and white bandanas stream through our security door.

I stop dead in my tracks.

The mob continues towards me. Afshin is not the ringleader of this group. I back up, frightened, feeling protective of Frankie at the security door. At the same time I sense someone creeping up behind me with purposeful steps from the depths of the garage's shadows. I hold my ground—eyes burning holes into the back of my head—fixed forward so as not to call attention to the slow, determined steps skulking out of the darkness. *Oh, please let it be Tim with his gun, or my father with his baton.*

Just as I wish, Tim strides past me brandishing his .38 caliber pistol. "Leave," Tim orders the group. The ringleader's long, black hair is pulled tight into a ponytail—his high cheekbones pop from his face like bone from broken skin. He stops short and raises his hands into the air slowly, turns around, shouting commands to his comrades in Farsi. The other men follow suit, retrace their steps back to the security door.

"Go on, get out of here!" shouts Tim.

My dad approaches. "We want no trouble here," he shouts. He extends his baton backward behind his head, his muscles visible in his veined biceps as if he would not hesitate to crack the skull of this malicious intruder—angry at the violation of our privacy, the potential harm to his young son, Frankie, to his precious daughter, if not physical—mental, to all his family.

"*Baleh*," the leader says, vitriol dripping from his mouth like saliva. "You the Colonel?"

"I'm the Colonel."

"Ah then, Colonel, you can be certain we will be back if you do not return to your own country. This day in history you feasted alongside American Indians, and after? You killed them like pigs. *Haram*! You stole their land like poachers stealing bush meat—ivory from slaughtered elephants—oil from harpooned whales. We have come this day to advise you to leave. Your government will no longer be allowed to poach our country's land, our oil, steal our values as easily as a crow pecks meat from road kill, and take what it did not earn. You can bet we will be back," he threatens, lips pulled into an ugly sneer.

The group spins away, chanting, "Infidel! Go home! *Marg bar Carter*! *Marg bar Shah*!" I motion for Frankie to run along the opposite side of the pool, mouthing, "Bud, run!" He does, flying into my arms in terror.

And then, finally, the security door slams shut behind them. And they are gone.

Back inside, I gather my emotions, wrap my arms around Frankie who is terrified and sobbing; his little boy shoulders are trembling uncontrollably.

I blow out a ragged breath. "Frankie. Those people would not have done us harm," I say without conviction. "They were just bullies. Like the kind at school? Angry at something and taking it out on someone else. All words and no serious action. We'll be all right. Don't you worry. You'll see."

Frankie looks at me as if he can't quite believe it.

"They're trying to frighten people. Make them go home. Like Jeff at school. The one with the Mohawk?"

"Can't we go home, too?" asks Frankie.

Mother's back is positioned to us the whole time; her palms are gripping the edge of the sink. But after she's steeled herself—arms crossed against her chest, as if to protect herself from intruders, or from vile thoughts of them—she tries to regain calm in our frightened household by throwing around orders.

"Annie, you can start by mashing the potatoes and assembling the green bean casserole. Frankie, help Annie by sprinkling the green bean casserole with those dried onions in that can on the counter—Debbie, where are you?!"

Frankie stands close, watching, still crying; but the act of mashing, and my frenetic pounding calms me. I hand Frankie the potato masher now slathered with cream and butter for a lick, drain the green beans into a copper colander. I slide the dish over to Frankie. "Sprinkle away, Frankie." Soon after, Frankie's sobs quiet.

Dad grabs the phone to report the incident. It is promised that a military patrol car will patrol our neighborhood. Dad reminds Frankie he should never open the security door without first asking who's there. Frankie nods yes, seeming desperately sorry. My father pats his shoulder.

The phone shrieks in the family room. I hear Debbie rush out of her room to grab the call.

Staring down at the mass of green beans and dried onions I am preparing, I ask, "Should we call off the party?"

Mother checks the clock, thinking. She sighs, says, "Our guests are probably already on their way."

Debbie enters the kitchen, glum. "Mahjid is not coming," she says flatly. She gazes moodily out the back window.

"Why?" I ask.

"His parents don't think it's a good idea to come to an American's home."

"They're probably right based on what just happened."

"What just happened?"

"Didn't you hear the commotion downstairs?"

"No, I was blow-drying my hair."

I explain to her about the confrontation with the intruders, their threats. We overhear my father speaking with Tim and Carol in the living room.

"Shhh." I put a finger up to my lips.

"I have to wonder if our driver's behind all of this," my father is saying.

"The driver or the bodyguard?" asks Tim.

I remember Debbie's accusation about Amir being a spy for the Shah and for SAVAK.

"I saw first-hand the hatred of Mohammad for the Shah at our Fourth of July picnic. As for our bodyguard, it would make sense he is sympathetic with the Shah. He might just be confirming our allegiance with him and the regime. But you may be right that both could be sympathetic to Khomeini," my father says.

"Jesus, who knows anymore," Tim says.

"I swear to God, this distrust is ridiculous. In a democracy, you decide not to vote for a leader if you're unhappy with his performance. You don't topple his presidency. Call for his death. I was convinced we were doing something valid here. Teaching the Iranian Air Force to build up its military power. And I will tell you how frustrating the language barrier has been for my team."

"At the same time, you wouldn't be happy about a foreign government helping you to negotiate and write up procurement contracts, would you?" asks Carol. "Courting you for your oil?" She flits her eyelashes.

"It's not the same thing," my dad says.

But I can't help but wonder why not.

"Colonel Ross was also targeted."

"No way."

"Yes, he said he received a note and a phone call at his house, but he's never identified his residence anywhere, as a matter of security. Someone knew where to find him."

Now in the foyer, I shiver. My sister's eyes widen. Frankie has clamped his eyes shut and clenched his fists. The intercom buzzes. We jump up and rush into the family room, frightened, thinking we should look out a balcony door. Frankie runs ahead of us, raising his hands into the air and shouting, "No way, I'm not going down there." It was chaos in this apartment.

Tim rises up from our living room couch. He puts a hand on Frankie's shoulder, says, "I've got it covered, young fellow. Wait right here."

Mother scurries to the foyer to press the intercom button. "Moshdeh?" she asks, erratic fingers twirling her hair. Hand at her heart.

"*Salaam*! Yes, it is I, Moshdeh, and Ali, Amir, Reza, and Nouri—we have arrived right on time, as being punctual is a virtue here in Iran!" I hear loud male snickers. Mom seems to sink into herself in relief.

"Excellent. We've anticipated your prompt arrival and so we're ready! See you upstairs!" Mother seems subdued compared to Moshdeh. She calls out, "Annie, please bring out the fruit platter. Put the tea on! Everyone! Our guests are here, come, let's greet them!"

When we've all gathered in the foyer, she says, "Let's not discuss the events earlier, okay?" Mother always wanted everything to be so pleasant.

Minutes later, Moshdeh breezes into the apartment escorted by the men. In her customary manner, she kisses everyone several times on each cheek; Ali, Amir, and Reza hug the men with one arm, pat shoulders several times and muss up Frankie's hair. Amir stops short of me, blushes and says, "Hello there, Annie."

"Amir, it's so nice to see you again." I blush back. I want to hug him, but we only shake hands. He bows to my mother, as does Reza, who winks at me.

"May I inquire after everyone's health and well-being?" Moshdeh asks while Frankie prepares to take the guests' coats to the bedroom.

"We are well. Everything is good," Mother says loudly, throwing a threatening look at Frankie who appears to be on the verge of recounting the tale.

The adults adjourn to the living room to drink tea, eat fruit and talk. The rest of us linger in the family room. Funny how nervous I felt. But then I relax when Nouri, Reza, and Amir begin peppering us with questions about our tradition of Thanksgiving.

"Get the photo albums out, Annie," Debbie says. I find the one filled with photographs of the Mayflower, Plymouth Rock, and Plimoth Plantation, when my father was first in the Air Force at Hanscom AFB and would take us on sightseeing trips throughout Massachusetts—my mom and dad taking turns to smile brightly at the camera, Debbie and me each bundled into our bulky strollers.

Nouri, Reza, and Amir pore over our photographs. "I am even more certain I would like to visit America one day," Amir says. Excitement burns like fire in his eyes.

I am on the verge of tears from memories of the good old U.S.A.—where no one ever forced their way into our house.

"Sit. *Beshinid*," invites my mother when the turkey is roasted to a spectacular golden brown.

We hold hands and say grace. Mother expresses gratitude for the wonderful friendships made here in Iran—the dearest few seated here at our very table. "May the current unrest be resolved diplomatically and in peace. May all of us stay safe. Amen."

"*Befarma'id*," murmurs Moshdeh.

"I want you to meet my family," Amir says after dinner. "You would love *Noruz*, the Iranian New Year." Amir squeezes my hand. "I shall invite you to feast with my family then—on the first day of spring. There will be parades, children dressed up in costumes who will beat on pots for candy or money. There will be fireworks, fires in the street—but it will be a happy occasion for burning, not what the protestors are doing now, just a contest to see how high one can jump over the flames. I am the master leaper of my street, like a flying frog, I kid you not! I win every year." Amir beats his chest with his fist. "Our ancient Zoroastrian fire-keeper looks like your Santa Claus, but he wears a soot face. There are gifts and brightly colored eggs and an all-day picnic because it is bad luck to remain inside that day. We shall picnic in your favorite spot, Darband, yes?"

"Darband? I will count on this then, spending *Noruz* with you and your family. It sounds like our Halloween, July Fourth, Easter, and Christmas all rolled into one." I laugh at the description of yet another superstition. And who wouldn't like an all-day picnic? And with Amir.

Later, Reza corners Tim in our living room for war stories, as if war to him is a Hollywood movie set. I know from all the war stories I'd ever heard that it most certainly wouldn't be theater to Tim. And so I stare, worried, while Tim carefully picks his words. "Vietnam?" comes his rhetorical question. "I could tell you stories about Vietnam, Reza, I could ... the way the fog rolled off the mountains in the morning in a dense veil of cloud. Running bivouac through dank rice paddy fields, trudging through paths so muddy they smelled worse than rot. I could probably tell you about the sounds of the jungle at night, the tangled vines, the creepy-crawly bugs and the venomous snakes; the wet humidity that hung thick in the air like a suffocating blanket—way worse than the dry heat here. You see, there are degrees of suffocation," he says, shoulders slumped. "But war is ugly. So I won't tell you a thing." Tim laughs, shrugs and falls silent, and the light in Reza's eyes dims a notch, but Tim has told his story, however brief—his message that war is real and horrible is clear.

I've missed my usual breakfast meeting with Khoda, too busy with Thanksgiving prep the morning before. But I'd remembered to save some dark meat from the turkey's carcass to feed him the next morning. Khoda considers it a delicacy.

Four days after our own Thanksgiving feast, millions of Iran's countrymen convince themselves they've seen Khomeini's face in the moon—a lunar eclipse that last night— the creeping earth's shadow thought to be the Imam. People cry and moan, certain it is a sign from the heavens—that the stern Ayatollah is calling them to action from his Paris post.

Ironic that a speaker named Mr. O'Neil had come to our English class that very same day to talk about active listening. I am becoming more and more convinced that we should be actively listening to the Iranian people.

My father informs us that his detachment head—Colonel Ross and the heads of ARMISH-MAGG—had warned the serving American military and their families to be extra cautious from December eleventh through the start of the Islamic holy calendar.

CHAPTER 11

DECEMBER 1978

Good-bye, proud world! I'm going home:
Thou art not my friend, and I'm not thine.
Long through thy weary crowds I roam;
A river-ark on the ocean brine,
Long I've been tossed like the driven foam;
But now, proud world! I'm going home....

"Good-bye", Ralph Waldo Emerson

Riots continue in Tehran. The Roller Palace is burned to the ground, news that devastates me. On the second day of December, more than two million people gather in Tehran's Shahyad Square to petition for the Shah's overthrow, the return of Grand Ayatollah Ruhollah Khomeini. On December third, more riots occur, and then resulting casualties.

Amir begins to meet me at the bus stop each morning. Each afternoon he walks me home after school. Most times we stand outside the security door and kiss good-bye, still awkward around Debbie. Other times we sit with our backs resting against the wall and talk as Amir absently strokes my ravishing rose nail polish, speaks about work—the lack of it—how his mother is frightened about everything that is going on—Maryam's dangerous relationship with Afshin.

On December sixth, I go to school fully expecting to attend the entire day. But just after lunch, the school officials decide it would be wise to close school, at least through the holidays. The expected start up date, assuming all unrest has magically ended, is January sixth, after *Moharram* and *Ashura*. The classmates become wild at the news; a group of football players run into the school courtyard and moon the students lined up for their buses. There couldn't well be detention now, could there? Worried we'd have to drive through the same rebellion-filled streets of November fifth, I climb on my bus subdued, too pre-occupied for good-byes to those classmates who didn't ride my bus.

After the bus had returned me to my stop early and without conflict, I walk the short distance home, my gaze nervously sweeping the main boulevard. I find my parents at home, each wearing serious expressions. Debbie is sprawled out on the couch, flipping through a magazine; her work had been canceled indefinitely several days ago. Frankie has beat me home.

At once, my parents sit us down.

"We've received official word—we are expected to leave Iran immediately—in just a few days."

My mouth drops open. "But, we'll be back?" I ask, thinking of Amir. Remembering Khoda.

"Yes, a temporary relocation for military dependents, that's all. We selected Germany because of our ski vacation plans." We sit quietly and listen to our parents talk about something fun like skiing so solemnly.

"An early start to our ski vacation," Mother says with false enthusiasm, tears pooling in her eyes. "We'll each receive a per diem allowance so our vacation will be all paid for, except for ski tickets! And more good news—we'll be air lifted to Greece—we'll get to see it again!"

Frankie and I can't believe our good luck—to be out of school for a full month at Christmastime. "Hurray!" yells Frankie. The prospect of seeing Greece again excites me; this time I plan to remember it.

"We've been instructed to prepare a thousand pounds of household goods for shipment. We'll be doing just that for the next few days, what Dad will be doing while we are away vacationing for a month." Mother waves to all the *stuff* around us.

Dad chimes in, "We've placed large boxes in each of your rooms; please pack everything you consider important or precious to you. We'll have to leave some items behind. Please tuck away your passports into your purses—Debbie, Annette. Frankie, I have yours."

"What will we leave behind?" I ask.

"Some of our furniture. We came with thirteen thousand pounds."

This is sobering information for me. Although I'm not married to my pink-painted wood dresser, the Levitz dining room table, or our walnut stereo cabinet, it feels wrong to leave belongings behind.

"What about our car?" asks Frankie.

"No car," says my father, shaking his head. "It'll stay."

Frankie squeezes his eyes closed. "I love that car," he wails.

Mother gathers Frankie in a large bear hug. "Germany has such good public transportation we won't even miss our little blue Honda."

"The thing is," Dad says, "The *temporary* relocation is for military *dependents* only."

"But aren't we sending out our things?" I ask.

"A few things now, just in case."

"But what about you? And what about these?" I ask, pointing to the beautifully rich hand-woven carpets spread out on our cold marble floors, the rugs that Dad had brought home from the rug vendor to test, pair with our furniture.

"These are our shipping priority," Mother says fiercely. "The Levitz dining room table and matching hutch can be chopped up for firewood for all I care."

"I think these carpets suit us. I'll pay the rug merchant before joining you in Germany." Dad was scheduled to take a military hop to Berchtesgaden three days before Christmas. "The James's also chose Germany as their temporary relocation spot. Isn't that nice? They'll be joining us on our ski vacation to Berchtesgaden!"

Really? Joining us? I'm not sure how I felt about this.

Dad turns to me. "Do you have Amir's phone number?"

"I do, why?"

"I have to run some things by him. I think we're going to need his help."

"I'll tell him you need to speak to him at the bus stop this afternoon. He always meets me there."

"I'll go with you."

Amir arrives at my bus stop, sees me standing there with my father. At the wretched expression on my face, he asks, "Are you leaving?" He guessed it.

"Yes, in a couple of days."

"No, *nakon*, Annie!" His eyes say it all.

I grab his arm. "I'm sorry. It's true…. But it's just for a while." His gaze is beseeching. It hurts to return it.

All the while, my father is staring at his feet, but then he looks up. "Amir, come for dinner."

"Yes, Amir, come," I say. We are overwhelmed with emotion. At dinner, we tell Amir about skiing; he wishes he could take us to Dezin, where he once saw the Shah and Empress Farah skiing. When things were so different, so much nicer.

The next morning each of us go to work packing, an all-day affair. Mid afternoon we stop to rest. I find some gardening tools in the garage.

"Do you think Mr. and Mrs. Jamison might like these?" I ask my mother. Rose clippers and a spade.

Mother regards me sadly. "Didn't I tell you? Mr. and Mrs. Jamison have left the country." She fiddles with her shirt.

It surprises me she hadn't told me. But she is explaining now.

"Mr. Jamison has resigned as professor of Chemistry at the Community School. The danger finally hit home after those students invaded their apartment."

"I can understand that."

"The Jamisons have asked us to check on their home every so often until he manages to sell it." She pauses, smiles secretively. "I must show you something the Jamisons left behind, Annette." Her smile widens. "Annie, go grab the keys on the hook in the foyer; they're on the green key chain."

That night my father is in the living room reading the Info-Grams that the Public Affairs Office has been sending out. Mom and I have just returned from the Jamisons' house, practically running from their security door to ours; Mother is out of breath, not feeling the least bit foolish about our skittishness as we climb the stairs and rush into the apartment.

Dad looks up. "Good, you're home." His expression is grim.

"What's wrong?" I stride over to his seat on the couch, grab a corner of the paper. "Can I see?"

"Annie, it's frightening." He shoves his shoulder at me and hides what he's reading.

"I can handle it. Please?"

"If you must." He hands me the December sixth Info-gram with a sigh.

I read:

At 12:15, there was a large demonstration in the Tajrish area, which reportedly involved an undetermined number of casualties. The demonstration covered the Tajrish, Niavaran and Darband areas.

There was a large demonstration in the Chizar-Geytarieh area, which involved an undetermined number of casualties.

At 22:40 hours, people walking in the street and sporadic gunfire were reported in from Nesa Alley near Pahlavi Boulevard and Old Shemiran. Power went off at 22:00 hours and returned at 22:40 hours in that area.

The door was broken down by demonstrators at the residence of a U.S. citizen near Pahlavi.

I gulp back saliva.

Small arms and automatic weapons fire reported in the Golestan Two and Five areas at 23:00 hours.

A firebomb was thrown into an apartment building on Farmanieh at 22:00 hours; a U.S. citizen lives on the third floor, but only the first two floors were affected. No injuries reported.

Crowds and firing were reported in the area of the Blue Mosque at 21:40 hours.

At Farmanieh, Kamranieh, two teenage boys painted "I will kill you and the King" on a telephone pole. Automatic weapons fire was also reported in the area (at 21:45 hours).

And finally:

Isfahan reported that the residence of a U.S. officer was firebombed. The officer had moved out on 4 December after his landlord received a threat on 3 December that if the American did not move, the house would be destroyed.

My shaking hands wrinkle the bulletin involuntarily. "Well, that's certainly scary," I say, handing it back to Dad, rushing from the room, tears prickling behind my eyes.

Later in bed, I listen to what could be my final evening Call to Prayer—tonight, thankfully, not accompanied by gunfire. Why was one night quieter than another? I drift off to sleep, but then the Call to Prayer entreats me to stay awake—like a lover wanting more.

The next afternoon, when Amir arrives at our security door, I am ready for him. I have dressed carefully, combed my hair until it shone like spun gold. I grab a set of keys from the hook in the hallway and skip downstairs to greet him, steering him out of the doorway and down the alley to the Jamisons' apartment.

"How's the packing coming?" he asks.

"Eh," I say. "It's never fun."

I open the Jamisons' gate and point to the bare branches of the hardy rose bush in the poolside garden. "Transplant it into your own garden for me, will you?"

"Yes, Annie, certainly," Amir says, "But you will be back?" His part statement/part question is filled with undisguised hope.

I nod yes through a blur of tears, hoping. "Let's go upstairs. I want to show you something."

In the light of day, it is clear that dust is taking up space on the bookshelves now instead of leather-spined novels and chubby Buddhas. The blue-tone Persian carpets are gone. The ivory-tusked elephants are off to other adventures. Our footsteps echo over the marble living room floor, where recently we'd celebrated Mr. Jamison's homecoming. There, still spanning the room's width is the Jamisons' large, grand piano.

"For you," I say to Amir. "Mr. Jamison would like you and your family to have it. To keep it, or sell it for money, or a vacation—to help pay for Maryam's university. It's entirely up to you." I lift the piano cover to snatch an envelope with Amir's name on it in Mr. Jamison's shaky handwriting. "Money, to move it." Emotion swells in me at the generosity of the gift.

"Ah, this is so very nice of Mr. Jamison, but I cannot accept this wonderful gift."

"Yes, you can. It's Mr. Jamison's expression of gratitude for keeping us all safe." I smile, anticipating his next sentence.

"No, I cannot." Amir shakes his head. An impish smile tugs at the corners of his mouth.

"Yes, you can," I repeat, laughing. "He wants you to."

"No, I cannot."

And I have counted three refusals already….

"If I must ... I accept," Amir says next, flashing a smile brimming with gratitude. He stares at the large black piano in disbelief, walks hesitantly over to it, plays a tune I recognize is the Persian song from Debbie's birthday party:

Tavallod, Tavallod
Tavallodet mobarak
Mobarak, Mobarak
Tavallodet mobarak

After he has finished playing, and he has rubbed his hand over the shiny exterior, he pulls me to him. I kiss him and tears stream down my face. "Let's not say good-bye yet." My voice sounds rough like sandpaper.

"You'll be back?" Amir's gaze is hopeful and sweet, and my heart aches. I feel my eyes sting.

I shrug my shoulders. "I hope so."

Amir runs his tongue along his top lip. I stand still, but the feeling of lust is like bath water between my legs. Without thinking, I reach up with aching fingers and begin to unbutton the delicate seed pearl buttons on the front of my sheer white blouse. My smile turns serious. "Would you like?" I almost breathe out the question.

Amir swallows hard, but does not step away.

"Would this be nice?" I ask, pulling my shirt open, letting it hang. I reach behind my back and unclasp my bra, which falls loose and open. Amir stares, and my skin burns as much as my thoughts. And he moves into me, pulls my blouse down and off, kneels and tugs me down to my knees, pressing his warm lips between my chilled breasts. Suddenly, I'm on my back on the marble floor, and I don't mind, and then he's on top of me, the warmth of his skin radiating through his clothes. I reach up for the tarnished gold button on his jeans, inches above my thighs. And he lets me. My fingers shake as I tug at his pants, wriggle out of my own skirt, and my underwear. And he's back down on me, hips pressing hard against mine. And then it's all heat and fire.

He does everything I had always imagined and more. I am terrified, but it is lovely and painful, the grace he uses on the soccer field and on the dance floor is there in his moves, all a hasty blur, until we push away, breaths stuck in our chests in amazement, eyes willing the other to look away, kisses as deep as the feelings between us. And when a single tear wets my bare breast, I bolt up from the floor, scurry for my clothes, flushed red with an emotion so raw, it feels like love.

The morning of evacuation day I awake early before the light erases the pre-dawn darkness to memorize my life in Tehran. As the morning brightens, I climb up onto the sturdy flat roof, to gaze over our crowded neighborhood streets, the now fruitless pomegranate orchard to the west, the barren dusty soccer field to the east, the majestic snow-covered Alborz Mountains. I will miss them.

It is misting outside and cold, so I return inside and wander around, careful not to wake Carol on the family room couch, Tim on the living room one, committing to memory the orange discs in the kitchen, the gray-veined marble floors, the view out the window, the Levitz dining room table and matching hutch I may never see again. I gaze down into the vinyl-covered pool my father had only recently drained. I drink it all in, certainly feeling different than I'd felt six months ago, when we first arrived, fresh with anticipation, in hindsight, naive?

Last night plays over and over in my mind. I giggle. My back is sore; a yellowish bruise has formed on each of my shoulder blades that I'd noticed after my shower this morning. But I am able to ignore the pain for memories of Amir's tender touches, thoughts of his gaze, how right it felt to do what we had. But at the same time … irresponsible. I take a breath. But I have knowledge of my own body, how feelings of sadness are magnified in me today two-fold; the puffiness of my normally flat stomach makes me check the calendar, reach into my toiletry bag and rush to the bathroom. And afterward, I'm able to breathe a sigh of relief, promise myself I would be more careful in the future, responsible, if there's ever a next time. With Amir.

Last evening, after I'd returned home from the Jamisons, starry-eyed and pre-occupied with thoughts of Amir, guilty in the harsh light of our kitchen, and facing my parents who had asked innocently for Amir's reaction to his gift, Moshdeh surprised us with a visit, a good-bye "for now". She brought us her favorite meal, *Khoresht Fesenjan*, a Persian chicken stew made with pomegranate juice and walnuts, which she sat and ate with us. After dinner, I could hear Moshdeh's lofty laugh, Mother giggling in the living room as they sipped *Pomtinis*, a cocktail beverage made with pomegranate and grapefruit juices, vodka, and sour mix. I heard Moshdeh comment on how difficult it was becoming to find alcohol.

"Alcohol is disappearing from the stores' shelves like prisoners to Evin Prison," she'd complained. "Along with kerosene, gasoline—food."

"Who needs food?" teased Mother. "Before, it had only been toilet paper," she said, spilling into a fit of giggles fueled by alcohol.

Last night I'd also heard the muffled sounds of Debbie crying after she'd said good-bye to Mahjid by phone—his parents still forbade him to come to our house. I'd also called Alika to say good-bye. It was a night of melancholy.

After my usual powered milk and cereal for breakfast, I neatly pack my toiletries into a small bag and head downstairs. Amir had said he'd come over this morning to say good-bye, and I knew he'd be waiting. And he is.

"Amir."

I startle him. He is sitting on the ground, back resting against our security wall, eyes closed.

He scrambles to his feet. "Annie."

"Come on up. We're getting ready to go to the commissary where I guess buses will take us to the airport. Everyone wants to say good-bye to you." I check my watch. Khoda's feeding time. And sure enough, there he comes rushing towards us, down the alley.

Amir steps back, stunned, watching curiously as I bend to pat Khoda's head.

"Wait one second?" I leave to gather Khoda's food in the garage. Amir looks as if he doesn't know what to do, left alone with a dog. I return, set the food bowl down in the alley. Khoda woofs it down in a few gulps.

"The dog from the pomegranate orchard?"

"Yes. One in the same. Khoda, *now*. We've been feeding him. He's going to miss me." I gaze down at my beloved *jube* dog, and my stomach knots.

"I'll look out for Khoda for you while you are gone." Amir's brow is furrowed. He eyes Khoda with a mix of interest and distrust.

"Thanks." Emotion swells in me for Amir. I sit with Khoda, grab his scruffy neck, kiss him on his black button nose. "Be good, Khoda." I sigh, rise up. "Let's get this over with."

Amir follows me upstairs. He closes his eyes at all the boxes. Mom joins us in the kitchen, then Frankie and Debbie wander in.

Amir hoists Frankie into the air and flies him around in circles. "I'll miss you very much Frankie, *Kheili*, if you don't come back. You will keep up with your soccer?"

"I will!"

"Debbie, you will be certain to keep out of trouble? Keep taking those very good photographs?"

"I will. Thank you. Tell Reza good-bye for me, if you see him, will you?" Debbie asks.

"Tell Reza bye for *all of us*," I say. "And Nouri."

Amir nods firmly and says, "Reza has convinced himself you will be back. He says he shall see you after your ski vacation." Amir turns to Mother. "Mrs. Patterson, I hope to sell your Levitz furniture for you. Aunt Laleh is very interested in both pieces, the table and the hutch—I hope that you will find the antique furniture you have always desired to replace them with if you cannot come back, *Inshallah*," he says, bowing to her.

Dad enters the room, carrying a roll of packing tape. "Amir, my friend, I'm afraid you'll be seeing more of me during the coming days."

Amir grins ear to ear. "We have lots to do, Mr. Patterson— carpets are our priority." Amir glances over to Mother who grabs him up in a tight bear hug.

"You know how much we appreciate you? All your help?" She kisses Amir's cheek. Embarrassed by Mother's affection, he smiles back shyly. "Amir, I have a gift for you." She reaches up into the cabinet and brings down Vladlena, the tea cozy from their trip to Russia.

Amir starts laughing, thanks Mother. "I will perch it on top of my *samovar*," he says. Still, he seems pre-occupied.

Reserved. He turns his attention towards me. He blows out a sigh. And then my family leaves the kitchen to give us privacy.

"Annie … my dear."

"Amir."

"Please don't forget me if you cannot come back."

"How could I ever forget you?" I say, moving into him. "You're the sun in my sky; you got that blinding aura." I smile gently, noticing the creases around his brown eyes. We hug tightly, reluctant to separate, standing beneath the large orange discs I had come to love, the pale-yellow radio that had so often been the bearer of unwelcome news.

"But you never met my family," he says sadly, as we pull away.

"I know, but I've heard stories. I love your mother and father for creating *you*." I stab a finger into his chest.

Anguished, Amir says, "I'm sorry about all of this," hands outstretched.

"I know."

"Ready?" my father calls from the other room.

"Ready." I sigh, touch Amir's lovely and familiar face and kiss him deeply.

He pretends to stumble backwards, wipe imaginary sweat from his forehead. "Annie. Open up your hand." He pulls something from his pocket, curls it into his fist.

I hold up my palm.

Gently, he drops a white gold puzzle ring on my hand.

"You didn't?"

"I did," he says, sheepishly.

I slide the shiny intertwined bands of gold on my shaking finger. "I shall cherish your gift always."

"You like?" Amir asks, smiling widely.

"I love."

Choking down a lump in my throat, I walk backwards, waving. Amir chooses instead to study the misting rain outside the window, swiping at his eyes with the back of his hand.

"Till we meet again."

He smiles back, nods firmly, and says, "After vacation." Willing us both to believe it.

Reluctantly, I leave Amir alone in the kitchen staring out the window. After my tears had abated, I see that Tim is awake and is carrying luggage downstairs. Carol is also up but still in her pajamas, sleepy-eyed. She gives us all a warm hug. "Careful Pattersons."

"Careful, back," cautions my sister.

"See you on the flip side," Carol says.

Mr. Ned meets us in the stair hall to say good-bye, grab Amir so he can show him his apartment—chock full of wood furniture like ours that might interest Amir's aunts, uncles or cousins. I hug Mr. Ned good-bye, tears filling up my eyes.

"Take care of yourself, darling, you hear?" he says.

I nod, turn to my father, hold up a finger and ask quickly, "Wait one second?" Already jingling his keys, Dad nods to me as I brush past Mr. Ned and rush back into the kitchen. I throw my arms around a surprised Amir's neck. "Bye, *Delbar*, Amir. *Dúset daram*," I say. I grip his hand, then let it go. The burden of grief in his eyes looks like a weight he can no longer bear to lift.

Moments later, we are packed like sardines into our Honda with our over-stuffed suitcases. My father exits our underground parking garage, drives us past our pool through the once feared, now beloved security door. It closes behind us with a firm click. A sound so final.

The streets are quiet at this hour and on a weekend—even demonstrators needed their rest—and so we head to the commissary without conflict to await "evacuation", a word that seems an exaggeration to me, but is apt.

My father deposits us and our suitcases beneath the entrance canopy and pulls away to find a parking spot. A line is forming outside to gain entry to the buses when they come. A woman near me wears a flag-embossed blue and red rain jacket. Another has on a gauzy, flowered head scarf over a beehive hairstyle like my mother's; she wears dark eye liner and mascara that have run in streaks from either the rain or her tears.

We take turns milling about the commissary and holding our space in line. It had opened to such fanfare and now had thinning inventory. A final sad hurrah to have so many people here again.

We are wearing warm winter jackets, and it is cold and raw outside, like our emotions. Mom spies Mrs. James, John, and Kelly at the front of the line. I wonder if we should go speak to them, but figure we'd have plenty of time to talk in Germany. I don't feel much like conversation.

Around lunchtime, a caravan of five buses pulls into the lot, and a cheer erupts from the crowd: "*U.S.A. U.S.A!*" Reluctantly, Mother gives Dad an emotional hug and Debbie, Frankie, and I follow with bear hugs and kisses. He steps back to hide his tears, and then lets us board the bus as he takes shelter again beneath the commissary canopy.

John, Kelly, and Mrs. James grab the first bus in line, and we board the last. As the bus pulls away from the curb, I wave out the half-opened window to my father like a zealot, wanting to wave good-bye all the while he appeared smaller and smaller the further we went. Tears begin to pour from my eyes, and I continue to wave like a maniac until he is out of sight.

Now apprehensive to be riding on a large bus filled with Americans, I search the landscape for a would-be assassin looking to throw a pipe bomb into or underneath our bus from a speeding motorcycle. My stomach is in knots. The trees outside the bus are leafless and the sky is spitting rain. Garbage still litters the streets. Burned remains of buildings become ugly reminders of the tumult we are now permitted to leave but our "non-dependent" family members still face.

Several yards behind the bus, there is indeed a speeding motorcyclist, a young sun-glassed clad Iranian man, a backpack slung over his shoulder. He's traveling fast, weaving in and out of traffic and gaining on us.

But no one but me seems worried. The armed guard at the front of the bus is cracking jokes in Farsi to the driver and smacking his gum; the guard at the rear watches out the back in the general direction of the speeding motorcyclist, but so far his gun remains at his shoulder. The bus is sandwiched between two Iranian military escorts from the American/Iranian motor pool. *Why worry?*

The motorcyclist catches up to the bus and shifts to the left lane to pass. The cyclist lifts his hand from the handlebars, reaches up behind his shoulder, pulls out from his anchored backpack a small American flag, the kind you'd wave at a Fourth of July parade, my bed tent pole. A wide goofy grin fills his face.

"*Mahjid*?!" Debbie cries. She hangs out the bus window and waves. The armed guards on the bus shout in Farsi, point both submachine guns out the window, but Mahjid only shrugs and blows Debbie a kiss, mouthing, "Good-bye!" Mahjid is our Star-Spangled Banner, a cheering sports fan in the stands, a boy expressing loyalty to his girl. Tears stream down Debbie's face like the rivulets of rain flowing down the bus windows.

We reach the airport gates. The bus driver races across the tarmac to a waiting cargo plane. A second cheer erupts from within the bus. But delighted cries soon turn to moans of despair as we board. Two rows of strung up seats made of woven orange fabric face each other in a cramped unembellished interior. It is obvious we are the cargo on this flight.

"Passengers, please deposit your passports into the bag we're passing around. It'll speed up the process of our leaving," an officer in a khaki flight suit tells us. I drop my passport into a large plastic bag along with all the others.

The slight muscle pull Mom had suffered when she lugged her suitcase on board is bothering her. She is becoming hysterical without my father. Her usual determination to mask her feelings for us is failing her. There are no flight attendants to calm her down or give her aspirin. No drinks or peanuts. Beads of sweat have formed on her upper lip and sweat has darkened her bangs black. "Not only does my back hurt," she hisses, "Moshdeh's *Pomtinis* gave me a headache! And my stomach," she groans, "the grapefruit juice has given me acid reflux."

And I wish I could order tomato juice for her like on a commercial flight, a possible cure for hangovers. I dig around in my purse, find some Ritz crackers beneath my copy of *The Thorn Birds*. "Here. Eat. The crackers will help to settle your stomach."

I fan my face with my book. But we continue to sit on the runway. Debbie is asleep across the aisle in a Dramamine-induced coma, mouth agape. Frankie is also napping. We wait. And then we wait.

After several hours and my mother having complained so much about her back that the gauzy-scarfed woman with the dripping mascara hands Mother some Vicodin, there comes the sound of static and the pilot's voice over the loud speaker. "Passengers, prepare for take off." A low gasp sounds in the airplane.

Once the steel stairs are moved away, cheers erupt in the cabin. *U.S.A, U.S.A.!* A rush of patriotism overcomes me. I give my mother a hug as best as I can from my strapped-in orange-netted seat and look around. For many people, cheers are now turning to tears, each of us wondering if there were a Plexiglas window we could look out, would we still see the Alborz Mountains? The rooftops of Tehran? Will our abandoned husbands and fathers be okay?

Three hours later, we land in Greece. The wheels skim the tarmac smoothly. Our entry into the airport is orderly; through customs, it is seamless. We gather up our passports. I stare at the blue-vinyl book, open it, and the royal blue swirls and dots of Persian making our exit from Iran official are there like I knew they'd be.

Despite the order at the Athens airport, Mother's back pain is unbearable for her. Her hair is sticking up untidily, but she doesn't seem to care. Debbie, Frankie, and I are left to struggle with all of our suitcases on our own, and to wrestle with our feelings about the life change that has suddenly been thrust upon us.

Through the open window of our hotel room, the familiar fragrance of grilled meat floats in the air, but this time the aroma is tangy. We are staying overnight in a seaside hotel called the Apollo Palace, which gets me thinking about the Roller Palace. Waves of nostalgia break over me. And though it is a seaside resort, Mother retires to bed immediately in a Vicodin-induced fatigue, but good for her to be numbed without my father.

But for us, it was not like she'd promised at all—that this temporary relocation would be a chance for us to remember Greece. My dreams of running out for a glimpse of the Mediterranean Sea, to buy sponges in a Greek market, or sample a Gyro or Souvlaki, are dashed. Mother's empty promises are just that.

My bedside radio plays "The Girl from Ipanema", a song that always brings me back to my childhood: *Tall and tan and young and lovely, the girl from Ipanema goes walking…. But each day, when she walks to the sea, she looks straight ahead, and not at me….* And is this how John thinks of me? That I am always looking past him, to Mike Morales, and now to Amir?

Germany, beautiful Germany, allows me to capture the spirit of Christmas despite my missing Amir. Often, John and I take to strolling the Walking Strasse's snow-covered cobblestone streets.

Each night in the sterile hotel room I share with my sister, Debbie listens to her shortwave radio in an effort to uncover news about Iran. Each of us is concerned for our father, all our Iranian friends, and especially worried about Amir and Mahjid. I remember how the arm-banned intruder had said, *"Colonel,"* with dripping sarcasm, the hatred that had darkened his eyes black.

But in Wiesbaden, there was always something to do—shopping, cafés, museums, restaurants—all at our mothers' fingertips. Mrs. James never mentions her unkind words to me. I understand them to be a result of too much wine, and her apology lacking because of no memory of it.

Hotel living is a novelty for us—the game room, the snack machines, taking all our meals in the hotel restaurant, including crocks of cheesy French Onion soup at suppertime. And our mothers enjoy the break from meal planning and preparing, take to sipping tea or an occasional glass of Blue Nun Riesling in the hotel bar after a day at the museum, or shopping for leaded German crystal in glitzy shops.

My father calls periodically, depending on the reliability of the telephone service, tells Frankie and me that the day after our evacuation it snowed in Tehran for the first time that year. Frankie smiles politely, now used to the pure white snow in Wiesbaden.

Just the sound of Dad's voice makes me miss him. He tells Mom about a disturbance at Lavizan. I hear enough of Mother's one-sided murmurings and gasps to grasp that there had been a shoot-out there that had killed several Iranian officers. Instead of this, Mom describes Dad's haggling with Amir's family, how much furniture they are buying, how he travels immediately to the Office of Finance to convert their rials to American dollars, how the funds are already on the way to us. Dad and Mr. Ned have moved out of our apartment house to the James's, so they can be closer to the Gulf District and work and should the roving group of demonstrators return, and to save on gas because lines at gas stations are miles long. I missed Dad so much, I couldn't wait for our family ski trip to Berchtesgaden. Berchtesgaden's General Walker Hotel, which offers reduced rates for government personnel, the reason Dad chose it, was to become my first stay at a European "luxury" hotel, and I'm excited.

We arrive in Berchtesgaden by bus Christmas Eve afternoon with Dad. He had joined us in Germany two days before, as promised. The relief is palpable—our father is off Iranian soil—at least for now.

The impressive lobby area is as big as a truck; underfoot is a large oriental carpet and I wonder if it's from Iran. Off the lobby is a fancy restaurant, all decorated to the hilt in Christmas finery, including a tall Christmas tree weighed down to the hardwood floor with ornaments as big as softballs and lit up like the Tehran night sky. Our room is large enough to accommodate the family, unheard of in a conventional hotel.

"No Christmas presents or Christmas tree this year." My parents tell us that a Christmas trip to a Bavarian hotel is a suitable substitute for the Christmas gifts we'd ordinarily receive. "The hotel's lobbies are filled with all the Christmas trees you'd ever want to see and fireplaces you can curl up next to with a good book."

But I decide I do not share the same opinion. I find a small Charlie Brown pine in the woods outside our hotel and drag it into our room. Kelly places the only tangible Christmas gift we'd receive that year under it, a wooden manger Christmas ornament she'd lifted from a store on the Walking Strasse. She places a couple of ornaments smuggled from downstairs off the lobby tree. We stand back, proud of our handiwork. When news of her five-finger discount breaks, my mother returns our one and only Christmas present to the Christmas shop downtown and sneaks the ornaments back downstairs.

On Christmas Eve, my parents learn a Texaco executive in Iran had been assassinated two days earlier, by a group called the Mujahidin, gunned downed as he drove to work. They'd talked about it in hushed tones, and we already knew that muted conversations never meant anything good, which made us listen carefully, pretending not to. Our pre-planned Christmas Eve celebration to the hotel bar for hors d'oeuvres and drinks, though, was to go on as planned. But when we were all gathered around the mahogany bar table, our parents had only stared absently into their wine goblets, unable to muster any real enthusiasm for our modest family party.

Christmas Day we attend an open air mass in the woods. Dad prays for his fallen comrade from Texaco. I stare up at the tall fragrant pine trees that tower above us like the spires of minarets from my bench-like pew, scarred and mottled by carpenter aunts and worms, similar to how I felt without Amir. After mass, Dad and I spend hours exploring the hotel grounds, and chunky snow flakes begin to fall around us like the paper bits and soot that had floated out of burning buildings in Tehran. Dad imagines Hitler plotting his horrific genocide and ethnic cleansing, smoking a corn cob pipe, and nursing a crystal glass of golden brandy before he tousled with his lover,

Eva Braun, in a cabin hideout outside the complex's main buildings. But then Dad shivers in his thin navy pea coat.

Late afternoon, we feast on stuffed roasted goose and fingerling potatoes, piped acorn squash baked to a crusty glow. And after dinner, I am stunned to receive special permission to call Amir, but not before my father receives his own telephone call about a disturbance at the United States Embassy—a group of students have driven a Paykan through the embassy gates and set it on fire.

Now alone in our hotel room I dial Amir's phone number. Within seconds, Amir's mother has answered. "*Salaam*, Annie!" she shouts in a high-pitched Farsi titter. She beckons Amir to the phone, "Amir, it is Annie! *Ajaleh kon!*"

And the sounds of approaching footsteps come through the receiver. A breathless and happy Amir shouts into the phone, "Annie! *Salaam*! You called! Merry Christmas, *Delbar!*"

"Hi, Amir! This telephone call is my one true Christmas present this year. How are you? Are you okay? Are things dangerous? How's work?" I shower him with questions. "Did you and your family have a peaceful *Moharram* and *Ashura*?!"

"*Ashura* was very good." Amir knew, and my father had said, that there had been a large demonstration a week and a half ago in Shahyad Square, on *Ashura*. And the demonstrations were surprisingly peaceful. Many had the opinion that the Shah's days seemed numbered. Amir laughs at my barrage of questions, tries to answer them one by one. "Yes, I am well. Very good. Conditions are deteriorating, but me? I am always avoiding trouble. Work is slow. Sometimes, I repair protestor-damaged cars. But these days I sell nothing. No cars. Little money. Gas lines run miles long. The Buick dealership was burned. All the cars ruined, finished. Just like that. The electricity and telephone never operate. I am so grateful we speak today. There was rioting again today in

Tehran. Burning and rocks again through all the buildings. It seems there is no more peace."

It had already been declared that the Ayatollah would be the Iranian people's new leader. The Shah would appoint a new prime minister, Shapour Bakhtiar, a former high-ranking member of Mossadegh's National Front, who once opposed the Shah who was planning to leave soon. The Shah would be calling it an extended vacation. It was only a matter of time.

"Is Mr. Patterson getting his well-awaited R&R?" Amir asks.

"Yes, he is." I laugh.

"Annie, I miss you. All is very bad here. Nothing is the same. *Deltang'am.*"

I close my eyes, whisper, "I miss you, too," reveling in the voice that once was so foreign to me and now is music to my ears. His endearment of *"Deltang'am"* meant he longed for me. I smile into the phone.

"How's Khoda?" I ask.

"Your mangy dog? Khoda, he is very good," Amir assures me, a smile in his voice. "I'd arranged for Azar, the gardener, to feed him. Khoda now sits in his lap, plays Frisbee with him all around the pomegranate orchard, sleeps in the hut on cold nights on a dog bed Azar's *bhaji* made for him. Azar cannot take him home because their Persian cat would not tolerate it."

"A huge outcome for Khoda, then," I say, grinning into the phone, consulting my watch. I fiddle with my sweater, pick at a loose thread. Without wanting to, I say, "I have to go."

"*Nakon*, no! It is much too early!" Amir complains.

"Money, you know. My dad. Gave me a time limit."

"Ah yes, your dad. He negotiated the sale of your furniture with Aunt Laleh. But wait. Tell me about you. You like it there?!" Amir asks.

"It's okay," I say, my voice small.

"Is anything wrong?"

"No, I'm just lonely."

"New things take getting used to. Like when you first came here? Remember to think of me though, *baleh*? Tell John to leave you alone with his Texan charms, sneakers, and baseball cap!"

"*Baleh*. Not a single worry."

And Amir's laughter turns serious. "He may be your friend if you feel you need them. *Dúset daram. Ashe gh etam.*"

An involuntary gasp escapes me before I can contain it. He hadn't said, "I love you" before. *Dúset daram* in Farsi is considered a gentle I love you, but *Ashe gh etam* is serious. "*Ashe gh etam,*" I say. "*Careful.*"

"Annie. I will be careful."

"Promise me?" I sit still on my hotel bed, worried. Bleak with the knowledge that we have nothing left to say to each other but good-bye. But the words catch in my throat. "*Khoda ha fez,*" I say. Good-bye is much easier in Farsi.

"*Khoda ha fez*, Annie. I promise I will be careful."

The phone line goes dead, and I linger in quiet desolation— worried for Amir in the chaos of the faltering regime. *What is the embattled Shah thinking now, as he listens to gunfire, the shouts of his people calling for his death through the walls of his gilded palace.*

CHAPTER 12

JANUARY, FEBRUARY 1979, GERMANY

*"Edelweiss, Edelweiss
Bless my homeland forever"*

Rodgers and Hammerstein, *The Sound of Music*;
Irving Berlin, composer

January sixth is fast approaching and TAS is still closed. The official word comes. Our temporary relocation is, in fact, permanent. Therefore, one cold January day John and I travel with my mother and Mrs. James to register to finish out the school year at the American high school in Wiesbaden, Germany—coincidentally, the school Priscilla Presley had attended before she married Elvis. And my mother likes this fact because Dad resembles the younger Elvis. It made sense; we had to go to school. There were several other Iran evacuees already registered, and the school administration promised to be sensitive to our dilemma. The school secretary touches my hand, murmurs, "How awful for you, honey, how scary; welcome to Germany, you'll be safe here, now." I begin to cry.

My father and Mr. James have already grabbed a hop back to Iran after Christmas vacation. We are nervous. While Dad was away, there were mass killings and firebombs at demonstrations in Meshad and Shiraz. Mobs turned on the secret police—ransacked a SAVAK safe house, hanged agents, displayed torture equipment and instruments they'd discovered. There was also news of the killing of a twenty-seven-year-old Tehran University professor and demonstrations surrounding his funeral procession. Amir had been right when he'd said that peace had been short-lived.

Despite my worry for Dad, Mr. James, and Amir, I feel an overwhelming unease about my own life. Unlike in Iran, where we'd shopped shoulder-to-shoulder at the commissary among the three branches of the military, here in Wiesbaden, a peroxide blonde army brat is after me at school. And I am terrified of her, understanding now how being bullied can make you feel hunted, like a wild boar at the Caspian Sea. I tell John about her, but he is no help, settling into the routine of school with ease—making the basketball team, *liking school*. Wanting me to be positive. But while he is able to saunter to practice every afternoon after school happily dribbling a basketball, I am forced to plan my exit strategy to my bus, to avoid an encounter with the peroxide blonde girl-bully, who I eventually learn is named Tammy. Anytime she passes me in the hallway, she says, "Hey, you, *Iranian chica*, meet me after school. I have a *bone* to pick with you." And I usually run in the opposite direction, ashamed of my cowardice while her sarcastic snickers follow me down the hall like a bitter aftertaste.

Meanwhile, we become minor celebrities as Iran evacuees, now such a newsworthy region. And I believe that we don't deserve such glory. But in some ways, school in Germany is easier than in Iran—the bus ride is short, minutes from the hotel, and it's a typical school bus—army green with shredded vinyl seats patched up in gray duct tape. John and I meet for lunch daily. School days are back to the usual Monday through Friday. And Mademoiselle Zehring, my new enthusiastic French teacher, has kinky blond ringlets and a mouth full of new beautiful teeth after a crash on the Autobahn. And she's cool. She takes joy in reading the pages of my French diary I'd continued where I'd left off, writing about the day the Shah left Iran with his wife, Farah, for medical purposes, saying it was a long-needed vacation. How the Shah had recently appointed Shapour Bakhtiar to run the country, and before he boarded the plane that would take him from Iran, he'd grabbed soil as a bittersweet souvenir. Oh, and how the Iranian people had celebrated with all their hearts and souls; jubilant masses had gathered in the streets, crying, moaning, dancing, and burning money that held the toppled Shah's picture as they kissed and hugged one another, raised their arms in victory. And Miss Zehring would often add notations in the margin, "*Bon! Annie, quelle lecon du lesson d'histoire!*" And, "*Merci* est thank you (également) en Farsi, *aussie*?! But all I felt was melancholy and fear.

"But why is Dad still there when the Shah is gone?" I ask my mother one day.

"Because the Shah's government is still there, and we must support it. You understand?"

But the Iranian people are calling for Khomeini, their voices are beckoning, calling him home, even with poetry:

The day the Imam (Khomeini) returns,
No one will tell lies anymore...
People will become brothers,
They shall share the bread of their joy together
In justice and in sincerity...
The Imam must return
So that justice may sit upon its throne,
So that evil, treachery and hatred
Are eliminated from the face of time.
When the Imam returns,
Iran, this broken, wounded mother,
Shall forever be liberated.

The news we receive now from Dad is usually bad—no gas, no power, a foot of snow one January day. I am relieved to hear that Carol and Tim have been sent to other assignments—Carol back to Pease Air Force Base in New Hampshire near her family, Tim to Lackland Air Force Base in Texas. After Mom drags it out of him, my father confesses that an American executive in Kerman had been found dead in his apartment, his throat slit. The killers had written in his blood on the bedroom wall, "return to your country." Two days later, the Chief of Staff of ARMISH-MAGG, an Army Colonel I didn't know, and my father had only heard of, had been found hanged in his home, apparently a victim of suicide. Mom whispers about it with Debbie in our cramped hotel room. And how I remember those exact words from our own Thanksgiving Day, as if they'd been iron-branded on my brain, "return to your country." But here we sit in Germany, still gone.

Events become fluid in Iran throughout February. On February first, Khomeini returns to Iran from exile to a great display of emotion from the Iranian people. Fear fills my heart. *What will happen now? Will he be righteous? Just?*

"Final victory will come when all foreigners are out of the country," he tells his people, and then he threatens to cut off the hands of all foreigners who still remain in Iran. Finally, the United States Ambassador orders all United States dependents out of Iran. But only dependents. On February fourth, Khomeini appoints Mehdi Barzargan as prime minister of "The Interim Government of Iran." On February ninth, fighting breaks out between pro-Khomeini technicians of the Iranian Air Force and the Imperial Guard. We are sick with worry about Dad, until he manages to call, from a pay phone down the street from the James's apartment.

Dad tells Mother that the Shah's army is fighting the militants.

"We've heard," Mom says, curling the telephone cord tight around her finger, impassive to the lack of circulation.

He tells Mother that curfew now begins at four thirty in the afternoon—that he's safe, holed up with Mr. Ned and Mr.

James in the James's apartment, unable to get to work, exiled to a back room, away from windows. He's glad to be away from work because it is bone-chilling cold without electricity; there is little to do without lights and working typewriters.

After Mother hangs up the phone, her face is ashen. "The thing is ... I thought I heard booms, shouting, gunfire in the background, the sounds of Dad ducking and clamoring around in the metal phone booth, air whooshing—then Dad laughing nervously, telling me how foolish he feels to duck when the sounds he hears are so far away. But were they? I told him he should always duck, no matter how foolish it seems!" Mother folds her arms across her chest, thinking, but also trying not to.

On Saturday, John and I head to the Walking Strasse. The winter chill smells fresh and crisp, like just-washed linens. Behind us on the sidewalk are narrow, crooked Tudors. Some of the rooftops are faced with blue-gray slate; others rise up to form copper turrets that are weathered to an elegant patina that matches summer moss turned dormant, silver in the winter cold, so different from the flat mud-colored roofs of Tehran. The buildings look happy almost, in their brightly colored shutters, relieved to forget about any ugly war that had come before.

John says nothing during lunch. We eat in silence. Today, he is gulping down his McDonald's hamburger for the umpteenth time after we'd discovered the restaurant on the edge of the Walking Strasse. The franchise was American as could be, but the workers were all German, and we had difficulty ordering. Somehow with John, I never minded the silence.

And as I people-watch, every dark-skinned man becomes Amir to me. My stomach flips at the handsome man who strolls past our table, says *Ciao* before lighting a Marlboro. The Frenchman with a cappuccino. Two lovers saunter arm-in-arm, hips knocking together, unaware of me watching—anyone watching—when they embrace.

I gaze down at my lunch, stab a round sausage chunk with a toothpick, lean over to pop it into John's mouth. But he wants none of it, and he obstructs the trajectory of my hand with his. A flattened sausage skewered on a bent splintered toothpick now lays between us, a reminder of our romance-less status. "What d'ya do that for, Annie? Now I've got ketchup all over me." What was I doing, feeding him, for God's sake? John grumbles, rises up to wash his hands in a nearby fountain, then gathers up the trash.

I see the two lovers meander down the cobbled sidewalk and dip into a store—one I wanted to visit, to browse for cards to send to Amir—those clichéd kind, imprinted with orange sunsets and black silhouettes of flying seagulls and poems about love, or longing.

Without John now, who is off shopping for more basketball shoes, I wander into the store. The shelves are filled with ruby red Valentine's Day cards; hearts hang everywhere from strings scotch-taped to the ceiling. I had wanted to send my father a card, but he'd told us that it was becoming too difficult to retrieve mail from the APO. *Difficult or dangerous*? I wasn't sure.

I select a card imprinted with a fluffy cartoon rain cloud crying heart-shaped raindrops—"Missing you"—it says in German. As I walk over to the register, the doorbell jangles behind me.

"I found the coolest pair—"

John stops dead in his tracks; he has placed the box top cover beneath the royal blue shoe box and his Converse High-Tops are threatening to spill out. His breath comes in excited bursts as if he'd been running. "Whatcha got?" John asks tentatively, hopefully. His eyes flit from my face to the card.

"Nothing," I say quickly as John's face registers he's better off not knowing, like at the Officers Club, or at his parents' bedroom doorway, a look that had always stopped me from the truth before. But this time, he wants to know.

"Yeah, it's something," he says, pacing. And a bunched up piece of tissue paper has fallen out of the tilted shoe box. He flattens it with a hardly worn Adidas.

"No. It's just a card." I hide it behind my back, my gaze defiant.

"May I see?" He acts as if all the trips to the Walking Strasse and school lunches give him this right.

I open my mouth, then close it. I give up. I show him the card.

"Not meant for your father, I take it? Or me?" John crumples the card into a ball with his one free hand, shouts, "Why can't you recognize a good thing when it's right in front of you?" He flings open the store door, bells jangling. He disappears through the glass storefront down the cobblestone street, walking quickly, head down, fumbling to close the shoe box, stuff it under his arm and wipe at his eyes with an elbow, thrust his hands deep into his pockets, away from the cold.

"Excuse me?" someone behind me says in a thick German accent.

I wheel around. It's the woman at the register.

"You *veel* have to pay for *dat*."

Mid February, Mother arranges a ski vacation to Austria for our school break—a tour to Salzburg to visit Mozart's house, and the place where the *Sound of Music* was filmed. Although Mom doesn't say it, I know she is trying desperately to keep herself busy so that she won't sit and worry, make up situations in her head about Dad. Before we'd left, John had presented me with a large red-suede, heart-shaped box of chocolates, with a note that read, "I'm sorry."

On the way to Salzburg, Mother tells us stories, about how as a young child I'd serenaded my parents on a plastic banjo in my Julie Andrews' haircut, already smitten with Christopher Plummer at the ripe old age of five. How I'd hoped he'd marry me if I could sing like Maria.

"Oh, how I can't wait to see the Von Trapp's Salzburg!" Mother squeals. "Do you remember Maria in her brown dress dancing through the streets of Salzburg, swinging her black guitar case?!"

"Can we visit the gazebo?" I ask. "The one where Liesl danced in that pink filmy dress with her boyfriend traitor and sang, 'I am sixteen going on seventeen'?" This part of the movie never failed to make me swoon, allowed me my first pre-occupation with romantic dancing in filmy, swirling dresses.

"Boyfriend traitor?" Frankie asks.

"Yes, Rolfe, the Nazi soldier who blows the whistle on the entire family when he discovers their hide-out." I think again how Debbie had labeled Amir a traitor, and my blood boils.

"They escaped a country, too, like us." And Frankie seems to like this thought. That the Pattersons are like the Von Trapp family.

Meanwhile, Mother is talking animatedly with the blonde army wife sitting next to her who is temporarily staying at our hotel until their duplex unit is ready. I hear them discuss movies—*The Sound of Music* and Jill Clayburgh's new film, *An Unmarried Woman*, which John and I had gone to see at the base movie theater last month. John had been snacking on a roll of cherry lifesavers, and when I'd asked him for one, he bent over quickly in the dark and snuck one into my mouth. "Not a used one," I'd complained, recoiling. *Really?* And he'd only just laughed at his brazenness, shrugged his shoulders, and continued to watch the movie. But again, I was ashamed to admit that I had felt something after. *Gee-sus, God, was I flitty like Debbie?*

Now the bus trip is long, but the charming village is worth the drive, replete with a babbling, but ice-filled brook running beneath centuries-old stone bridges, bakeries, restaurants, and clubs, so I don't mind. Our B&B is nestled down a narrow, medieval alley. We sleep in lumpy feather beds at night, the loud ticking clock at our bedsides the substitute for a telephone. Each morning we rise early to a breakfast of warm *Broetchen* rolls slathered with tart raspberry jam—thick and sweet, accompanied by a steaming mug of creamy hot chocolate.

During the day, Frankie and I ski the intimidating treeless bowls as best we can with our limited skill, basins of fluffy white snow. Often we'd spot Debbie flitting about below the chair lift with some Austrian man she'd met in the lodge. Mother could be found reading a novel, tucked beside some fireplace, sipping hot wine with floating oranges.

In the evenings, dinners are large and guiltless after long days of skiing—cuts of breaded lemony Schnitzel, thick fries or creamy spaetzel, and plates of apple strudel or dense slabs of German chocolate cake. At night, Debbie drags me out to the Austrian disco of choice to meet up with whatever boy she had romped around with during the day, and encourage me to drink shots of Apple Schnapps.

"But this tastes like cough syrup," I'd gasp. Silent, Debbie would only roll her eyes, hold up her shot glass high into the air and shout, "To Austria!"

And then the Austrian boys at a nearby table would toast back. "To America!"

"To Iran!" I'd shout. "To world peace!"

And the Austrian boys would throw us curious glances. Iran?

Haven't you heard? Don't you care? A country where people we love still live. In danger if you'd really like to know. "To Apple Schnapps!" I'd ignore my thoughts and toast again, sloshing my drink across the table like a drunken sailor. Guiltily, I'd imagine Mom back at the B&B under her down coverlet, reading a novel while Frankie slept, Mom so unfocused lately, looking tired and haggard, as if she never slept, not caring about much, even when her two alcohol-breathed daughters stumble in late. Salzburg Square had failed to move her; Mozart's house hadn't even stimulated her. She'd tried to call Dad from a phone booth outside a pub on Wednesday, and then again on Friday. Each time she'd been unable to get through. And after each failed phone call attempt, Mother retreated into herself more and more, still attempting to show us a good time, but her brow was becoming perpetually furrowed.

Meanwhile, all the drinking had resulted in an alcohol-fueled kinship with Debbie, which had made us momentarily close, so close that one night I confess my problems with the girl-bully, admit how terrified I am to go to school. And after my confession, Debbie had held up her glass of Apple Schnapps and had toasted "To Sisterhood!" and a fierce look had been stamped on her face, which had made me smile.

We return to Wiesbaden late Sunday night. I am tired, but wound up like a top from the bus ride back to the hotel.

"Annette, Debbie. Could one of you—bring my luggage to my room?" Mother winces. "My back."

Debbie pretends not to hear, and I grab my mom's pink plaid suitcase without rollers, struggle out of the elevator.

"You forgot Frankie's!" Debbie grabs his lightweight suitcase.

"Do you have the key?" I ask Mother over my shoulder as I approach her room, but the door is slightly ajar. I wonder now if the room would be cleared out of the only possessions we still owned.

I push the door open wider, peek inside.

"Painting the town red in my absence?"

My hand flies to my mouth. "Dad!" I scream.

"Jack!" Mother shrieks from the doorway.

"Dad!" Debbie shouts and we pile around him—Frankie jumps into his lap.

Dad is laughing, but tears are settling in his eyes; he looks so thin, gaunt like a scarecrow; the skin on his face is pulled so tight that his eyes bulge, and his teeth appear larger.

"On a whim, I took the kids skiing to Austria," Mother says, staring at him in disbelief, as if he were a ghost. "I'm so sorry. We had no idea. Of course, we are so relieved!" She stretches out her hand, lays it on his shoulder. "You look so tired!" She regards him closely. "Are you sick?"

"No. Not at all, just relieved to be here. I suppose I'm hungry for a large meal." Dad laughs a little, says quietly, "I got most of our belongings out. The Air Force dumped a large wooden crate outside our security wall, just in time; Amir had let me know it was there."

My heart seesaws at the mention of Amir's name.

"I piled the crate high. Made an appointment that day to have it carted away. It's supposed to be on its way to a Watertown storage facility near Mom and Dad. All our Persian carpets fit into that crate." He sits up a little taller in his chair.

"And our car?" Frankie asks. I smother a smile, imagining the Honda in a wooden crate.

"I gave it to Amir."

And Frankie lowers his eyes to stop his tears.

"Yes, Frankie, I did. No cars were permitted out, just household goods. Amir was such an immense help, you see? While we were holed up at the James's apartment, another band of demonstrators came by looking for us. Amir went to the door with our Pete Rose bat we'd brought from our apartment, saved us once again by telling them no Americans lived there."

"When did you get out?" Mother asks.

"On the eighteenth of February. The same day Khomeini met with Yasser Arafat and dispelled all Israeli's out of Iran, recalled all Iranian diplomats back from Israel—just after Valentine's Day—same day the American Ambassador to Afghanistan was kidnapped in Kabul and murdered." Dad snorts.

"Oh, dear, God no. I hadn't heard. This is terrible. I'm so relieved you are safe. Why are you out? Weren't you supposed to help with the new government if they needed you?" Mother asks, handing him a glass of Blue Nun wine from the corked bottle on the hotel dresser.

"They don't need us. Have you heard any news?"

"No. Our Austrian B&B had no telephone—no newspapers we could read. What happened?"

My father's expression tells us that everything had happened. "Remember the last time I called? I told you about the disturbance at *Doshan Tappeh*?" We nod.

"Because of that small skirmish, there were more tanks parked on the base than usual. The next day, when Colonel Ross got to work, he heard gunfire around eight in the morning. He called to stop the work buses from coming in. Thank God because we were scheduled for the later shift. My only task really had been to shred classified documents, destroy equipment we wouldn't want to fall into the hands of a hostile government."

Mother twists her wedding ring, pulls at a lock of hair.

"By mid morning, heavy tank fire sounded outside the office building. Ross explained that when he'd belly crawled to the window to peer out, he saw three *homafaran*—contract technicians in the Imperial Iranian Air Force—they're like warrant officers—open fire with their machine guns on the Imperial Army tanks, just outside the window. They had defected! Marble was blasting from the exterior walls like hail from all the gunfire. Ross and about thirty-five others were forced to barricade themselves into an interior office."

I sit perched on the hotel bed's edge in suspense and disbelief, imagining what might have happened had Dad been at work. His simple short phone call that February ninth did not convey the chaos that had occurred or was about to unfold.

"When Colonel Ross peered out the window onto *Farahabad* Avenue, he noticed that the guards at the entrance gates to the base had vanished from their posts. At the armory across the street, where the Iranian Imperial Air Force stored their weapons, dissidents were streaming from the building juggling stolen hordes of weapons. Everyone had a gun that day."

Mother gasps, ironically, at something that had already made the history books.

"About mid morning, Brigadier General Aziz Salahi, Ross's counterpart in the Iranian Air Force, takes off his uniform, puts on his street clothes and abandons the base with his colleagues. They just left. Hundreds of people streamed out of the front gate of *Doshan Tappeh* Air Base in their civilian clothes."

"I had no idea—I should never have taken that ski trip while you were going through this," Mother cries.

Dad gulps his wine. "Anyway, the four-thirty p.m. curfew was fast approaching and Brigadier General Kertesz, Chief Officer of the MAAG was still at the base with Ross, wondering how everyone would get out. He called the Imperial Air Force commander, General Rabii, who dispatched a helicopter to *Doshan Tappeh*. Rockwell International and Pan Am were also on the base that day. Roughly one hundred people at a time were loaded up on buses, all amid gunfire and soldiers changing sides. The helicopter made three trips, landing successfully each time on the softball field at the Gulf District, which he thought would be a safe location."

"Our softball field?" I ask.

"Yes, where you and Debbie played all your games." Dad reaches into his pocket. "Frankie, here's some change," he says. "Run and get yourself something out of the vending machine—a package of cookies or some candy?"

"A diet Pepsi for me?" asks Debbie.

Dad waits for Frankie to leave the room, then continues. "But when the Colonel and his group got to the Gulf District, they found it had already been attacked, taken over, and locked. Ross and his team were trapped again inside the Gulf District's locked gates."

"Attacked? Dad?! The Gulf District?" I ask. My recreational haven and place of work.

"Yes. Sadly, the revolutionaries had also captured other American facilities, the commissary, the APO. Every foreign-owned or operated building was under attack. Some of our people were blindfolded and carted away for questioning. All the revolutionaries kept saying was, 'CIA! CIA!' while demonstrators soaked vehicles and buildings with gas, set them on fire, even the Bell Helicopter office building downtown."

I thought of Mike Morales's dad, Janice's father. I hoped they were safe.

"Ross and his team spent the night on the Officers Club floor."

"Lucky for them to be in a building with a kitchen and food!" Mom always wanted her men fed. "Maybe being inside the locked gates of the Gulf District was a good thing."

"My thought, as well. That night there was a shootout at the Imperial Guard barracks next door to the Gulf District, firing all night. The gunshots that filled Mr. James's apartment were louder than the roar of a European soccer game."

"How did Ross and his team get out of the Gulf District?"

"The next morning they managed to get ahold of church buses, left after the gates were unlocked by revolutionaries." I picture them bursting out of the untethered gates in Christian buses, hoped it hadn't happened that way.

"We had no idea how dangerous all of this was for you," Mother cries.

"Donna, we were fine—we were safe at the James's, just frightened. Mr. Ned barricaded himself in a closet." Dad inhales sharply, remembering. "From the closet, I heard Ned sobbing! I'd never heard of a special operations officer crying before, but, you know, I almost wanted to weep myself. We managed to coax him out of the closet for drinks. Once we broke out the *Boomerangs*, we all relaxed." Dad smiles. "We knew to stay put, ignore the commotion outside the best we could."

I remembered the sound of heavy gunfire vividly, that night in Jamshid's apartment. How tough it was to ignore it. How my own drinking had numbed the fright.

"In the morning we learned the Bakhtiar government had resigned. We were beside ourselves, thinking, what now? Armed revolutionaries were all over the streets. We couldn't leave for fear of being recognized as Americans. And Amir's mother had become hysterical as the days wore on. Amir left us to try to get home. We were shut off from all news—nothing from ARMISH-MAAG, Colonel Ross, the State Department, even the president. All airports in the country were closed. Our food supplies were low. Let me tell you, we were starting to feel pretty desperate."

"Amir. Do you know if he ever made it home safely, Dad?"

Dad's gaze is serious. He shakes his head. "Honestly, Annie, I don't know."

I sigh, blow out a sharp breath.

"Finally, we heard news from the BBC that the airport would re-open for evacuation flights in six days. Pan Am, Air France, British Airways, and Japan Airlines would all be open to get their people out. Eventually, we received official news from the work on the 'alert net.'"

Dad stops talking, as if he had nothing left to say. But then he sighs, continues, "On Valentine's Day, a detachment member who lived opposite the embassy saw it was under attack. Armed intruders were tumbling over the ten foot high brick embassy walls like Indians. Took about a hundred Americans hostage, captured Ambassador Sullivan and General Gasky. But after several hours, Khomeini and pro-Khomeini guards asked the intruders to let everyone go. The armed intruders were Fedayaen-E Kalq guerrillas we found out later, their hatred for the Shah worse than their anti-Islamist beliefs."

"Guerrillas?" Mother says, mouth agape.

"It seemed everyone who had a gun that day was a guerrilla ...." Dad clears his throat. "Finally, we got orders to be on an evacuation flight out of Iran on the eighteenth—if only we could get ourselves to the embassy. Our suitcases were packed, and we cursed our bad luck that Amir had only just gone home. We didn't know what to do next."

I think the question, again, was: had Amir ever arrived home safely?

"But then we hear a frantic knocking on the door, a woman's high-pitched voice speaking Farsi, '*Salaam*, hello, it is Moshdeh? I have come for you'." Dad describes how Mr. Ned moved piles of furniture blocking the door to usher the *chador*-cloaked Moshdeh into the apartment.

Frankie returns with an arm full of candy and two diet Pepsis. "Moshdeh?" Frankie asks, handing us our drinks.

Debbie and I smile.

"Thank you!" I say, not expecting a soda. I pop open the can with a jolt, loud in the room.

"We almost didn't recognize her," Dad says. "Nothing visible but her eyes. She'd heard the same BBC news about evacuation flights from the airport, originating from the embassy. She told us we had to get there, now." She herded us into her black Mercedes parked inside the compound. We scampered into the car, lay flat beneath the suffocating blankets, and Moshdeh drove like a bat out of hell, let me tell you, gunfire whizzing around the car," Father says, laughing, quickly scrutinizing Frankie, who was immersed in his bag of gummy bears, paying no attention. "Moshdeh deposited us safely at the back entrance to the American Embassy."

Frankie looks up at the mention of Moshdeh and smiles now with reddish-green teeth. Secretly, I think Frankie has a crush on Moshdeh, like I'd had on Christopher Plummer when I was young.

"We spent the night at the embassy. Woke up at four thirty in the morning to board buses to the airport. When we got there, the security guards gave us an attitude, searching us over and over again, poring over a list of names, but finally, they let us go."

Frankie disappears into the bathroom as Dad shakes his head, remembering. "Some of the leaders of the dissidents at the airport were Iranian Imperial Air Force Logistics Command personnel we worked with every day. Can you believe it? Mohammad, our driver, was one of them."

"Mohammad? You've got to be kidding me." Mother's eyes grow wide.

"Yes, Mohammad. At least he had the courtesy to look down as we passed." Father pauses, shaking his head. "A funny thing happened—honestly, I was relieved I could see any humor in any of this—but, as we were being bused to the airport, some of the carpet dealers ran alongside us, looking to collect their money."

We all begin to snicker. I imagine bearded carpet vendors running after the departing buses, shouting, "*Ahh, boro gom sho!*", scolding themselves to have been so foolish to let the bad Americans *test the carpets*.

"But you paid, Dad," I say, proud of him.

"I did. I'm so honest, Annie. Even returned your cheerleading uniform to the school before I left."

"No way?! You're the best, Dad." I walk up behind his chair, wrap my arms around his neck, amazed at what he had endured. I am proud he had remained true to his own code of honor. "I hope bullets weren't flying around you when you did that, Dad?" My voice is like a scolding parent.

Frankie comes out of the bathroom, clicking off the fan. He flips on the television set, but then Debbie and he begin to argue about the channel. Dad smiles emotionally at the banality of it, his kids fighting about TV.

"Turn that television set off right now," Mom demands. She grabs for the remote control while my father whispers to me, "Amir was so depressed without you. I thought you might like to know that." I smile to myself, but am beside myself with worry for him.

CHAPTER 13

APRIL—NOVEMBER 1979— FEBRUARY 1981

After you we went to the squares and shouted:
'long live ...
and down with....'

and in the clamor of the square we applauded the little singing
     coins,
which had insidiously come to visit our town.

After you, us: each other's murderers, judged love
and while our hearts were anxious in our pockets,
     we judged love's share.

After you
we resorted to cemeteries
and death was breathing under the grandmother's veil.

We lost everything ...
How much must one pay?...

Sections of "Age Seven", Forugh Farrokhzad

After my father's late-night surprise, I grab up all the old newspapers I can find—the ones left unread when we were in Austria—it is all there. Everything that Dad had explained and more. Reports about how Shapour Bakhtiar had re-invoked martial law, how Khomeini had ordered his "people" to dismiss it and had called for a *Jihad* against the Iranian army if they did not surrender to the revolutionaries. Articles about how leftist guerrillas and revolutionaries had joined the rebel troops in the streets, looting buildings, police stations and other government facilities, just like Dad had said. How Shapour Bakhtiar had gone into hiding, and the beginning stages of the Islamic Republic were underway. How committees were being set up to interrogate people, and the structure of a new government was being formed.

Later, I learn that the United States State Department had chartered thirteen commercial Boeing Seven Forty Seven airliners that flew out an additional four thousand people during those last days of February. By March first, the U.S. government had decided to evacuate all United States citizens still in Iran, except for a skeleton crew at the embassy and several corporate headquarters.

My father received his new assignment quickly—England, a fairy-tale tour of duty for my family—an F-16 RAF base this time—which would mean saying good-bye all over again, to John and the James, and missing my end of June graduation, because Dad was expected to begin work the first day of May; proof that moves were never timely in the military, never convenient. And although Debbie had not predicted it—that Dad would miss my graduation—no one ever thought that I'd miss it too, and this chain of events has upset her, surprisingly. She feels sorry for me. The high school administration allows me to finish up early, and I load up on homework, meet with all my teachers to arrange a special schedule. And somehow, I am not upset like Debbie is for me. The novelty of living in a hotel has worn off. I yearn for a house where I can spread out and have some privacy, rather than exist in limbo with another family, Kelly always hovering around, Mrs. James always annoyed with Mr. James, who had failed to get their expensive oil paintings out of Iran—who could never do anything right in her eyes, or so it seemed.

Today, I am navigating the schoolyard to avoid the dreaded girl-bully. How ridiculous for me to feel compelled to rush to my bus every afternoon after the dismissal bell, eyes darting around like I'm hunted game.

But this time, I feel a tug on my scarf, hear a sarcastic snicker behind me.

"Hey, *Iranian chica*, what's your hurry?" Tammy holds me in place with a firm pull of my scarf.

I turn around, and she is wearing an ugly sneer. Her yellow hair is spiked stiff with hairspray, springing up from black roots like scorched grass from dark pungent earth.

"Ready to fight, huh, *Iranian chica*?"

I start sweating, gulp back saliva. "Uh, can we stop this thing? Whatever it is. I'm a pacifist, you know. What did I ever do to you?"

She spits a wad of green gunk on the pavement. "You and some girl made fun of my hair. That day at the PX. No one makes fun of me and gets away with it."

"Me?—I did?" I sound whiny. I'm confused, but then it comes back, how my sister and I were shopping in the PX, and Debbie had grabbed a box of Clairol hair coloring from the shelf, had pointed it to a rough-looking girl with tattoos spreading up her bare muscled arms, laughing. I laughed too, but more to attain the sister camaraderie so elusive with Debbie than to make fun of anyone.

My stomach drops. This is not good. My eyes dart to the bus to see if someone might help me. But no one is paying any attention to our little standoff.

"Your hair is just fine," I say, wondering if I should bolt, but she is still clutching my scarf, glaring.

And then comes one of those times when the unthinkable happens, a huge coincidence or just beautiful karma. Debbie appears around the side of the bus, "*Hey!* You leave my sister alone. You hear? Drop that scarf. *Now.*"

"Oh, another *Iranian chica*. You the *chica* sister who made fun of me?" Tammy laughs.

"Do I look Iranian to you?" Debbie shouts as she gallops towards us. Even I am frightened of Debbie now, the way her eyes are narrow, her brow furrowed into angry darts. Then, Debbie takes her own muscled arms, arms that could fling a softball seventy miles per hour, and pushes the girl-bully, who lets loose of my scarf as she falls backward on her elbows onto the pavement, stunned. She rises up from the ground stiffly, raises up one arm to inspect the new rip at the elbow of her camouflage coat. "Now look what you've done," she shouts. "I'm going to tell my Dad on you."

Debbie steps forward. "Go on and tell your Dad, *German chica*. Also tell him how you've been bullying my sister. And if you keep it up, you'll have something much worse than a ripped coat next time, okay? Got it?"

"I'm not German!" shouts Tammy.

"See."

Wide-eyed and pursed-lipped, Tammy nods her head a few times, then shakes it sideways, as if *we* were the crazy ones. Debbie and I watch her scramble up her bus stairs wearing a stiff upper lip.

"Come on Annie, forget about your bus, I'll buy you a Baskin Robbins ice cream. Pecan Praline? Gummy bears on top?" Debbie grabs my arm protectively. Arm in arm, we walk across the playing fields to the PX.

"How'd you know?!" I ask.

"I just had this feeling."

"Maybe I deserved it?"

"But Annie, no one deserves to be bullied." I smile gratefully. "And Annie? I'm sorry I called Amir a spy. I was just jealous he liked you better than me."

We keep abreast of the deteriorating situation in Iran by reading more newspapers. There are no other words for what is happening in Iran but "The Purge."

I read in the paper about Colonel Ross's counterpart, and my eyes tear frantically across the paper: "*General Amir*

Hossein Rabii, former commander of the Imperial Air Force, was killed Monday, April 9, by the new government of Iran, supported by the Ayatollah Khomeini. General Rabii was executed for his supposed crimes against the nation. The reasons for this postulated treason are mysterious. General Rabii was not a SAVAK agent, not an interrogator and torturer, not a politician, not a socialite, not a self-aggrandizing influence in the Shah's court. He was an airman, fascinated by aircraft...During the February conflicts between the Khomeini and Bakhtiari forces, he counseled his men not to shoot to kill their brothers on the other side."

General Rabii had dispatched the helicopter that had transported my father's detachment and hundreds of others off *Doshan Tappeh* Air Base that fateful February day. Now he was *dead. Executed. Oh, my God.*

Next comes the purge of Iranian Air Force officers. "Ali?" Our family begins to worry about him to the extent we place a phone call to Amir. I ask if I can also talk to Amir after my father. I can't believe I will finally learn if he's okay; my heart is in my throat.

Immediately, I recognize the call is bringing awful news. But not regarding Amir.

"*Ali?*" Dad's face looks stunned. Then he wails "*Moshdeh?*" His face whitens like chalk. And at once Dad sinks to his knees, head hanging low, body curled into itself, sucker-punched, like a boxer in the ring. "God, no Amir. This can't be true." He hangs up the phone, quiet, devastated, back turned to us. I sense that this certainly was not the time to complain about my lost opportunity to speak with Amir.

"Jack, what? What? What has happened?"

Dad turns to us.

.... "Khomeini's council committee members went in search of Ali. They found him—"

"Found him?" Mother asks.

"Yes. Found him at Moshdeh's apartment one night while they were sleeping."

"Together?"

"Yes, together." Dad avoids her eyes.

Mother asks with a jagged breath, "And?"

"Ali was taken. Dragged before a revolutionary tribunal."

"And?" her voice wavers.

"There's no easy way to say this … He was executed for crimes against the state. A gunshot to the back of his head. *Our Ali.*"

The room rotates.

"God, no Jack," Mother screams. Mother's eyes are wild. *"Moshdeh?"*

"Moshdeh…." Dad can barely speak. His mouth opens, but words escape him.

No. No. Don't say it then. Tears are streaming down Dad's face. I cover my ears, but it doesn't help.

"Moshdeh … Moshdeh was stoned … to death—"

"To death?!" Mother wails.

Father nods. "In the bazaar square … for sleeping with Ali … outside of marriage. For being *corrupt on earth.* In allegiance with the Great Satan and the den of spics. Her association with *us* brought the end to her. Our Moshdeh. I don't want to believe it."

"I won't believe it!" Mother sobs, falls to her knees.

Dad bends to rub her back, wipe away her tears. "Amir is terrified. And not without good reason. Khomeini's revolutionary guards have also executed his tenant, Jamshid, for homosexuality. Amir is worried about how he's helped us. We shouldn't be talking on the phone with him."

"Murdering for sexual *orientation*? Killing two wonderful souls like Ali, and Moshdeh?" Hadn't Moshdeh been through enough after her beloved husband's early death? To die after being given the gift of love again? "I'm sick, Jack, just sick."

Mom punches her fist towards the sky. Suddenly, she remembers us, wheels around. Shock is written all over her face. Frankie sobs soundlessly. And Debbie stares back in a wide-eyed stupor.

I take off down the hall to my room, wailing. *No! No!* I throw myself on my bed, punch my pillow. Our Moshdeh? The bearer of good news? A springtime breeze? A woman's advocate. Our dear, dear friend. *Dead?* Stoned to death in a town square without dignity? *Who does that?* This is 1979, for God's sake, not seventeen hundred's France. France? The same country that had harbored the man who killed our friends and brought him back to Iran via Air France airlines.

"*Assholes!*" screams Debbie down the hall.

Persecute—purge. This is pious? My fear for Amir's welfare is intense.

And as the regime begins to slaughter those Iranian people with connections to the Shah, and as women begin to cover up again, and as groups of prostitutes are lined up and executed one by one in the name of the new Islamic Republic, I wonder how all of this will ever turn out well. How was this better than the Shah's SAVAK if it is producing similar horrific injustices, torture, and public executions worthy of ancient rituals or law-less governments? The Family Protection Law, which was instituted by the Shah, restricting polygamy and raising the minimum age of marriage for girls aged thirteen to eighteen, is repealed; the legal age of marriage for girls becomes just nine years old; women judges are disbarred; and beaches, gathering places, schools, and sports games are all segregated between men and women. Iranian Jews and non-Islamic Baha'is run scared for their lives, Tudeh party members later, all scrambling to flee the country before it's too late.

In April, my father's boss, commander of his detachment, says in an interview, *When you sell something to somebody, he owns it, and when he owns it, you lose control of it.* He describes how all the planes the Shah had purchased during his reign are sitting still, grounded on Iranian soil, rusting and rotting in the elements. But it sounds like he's describing Iran, how its soul has been sold to Khomeini. Donated rather with fanatical belief, some of them now being executed.

And in just a few short weeks, we'd be loading up our new Saab, bought at a fantastic in-continent price, to head for RAF Upper Heyford in Oxfordshire, England—to drink yet more tea! Still, it would be difficult for me to say good-bye to John—a comfortable old slipper that would be sorely missed.

Now that it's spring, Debbie and I sleep with our windows open, and the groaning city traffic in the morning acts like an alarm clock, though we allow ourselves the luxury to remain in bed for just a few minutes, cozied by the flutter of the thin curtains at the window, like a serenade, whispering to us that all will be fine now, as Moshdeh would do if she were here, in that breezy optimistic manner of hers.

My last day with John is beyond sad. We bid our formal good-byes to the James at a downtown restaurant. Mrs. James presents me with a crystal vase, a card imprinted with *Good friends are hard to find,* and in her strong, pragmatic penmanship, she has written: *Annie, thanks for being such a good friend to John and our family, Mrs. James.* My eyes moisten when I read her note. She has changed her opinion about me.

While the others return to the hotel, John and I set off walking, reluctant to say good-bye just yet, past the quiet town square, through the park to our usual spot on the bench where the Weeping Willows are bending sadly. We sit in comfortable silence as darkness envelopes us. Purple-winged pigeons waddle on the pavement before us, searching for seeds or pieces of bread we didn't have to offer them. After a while we continue down the Walking Strasse, past the pizza bistro we'd sometimes go for dinner, stopping into a store for John to buy me a parting gift, which he does, a heart-shaped wooden box, then to another store where I buy John a pair of bright white sneakers. And he slips them on, hanging the old grayed sneakers by their blackened shredded shoelaces across his arm, holding my waist with his other. But tonight I am comfortable with his expressions of affection. We wander back to the hotel on streets brightened yellow by the glow of old-fashioned gas lanterns.

Outside my room, John reaches for my hands.

"Annie." His eyes are moist.

"John." I gulp. "Our unfortunate Islamic Revolution created this." I wave my hand between us. "Our wonderful friendship. "

"Good can come out of everything, even bad, right Annie?" John looks pained. I nod, wordless, unable to hold back tears. "Oh, Annie. Don't cry. We'll write." He attempts to comfort me, strokes my shoulder ineffectually.

I nod, biting back sobs. "You'll be going back to Texas— your mom to her horses—you to your sports—"

"But I won't have you," John says.

I clutch the doorknob to my room.

"You'll do great in England. At least you'll know the language. I'll miss you at graduation; I'll think of you when I throw my hat high into the air."

I stare down at my feet, thinking that the events of the last year have made the physical act of receiving a diploma in a formal ceremony meaningless. "I have my diploma; I grabbed it from the office yesterday."

"Grabbed it? Sounds like a let down to me; especially since you finished up all your classes early, not to mention your entire school career."

I laugh. "It's okay. Dinner tonight doubled as the celebration."

We fall quiet, waiting for the inevitable.

"I've been allowed one year off to travel throughout Europe before I begin college, which is something to celebrate."

"Yeah. Come to Texas."

"Maybe." Then, surprising both of us, I sneak John a soft kiss. Startled he beams, backs away from the door, waves all the while I close it on his sweet, smiling face. My throat closes at the sight of his fingers pressed to his lips, and his generous smile, a memory I'd carry with me always.

"Bye, John."

"Bye, Annie." I clip the door shut behind me, fasten the door chain in the lock.

"You sad?" asks Debbie.

I nod, crying softly.

In the fall, the United States lets the Shah receive treatment for his end-stage cancer. For a second time, on the fourth of November 1979, a mob of angry Iranians storm the American Embassy, this time referring to it as the *Conquest of the American Spy Den*. Sixty-six hostages are taken, the number later thinned to fifty-two. Their captors demand the Shah be returned to Iran for trial and execution. This time, Khomeini supports the rebels and does not intervene. I find it unimaginable how only nine months earlier my father had been evacuated from that same American Embassy—*thank God*—but then Moshdeh and Ali were still alive.

My family and I cease to be living the news, just reading about it in inky newspapers. We bury our heads in the sand like ostriches during the coverage of the Iranian Embassy siege in South Kensington in late April, early May. We are unable to watch as an Iranian Arab group demands the release of Arab prisoners in Khuzestan jails, kill a hostage and throw a lifeless body out onto the streets, all televised. We absorb the news of the Shah's death from cancer without letting the reality of it sink in—that he is dead, so soon after his overthrow. We note the execution of the manager of the Cinema Rex by the new Islamic regime, even though Iraq had picked up someone fleeing Iran who confessed that Khomeini and a team of clerics had engaged him to do it, to make the Shah appear blood thirsty—inhuman.

Instead, my mother, sister, and I focus on the upcoming wedding of Prince Charles and Lady Di, as all of Britain is doing, hoping for a fairy-tale marriage, but settling for the chance to gaze at beautiful Diana in her various cloaks, ball gowns, and smart suits.

And as life seemed to continue with the premise that hope, love, and goodness are still alive and well in the world, we begin to live with the complacency that comes with feeling safe and comfortable. The worst thing that might happen to our family now would be a pick-pocket in Rome, or a Frenchman hassling Debbie and me in the restaurant district of Paris. We travel around Britain, then back to Europe—to Spain, Belgium, West and East Berlin, where my father accidentally stumbles into a wedding reception. And after the unfamiliar bride requests a handout, we focus instead on the bride's beaming smile, her simple no-nonsense gown, what the American currency could bring her, rather than her request for a handout in the first place. We worry about her life behind the imposing Berlin wall.

From this point forward, we focus on the positive. We do not dwell on Moshdeh and Ali's brutal end. Attempt not to wonder about Amir or Reza during the Iran-Iraq war. Especially since there's been no word from Amir. Not a peep since the devastating news of Ali and Moshdeh.

But with the passage of time, more time spent in typical pursuits amid a fertile, verdant countryside that smells like hope, rose-covered thatched roof cottages and fields of yellow that lend an old-fashioned sense of security. Wheat and barley-fragrant British pubs, trips to Oxford to pick up the new "U-2" album and wander the hallowed arched hallways of the University, trips to bustling London and ritzy Harrods to shop—life in Iran becomes a distant memory. How nice it feels to be conventional now.

We leave ourselves no free time to dwell on any anxious thoughts of our Iranian friends—Amir, Reza, and Nouri, and their welfare—left behind in a country no better off with Khomeini at its helm, in fact, worse. We are frightened to call to discover if everyone is okay. *Just in case they weren't.*

CHAPTER 14

SEPTEMBER 2001

*"There comes a time
when the world gets quiet
and the only thing left is your
own heart."*

Sarah Dessen, *Just Listen*

That day, that awful day, I'd awoken with a splitting headache and a bad cold and called in sick, the single best decision I'd made in a long, long time. It was something too horrible to think or talk about, all still floating around in my head. Afterward, Lower Manhattan was inaccessible and our publishing group was closed awhile, so I didn't have to make any decisions about going into work anytime soon.

Never minding my cold, prior to all that had happened two weeks ago, I'd been constantly tired and stressed, having difficulty juggling work and family. Colin was just thirteen months old and Liam was in kindergarten. Each evening I'd race home from my commute on the Long Island Railroad to tuck sleepy Liam into bed for a nighttime story before he fell asleep. Sometimes I didn't make it home in time. Colin, on the other hand, was always asleep. Once *Scooby Doo* was finished, and my husband, Ryan, had played around with Colin on the family room floor, letting him cruise around the coffee table— still needing that crutch to walk—Ryan would give the kids a bath in our white-tiled bathroom. Colin would have been placed carefully in his crib after his long day at day care, while Liam would have gone to the bathroom to brush his teeth with his Barney toothpaste to wait for me, patiently, to rush into the house. When I had finished reading Liam *Go, Dog, Go* or

Green Eggs and Ham, still fully clothed in my work suit and heels, lying supine in Liam's race car bed, and after I had planted a kiss on his sweet little boy's head, hair fresh from his bath, I would wander down the hall to Colin's bedroom. Often I'd open the door tenuously, worried Colin would wake up and cry. Usually, he'd be lying on his stomach, fast asleep, head turned to one side, lips puffy and drooling, so precious with his padded bottom rising high into the air, bulky in a fresh pajama-covered diaper. My husband had long been picking Liam up after work at the after school program, then dashing to retrieve Colin at day care. He'd make them dinner, give them baths, prepare my supper, all in the time I was commuting home from my publishing job in Manhattan.

My office was three blocks east of the World Trade Center, on the Lower East Side of Manhattan. I tried to remember the last time I had felt such horrific grief similar to what I'd been feeling the last two weeks. Probably when I heard about Moshdeh and Ali. My grandmother's death. Then my grandfather's. How Beauty and Betty had been sold. And, to a lesser extent, after Princess Diana's car crash in that Paris tunnel—a kick in my stomach when I first heard news of it. Horrendous disbelief. Numb shock as I stayed up late into the night to watch the news coverage on some cable news channel, only to hear Brian Williams in his black tailored suit—so crisp it appeared a second skin—announce she had, in fact, died, that early August morning. She had been such a good mother. So beautiful. I remembered that after I'd flipped off the television set in disgust and looked up to the heavens to ask, *why?* I'd crept into Liam's room at 1:15 in the morning to watch him sleeping in his crib; my tears had drenched his pajamas as I bent to kiss him. But hers was a tragic accident, not cold-blooded murder against thousand of innocent victims who were only at work.

Today, I am taking the kids to Jones Beach, even though this simple recreational trip seemed inappropriate in the few weeks that followed September 11th. It is warmer than usual, a high of eighty degrees is expected but with a slight inconvenient cloud cover. Luckily, Liam had posed no questions for me about the events that had transpired a few weeks earlier, at his tender young age of five.

The van is packed to the brim with beach paraphernalia, an umbrella, blankets, a fold-up vinyl crib and toys for Colin, shovels and sandcastle-making tools for Liam. Ryan had watched the preparation of the beach trip early this morning while he was drinking coffee, and the kids were still sleeping, having difficulty hiding his envy.

"Take the day off. *Come on.* Come with us," I'd pleaded to him, before he'd left for work.

"I can't. I have too much to do. That investment piece, you know, the one I told you about? It's due today." Ryan worked in the marketing department of Merrill Lynch near our home in Garden City, in a large glass office building on Franklin Avenue.

"Come on. I took the day off for you. It's your birthday! Don't we all have too much work to do?"

"Annie, I can't!" he said, laughing. "I wish I could! You had to take the day off. Liam's teacher's in-service day and no school? Remember?"

"Right. Okay, Ryan," I said, also laughing, letting him off the hook. "Be careful out there in the world. We love you and rely on you." I had been feeling so emotional lately.

"I will." Then Ryan kissed me. "And I love you guys more than anything in the world."

Now I sit sunbathing on Jones Beach with my two precious children, Liam and Colin, on what should have been a work day. *I could get into this.* The clouds filter the sun's hot rays, and Colin remains deep asleep in his vinyl portable crib. His sleep-fattened lips flutter like butterflies, and every once in a while he blows out a tiny bubble of saliva, which sends Liam off into a fit of silly giggles. He moves to pop the bubble, and I swat away his arm playfully. I had placed an umbrella strategically over the crib, another smaller one over Liam's purple Barney beach blanket, but I'm still worried. I look towards the sun, which is dimmed by a haze that is sadly the aftermath of *that day*, the dust plume lingering. Liam sits reading a palm-sized cardboard book about Barney, his favorite purple dinosaur, collecting starfish in a bucket at the beach. Liam wanted to do the same. He shows me the bumps in the book making up the spines of the starfish you could feel if you ran your fingers along the page.

"See, Mom. *Touch* it."

I stroke the bumpy spines and the soft terry cloth fabric of Barney's purple beach towel, murmuring, "Mmm, Liam, Barney's blanket is so *soft!*" Liam beams.

It is such a pleasant, relaxing day. Colin is sleeping, lulled by the fresh air, the waves' soft rush instead of crying for a cookie. Liam and I search for starfish nearby, and I let him run to the water's edge to get his tiny feet wet in the waves. If he dares to venture out just a little too far, my heart is in my throat. I peer back at the port-a-crib and Colin, then shoot my glance back at tow-headed Liam, surely a recipe for whiplash.

"Liam!" I shout with my scratchy throat, "Don't go out too far!"

My warning awakes Colin, so I let him out of the port-a-crib to toddle around in the water, scream in delight as the cool waves touch his toes. Staring out at the calm gray ocean while holding Colin's two chubby arms over his head as he splashes around in the water with his flat, thick feet, I wonder, when had I been here last? Not since the final day of our honeymoon, after we'd returned from Nantucket, before kids and the first days of our new jobs when we'd worked in the trenches, hardly up the ladder. Lately, we'd been so busy at work, paying no focused attention to each other—no dinners out, no trips to the beach, to museums that didn't involve kids and petting zoos. But two weeks ago when everybody and everything important in our lives became someone and something to be cherished, I knew we'd find a way to make this simple change. But for today, Ryan still toils at work, and I am celebrating his birthday at the beach without him. I lay back on my towel and doze.

"Mom, can we have macaroni and cheese for dinner?" Liam asks.

I smile sleepily. And then I dream I am the perfect mom.

CHAPTER 15

MAY 2013

"the past increases,
the future recedes.
possibilities decreasing,
regrets mounting."

Haruki Murakami
Dance, Dance, Dance

We make the decision to move. I'd grown tired of the long work days—the lack of family time that comes along with a job in the Big Apple, weary of the commute. I'd developed this superstitious fear about working there as a mother of small children—that I needed to protect myself for *them*. My children are older now, but my husband and I want something more manageable for them, and for us, a smaller city where Paul Revere had lived and roamed, where he had warned the general public that the redcoats were coming—a home closer to my parents.

We settle near Boston, a city of red brick and mortar, the Italian North-end, the tall buildings in the Financial District and the Back Bay. Just tall enough for us not to fret, where there are no lofty Twin Towers, just a fifty-two-floor Prudential Center and a sixty-floor John Hancock Tower, and my husband's building, forty-six stories tall. Ryan had landed the perfect job—interesting work, executive meetings, lavish holiday parties, a high salary and perks to die for. We'd meet for lunch, wander past the narrow brownstones that faced the public garden—chock full of fanciful things like swan boats, duckling statues from my favorite children's book. And there was Faneuil Hall and Quincy Market, Charles Street, Regina

Pizzeria, and the Red Sox. And being a former military brat, I'd been itching to move after years in New York.

We find the perfect seaside town and buy a comfortable bay-view, gray-shingled Cape on a marsh—our new town blessed with its own long and narrow barrier beach where I begin to collect smoothed shards of colorful sea glass, which I take to rubbing, like worry beads. And I can breathe a sigh of relief now ... relax. Even if it had meant resigning my cushy publishing job to concentrate on writing a novel instead. But who could complain about sipping a cup of hot dark roast coffee at the kitchen table while the kids were at school? Not much stress, just self-imposed, relating to publishing something.

This morning I power up my laptop to check e-mail and Facebook; admittedly I am playing with social media. I have set up an author's page, using my maiden name as a pen surname. An "Other" message is buried in the in-box of my Facebook page, from a "Firouzeh." I open the message, interested. I also belong to a Tehran American School Facebook group, but this is different, a message from a TAS friend isn't usually classified as "Other."

Firouzeh begins her message by saying, *Annie. Hello. I hope you forgive this intrusion into your life by someone you do not know. But I am aware that you knew my father, Amir, many, many years ago, in Tehran, Iran.*

I gasp, stop reading for a moment to compose myself. My heart thumps in my chest.

He has spoken of you fondly and often over the years. I'd like to meet you if you'll have me. I live in Maine, and my father lives on a farm near me, the farm he bought with his wife of more than twenty years. He loved his Iranian upbringing, though his roots have been steeped in the "American experience"—off Iranian soil—for so many more years than he'd lived in Tehran. He has a large American flag pinned to his post and beam barn at the back of his property. He participates in elections and has strong political opinions about the candidates. I know you cared for the Iranian urban cowboy. Listen, I'll be in Boston for a conference beginning this Saturday. Would it be possible to meet there for dinner Sunday night? Write back if you are amenable to this and may peace be onto you. Firouzeh.

I'm shaking like a leaf. *Amir's daughter?* Thank God, he's alive.... *Married for more than twenty years? In the United States?* I gather my emotions, remember that my life has also progressed forward, and I shouldn't be reacting so viscerally.

Fingers poised over the keyboard, I struggle with what to say back to her. I think I ought to be brief and casual. I type: *Hello, Firouzeh, how nice to hear from you. What a surprise, my goodness! Yes, I'd love to meet you for dinner in Boston, say six o'clock?* I include my phone number in case she wants to call.

I stare at the small square that is her Facebook profile picture. She is stunningly beautiful. She reminds me of our precious Moshdeh, tumbling black hair, olive skin, and bright, sea-blue eyes.

Soon after, I receive a reply:

Wonderful, meet me at the Langham Hotel's bar in Boston this Sunday, if a six p.m. dinner sounds okay, and we shall chat. I've made reservations, she wrote.

Okay, not much detail there, I think, but the curiosity is unbearable. *What does she have to say to me?*

I arrive at the Langham Hotel's bar, The Bond, on time on Sunday evening; I walk into a chic modern space that cries out old money, like a bank—dark walls, several large impressive chandeliers, long posters of old-style currency, red velvet covered bar stools, rich golden brushed-velvet lounge seats. I recognize Firouzeh right away from her Facebook photograph.

She is sitting at a leather banquette in the corner sipping a cup of tea.

She looks up and smiles when she sees me, obviously also recognizing me from my Facebook photograph.

She stands up when I approach, extends her hand for a shake with a warm smile, "Annie. Welcome. Please, sit."

I sit down on the yellow banquette, facing her. She is beautiful, more so in person. Thin as a rake. Nervous.

"I hope you don't find this awkward."

"I don't."

"I'm attending a writing seminar here, believe it or not."

"You are?"

"I am." We discuss the author and his books, the breakout sessions and individual writing periods during the morning, followed by afternoon critiques. "We read out loud everything we write in the morning, then the class members critique us. It can be a bit harsh sometimes," Firouzeh says. "The teacher acts as moderator—he supplies tips on writing." She sips her tea. "You're in publishing? Your Facebook profile mentions that." I study her as she talks. I see Amir in her long aquiline nose, her thinness, the shape of her eyes, although startling blue. Her skin is olive like her father's, an identical impish grin.

"Yes, I was in publishing in Manhattan, but gave it up recently to move here to the Boston area. I'm also trying to write—a novel."

Firouzeh smiles, excited we have something in common.

"I asked you to meet me here today because I wanted to talk to someone who knew my father before."

"Before?"

"Before the Islamic Revolution. Before he left Iran."

"I think that would be me. He was our family's good friend in Iran."

She nods. "It's just that … my father has been perpetually sad. Ever since I can remember. Was he like that when you knew him, Annie?"

"No," I say, surprised. "He was always happy, silly even, driving around Tehran on his motorcycle, or in his Mercedes, a cigarette always hanging from his lips."

"He was?"

"Yes, he was."

"I want him happy again," Firouzeh says. "Perhaps he was happy when we were little, and he was showing us soccer moves—we all played. My sisters. My brothers. But since we've grown older, and he doesn't have the chance to play games with us, he's grown more reserved."

"How many brothers and sisters do you have?" I ask.

"There are five of us, three girls and two boys."

I smile, remembering how Amir had told us at the Khwansalar restaurant that he would have five children, *Inshallah*. Yet my heart aches. "And your mother?"

"He met her when he arrived here. She's American."

"But you look so Iranian," I exclaim.

"Yes, I do. Of all the kids, I look most like *Baba*. My brother, Ali, is blonde." Firouzeh smiles.

"You are certainly beautiful."

"Thank you, Annie." She continues, "I'm in college—won a scholarship for good grades, a big help to my parents. I also have a work-study job for spending money. My mother works in the administrative office of my former middle school. My father tinkers on our farm, fixing cars and trucks. We have a large barn. One side is for drying flowers, and the other is for working on automobiles," Firouzeh says. "I'm so happy I found you on Facebook."

"Yes, Facebook is great for that," I say. "In fact, my best friend at Tehran American School found her birth mother on Facebook. She talks to her almost daily. I also got back in

touch with someone else I knew in Iran—my friend John—
your father knows him. He also escaped Iran with us, lived in
Germany at the same time we did."

"What did you find? About John, now? Was he the same?"

"Yes. He's a coach in Texas, teaches Chemistry—is doing
exactly what he told me he'd do back on a lonely rooftop in
Tehran," I say.

"What a nice story."

"Mostly nice. His parents got divorced once they returned
to the United States. But his mother remarried, a rich oilman
this time—the two of them live on a ranch outside San
Antonio, a dream come true for his mom who loves horses."

"Divorce is unfortunate, but it happens," Firouzeh says.
She shifts uncomfortably in her seat, stares into her tea.

"Anyway, enough about them. Firouzeh, I remember your
father was hilarious. He loved sweet and savory and thought
eating eggs would cause bad skin."

"Oh, that. Yes. He does think that. Loves eggs with quince
jam." She smiles, satisfied I did have knowledge of her father.
She looks at her watch, picks up a gauzy red scarf similar to the
hijab I found in Amir's car's back seat, long ago in Tehran,
when streets were crowded with tire-burning demonstrators—
after Amir and I had enjoyed a romantic lunch at the *Chelo
Kebab* restaurant on *Lalehzar* Avenue.

Firouzeh wraps the scarf around her head. She smiles
enigmatically, sips her tea, glances at her watch again, stares
across the room before a look of recognition flashes upon her
face. She nods over my shoulder, lifts her hand in the air in a
slight, halfhearted and nervous wave. As if she were offering
an apology.

I turn to a confused, older man approaching us. He looks
Iranian. As he draws closer, Firouzeh stands up.

"*Delbar, Firouzeh*, what have you done?" the man asks
when he reaches our table.

"*Baba*, Happy Birthday! Say hello to Annie."

"*Amir*?" I ask, at once uneasy from being caught off guard. I touch my hair, tuck a strand behind my ear.

"Annie, *Baba*, forgive me, please, but I must go, I have classwork to finish before tomorrow morning. I will leave you two alone to catch up."

"*Firouzeh*," Amir says sternly, holding his palms up in the air.

"*Baba*, you know I have booked an adjoining room for you to stay overnight at the class discount. You have plenty of time. The night is young. Please enjoy yourself tonight. Remember, you used to be an urban cowboy. Country life has made you timid. It is time for you to shed your pride and come to see an important friend."

She leaves us silent, awkward at the table. Amir continues to stand. We watch her leave. I take a deep breath. I can't believe he is standing in front of me.

"Amir."

"Annie."

"Sit. Please. I'm so sorry. I had no idea what Firouzeh was planning."

Amir sits down, scooting into the leather banquette vacated by his daughter. He smiles, begins to laugh, shaking his head. "That daughter of mine." He sits back in his seat, still laughing, studying me. "Annie, you look so much the same. More beautiful now compared to then."

Thoughts are tumbling in my head, and my breath is ragged as if I'd been running a race. "This is such a surprise. You look wonderful—also so much the same!" His hair is speckled gray. The lines around his eyes have increased and deepened—he's still so thin, but his smile is nearly the same; the separation of his eyetooth from his incisor, though, has been corrected by dentistry. "When did you come to the United States?"

"Annie, I've been here for decades."

My stomach hurts. "For decades?" I pretend not to be offended.

"Left at the start of the Iran-Iraq war. I had to leave. A close friend of my *Baba Borzog* told my grandfather that my name was on a list. *Baba Borzog* was convinced I'd be found, carted off to a revolutionary tribunal, and summarily executed. For my association with your family. For the Honda I was foolish enough to drive all over Tehran with the American military license plate. For the letters I sent you in Germany."

Letters? "I never received your letters. Did you receive mine?"

"No, I never got your letters, either, Annie. Someone else must have read them."

I sit still, wondering if Khomeini or some revolutionary guard had appreciated the seagulls on the special clichéd cards I'd sent. The poetry? "Is that how you got on the list? The letters?" I ask.

"I think it may have had something to do with that, or with Afshin. I'm not so sure. Or a friend of my father's, *Agha* Moaveni. He was dining at the *Chelo Kebab* restaurant that day we were there for lunch. He may have noticed the tension between us," Amir said, blushing now. "His imagination probably had us doing things far worse that day. That came later."

"*Oh.*" I kick the table leg with my foot, shake my head. "Amir, how did you manage to get out of Iran? If you were on this list."

"This Iranian urban cowboy rode a mule over the mountains and escaped over the border into Turkey." His proud excitement fills the nervous space between us.

"You did?" I laugh at his expression. He had been a cowboy of sorts. Our hero. Battling the bad guys in our honor. A savior who hadn't believed in our savior. "How frightening!"

Amir nods. "It all seems ages ago. But, yes, terrifying. I was hiding out in my parents' apartment. Everyone knew the revolutionary guards were looking for me. We talked and talked about what we should do, what might be in store for me. And for them. I couldn't hide forever, or continue to live in a country I couldn't trust. No political ideals were floating around in this head, believe me, I was as innocent as a child. But the inevitable became my only choice."

"To escape?"

Amir nods. "Yes. My parents drove me to Tabriz hidden under a thick wool blanket covered by empty gift-wrapped boxes. Outside the city, revolutionary guards stopped my parents' car and asked them their business. 'Heading to my brother's house in Tabriz', my father said, lying like a con-artist, 'for the birth of my nephew.' He even smiled like a proud uncle at the revolutionary guard. 'Yes, fortunate for them they had a son,' the guard replied. The wool blanket tickled my nose while the guards poked around. I had to sneeze. I almost did. Instead, though, I thought of you, Annie, our long, drawn-out kisses. How I'd hold my breath when I kissed you. Once in Tabriz, we met an undercover guide. He supplied me with a fake identity and false papers—"

"To smuggle you over the border?"

"Yes."

"Was it expensive?"

"Yes. More than *Maman* and *Baba* could afford." Amir paused, eyes downcast. "I'm sorry to have to tell you this, Annie, but my parents sold Mr. Jamison's grand piano to pay for my escape, my living expenses, beyond what there was in savings."

"That's okay, Amir."

"I said good-bye to my dear parents for a horse and mule caravan towards the Zagros Mountains, never to see them again."

"I'm sorry." I feel somehow responsible. I reach over the table, touch his hand, then snatch my hand back reflexively. I move the conversation away from his parents. "Tell me about your escape."

Amir still looks pained. "That first night we slept outside against scrub-covered rocks and a full moon, so yellow, so bright. The next day, I contracted altitude sickness, vomiting endlessly over my saddle. But we had to move on. Luckily, a doctor who had treated the Shah's Imperial Guard was traveling with me. Nice man. Human. When we'd run out of water, he'd discovered pure mountain streams we could drink from—and we guzzled the cold water so rapidly, our throats ached. Breakfast, lunch, and dinner were out of tin cans until we reached the villages and the network of underground smugglers—refugee protectors who risked their lives working for the *cause*. And then the meals were generous plates of rice, kebab. How thankful I was that *my* life was worth something to them."

I touch Amir's hand, "Your life was … is … worth something, Amir!"

Amir sighs, eyes distant, as if he were wondering if it really was. "We crossed the border. Met another undercover escort who wanted even more money. We paid it. The next morning he took us by van to Ankara, Turkey and the United Nations where I registered for refugee status. Turkey wouldn't offer me political asylum. I was told I could arrange it through Canada or the United States. Learned I'd have to wait awhile for my papers. So I worked for a time as a mechanic in Istanbul until I received them, until I could save enough money for my flight to the United States. But living in Turkey was difficult, not understanding the language. The Turkish people resented refugees from Iran, but accepted them, you know, the alternative would have been Saddam Hussein and Iraq on their border." Amir smiles. "I was your Swiss Family Robinson cast-a-way." Amir sighs. "And here. I've summoned the courage to be a lifetime away from my family, rather than just on the border."

"Did you ever try to contact me once you arrived in the United States?"

"I did—contacted your grandparents—remembered they lived in Watertown, New York, not New York City." Amir smiles. "So I called."

"My grandparents never mentioned it."

"I begged them not to. They told me you were married."

"Oh."

Amir shuffles his knife and fork. He looks up, and I see that his eyes are moist. "But, thank you Annie. Thoughts of you kept me motivated on my journey. Guided me to safety like a shining beacon. To hold a sunny, silky blond strand of your hair in my hand was incentive enough." Amir's pupils are wide and soft, shiny, reflecting back light from the massive crystal chandeliers suspended overhead. Precarious back then. Precarious now. My feelings.

I remain silent, fidgeting in my seat. I take a sip of my water to quench my quicksand throat. "But, you did marry?"

"I did. But, I'm separated now ... the kids ... the separation's been hard for them."

"I can only imagine. But at least you have the five lovely children you'd always wanted, *Inshallah*," I say, smiling. Trying to encourage him.

"Yes. You are right. Their names are Firouzeh, which you know, Fatima, Maryam, Ali, and Parviz." He brightened just speaking their names.

"*Wonderful.*"

"And you?"

"I have two boys," I say, straightening in my chair. I begin to smile as I speak. "Liam is my oldest. He turned seventeen in April. My youngest is Colin; he's twelve—thirteen in June.

Had them when I was older. Spent my twenties throwing myself into my job in Manhattan. Some time after the World Trade Center attack I told myself I had to slow down. Feed my soul. Be home for the kids. Help to feed their souls. So I left the business." I gaze down at my water glass, nostalgia filling me like liquid for the energy of working in a large city, with intelligent people. "And Reza?"

Amir looks into Firouzeh's tea. The waitress approaches with an order pad. "Sorry to interrupt, but I want to get you two started. Here's a drink menu." The waitress hands over a thick, leather bound book.

I laugh. "This is a drink menu?"

"Yes," she smiles. "We have quite the selection of martinis here."

I scan the menu. "Oh, how ironic, Amir, they have a *Pomtini* on the menu!"

"A *Pomtini*?" he asks, eyebrows raised.

"Moshdeh's favorite drink, pomegranate juice, vodka, grapefruit juice, and sour mix!" I show him the menu.

"Would you like one?" asks the polished waitress with a shiny black bob and rum raisin lipstick. She smacks her lips together. "They're delightful!"

"No, I'll stick with my tea for now," I say.

"I'll have what the lady is having," Amir tells the waitress, winking at me.

"The young lady, Firouzeh, assures me you two will be having dinner. That it's all set. Dinner is on her." The waitress also winks. "Let me retrieve your tea, bring back some dinner menus."

Amir sits helplessly, his grin turning sheepish. "I guess we do have a lot to catch up on, Annie, don't we?"

"We do indeed, Amir."

"You asked about Reza? Annie.... I don't have an easy way to tell you this, but Reza died a week into the Iran-Iraq war."

I inhale sharply, gulp down the lump in my throat. "God, no. How?"

"He crashed an F-14 into the mountains, ironically bought by the Shah, a plane that had sat unused and not maintained ... out in the sun, rain, and snow, but ordered into action once the Iraq war began. Everything was chaotic in the war's early weeks, anyway, when Reza died."

When Reza died. I sit still, mourning the boy I remembered, his practical jokes, dancing with him at the Persian wedding reception. I never had the chance to say good-bye to him.

"That's not all," Amir says, eyes darkening, lips pursed. "Nouri."

"*Nouri*?" I want him to stop.

"Yes. Annie, Nouri was ordered on the front lines, believe it or not, at the start of the Iran-Iraq war by Khomeini."

"Front lines? What was he? ... Thirteen ... Fourteen?"

"Yes, something like that."

"And?"

"He was killed, clearing minefields."

"No!"

"His first duty." Amir snorts, looks away.

"It's not possible. All these years, Reza and Nouri have been gone?!"

"Yes." Amir glances down at his hands, silent.

I absorb the news. *Nouri clearing minefields.* My own Colin's age? I can't bear to think of it. And we had tried to protect Nouri from malnutrition? Nurtured and tended to Nouri as if he were Mr. Jamison's hybrid rose. Concerned about bare spots and scars. Clearing *minefields*. I shudder. Suddenly, I want a drink. *A glass of wine. Maybe even* a *vodka Pomtini.*

The waitress brings over some dinner menus.

I raise my hand like a schoolgirl. "On second thought, I'll have a Merlot. The house."

"Still tea for me," Amir says. She leaves to retrieve our drinks and Amir explains, "I don't drink. Gave it up several years ago. I'm trying to be something of a purist."

I think for a moment. "Your daughter wears a head scarf?"

Amir nods. "She has adopted some of my views of Islam. Of all the children, she feels the most Iranian-American, even though she has never set foot on Iranian soil. She is happy to wear it."

"Yes. It's always a woman's choice to wear what she wants. Right?"

"Not in the Islamic Republic. A *chador* or a *manteau* is required if you are a woman or the morality police will be knocking on your door. Or carting you off the streets to prison."

"Morality police?" I start laughing, but stop at Amir's serious expression. He was not kidding. "Sorry. Is there such a thing as the morality police now in Iran?"

"Yes, there is. There has been," he says, expression blank.

I frown. "Firouzeh wasn't wearing the headscarf until just about the moment she thought you'd arrive."

"You don't say so?" Amir sits contemplating this.

"How's Iran these days? Any family still there?"

"My uncle gives me all the news of Iran. My cousin had to fish his daughter out of detention for having tea with her boyfriend on a bench along *Pahlavi*. Only the street name isn't *Pahlavi*. They've changed all the names to Islamic clerics. Eisenhower Boulevard is no longer. The Shahyad Monument is now the Azadi Freedom Tower."

My wine is delivered to me with a flourish by the smart looking and attentive waitress.

"Thank you," I say, guilty at the ample pour presented to me. The waitress smiles back. "I hope you like it. It's on the low side of fruity, for a Merlot."

"I'm sure I will."

"All set to order?"

Lamb is on special tonight, even saffron-lobster with heirloom tomatoes. I smile. "I'd like the lamb." I snap shut the menu, hand it back to the waitress.

"The same for me," Amir says.

I raise my Merlot to my lips, but stop to ask him if he minded.

"No, Annie, I'm sorry, I do not mind that you are having a glass of wine."

"Remember all the wine we had at Jamshid's?" I cringe at the mention of his former tenant who had also been executed.

"Yes. Not too smart considering what almost happened after, was it, Annie?"

"I found it to be lovely?" My statement becomes a confused question.

"I hope my daughter Firouzeh does not fall victim to a man with a bottle of wine." Amir laughs softly.

"Or a Grand Piano," I say, laughing, thinking that no wine was involved in that moment. Amir is not amused.

I frown. *What was I doing here, ruining my memories of the past? Thoughts of us together were Amir's scar tissue?* But it is true, we were much too young. I think of Liam, eighteen next year. "From what I gathered from the few minutes I was fortunate to speak with your daughter, she seems intelligent with a solid head on her shoulders. A lovely, generous woman. I am amazed you produced such a beautiful, smart young woman!"

"Amazed?" Amir asks, feigning insult, but smiling. "Yes, how could I impress you with any knowledge when I could barely speak your language, Annie? Ironically, Maryam was forced to leave Khomeini's Iran to become a journalist—now all the censorship. She is the only one in my family I am able to see regularly. My former activist sister married a physician. A *Christian*." Amir pauses. "They live in Canada and have two girls. She writes magazine articles and short stories on a freelance basis. To be home for her children. She paints brightly colored eggs at Easter now, rather than *Noruz*—"

"*Noruz*?" I interrupt. I remembered how Amir had invited me to meet his family and feast with them on *Noruz*. I smile.

"Yes, *Noruz*. I don't celebrate those secular holidays anymore," Amir says.

"What? No! Not *Noruz*? But you loved it!"

"Maryam celebrates Christmas now," Amir says, resigned. "I'm the one that must be the good Muslim in the family, now." Brightening, he says, "Annie, I can hardly believe I am sitting across from you. Now after all these years."

"Yes, I agree, it's surreal," I say, the large, crystal chandelier above my head dripping light like melted gold.

"You'll appreciate this. I read a lot now. I remember how your nose was always stuck in a book."

"You sound like Debbie." I laugh.

He nods, grinning back. "Anyway, my wife... Jenny..." Amir stutters.

"It's all right, Amir, go on."

"Jenny... She's a health teacher/administrator. She'd always bring me books to read from the school library ... before our separation."

"You once said you wanted a wife with books in her head?"

"I did. And that same wife has asked me for a separation. Now we live apart in the same town," Amir says, throwing back the last of his tea.

"Oh." I shift in my brushed-velvet seat.

Amir sighs, fiddles with his napkin. "I suppose it's because she desires to be married to someone more successful than a janitor. More than a mechanic who just plays around, barely makes a living at it." He snorts. "My last job involved picking up trash along the highway. Wearing an orange vest. My wife has supported the whole family for years. I've never contributed much … I suppose she's tired of it."

"But you work on cars now! Firouzeh said."

"Like I said, in my barn, playing around; I barely make a living at it."

"Still, you work on cars."

"My wife deserves someone better than a grease monkey, someone who picks up trash."

I can't help but wonder, *what happened to Amir? The enthusiastic Amir I used to know? His passion? His impish smile? Kheili khoobe, with his guttural "K"?* Firouzeh is right. Her father's unhappy.

"When I arrived here after the storming of the American Embassy and the hostage crisis, I had to hide I was from Iran. Pretended I was Italian. But everyone always caught on once they'd watched news footage of dark, large-nose guys like me shouting death threats outside the American Embassy. I couldn't get a job. No one wanted me to work for them. And when I did become employed, every job was beneath me. I washed dishes in a restaurant. Made pizza. Emptied trash. Annie, *in Iran I was my own boss.* A landlord. *At eighteen.*"

"You were, Amir, and quite happy. I was proud of you."

"But now, I should be a respected business owner. Able to provide for my family. That should be the natural order of things. Even years later I am distrusted for my coloring and my accent, people wondering if I'll be the next suicide bomber, or a plane hijacker."

I gaze at his pale olive face, still generous lips, brooding eyes like pools of melted chocolate. If only I could have rearranged his story. What if Amir had been given the opportunity to heal? Stay somewhere rent-free. Move into a job he could do well. Repair cars like he had in Iran? But in a garage. Earn some cash. Move into sales—Audi's, Mercedes or BMW's? Grease-covered jeans and cotton Bowdoin sweatshirts might have been replaced with tailored suits and thin ties. Self-esteem and confidence could have pushed him forward, especially without prejudice or ugly words to stifle his success. Money might have begun to trickle in, fatten the slim bulge of his wallet. Dinner parties with friends. A new best friend to take the place of Reza.... Yet he never asked for help.

Or what if his story was this? Amir had never been gifted our Honda Civic. Nosey mullahs had never pawed his derailed love letters to me. One of his father's former friends would have ignored Amir and an American blonde kissing after a romantic *Chelo Kebab* lunch, ignoring his own distaste to see Amir kissing an *Infidel* rather than courting a *chador*-clad woman. Not minding at all as we disappeared from view for a long, arduous kiss on the flat of the leather seat.

Suppose there had never been any tragic events chipping away at the innocence that had come before it? The chip, chip, chip of bullets blasting marble from buildings. The clink, clink, clink of ricocheting bullets shot at steel tanks. What if Amir had remained in Iran, without ever being put on the *list?* Would this have changed the course of time? Altered actual events? Would Amir have lived on in Iran as a gentle and wise man in a villa in the countryside? With a courtyard garden and bubbling fountain? Out of the way of danger? Would he have convinced Nouri of Khomeini's trickery? Could he have hidden him away behind the bookcase of his house like a boy-Anne Frank?

And what if Khomeini had been kind? Like Mother Teresa? *Not.* Anyway, this could never have ever played out successfully. There was no way. Amir would have become a casualty of the Iran-Iraq war. Like Reza. Or forever designated a *Corrupter on Earth*. Why did he seem so pious now?

My reverie is ridiculous. Only dreams now. Everything had turned out the way it was meant to. "How did you end up in Maine?" I ask.

"Drove north from LaGuardia when I first arrived here, once I toured New York City, of course, the Statue of Liberty, the Empire State building, met the INS (Immigration and Naturalization) contact. Went in search of the tall snowcapped mountains I knew in Tehran—ended up in Maine. I took a janitor's position in a school. And there I met my wife."

"And you've been blessed with five wonderful children," I say, an ache in my heart.

"Without my courtyard garden and mulberry tree—my mother, father, and sister who should have lived in our house, or near to us—available to share tea, have lunch, and celebrate Ramazan together," he says bitterly. "And how are your parents?"

"Meester Patterson is just fine, living in Vermont with my mother, who is also just grand. She got her wish for antique and sturdy wood furniture while we lived in England. Dad retired from the military years ago after they passed on that promised promotion. He decided to go into farming like my grandparents always had, buy and sell antiques. Mom and Dad travel to Europe each year for inventory, sometimes they go some place tropical ... Are your parents still alive?"

Amir shakes his head, begins to speak. "The Iran-Iraq war. The bombing...." He stops, unable to talk about it. I change the subject; my heart bleeds for him.

"What's it like having a daughter?" I am thankful I have two boys who can play sports together in the yard, be friends, but have always wondered what it might have been like to have had a daughter.

"I'm having trouble with Firouzeh."

"Trouble, what trouble?"

"She wants to date."

"So? She's smart and beautiful and worthy of love. How do you say it, *Dúset daram*?" I smile at him across the table.

"But she should wait. Be ready for marriage."

"I disagree; she needs to sow her seeds. Play the field. So she doesn't regret the person she finally chooses. Right?"

"Sowing seeds is dangerous. I have found a suitable marriage partner for her, but she wants nothing of it. An Iranian boy in Bar Harbor. But, she's in love with a boy by the name of *Chuck* in her journalism class at school."

"Amir, don't you remember love? Don't you remember how we felt back then? Or if you don't, then don't you remember the love you felt for your wife when you asked her to marry you?"

Amir's face is stone. "Yes, I have thought of us. But we are talking about my daughter."

"Right now, it's a sore subject for you. Even Tehran is accepting new shiny office towers. The *chador* can now be traded in for a *manteau* with leggings. Right? A little rouge on a woman's cheek? Lipstick and mascara, but with a veil and bangs escaping it. Shopping malls and luxury, despite sanctions. Home-brewed wine behind closed doors. Sneaking television from forbidden satellite dishes. Kentucky Fried Chicken in Iran. Right, Amir?"

"I know none of this, Annie. Only that there are segregated teahouses and schools. The Koran has stated that this is as it should be. The Kentucky Fried Chicken store is a reproduction, a knock off, no real affiliation. You can order kebab there."

I am grappling with this different version of Amir, unhappy and *pious*? But, didn't he tell us he was "medium" religious back then? Could it be that his faith intensified after being forced to leave a country and family he loved so desperately, so long ago? Or was he always destined to be this man? Did youth's verve change to bitterness with age? Had it for me? Maybe, a little. Does having children change us? With the gift of them, do we become more distrustful of the world? Maybe.

Our meals arrive. We busy ourselves cutting our meat, tamping down butter-puddled mashed potatoes in focused silence. I take a bite, roll my eyes to the ceiling. The lamb is succulent. Redolent with flavor. I remember the Khwansalar restaurant and how Amir had shocked me with his order of brain or tongue; I couldn't recall which just now.

"Remember the Khwansalar?" I ask. I almost make the joke—which would have been in complete and utter poor taste—that at least The Bond wouldn't be bombed in two weeks. But now after the marathon bombing, I can't be so sure.

"I do remember that night of Debbie's birthday party," Amir says.

"Remember when Debbie was offended by your gifts?"

"Everything offended Debbie. How is she?"

"She's well. Been married several times. No children." I spoon at the potatoes on my plate. "She's happily married to a wonderful man this time. They live out West. Constantly doing those western activities." The word western stops me: 'Death to the west; death to Carter; the great Satan', leaping in my brain before I could go on. "She rides canvas-covered jeeps with roll bars in the country. Recently, she rode a donkey over and down steep treacherous trails at the Grand Canyon. To help herself overcome her fear of heights—"

"That's right, she had that," Amir interrupts, laughing.

"Yeah. Debbie, of all people, feeling fear."

"I think she just hid her fear, her low self-esteem, the thought she wasn't pretty enough always hidden by her boyish clothes. When she was. Pretty, I mean."

How astute of Amir, I think. "Anyway, she's a wonderful aunt. Couldn't imagine anyone better. Sends inventive presents. Flies out from time to time to visit. Takes the kids fishing."

"Does she work?"

"Shoots wilderness photos for a living—elks, buffalo, scenery—mountain shots in the mist or at sunset. But she's still not much for domestication. And that's all right. She makes a mean buffalo chicken salad from pre-cooked chicken she buys at her gourmet grocery market."

"Does she prepare real buffalo?" Amir asks, grinning. "I knew she'd turn out that way. And Frankie?"

"Fine, doing well. His beautiful white blond hair has darkened and thinned. He's an elementary teacher in New Hampshire, coaches soccer." Amir smiles and I say, "You know, he once thought he saw your identical twin at a car wash in Portsmouth, New Hampshire."

"That was probably me," Amir says, laughing.

I also laugh. "Oh, my God. Then, it is such a small, small world."

"Yes, it can be. But, on the other hand, I wish I could go back to Iran and see my family. In that respect, the world is much too large for me."

"Maybe you could. Now?"

"No. I sought political asylum. I can't go back."

"I'm sorry, Amir."

"I know. It is as it was designed to be. Don't you think?"

I didn't, but I take a scoop of buttery, garlic-infused mashed potatoes, sample the steamed yellow squash. "The food is delicious. But I can't accept this generous gift from Firouzeh. I must pay her."

"Yes, you can, Annie."

"No, I can't, Amir."

"Yes, you can."

"No, I can't."

We both start to laugh. *Taarof.*

A feathery light breeze lifts my hair from my shoulders, and, as if on cue, Firouzeh appears at our table.

"Firouzeh, hello! Thank you for the lovely surprise of dinner. Will you join us?"

"I will, thank you."

She sits on the leather banquette again, this time next to her father, laying her head on his shoulder, still covered by the pretty red and gauzy scarf. "*Delbar*, Firouzeh *Joon*, how's the studying coming?"

"Not well, *Baba*. I have writer's block."

"You never have writer's block, *Delbar*, Firouzeh. *Azizam*. Come have some dessert with Annie and me. They have fruit and mango sorbet!"

"Mango sorbet it is then."

I look at the two of them together, stunned by their affection, their love for each other, despite my perceived notions about Amir's beliefs and austerity. Now there comes that impish smile.

The waitress comes around again; we order three mango sorbets.

"Annie, tell me about your husband," Amir encourages.

"I met him in college. Both of us catered a school event for spending money. He prevented me from spilling prime rib juice on the college's president by skillfully tipping my tray up as he whisked by with his own tray of food."

"How did you know he was the one for you?"

"Dinners out." I laugh. "He wined and dined me—Shrimp Scampi at the Fox Hollow; Filet Mignon with béarnaise sauce at Tavern on the Green. Bought me wine; gave me pearls. Once we got to know each other, we realized how much we had in common. Same taste in movies and books. Same religion. Similar dreams. For us, the old adage that opposites attract was not true. We were and are so much alike. Two peas in a pod. Except that he has dark black hair and is very thin." I grin, stop talking; thinking for a moment about what had first attracted me to Ryan. "Ryan had this shy smile, and the first thing I noticed about him was that one of his teeth stuck out in the front. That imperfect grin sealed it for me." I smile to myself.

Amir looks at me, pursed lips breaking into that impish grin I so recognized, nodding as if he understood something I did not.

I smile back, but I had definitely understood it. "Patterns do define us, don't they? What about your wife, Amir?" Firouzeh also smiles, biting her lip and looking up at her father.

"She was … is … smart." He shrugs. "I don't know." Chuckling awkwardly, he continues, "I must admit a little shallowness. She is blonde with blue eyes … patterns do indeed define us."

Firouzeh sits back in her seat; a half smile plays on her face. "Old habits die hard?"

"Exactly, Firouzeh," I say.

"*Baba* liked that my mother would wear a veil or a *chador* on special occasions."

"She doesn't now," Amir declares bitterly.

"But she *used* to *Baba*. For *you*."

Firouzeh turns to me and asks, "Annie, do you have pictures of your children?"

I extract two photographs of Liam and Colin from my wallet, show them to Firouzeh and Amir.

Amir sits still. He stares at one photograph for a long time. Looking up with tears in his eyes, he says, "Annie, Liam looks just like you did when you were a teenager. A handsome version of his lovely mother."

"Thank you."

"Colin is cute, also. Still a young boy in the face. He could be Iranian with those heavy eyebrows, strong nose, and dark hair."

After the iced mango sorbets are spooned dry, and the bill has been paid with much argument between Firouzeh and Amir, and Amir looks at me with moist eyes, we walk out into the night. The air smells of lilacs and sweet roses, with a hint of vanilla thrown in. I breathe it in deeply, turn to Firouzeh and hug her.

"Thank you, Firouzeh. For this," I say, pointing to her and her father.

"Thank *you*, Annie. I've very much enjoyed meeting the grown-up version of the Annie my father spoke of so fondly. May peace be upon you." Firouzeh bows ever so slightly, waves, and retreats inside the hotel.

"Amir. It was so nice to see you again. Lovely, really." The feeling of melancholy is profound.

"Annie, a thoughtful birthday present from my dear daughter. May peace be upon you." Amir's gaze is raw.

"Remember when you said long, long ago that you were trying to make Debbie see happiness, and you feared you were failing?"

"Yes, I do recall that."

"Firouzeh would like you to see happiness, Amir."

He pauses for a split second, then seems to consider what I'd said. "Thank you. I will try harder. If not for me, for her."

"You do that. She's the sun in your sky."

"The light of my life," he counters, smiling. "Could anything have turned out differently?" He waves his hand between us.

I knew in my heart of hearts it would never have turned out any differently. "Amir, no, because then you wouldn't have been blessed with your precious daughter or your other children." I nudge my head against his shoulder, grasp him in a bear hug, realizing that now in Iran, men and women were forbidden to do this on the streets. I remember my mom's affectionate hug to Amir the day we left.

"Oh, Annie." He hugs me back tightly.

"I like the way my life turned out," I whisper, wishing the same for Amir. I trace the olive skin on his cheek, softly—tenderly. "You take care of yourself?"

He holds my hand at his face. "I will. You too, *Delbar,* Annie?"

I close my eyes, remember how he'd whispered those words to me long ago, in a faraway land, before everything changed.

Suddenly, Amir grabs me by my arm, pulls me away from the street as the valet parking attendant swings my car up to the curb with a screech. I stumble, throw the young ear-phoned attendant a few dollars, hop into my car and roll down my window. I nod over to the flower shop in the hotel window where earlier a homeless woman in a red rain slicker had sat sprawled out on a mat. She'd been mumbling to herself and was dirty, legs crossed at her ankles, feet bare—her gaze pensive and sorrowful, looking side to side for a kind soul who might throw some money into her own tarnished silver tin. The woman was gone now and without her, the flowers fill the window in a vivid display of color—bunches of red, orange, and yellow roses, buckets of tall stems of multi-colored snapdragons, and bouquets of white daisies and lavender pansies. I motion to the window. "See the flower shop over there?"

Amir turns to look, confused. "You want flowers?"

"No, silly. Bring a bouquet of roses to your wife." I wink at him.

Amir nods, wisely, graciously. "Ah yes, Annie, I should be more tolerant there, too, you are saying."

"I don't know your marriage, but if you think you should, then yes," I say with a grin and an impatient driver taps his horn behind me. "You've got five children and a wife with books in her head—what more could you want?!"

"Yes, you are so right."

"Bye!" "Bye!" we each say, simultaneously.

"Jinx!" Amir flashes his impish, repaired grin.

"Jinx. *Khoda ha Fez!*" I blow him a kiss.

"*Khoda ha Fez*, Annie!" Amir throws a kiss back at me, approaches the car. His voice is like gravel, and he says, "*Maman* always said that Mr. Jamison's rose gave her so much pleasure and never any trouble. It would flourish in drought, stand tall in storms, never required any chemicals to sustain it, had the most beautiful petals you could ever image. Luxuriant like velvet. If only everything we love would give us no trouble." He steps back from the car, tears in his eyes. I sweep at my own eyes with the back of my hand, wave and pull away from the curb.

And as I drive away, looking for signs to Interstate 93, I see Amir in the rear view mirror waving, smiling his wide, generous grin, wearing his signature black sport jacket, crisp white dress shirt and pressed jeans, polished brown dress shoes. And I am seventeen again, on a Tehran sidewalk, the smell of saffron and grilled lamb floating in the air, anticipating the endless possibilities within easy reach of my *Ravishing Rose*-lacquered fingertips. "*Dúset daram*, my dear, Amir." A single tear slides down my face and onto my lap as I turn my steering wheel towards home.

ACKNOWLEDGEMENTS

I would like to acknowledge all who have encouraged me to write this story or have helped me with my embellished memories of Iran: my girlfriend, Isabelle, also an author, who prompted me to finish this book; to all of my good friends and "readers"—my husband (my number one fan), Greg, my brother-in-law Chris, Pam, Renee, Naomi, Barbara, Seth, Arnold, "that guy from England"; Mark, that other guy from England; you know who you are. And, in loving memory of my faithful golden retriever, Fenway, who pawed me as I wrote, waiting for a pet, many pets, but happy to accept a place on the couch by my side. *To Iran, delam barat tang shode bood.* I'd also like to thank my editor, Julie Miesionczek, who tweaked and polished my first draft with wonderful encouragement for me *to keep on tweaking on.*

PERMISSIONS

CPSIA information can be obtained
at www.ICGtesting.com
Printed in the USA
LVOW07*0031051017

551234LV00004B/31/P